IN MEMORIAM LU GUSUN MAGISTRI MEI (1940—2016)
LIBER HIC AMANTISSIME ATQUE GRATISSIME DICATUR

北京大学比较文学学术文库
Beijing Daxue Bijiao Wenxue Xueshu Wenku

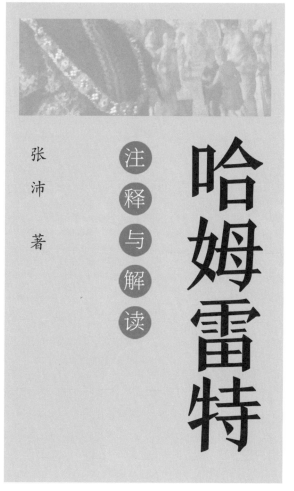

张沛 著

注释与解读

哈姆雷特

北京大学出版社
PEKING UNIVERSITY PRESS

图书在版编目(CIP)数据

哈姆雷特：注释与解读 / 张沛著. —北京：北京大学出版社，2020.12
（北京大学比较文学学术文库）
ISBN 978-7-301-31068-7

Ⅰ. ①哈… Ⅱ. ①张… Ⅲ. ①悲剧 – 人物形象 – 文学研究 – 英国 – 中世纪 Ⅳ. ① I561.073

中国版本图书馆 CIP 数据核字 (2019) 第 301246 号

书　　　名	哈姆雷特：注释与解读 HAMULEITE：ZHUSHI YU JIEDU
著作责任者	张　沛　著
责 任 编 辑	郝妮娜
标 准 书 号	ISBN 978-7-301-31068-7
出 版 发 行	北京大学出版社
地　　　址	北京市海淀区成府路 205 号　100871
网　　　址	http://www.pup.cn　新浪微博：@北京大学出版社
电 子 信 箱	bdhnn2011@126.com
电　　　话	邮购部 010-62752015　发行部 010-62750672 编辑部 010-62759634
印 　刷　 者	大厂回族自治县彩虹印刷有限公司
经 　销　 者	新华书店
	650 毫米 ×980 毫米　16 开本　29.75 印张　600 千字 2020 年 12 月第 1 版　2020 年 12 月第 1 次印刷
定　　　价	116.00 元

未经许可，不得以任何方式复制或抄袭本书之部分或全部内容。
版权所有，侵权必究
举报电话：010-62752024　电子信箱：fd@pup.pku.edu.cn
图书如有印装质量问题，请与出版部联系，电话：010-62756370

目 录

《哈姆雷特》的问题（代序） ········· 陆谷孙 1
引言 ························· 1

《哈姆雷特》注释 ························· 1
The Tragedy of Hamlet, Prince of Denmark ········· 3
ACT I ····························· 5
    SCENE I. Elsinore. A platform before the castle. ········· 5
    SCENE II. A room of state in the castle. ············· 19
    SCENE III. A room in Polonius' house. ············· 38
    SCENE IV. The platform. ····················· 48
    SCENE V. Another part of the platform. ············ 56
ACT II ···························· 71
    SCENE I. A room in Polonius' house. ············· 71
    SCENE II. A room in the castle. ················· 79
ACT III ··························· 122
    SCENE I. A room in the castle. ················· 122
    SCENE II. A hall in the castle. ················· 137

SCENE III. A room in the castle. ················· 166
　　SCENE IV. The Queen's closet. ················· 173
ACT IV ··· 190
　　SCENE I. A room in the castle. ················· 190
　　SCENE II. Another room in the castle. ········ 193
　　SCENE III. Another room in the castle. ······· 195
　　SCENE IV. A plain in Denmark. ················· 200
　　SCENE V. Elsinore. A room in the castle. ···· 205
　　SCENE VI. Another room in the castle. ······· 221
　　SCENE VII. Another room in the castle. ······ 223
ACT V ··· 238
　　SCENE I. A churchyard. ·························· 238
　　SCENE II. A hall in the castle. ·················· 259

哈姆雷特的问题 ·· 291
1. 悲剧 ·· 293
2. 比兴 ·· 302
3. 自杀 ·· 307
4. 恋父情结与死者神化 ···································· 315
5. 庭训和话语—权力 ······································· 321
6. 胡桃壳里的噩梦 ·· 330
7. 人是何物 ··· 344
8. 父仇焉报 ··· 354
9. 生与死 ··· 363
10. 哈姆雷特的命运 ·· 372

附录一 ··· 385
附录二 ··· 406

参考文献·· 433
后记一·· 439
后记二·· 443
新版后记一·· 448
新版后记二·· 453

《哈姆雷特》的问题(代序)

陆谷孙

张沛同志敏而好学,在复旦攻读硕士期间,我已发现此人审问、慎思的特点。士别三日当刮目相看。近读他的新著《哈姆雷特的问题》[*],深感张去北大攻博学成,复做博士后研究,素心焚膏,笃志穷道,融会中西,视界大开,器识已远非昔日可比。承他尚记当年在复旦莎士比亚课上逐字逐句精读《哈姆雷特》的心得,并以此剧为标本,从一曲审全貌,徜徉恣肆,既邃深商量旧学,又反复详玩新知,落笔十数万言,虽未必箭箭中鹄,但多洞见的论,我自叹弗如也。

这篇代序试以"《哈姆雷特》的问题"为题,改以考察剧本而非主人公楔入,拟根据文本罗列一些有趣问题(不局限于社会、哲学方面,当然也不展开求解),意不在质疑折冲,倒是想提供多方面的视角,以冀扩大全书容量。有幽默感的读者,不妨把这篇序文,看作当年的老师在此与当年的学生唱一出双簧可也。

先从问题剧说起。

《牛津英语大词典》收录的"problem play"首例见于19世纪末

---

[*] 编者按:即本书解读部分。

期，严格说来，"问题剧"是一种晚近的戏剧样式，所谓"问题"者，专指某个社会关注问题。如萧伯纳在《论戏剧》①中提到的自Mary Wollstonecraft Shelley（英国诗人雪莱之妻，《弗兰肯斯泰因》的作者）以还，社会普遍关心的妇女问题，直到挪威的易卜生写出《玩偶之家》才算是一部真正意义上的问题剧。萧本人也是写此类问题剧的好手，如《芭芭拉少校》，不但着墨讨论"救世军"等宗教问题，还涉及军火工业乃至战争与和平问题。

不过，萧伯纳又说，就任何剧作都或多或少提出社会问题的意义上说——如莎士比亚笔下的哈姆雷特琢磨自杀问题和卡西奥反省酗酒问题（后者见《奥赛罗》）——每一部戏又可被视作问题剧。而早在萧之前一个多世纪，就已有评家从更宽泛的意义上，用"问题剧"一词来指称莎士比亚在17世纪初年写成的几部剧作，即《终成眷属》《哈姆雷特》《一报还一报》和《特洛伊罗斯和克瑞西达》，理由是剧中有"反常的心智状态"和"复杂的良知问题"，到最后只能"采用没有先例的方法去解决"。②当然，还有宽泛无边因而不免舛讹的说法，即把全部莎剧，不管是喜剧、悲剧、历史剧或传奇剧，一网打尽，统称之为"问题剧"，即如莎士比亚出生地托管基金会主席Levi Fox之所言③。

《哈姆雷特》乃全部莎剧中篇幅最长的一部，主人公丹麦王子一人台词共1 506行，占全剧台词的39%，名列所有说台词的1 378名莎剧角色之首。130年来，前身为莎士比亚纪念剧院的英国皇家莎士比亚剧团（RSC）演出频度最高的是《哈姆雷特》，共82次（场数更多），而百年以来根据剧中故事拍成的影片有75部（仅次于《罗密欧与朱丽叶》），两种媒体相加，受众无计，从而使故事在全世

---

① Bernard Shaw: *Shaw on Theatre*. E.T. West (ed.), New York: Hill and Wang. 1958.
② Frederick S. Boas: *Shakespeare and His Predecessors*. Reprinted 1969, New York: Greenwood Press, 1896, pp. 14—15.
③ L.F. Salzma (ed.), Levi Fox in *The Victoria History of the County of Warwick (IV)*. Oxford: OUP, 1947, p.218.

界家喻户晓。从这样一部剧作和这样一个角色入手来诠释莎士比亚的各种问题，无论从文本本身的代表性，或从接受主义的广度来说，无疑是有的放矢的。

就挖掘并提出问题而论，《哈姆雷特》不啻是座"富矿"。问题中荦荦大端者如"生与死""知与昧""知与行""虚与实""盈与冲""貌似与本真""表演/化妆与自然""朝夕与永恒""樊笼与无垠""计谋与宿命""奸佞与仁义""牺牲与保全""吁天与亵渎"等。此类问题中有不少正是张著论述的重点，小序不赘。但犹有许多与文本或舞台演出有关的问题，至今尚阙圆满的答案，有的可能成为永远的谜团，窃以为相当一部分的莎士比亚魅力正在于此。

譬如说，已为后世耳熟能详的独白"To be, or not to be; ..."（III, i, 64—98）究竟本来行文面貌如何？《哈姆雷特》第一次印成文字是在1603年，形式是一剧一册的四开本（quarto）。这第一四开本史称"讹本"，是由几位甚至某一位演员（一说系扮演次要角色军官马西勒斯的那位）凭记忆拼凑而成的。必须注意，为防剧本外流到票房竞争者手里，当年的演员一般都只拿到自己饰演的角色的台词文本，全剧文本则掌握在舞台监督（时称book-keeper）手中，所以依靠演员回忆拼凑，准确性自然较差，但另一方面，按照当代某些莎学家的看法，这样的文本倒是可能更接近于"实时"（real-time）的莎士比亚[①]。第一四开"讹本"的那则独白开篇是这么几句：

> To be, or not to be, I [=ay] there's the point,
> To die, to sleepe, is that all? I all:
> No, to sleepe, to dreame, I mary [=marry] there it goes,
> For in that dreame of death, when wee awake,
> And borne before an euerlasting Iudge,
> From whence no passenger euer retur'nd
> The vndiscouered country, at whose sight

---

① Marjorie Garber: *Shakespeare After All*. New York: Anchor Books, 2004, pp.467—468.

The happy smile, and the accursed damn'd.

拿这8行与流传至今并引得学者们诠释不尽的文本作一比较，主要区别似在语速和用词；至于意象，"长眠""做梦""未被发现的天地，旅人不曾回归"都无变化，失落的是"命运的矢石"等大量的隐喻和对现世苦难的罗列，从而剥夺了后世学人阐释、解码破译、解构—重构的无穷乐趣；而 The happy smile 一语更是破坏了整段的基调。第一四开本是个"讹本"已有定论，但文本极为浓缩，长度仅及吾人今日所见文本之半，动作性和可演性强，不像今日所见文本前半部王子"延宕"复"延宕"（前四幕每一幕都有一大段独白），直到第三幕第二场的"戏中戏"开始，思考转向动作，剧情急遽推进，而"讹本"被认为没有这种结构上的瑕疵。因此专门研究"文字莎士比亚"（Shakespeare on the page）的学者，似也应注意"舞台莎士比亚"（Shakespeare on the stage），特别是英国伊丽莎白一世时代的"实时"莎士比亚。

我是个称铢度寸的微观型学人，兼之教过几轮《哈姆雷特》，脑子里还存有不少其他的琐屑问题，诸如幕启之时喝问口令的何以不是值班哨兵，反倒是行近的换岗人？这算不算文学中的一种"所指"，从戏一开始便埋下乾坤颠倒的隐喻？［后又为"地上打雷"（earthly thunder）等意象反复强化。］第一幕第一场鬼魂的缄口与紧接其后第二场僭主的雄辩是不是奇崛的对照，出自剧作家有意的手笔？（谁说"意图"一定是"谬论"？）鉴于剧中反复出现因应时事的内容，僭主口中"our sometime sister, now our queen"会不会激发当年观众对伊丽莎白女王的联想？——其父亨利八世曾违背《旧约》"利未记"训诫，占嫂为妻。同样，波洛涅斯的原型是伊后的某位宠臣抑或波兰使节，他在 II, ii, 400—403 对巡回剧团剧目的饶舌介绍（悲剧、喜剧、历史剧、田园剧、田园喜剧、田园史剧、历史悲剧、历史田园悲喜剧）是否是对戏剧学术化的讥讽？——特别是"历史田园悲喜剧"颇使人联想到今日里我称之为 pigeonholing 的学术细分，如bio-+x+y。剧中众哨兵追看鬼魂，观众看演员；哈姆雷特冷眼看僭主，观众看王子；还有"戏中戏"，众演员看戏中的演员，观众看演员——这是不是一种"大娃套小娃"的"俄罗斯玩偶"式的戏剧效应？有使用电脑专事莎剧中意象复现统计的学者发现，"ear"一词在《哈姆雷特》剧中使用最频，疑与施毒于耳及全剧多偷听刺探的剧情有关，基于同理，我们是否可分别统计关于"腐败"（rotten, cankerous, contagion, ulcer等）以及关于"伪装"（show, play, stage, face-painting, plast'ing art等）的意象，以期更接近全剧主旨？关于thou/you的换用，如幕启时两哨兵的对话（勃那多先说"get thee to bed, Francisco"，继问"Have *you* had quiet guard？"前者以私交身份，用亲切语气，后者则事关军务，语气自然涉公）以及III, iv母后寝宫的母子唇枪舌剑，是否可解今日读者之疑以利其他莎剧的阅读理解？莎翁创作《哈姆雷特》，除去已知的12世纪拉丁文《丹麦史话》、16世纪的法文《历史悲剧》和早些时候的佚失剧《元始哈姆雷特》（*Ur-Hamlet*）之外，还读过些什么古书？已有的考证指出，莎士比亚的"To be, or not to be"名段明显受了从古希腊普罗塔克和古罗马西塞罗到法国蒙田等人著作的影响，那么剧中的其他内容是否也有所本呢？如墓地郁利克骷髅背后有无第一部人体解剖教科书《人体构造》（*De humani corproris fabrica*, Andreas Vesalius著，1543年）的影响？溯源莎剧过去有Geoffrey Bullough的8卷巨制可供参阅，如今又出了一位苏格兰格拉斯哥大学的年轻教授①，断言莎翁读过郝林希特、普罗塔克、奥维德、贺拉斯、《圣经》、英国国教《祈祷书》《伊索寓言》等200多种参考书，其结论可靠性如何？出现鬼魂的莎剧不止《哈姆雷特》一部（读者可比照《麦克白》《理查三世》等），但唯有先王老哈姆雷特用词丽靡，且有塞涅卡古风，形容惨遭谋杀一段颇有伊甸园神话

---

① Stuart Gillespie: *Shakespeare's Books: A Dictionary of Shakespeare Sources*. London: Ahlone Press/ Continuum, 2001.

的意味，加上对忏悔、炼狱的描写，是否足见天主教教义对作者的影响？对于新历史主义宣称的莎氏在清教主义英国阴奉旧教的结论，算不算又是一证？剧中"globe"一词倘若兼有"脑袋""地球""环球剧场"的三重意义，"union"有"宝石"和"联姻"两重意思，那么"nunnery"（III, i, 131）除了"尼姑庵"以外，有无伊丽莎白时代俚语中"妓院"的暗指？鬼魂出现于暗夜，闻鸡鸣急遁，随后就是笔者吟玩不倦的关于旭日、朝露、青嶂的两句，由霍拉旭说出：

> But look, the morn in russet mantle clad
> Walks o'er the dew of yon high eastward hill.①

可以想象现当代演出中此时舞台照明由暗转亮，正如紧接其后的I, ii中，在富丽堂皇的宫廷，在远离金灿灿的王冠和珠光宝气的一隅，孤独地站着一身黑色丧服的王子。此类灯光和戏装的现当代常技，以伊丽莎白时代的标准衡量，是否迹近melodrama？反会导致莎剧诗之美趣（如上引两句）的失落？说到演出，还有一个有趣的问题：莎剧在伊丽莎白时代由全男班演出——女角由男童饰演——乃习俗使然，不足为奇（这一技术性障碍可能也是莎剧女角常常无母的原因之一，像《哈姆雷特》中似乎就缺了一个波洛涅斯夫人！），然而由全女班演出《哈姆雷特》就匪夷所思了。据记载，自1775年Sarah Siddons起，至少有五六名女士饰演丹麦王子，20世纪的Judith Anderson更是在73岁的高龄扮演哈姆雷特，一时传为佳话②。派定女角演哈姆雷特的用意是什么？难道有导演在王子身上发掘出了女性的细腻和阴柔？奥菲利娅是投水自杀还是意外溺水？王子给巡回剧团的戏文中加上dozen or sixteen lines（实指"几句台词"，与"一

---

① 在人民文学出版社1978年版《莎士比亚全集》中，朱生豪译作："可是瞧，清晨披着赤褐色的外衣/已经踏着那边东方高山上的露水走过来了。"

② Crystal, David & Ben: *The Shakespeare Miscellany*. Woodstock and New York: The Overlook Press, 2005.

打"或"十六"无关）究竟是哪些？……如此这般，关于《哈姆雷特》的问题诚如丝麻纷乱，要解开有的谜团可能是曲学多辩，钻奇凿诡，只会治丝愈棼。另一方面，如同其他学问一样，力至则入，钻研一下上述问题可能不是没有好处的。

哈佛女教授Marjorie Garber①说，阅读或观看《哈姆雷特》的功效之一在于唤起认同和回忆。诚哉斯言！给张沛老弟这部专著撰写序言时，我仿佛又回到了当年"Shakespeare in-depth"的课堂。在张沛他们是："学，然后知不足"；在我是："教，然后知困"。我还记得曾与学生分享自己认为极其重要的两个看法。一是搞文学的必须熟读第一手的作品，且要做到手披目视，熟诵其言，心唯其义，切不可丢下原著，盲目躁进，急急效模第二手文评，玩弄术语唬人，结果把学问做"僵"。二是搞外国文学的不可完全抛弃中国文人重性灵、机趣、兴会的传统，一味皮附欧美分析哲学的高论；即便是穿上了后者的"紧身衣"，写文章也还须挥洒自如，元气淋漓。我还提出，学生应向中国的钱锺书和外国的本雅明学习（后者自称是homme de lettre，即man of letters，类乎中国的"文人"之谓，嗜写随笔、杂感之类，少泡沫，有深度），最好达到Wonderlander加Wastelander的学术境界。

张沛老弟从严格的意义上说，非我弟子；除了复旦的一段因缘，他去北大之后，由于两人都不存学校之町畦，兼之时下电话和电邮又极方便，切磋反倒更频。尼采讲过宗师与弟子的关系，称"子将背其师，盖渠亦必自成大宗师也"。张年而立，可不勉欤！

---

① Marjorie Garber: *Shakespeare After All*. New York: Anchor Books, 2004, pp.467—468.

引　言

　　莎士比亚1564年出生于英格兰中部瓦维克郡（Warwickshire）埃文河畔的斯特拉特福（Stratford-upon Avon），1585年离乡到伦敦谋生，1590年参加剧团开始舞台和创作生涯，1599年与人合建"环球剧院"（the Globe Theatre），1612年回乡定居，4年后病逝，遗体安葬于故乡圣三位一体教堂。

　　作为诗人和剧作家，莎士比亚主要活跃于伊丽莎白一世（1558—1603）、詹姆士一世（1603—1625）统治时期。"这是一个颠倒混乱的时代"（《哈姆雷特》一幕五场），这句话在一定程度上也是当时英国社会的真实写照。这时英国经历着民族扩张、商业繁荣和宗教论战，处于神权政治与君权政治、封建农业社会与近代工商业社会、民族国家与世界性国家的交接点上。社会的发展与变化，带来了"英国文学的黄金时代"，而戏剧则是这个时代的骄子。从1580年起，英国产生了数十位卓有成就的剧作家，见于记载的剧本达一千部左右。莎士比亚的前辈、同侪与后学，如李利（John Lyly）、马洛（Christopher Marlowe）、格林（Robert Greene）、皮尔（George Peele）、纳什（Thomas Nashe）、基德（Thomas Kyd）以及弗莱彻（John Fletcher）等人，共同创造了复仇悲剧、伟人悲剧、浪漫喜剧、历史剧、宫廷喜剧、悲喜剧等戏剧样式；莎士比亚总其大成，更加纯熟地运用这些形式，从而奠定了英国戏剧的伟大传统。

莎士比亚20余年内共写了2首长诗、154首十四行诗和37部戏剧（如果加上《爱德华三世》则是38部）。他的创作大致可分为三个阶段[①]：

（一）1590—1601年：主要是富于乐观精神和鲜明信念的英国历史剧、喜剧和悲剧

（二）1601—1608年的"悲剧时期"[②]：多为反映深刻矛盾和表现怀疑情绪的作品，包括《哈姆雷特》等五部悲剧和三部"阴郁的喜剧"

（三）1608年后：倾向于妥协和幻想的四部悲喜剧和传奇剧

莎士比亚的戏剧是对恪守"三一律"（即时间、地点与行动的统一）的欧洲大陆戏剧理论的一个反拨。伊丽莎白时期的剧场采用类似中国传统"三面光"式的裙式舞台，不像现代镜框式舞台那样把观众与演员隔离开来，因此演员可以直接同观众交流。他们的表演既有歌舞玩笑，又有杂耍、特技，几乎包括了当时流行的所有大众娱乐形式。

当然，今天我们所欣赏的主要还是莎士比亚的剧本。莎士比亚是英语世界中首屈一指的语言大师：他笔下的972名角色总共说了884 647个台词[③]；在这17 000余词汇中（一说据电脑统计为29 066，最大数字更达43 566），既有文雅的拉丁语、法语和意大利语，也有时人习用的方言土语，甚至是不登大雅的粗言俚语。莎士比亚在写作之初并未打算作为文学作品出版，而是作为演出的剧本，因此有时难免产生疏漏重复、臃肿花哨的毛病（对此琼森、德莱顿、

[①] 亦有学者分为四个时期：1590—1595年、1595—1602年、1602—1608年以及1608年之后。（A. C. Bradley: *Shakespearean Tragedy*, London: The Macmillan Press Ltd., 1974, p.62.）

[②] Ibid, p.62.

[③] 科尔奈留·杜米丘主编：《莎士比亚戏剧辞典》，宫宝荣等译，上海：上海书店出版社，2011年，大卫·钱伯斯序。

伏尔泰等人先后都曾加以指责），不过这些缺憾在一定程度上正反映了他那汪洋恣肆、真气弥漫的原生性创作天才。和关汉卿、莫里哀一样，莎士比亚不是今天意义上的剧作家，而是一名写剧本的演员——他更多地代表了民间的风格、舞台表演（而不仅仅是写作）的传统。

莎士比亚是一名广博而深刻的人性观察者。歌德曾经这样评论他："莎士比亚是一个伟大的心理学家，从他的剧本中我们可以学会懂得人类的思想感情"，"莎士比亚已把全部人性的各种倾向，无论在高度上还是在深度上，都描写得竭尽无余"，"他把人类生活中的一切动机都画出来和说出来了！"《哈姆雷特》一剧为我们理解这些评论提供了最好的样本。写作于1600年的《哈姆雷特》被誉为莎氏四大悲剧之首（虽然R. A. Foakes认为《李尔王》是莎士比亚最伟大的作品[①]，而E. A. J. Honigmann则提议《奥赛罗》），也是世界文学史上最伟大的悲剧之一。

《哈姆雷特》讲述的故事是：丹麦国王突然死去，其弟克劳狄斯接替王位并娶王后为妻，回国奔丧的王子哈姆雷特对父亲的死因感到可疑，并对母亲急忙改嫁心怀不满。当他从父亲的鬼魂那里知道父亲被叔王害死的真相后，决心复仇。这时克劳狄斯授意王子早年的两名好友进行试探，王子则让演员在宫里演出一场弑兄夺嫂的戏进行反试探。对此叔王反应异常并有所觉察，于是指示大臣波洛涅斯的女儿、也是王子的爱人奥菲利娅去试探哈姆雷特。哈姆雷特装疯卖傻并故意表示冷淡。克劳狄斯再命波洛涅斯偷听哈姆雷特母子的谈话，波洛涅斯被王子误当作克劳狄斯刺死。在多重打击之下，奥菲利娅精神崩溃，失足落水而亡。其兄雷欧提斯闻讯从国外赶回为父妹报仇。这时哈姆雷特也通过修改克劳狄斯的密令，结

[①] A. C. Bradley也认为《李尔王》是莎氏"最伟大的作品"，但非其"最佳戏剧"。此说耐人寻味。

果了奉命押送他到英国的那两名好友,再次返回丹麦。克劳狄斯闻讯与雷欧提斯定计,安排后者与哈姆雷特比剑决斗,并在剑头上涂毒。斗剑时雷欧提斯处于下风,于是用暗剑刺伤了对方,但很快也被哈姆雷特刺中身亡。这时克劳狄斯赐饮哈姆雷特毒酒,王后抢过喝下,旋即中毒死去。哈姆雷特将叔王刺死后自己也毒发身亡,临死时他嘱托至交霍拉旭传达他的遗愿:推举兴兵来犯的挪威王子继任丹麦国王并把他的故事昭告世人。

《哈姆雷特》取材于13世纪初丹麦历史学家"博学者萨克叟"(Saxo Grammaticus,约1150—1220)所著《丹麦史》(*Gesta Danorum*)中的一段传说(托马斯·卡莱尔认为这个故事来源于北欧神话),在写法上明显具有古罗马剧作家塞内加(Seneca)"复仇悲剧"的特点,另外与1594年在伦敦上演的一部鬼戏(已失传)可能也有些渊源①。

在情节上,《哈姆雷特》沿用了复仇剧(其典型模式是主人公通过确凿的证据查明有人对他犯下了骇人的罪行,然后他克服重重艰险而终于报仇雪恨、伸张正义)与"血腥剧"的基本程式(例如《哈姆雷特》中先后死去八人,其中四人在最后一场殒命),但作者在主人公复仇的主线之外,同时又安排了雷欧提斯以及挪威王子福丁布拉斯为父报仇的两条副线,三条线索相互映衬而深化了对复仇行为的伦理思考。事实上,莎士比亚塑造的哈姆雷特王子并不是一个典型的复仇悲剧英雄。哈姆雷特在德国的维登堡城(Wittenberg)读书,而这里是马丁·路德新教改革的大本营,因此他身上具有"新人""自由思想者"的某些特点。在《哈姆雷特》中,莎士比亚探索了人类良知在特定的社会与历史条件下所面临的内心冲突。面对邪恶,哈姆雷特没有诉诸任何神灵或权威,而是召唤、思考和展示了人性的本质特征。这,正是《哈姆雷特》的永恒

---

① 另外Edmund Marlone提到(Preface to Robert Greene's *Menaphon*)1589年曾有一部老本《哈姆雷特》上演。

魅力所在。

　　《哈姆雷特》甚至也不是一部一般意义上的悲剧。古希腊悲剧源于祭神仪式，确切地讲是"牺牲剧"或"祭献剧"，因此按照西方传统的悲剧理论，悲剧主人公必然是一个品性高贵但遭到"命运"嘲弄的人，其遭受不幸或出于本人有意或无意的"过失"（例如《阿伽门农王》《俄底浦斯王》），或出于奸人的陷害（例如《奥赛罗》），或出于自身"性格缺陷"（例如《安提戈涅》）。前两者属于命运悲剧，后者则属于性格悲剧；而无论在何种类型的悲剧中，主人公都是奉献给命运——作为终极目的之"永恒正义"——祭坛上的美好牺牲。《哈姆雷特》可以说兼有上述三种悲剧的性质（哈姆雷特父亲被害、误杀爱人之父、被叔父设计陷害属于前两种类型，而他在复仇时犹豫不决而导致自己及其亲人死亡则属于后者），但同时也超越了上述悲剧类型，即主人公乃是出于明达而非无知、自感洞透了世界的本质而厌弃命运的终极目的，从而产生了一种形而上的、对于存在本身的绝望："To be or not to be？"

　　就语言而论，《哈姆雷特》取得了极高的艺术成就。它是莎剧作品中篇幅最长的一部（近3万字），其主人公哈姆雷特也因包括7 350个单词的1 506行台词成为莎剧人物中道白最多的一位。他和其他剧中人说的是16世纪早期现代英语，以抑扬格五音步的无韵体诗（blank verse）为主，同时也有相当多的散文道白成分（典型如五幕"墓地"一场的道白多为散文甚至口语；而在三幕二场"戏中戏"中，作者对雕镂堆砌的诗剧体还予以了丑化摹仿）。不过，其中大量的典故、文字游戏（例如双关）以及由于时代和印刷而带来的不规范与讹误，也为今人欣赏、理解和翻译这部作品带来了一定困难。

　　《哈姆雷特》的现存早期版本有1603年的第一四开本（Q1）、1604—1605年的第二四开本（Q2）、1611年的第三四开本以及1623

年的第一次对开本（F），各本间颇有出入①。今天通行的版本一般以1604年本第二四开本（Q2）为底本，参校1623年本（F），改用现代拼写和标点而成。

中国大多数莎剧都有不止一个单行译本，比如 *Hamlet* 一剧就有"哈姆雷特""哈姆莱特""汉姆莱特""罕秫莱德""哈孟雷特"等十数个译名，是中译最多的一部莎剧作品。

"越是民族的，就越是世界的"，这一论断在主题和内容方面或许可以成立，但就语言形式而言却不尽然。文学是语言的艺术，文学作品的表述形式在很大程度上就是它的内容。文学作品特别是诗歌作品的内容与形式可以说是同生共体、无法分割的。阅读《离骚》及其白话今译，或阅读 *Hamlet* 与《哈姆雷特》，是两种迥乎不同的阅读经验。翻译是用不同的语言形式表达同一内容，然而即便是最出色的译文也无法取代原文。就文学翻译而言，无论多么优秀的翻译都不可能等同于原作，它或多或少、有意无意都会偏离甚至改写原作；这种偏离或改写正是来自语言形式的改变，而异质文化中不同的表达形式就导致了各种合法的和非法的"误读"。即以哈姆雷特在第三幕第一场的著名独白为例，它的第一句话是：

To be, or not to be, that is the question.

这句话的翻译不尽相同，例如"生存还是毁灭，这是一个值得考虑的问题"（朱生豪）、"是生存还是消亡，问题的所在"（孙大雨）、"死后是存在，还是不存在——这是问题"（梁实秋）、"活下去还是不活，这是问题"（卞之琳）、"活着好，还是死了

---

① 以正文（对话部分）为例：Q1本最短（但也是唯一有可能用于舞台表演的），有15 983字；Q2本最长，有28 628字；F本有27 602字；F本中有1 914字不见于Q2本，而Q2本中有2 887字不见于F本；Q2有3 902行台词，其中与F本完全相同者仅220行（6%），同时有222行不见于F本，而F本中也有88行不见于Q2本。（*The Arden Shakespeare: Hamlet*, edited by Ann Thompson & Neil Taylor, London: Arden Shakespeare, 2006, p.80.）

好，这是个问题"（方平）等。这些译法各有千秋，但也都有不足之处：朱译朗朗上口，但"毁灭"不尽符合"not to be"的意思；孙译"问题的所在"语法欠妥；梁译似乎有些"过度阐释"；方译中同样出现了意义偏离；卞译虽然贴近原文，但是读来有些拗口。另外，他们都没有能够准确译出原文中定冠词"the"的含义。因此，翻译作品可以帮助理解原作，但要想避免误读，领会原作精神，最好的方法还是阅读原典，由亲熟形式达到内容的会解。

诚如哈罗德·布鲁姆（Harold Bloom）所说，莎士比亚是西方经典的中心。《哈姆雷特》又在莎士比亚的作品中占据了一个中心位置，可谓经典中之经典①。另一位布鲁姆（Allan Bloom）也告诉我们："莎士比亚对不同时代、不同国家里那些认真阅读他的人产生的影响证明了，我们身上存在着某些永恒的东西，为了这些永恒的东西，我们必须一次又一次重新回到他的戏剧。……一个思想共同体是由这位伟大的艺术家以及围绕他聚集起来的传统解释构成的。这是实际上存在的最接近'存在大链条'的东西。……正是这一解释传统为我们建立了文明。这一传统非'创造性误读'，也非对'影响的焦虑'所表现的空洞的叛逆，而是顺理而做的解释，并为有幸与比自己更优秀者相伴而快乐。"②

人生贵在知之而即行。现在，就让我们一起来阅读这部伟大的经典和"自我之书"吧！——

What do you read, my lord?
Words, words, words.
(*Hamlet*, II. ii. 206—207)

---

① 据统计，20世纪平均每年出版400部以上研究《哈姆雷特》的著作。（*The Arden Shakespeare: Hamlet*, Introduction, pp.1—2.）
② 阿兰·布鲁姆：《莎士比亚笔下的爱与友谊》，马涛红译，北京：华夏出版社，2012年，第156页。

Still be kind,
And eke out our performance with your mind.
(*Henry* V, Chorus. 34—35)

《哈姆雷特》注释

张　沛　注释
孟来燕　整理
陆浩斌　校读

The Tragedy of Hamlet, Prince of Denmark

DRAMATIS PERSONAE
CLAUDIUS, King of Denmark①
HAMLET, son to the former, and nephew to the present king②
POLONIUS, Lord Chamberlain③
HORATIO, friend to Hamlet④
LAERTES, son to Polonius⑤
VOLTEMAND, courtier⑥
CORNELIUS, courtier

---

① He is "Feng" in Saxo Grammaticus' *Gesta Danorum*, and Fengon in the 1608 English translation of Belleforest. His namesake Claudius (10BC—54AD) is the fifth Caesar of the ancient Roman Empire and the first Roman Emperor that came to England (he stayed 16 days). According to Suetonius's *De Vita Caesarum*, he was reputedly foolish (Lucian wrote in a comic dialogue that he became a pumpkin after his death), and was poisoned by his niece and third wife Agrippina (Their marriage was regarded as incestuous).
② He is "Amleth" in Saxo and "Hamblet" in Belleforest.
③ The actor playing Polonius has since 1730 often doubled in the role of the Gravedigger.
④ Horatio is not only a name with classical connotations—his name implies "ratio" (reason) on the one hand, and suggests "Horatian decorum" on the other—but also that of the loyal friend and murdered son in Thomas Kyd's *The Spanish Tragedy*.
⑤ Laertes is the name of the father of Odysseus in Homer's *Odyssey*. It is possible for the player playing Laertes to double in the role of Guildenstern.
⑥ It is close to Valdemar, the name of several kings of Denmark.

ROSENCRANTZ, courtier[1]
GUILDENSTERN, courtier[2]
OSRIC, courtier
A GENTLEMAN, COURTIER
A PRIEST
MARCELLUS, officer
BERNARDO, officer
FRANCISCO, a soldier
REYNALDO, servant to Polonius
PLAYERS
TWO CLOWNS, GRAVEDIGGERS
FORTINBRAS, Prince of Norway[3]
A NORWEGIAN CAPTAIN
ENGLISH AMBASSADORS

GERTRUDE, Queen of Denmark, mother to Hamlet[4]
OPHELIA, daughter to Polonius[5]
GHOST OF HAMLET'S FATHER[6].
LORDS, LADIES, OFFICERS, SOLDIERS, SAILORS, MESSENGERS, ATTENDANTS

---

[1] The name means "wreath or crown of roses."
[2] The name means "golden star."
[3] The name means "strong (in) arm" or "iron hand" in French.
[4] She is Gerutha in Saxo and Geruth in Belleforest. Possibly Shakespeare combines this name with that of Hermutrude or Hermetrude, Amleth's own second wife.
[5] Greek: ὠφελέω (help, aid, assist).
[6] Hamlet's father is called Horwendill in Saxo, Horvendile in Belleforest. Occasionally the actor playing the Ghost also plays the King.

ACT I
SCENE I. Elsinore. A platform before the castle.

FRANCISCO at his post. Enter to him BERNARDO

BERNARDO

Who's there?[1]

FRANCISCO

Nay,[2] answer me. Stand, and unfold[3] yourself.[4]

BERNARDO

Long live the King! [5]

FRANCISCO

Bernardo?

BERNARDO

5 He.[6]

FRANCISCO

You come most carefully[7] upon your hour[8].[9]

BERNARDO

'Tis[10] now struck twelve;[11] get thee[12] to bed, Francisco.

FRANCISCO

---

[1] **Who's there:** The play begins with a question, which establishes a foreboding atmosphere.

[2] **Nay:** but

[3] **unfold:** reveal

[4] **unfold yourself:** disclose your identity

[5] **Long ... the King:** It is the password, which sounds ironic because the King is dead in fact.

[6] **He:** Him. (Me.)

[7] **carefully:** punctually

[8] **your hour:** point hour.

[9] **You ... hour:** He may be ironic, or even reproving, as if Bernado is only just on time.

[10] **'Tis:** it's

[11] **'Tis ... twelve:** The play begins at midnight. (Cf. I. iv. 4—5: "I think it lacks of twelve.– / No, it is struck.") "Struck" is an anachronism, for clock was invented in early 14th century.

[12] **thee:** you

For this relief much thanks. 'Tis bitter cold,
10　And I am sick at heart.①

BERNARDO

Have you had quiet guard?

FRANCISCO

Not a mouse stirring.②

BERNARDO

Well, good night.

If you do meet Horatio and Marcellus,
15　The rivals③ of my watch, bid them make haste.

FRANCISCO

I think I hear them. Stand, ho! Who's there?

Enter HORATIO and MARCELLUS

HORATIO

Friends to this ground.

MARCELLUS

And liegemen④ to the Dane⑤.

FRANCISCO

Give⑥ you good night.

MARCELLUS

20　O, farewell, honest soldier.

Who hath⑦ relieved you?

FRANCISCO

Bernardo has my place. Give you good night.

Exit

---

① **'Tis ... heart:** It creates an eerie atmosphere that runs through the whole play. (Cf. V. ii. 208—209: "thou wouldst not think how ill all's here / about my heart.")
② **Not ... stirring:** a sense of uncanniness
③ **rivals:** partners (in buddy system), fellow sentries
④ **liegemen:** men who have sworn allegiance to the King; subjects
⑤ **the Dane:** King of Denmark
⑥ **Give:** May God give (optative)
⑦ **hath:** has

MARCELLUS

25 Holla[1]! Bernardo!

BERNARDO

Say—

What, is Horatio there?[2]

HORATIO

A piece of him.[3]

BERNARDO

Welcome, Horatio. Welcome, good Marcellus.

MARCELLUS

What, has this thing[4] appeared again tonight?

BERNARDO

30 I have seen nothing.

MARCELLUS

Horatio says 'tis but our fantasy[5],

And will not let belief take hold of him[6]

Touching[7] this dreaded sight, twice seen of[8] us.

Therefore I have entreated him along

35 With us to watch the minutes of this night,[9]

That if again this apparition come,

He may approve our eyes[10] and speak to it.

---

[1] **Holla:** hallo / hello
[2] **What ... there:** It is a pleasant surprise.
[3] **A piece of him:** i.e. his hand (It makes some comic effect, hence a switch of atmosphere.). Cf. *Twelfth Night*, I. v. 26: "a piece of Eve's flesh" (a girl); *The Tempest*, I. i. 56: "a piece of virtue" (piece: specimen)
[4] **this thing:** the ghost (Cf. this dreaded sight; this apparition). The word "thing" can be used as a euphemism for undesirable things, e.g. *seeing things, one of those things*, etc.
[5] **fantasy:** fancy, imagination
[6] **will ... him:** will not let himself believe
[7] **Touching:** about, concerning
[8] **of:** by
[9] **watch ... night:** keep watch through the night
[10] **approve our eyes:** confirm what we have seen

HORATIO

Tush①, tush, 'twill not appear.

BERNARDO

Sit down awhile,

40　And let us once again assail② your ears,

That are so fortified③ against our story

What④ we have two nights seen.

HORATIO

Well, sit we down,

And let us hear Bernardo speak of this.

BERNARDO⑤

45　Last night of all⑥

When yond⑦ same star that's westward from the pole⑧

Had made his⑨ course to illume⑩ that part of heaven

Where now it burns, Marcellus and myself,

The bell then beating⑪ one—

Enter Ghost

MARCELLUS

50　Peace, break thee off; look, where it comes again!

BERNARDO

In the same figure, like the King that's dead.

---

① **Tush:** Poof!
② **assail:** attack
③ **fortified:** incredulous (military metaphors)
④ **What:** with what
⑤ **Bernardo:** What follows is a flashback, a theatrical device prevalent in ancient Greek tragedies, such as the chorus in *Agamemnon*, who introduces what's happened before.
⑥ **Last night of all:** the most recent night
⑦ **yond:** yonder
⑧ **pole:** pole-star, Polaris
⑨ **his:** its
⑩ **illume:** illuminate
⑪ **beating:** striking, tolling

MARCELLUS

Thou art[1] a scholar[2], speak to it, Horatio.[3]

BERNARDO

Looks it not like the King? Mark[4] it, Horatio.

HORATIO

Most like. It harrows[5] me with fear and wonder.

BERNARDO

55 It would[6] be spoke[7] to.

MARCELLUS

Question it, Horatio.

HORATIO

What art thou that usurp'st[8] this time of night,

Together with that fair and warlike form[9]

In which the majesty of buried Denmark[10]

60 Did sometimes[11] march? By heaven I charge thee, speak!

MARCELLUS

It is offended.

BERNARDO

See, it stalks[12] away!

HORATIO

---

[1] **art:** are
[2] **scholar:** student
[3] **Thou … Horatio:** Medieval people believed scholars (philosophers, e.g. Faust) knew witchcraft and could communicate with supernatural spirits.
[4] **Mark:** observe closely
[5] **harrows:** lacerates, torments
[6] **would:** requires to
[7] **spoke:** spoken
[8] **usurp'st:** usurp: invade, encroach on (ironic, for it is the present king who is a usurper)
[9] **form:** shape, appearance
[10] **Denmark:** king of Denmark
[11] **sometimes:** sometime, formerly (i.e. when he was alive)
[12] **stalks:** moves in a stiff or stately way

Stay! speak, speak! I charge thee, speak!

Exit Ghost

MARCELLUS

'Tis gone, and will not answer.①

BERNARDO

65　How now, Horatio! You tremble and look pale②

Is not this something more than fantasy?

What think you on't③?

HORATIO

Before④ my God, I might not⑤ this believe

Without the sensible⑥ and true avouch⑦

70　Of mine own eyes.

MARCELLUS

Is it not like the King?

HORATIO

As thou art to thyself.

Such was the very armor he had on

When he the ambitious Norway⑧ combated⑨;⑩

75　So frowned he once, when, in an angry parle⑪

He smote⑫ the sledded Polacks⑬ on the ice.

'Tis strange.

---

① **'Tis gone … answer:** He is looking for his son Hamlet.
② **You … pale:** Cf. V. ii. 349: "You that look pale and tremble at this chance" etc.
③ **on't:** of it
④ **Before:** I swear before
⑤ **might not:** would not be able to
⑥ **sensible:** able to be sensed, confirmed by senses
⑦ **avouch:** avouchment, testimony
⑧ **Norway:** King of Norway (i.e. old Fortinbras)
⑨ **combated:** accented on the first syllable
⑩ **When … combated:** A foreshadow of the ensuing plot. This happened thirty years ago, in the very year when Hamlet was born. (How could Horatio possibly see him?)
⑪ **parle:** parley, talk; encounter
⑫ **smote:** past tense of smite, stroke
⑬ **the sledded Polacks:** Polish soldiers riding in sleds

MARCELLUS

Thus twice before, and jump[1] at this dead hour[2],
With martial stalk hath he gone by our watch[3].

HORATIO

80 In what particular thought to work I know not[4];
But in the gross and scope[5] of my opinion,[6]
This bodes[7] some strange eruption[8] to our state.[9]

MARCELLUS

Good[10] now, sit down, and tell me, he that knows,
Why this same strict and most observant watch[11]
85 So nightly toils[12] the subject[13] of the land,
And why such daily cast of brazen cannon,
And foreign mart[14] for implements of war;
Why such impress[15] of shipwrights, whose sore task
Does not divide the Sunday from the week;[16]

---

[1] **jump:** just, exactly
[2] **dead hour:** dead night
[3] **our watch:** as we stood on watch
[4] **I know not:** I don't know exactly
[5] **gross and scope:** gross scope (hendiadys)
[6] **in the gross ... opinion:** in my general opinion
[7] **bodes:** forebodes
[8] **eruption:** revolt or disturbance
[9] **This bodes ... state:** The state is the King's body politic. Cf. 128—130: "A little ere the mightest Julius fell" etc. I. iv. 99: "Something is rotten in the state of Denmark."
[10] **Good:** my good friends
[11] **watch:** vigilance
[12] **toils:** gives toils to, wearies
[13] **subject:** subjects, inhabitants
[14] **foreign mart:** foreign trade, expenditure abroad
[15] **impress:** impressments, forced labor, conscription
[16] **Does ... week:** work without rest (Cf. *Genesis* 2: 2—3; *Exodus* 8—11)

90　What might be toward①, that this sweaty haste②
　　Doth make the night joint-labourer③ with the day?
　　Who is't④ that can inform me?

HORATIO

　　That can I;⑤
　　At least, the whisper⑥ goes so. Our last king,
95　Whose image even but now appeared to us,
　　Was, as you know, by Fortinbras of Norway,
　　Thereto pricked on⑦ by a most emulate pride,⑧
　　Dared to the combat⑨; in which our valiant Hamlet,
　　For so this side of our known world⑩ esteemed him,⑪
100　Did slay⑫ this Fortinbras; who by a sealed compact⑬,
　　Well ratified by law and heraldry,⑭
　　Did forfeit, with his life, all those his lands
　　Which he stood seized of⑮, to the conqueror;
　　Against the which⑯, a moiety competent⑰
105　Was gaged⑱ by our king; which had⑲ returned

---

① **toward:** in prospect, about to happen
② **sweaty haste:** personification
③ **night joint-labourer:** night guards
④ **is't:** is it
⑤ **That can I:** Horatio plays the choric role who introduces antecedent happenings to the audience.
⑥ **whisper:** rumor
⑦ **pricked on:** stimulated
⑧ **Thereto ... pride:** provoked to do this by a proud desire to rival the Danish king
⑨ **combat:** single combat
⑩ **our known world:** all Europe
⑪ **For ... him:** an ironic comment
⑫ **slay:** kill
⑬ **a sealed compact** (accented on the second syllable): sworn agreement
⑭ **law and heraldry:** heraldic law (hendiadys), the law of arms
⑮ **stood seized of:** had possessed (his personal estates)
⑯ **the which:** which (i.e. the compact)
⑰ **a moiety competent:** an equivalent portion
⑱ **gaged:** engaged, pledged
⑲ **which had:** would have

To the inheritance of Fortinbras,
Had he been vanquisher; as, by the same covenant[1],
And carriage of the article designed[2],
His[3] fell to[4] Hamlet.[5] Now, sir, young Fortinbras,[6]
110 Of unimproved[7] mettle[8] hot and full,
Hath in the skirts[9] of Norway here and there
Sharked up[10] a list of lawless resolutes[11],
For food and diet[12], to some enterprise
That hath a stomach[13] in't; which is no other—
115 As it doth well appear unto our state—
But to recover of[14] us, by strong hand
And terms compulsatory[15], those foresaid lands
So by his father lost;[16] and this, I take it,
Is the main motive[17] of our preparations,
120 The source of this our watch and the chief head[18]
Of this post-haste[19] and romage[20] in the land.

---

[1] **covenant:** co-mart, mutual bargain
[2] **carriage of the article designed:** tenor of the agreement drawn up
[3] **His:** his land
[4] **fell to:** would be forfeit to
[5] **94—109:** Jungle law: might makes right.
[6] **young Fortinbras:** This is the first mention of Fortinbras (French: "fort en bras" = strong arm), the shadow of and complement to Hamlet.
[7] **unimproved:** unrefined, undisciplined
[8] **mettle:** courage
[9] **skirts:** outskirts, bordering parts
[10] **sharked up:** seized, gathered
[11] **a list of lawless resolutes:** a mob of desperadoes
[12] **For food and diet:** as cannon fodder
[13] **stomach:** appetite, spirit of adventure (a maw image)
[14] **of:** from
[15] **compulsatory:** compulsory
[16] **So by his father lost:** Hence a second revenging son-prince.
[17] **motive:** cause
[18] **chief head:** source, origin
[19] **post-haste:** urgency, rapid activity
[20] **romage:** commotion, bustle

BERNARDO

I think it be no other but e'en① so.

Well may it sort② that this portentous③ figure④

Comes armèd through our watch; so like the King

125 That was and is the question⑤ of these wars.⑥

HORATIO

A mote⑦ it is to trouble the mind's eye.⑧

In the most high and palmy⑨ state of Rome,

A little ere⑩ the mightiest Julius fell,

The graves stood tenantless⑪ and the sheeted⑫ dead

130 Did squeak and gibber⑬ in the Roman streets;⑭

As stars with trains of fire⑮ and dews of blood,

Disasters⑯ in the sun; and the moist star⑰

Upon whose influence Neptune's empire⑱ stands⑲

Was sick almost to doomsday⑳ with eclipse.

---

① **e'en:** exactly
② **sort:** accord, fit
③ **portentous:** foreboding some calamity
④ **figure:** the ghost
⑤ **question:** cause
⑥ "Valiant" old Hamlet has left his country in turmoil and peril.
⑦ **mote:** dust
⑧ **A mote … eye:** *Matthew* 7:3 "Why do you see the speck in your neighbor's eye, but don't notice the log in your own eye?" It is the first mention of the *Holy Bible*. There are altogether 39 biblical mentions and quotations, 28 of them made by Hamlet.
⑨ **palmy:** triumphant, prosperous
⑩ **ere:** before
⑪ **tenantless:** empty, void of corpses
⑫ **sheeted:** wrapped in shrouds
⑬ **squeak and glibber:** made inarticulate noises
⑭ **127—130:** Cosmic correspondence. Cf. *Julius Caesar*, I. iii. 63, 74 & II. ii. 14—24.
⑮ **stars with trains of fire:** comets
⑯ **Disasters:** threatening signs
⑰ **the moist star:** the moon, which governs the tides
⑱ **Neptune's empire:** the oceans
⑲ **stands:** depends
⑳ **almost to doomsday:** almost as if it were the end of the world

135 And even[1] the like[2] precurse[3] of fierce events,
As harbingers[4] preceding still[5] the fates[6]
And prologue to the omen[7] coming on,
Have heaven and earth together demonstrated
Unto our climatures[8] and countrymen.[9]
140 But soft[10], behold! Lo, where it comes again!
Re-enter Ghost
I'll cross[11] it, though it blast[12] me. Stay, illusion!
If thou hast any sound, or use of voice,
Speak to me.
If there be any good thing to be done,
145 That may to thee do ease and grace[13] to me,[14]
Speak to me.
Cock crows
If thou art privy to[15] thy country's fate[16],
Which, happily[17], foreknowing[18] may avoid, O, speak!

---

① **even:** exactly
② **the like:** the same
③ **precurse:** precursor(s), warning signs
④ **harbingers:** heralds
⑤ **still:** always
⑥ **the fates:** Goddesses of Fate
⑦ **omen:** ominous events
⑧ **climatures:** climes, geographical regions
⑨ **Unto ... countrymen:** Medieval Europeans generally believed in the doctrine of cosmic correspondence. (Cf. *Macbeth*, II. iii. 50—56; iv. 5—18)
⑩ **soft:** enough; be quiet
⑪ **cross:** cross its path; draw a cross (to ward off the supernatural)
⑫ **blast:** destroy
⑬ **grace:** do grace
⑭ **That may ... me:** make you rest in peace and bring me credit
⑮ **art privy to:** have secret knowledge of
⑯ **fate:** destiny
⑰ **happily:** haply (perhaps); fortunately
⑱ **foreknowing:** advance knowledge

Or if thou hast uphoarded① in thy life.
150 Extorted② treasure in the womb of earth,
For which, they say, you spirits oft③ walk in death.
The cock crows.
Speak of it! Stay, and speak! Stop it, Marcellus!
MARCELLUS
Shall I strike at it with my partisan④?
HORATIO
Do, if it will not stand⑤.
BERNARDO
155 'Tis here!
HORATIO
'Tis here!
MARCELLUS
'Tis gone!
Exit Ghost
We do it wrong, being so majestical⑥,
To offer it the show of violence;
For it is, as the air, invulnerable,
And our vain blows malicious⑦ mockery⑧.
BERNARDO
160 It was about to speak, when the cock crew.
HORATIO
And then it started like a guilty thing
Upon a fearful summons. I have heard,

---

① **uphoarded:** accumulated
② **extorted:** wrongfully obtained
③ **oft:** often
④ **Partisan:** halberd
⑤ **stand:** stay
⑥ **majestical:** majestic
⑦ **malicious:** are malicious
⑧ **mockery:** mock (ineffectual) malice

165 The cock, that is the trumpet① to the morn,
 Doth with his lofty② and shrill-sounding throat
 Awake the god of day③; and, at his warning,
 Whether in sea or fire, in earth or air,④
 The extravagant⑤ and erring⑥ spirit hies⑦
170 To his confine⑧; and of the truth herein
 This present object⑨ made probation⑩.⑪

MARCELLUS

 It faded on the crowing of the cock.
 Some say that ever⑫ 'gainst⑬ that season⑭ comes
 Wherein our Saviour's birth is celebrated,
175 The bird of dawning⑮ singeth all night long;
 And then, they say, no spirit dares stir abroad⑯;
 The nights are wholesome⑰; then no planets strike⑱,
 No fairy takes⑲, nor witch hath power to charm,
 So hallowed⑳ and so gracious㉑ is the time.

---

① **trumpet:** trumpeter, herald
② **lofty:** high-pitched
③ **the god of day:** sun-god
④ **Whether ... air:** Sea, fire, earth and air are the four elements.
⑤ **extravagant:** out of bounds
⑥ **erring:** wandering (e.g. knight errant)
⑦ **hies:** hastens
⑧ **confine:** proper home; place of confinement
⑨ **object:** sight
⑩ **probation:** proof.
⑪ **This ... probation:** This recent sight has just proved its truth.
⑫ **ever:** every time
⑬ **'gainst:** against, just before
⑭ **season:** late December
⑮ **bird of dawning:** cock
⑯ **stir abroad:** move beyond its confine
⑰ **wholesome:** healthy
⑱ **strike:** blast with misfortune, exert evil influences
⑲ **takes:** bewitches, puts under magical spell
⑳ **hallowed:** sanctified
㉑ **gracioius:** blessed

HORATIO

180　So have I heard and do in part believe it.①
　　But, look, the morn, in russet② mantle clad,
　　Walks o'er the dew of yon high eastern hill.③
　　Break we our watch up④; and by my advice⑤,
　　Let us impart what we have seen tonight
185　Unto young Hamlet⑥; for, upon my life,
　　This spirit, dumb to us, will speak to him.
　　Do you consent we shall acquaint him with it,
　　As needful⑦ in our loves, fitting our duty?

MARCELLUS

　　Let's do't, I pray; and I this morning know
190　Where we shall find him most conveniently.

Exeunt

---

① **So ... it:** He is less of a scholar now!
② **russet:** grayish, brownish
③ **But ... hill:** Cf. *Much Ado about Nothing*, V. iii. 27—29: "and look, the gentle day, / Before the wheels of Phoebus, round about / Dapples the drowsy east with spots of grey."
④ **Break ... up:** Let us bring our guard duty to an end
⑤ **by my advice:** I suggest
⑥ **young Hamlet:** the first mention of the title hero
⑦ **needful:** necessary

SCENE II. A room of state in the castle.

Flourish[1]. *Enter KING, QUEEN, HAMLET, POLONIUS, LAERTES, VOLTEMAND, CORNELIUS, Lords, and Attendants*

KING
Though yet[2] of Hamlet our[3] dear brother's death
The memory be green[4], and that[5] it us befitted[6]
To bear our hearts in grief and our whole kingdom
To be contracted in one brow of woe,[7]
5   Yet[8] so far hath discretion[9] fought with nature
That we with wisest sorrow think on him,
Together with remembrance of ourselves.
Therefore[10] our[11] sometime[12] sister[13], now our queen,
The imperial jointress[14] to this warlike state,
10 Have we, as 'twere with a defeated[15] joy,

---

[1] **Flourish:** a fanfare of trumpets
[2] **yet:** still
[3] **our:** the royal plural
[4] **green:** fresh
[5] **that:** though; consequently
[6] **befitted:** would have been appropriate for us
[7] **To be ... woe:** personification
[8] **yet:** a shrewd turn
[9] **discretion:** reason
[10] **Therefore:** a second turn
[11] **our:** the royal plural (a clever pun)
[12] **sometime:** former
[13] **sister:** sister-in-law
[14] **jointress:** a widow who is a joint inheritor (it recalls Elizabeth I)
[15] **defeated:** frustrated, overcome

With an auspicious[1] and a dropping[2] eye,
With mirth in funeral and with dirge in marriage,
In equal scale weighing delight and dole[3],
Taken to wife.[4] Nor have we herein barred[5]
15 Your better wisdoms[6], which have freely gone
With this affair along.[7] For all, our thanks.[8]
Now follows, that[9] you know, young Fortinbras,
Holding a weak supposal of our worth[10],
Or thinking by our late dear brother's death
20 Our state to be disjoint[11] and out of frame,[12]
Colleagued[13] with the dream of his advantage[14],
He hath not failed to pester us with message,
Importing[15] the surrender of those lands
Lost by his father, with all bonds of law[16],
25 To our most valiant brother.[17] So much for him.
Now for ourself and for this time of meeting.

---

[1] **auspicious:** joyful
[2] **dropping:** tearful, drooping
[3] **In equal ... dole:** balancing joy against an equivalent quantity of sorrow
[4] **Taken to wife:** He deliberately postpones the information.
[5] **barred:** excluded
[6] **wisdoms:** wise preference
[7] **With this affair along:** He justifies his action and shifts the burden.
[8] **For all, our thanks:** It is a vigorous ending that bespeaks "a certain appropriate majesty" (S. T. Coleridge).
[9] **that:** as
[10] **a weak supposal of our worth:** a poor estimation of my ability
[11] **disjoint:** disjointed
[12] **Our ...frame:** Cf. I. v. 208: "The time is out of joint."
[13] **Colleagued:** allied
[14] **advantage:** superior position
[15] **importing:** demanding
[16] **bonds of law:** legal bonds
[17] Cf. I. i. 98: "our valiant Hamlet" (From "the general censure" we can roughly tell what old Hamlet was like in his lifetime.)

Thus much the business is: we have here writ[1]
To Norway, uncle of young Fortinbras,
Who, impotent[2] and bed-rid[3], scarcely hears
Of this his nephew's purpose, to suppress
His further gait[4] herein; in that the levies,
The lists and full proportions[5] are all made[6]
Out of his subject[7]; and we here dispatch
You, good Cornelius, and you, Voltemand,
For[8] bearers[9] of this greeting to old Norway;
Giving to you no further personal power
To business[10] with the King, more than the scope
Of these delated articles[11] allow.
Farewell, and let your haste commend your duty[12].

CORNELIUS VOLTEMAND
In that and all things will we show our duty.[13]

KING
We doubt it nothing[14]. Heartily farewell.
Exeunt VOLTEMAND and CORNELIUS
And now, Laertes, what's the news with you?[15]

---

[1] **writ:** written
[2] **impotent:** incapable
[3] **bed-rid:** bed-ridden
[4] **gait:** course, proceeding
[5] **The lists and full propotions:** the troops and the supplies
[6] **made:** drawn
[7] **subject:** subjects
[8] **For:** as
[9] **bearers:** messengers
[10] **business:** negotiate
[11] **delated articles:** detailed items
[12] **let ... duty:** prove your duty by the speed with which you accomplish your mission; let your speedy departure take the place of ceremonious leave-taking
[13] **duty:** the medieval society is a duty-based hierarchy.
[14] **We doubt it nothing:** we have complete confidence in you
[15] **you:** "You" and "thou" indicate different social distances. "You" is more formal.

You told us of some suit①; what is't, Laertes?
You cannot speak of reason② to the Dane③,
And loose your voice④. What wouldst thou beg, Laertes,
45 That shall not be my offer, not⑤ thy asking?⑥
The head is not more native⑦ to the heart,
The hand more instrumental to the mouth,
Than is the throne of Denmark to thy father.⑧
What wouldst thou have, Laertes?⑨.

50 **LAERTES**

My dread lord,
Your leave and favour⑩ to return to France;
From whence though willingly I came to Denmark,
To show my duty in your coronation,
Yet now, I must confess, that duty done,
55 My thoughts and wishes bend again toward France
And bow⑪ them to your gracious leave and pardon.

KING

Have you your father's leave? What says Polonius?

POLONIUS

He hath, my lord, wrung from me my slow⑫ leave
By laboursome⑬ petition, and at last

---

① **suit:** request
② **speak of reason:** make a reasonable request
③ **the Dane:** king of Denmark
④ **loose your voice:** speak in vain
⑤ **not:** without
⑥ **That ... asking:** "My" and "thy" are both terms of endearment.
⑦ **native:** obliged, connected
⑧ 46—48: It is an indirect compliment to Polonius.
⑨ 41—49: There are altogether 4 Laertes's, 2 thou's and 2 thy's.
⑩ **Your leave and favour:** the favor of your permission (hendiadys)
⑪ **bow:** submit
⑫ **slow:** reluctant
⑬ **laboursome:** repeated

60 Upon his will I sealed my hard① consent.
I do beseech you, give him leave to go.
KING
Take② thy fair hour③, Laertes; time be thine④,
And thy best graces spend it at thy will!⑤
But now, my cousin⑥ Hamlet, and my son—⑦
65 **HAMLET**
[*Aside*]⑧ A little more than kin, and less than kind⑨.⑩
KING
How is it that the clouds still⑪ hang on you?
HAMLET
Not so, my lord; I am too much i' the sun.⑫
QUEEN
Good Hamlet,⑬ cast thy nighted⑭ color⑮ off,
And let thine⑯ eye look like a friend on Denmark⑰.

---

① **hard:** unwilling
② **take:** enjoy
③ **fair hour:** youth (Cf. Edmund Spenser: "Make haste while it is prime.")
④ **time be thine:** let time be yours
⑤ **And … will:** May your virtues control the way you spend it.
⑥ **cousin:** kinsman
⑦ **But now … son:** He is hesitating how to orientate their relationship.
⑧ He refuses to answer, hence an embarrassing change of atmosphere.
⑨ **kind:** of a kind (a son here); benevolent.
⑩ **kin, kind:** The nearer in kin, the less in kindness. "Kin" alliterates with "kind". A. C. Bradley: "Hamlet … is fond of quibbles and word-play, and of 'conceits' and turns of thought"; this tendency "betokens a nimbleness and flexibility of mind which is characteristic of him and not of the later many-sided heroes." (*Shakespearean Tragedy*, London: The Macmillan Press Ltd., 1974, p.120)
⑪ **still:** always
⑫ He puns on "sun" and "son". There are many interpretations for this line, such as "You have given too much avuncular love (for me to be gloomy)", "I have been a son for too long a time" etc.
⑬ **Good Hamlet:** Her first words addressed to Hamlet. Cf. her last words: "oh my dear Hamlet" (V. ii. 323—324)
⑭ **nighted:** dark
⑮ **color:** mourning dress
⑯ **thine:** "Thine" is more familiar than "your".
⑰ **Denmark:** the King

70　Do not for ever with thy vailèd① lids②
　　Seek for thy noble father in the dust.
　　Thou know'st 'tis common; all that lives must die,
　　Passing through nature③ to eternity.
　　HAMLET
　　Ay④, madam, it is common.⑤
75　**QUEEN**
　　If it be,
　　Why seems it so particular with thee?
　　HAMLET
　　Seems, madam!⑥ Nay, it is; I know not 'seems'.⑦
　　'Tis not alone my inky⑧ cloak, good mother⑨,
　　Nor customary suits⑩ of solemn black,
80　Nor windy suspiration⑪ of forced⑫ breath,
　　No, nor the fruitful⑬ river in the eye⑭,
　　Nor the dejected⑮ 'havior⑯ of the visage⑰,
　　Together with all forms, moods, shapes of grief,
　　That can denote⑱ me truly. These indeed seem,

---

① **vailèd:** lowered
② **lids:** eyelids
③ **nature:** natural life
④ **Ay:** yes
⑤ **it is common:** It is an ironic agreement.
⑥ **Seems, madam:** He takes up the word "seems" and twists it against the speaker.
⑦ **seems:** a pun on "seams".
⑧ **inky:** dark
⑨ **good mother:** a term for step-mother or mother-in-law (used sarcastically here)
⑩ **customary suits:** garments, clothes
⑪ **windy suspiration:** sighs
⑫ **forced:** strong; affected
⑬ **fruitful:** copious
⑭ **the fruitful ... eye:** abundant flow of tears
⑮ **dejected:** depressed, dowcast
⑯ **'havior:** behavior, appearance
⑰ **visage:** face
⑱ **denote:** indicate, express

For they are actions that a man might play;
85 But I have that within which passeth① show;
These but the trappings② and the suits③ of woe.
KING④
'Tis sweet and commendable⑤ in your nature⑥, Hamlet,
To give these mourning duties to your father;
But, you must know, your father lost a father;
90 That father lost, lost his, and the survivor bound⑦
In filial obligation for some term⑧
To do obsequious⑨ sorrow. But to persever⑩
In obstinate condolement⑪ is a course⑫
Of impious⑬ stubbornness; 'tis unmanly grief;
95 It shows a will most incorrect⑭ to heaven⑮,
A heart unfortified⑯, a mind impatient⑰,
An understanding simple⑱ and unschooled⑲:
For what we know must be and is as common

---

① **passeth:** surpasses
② **trappings:** accoutrements
③ **suits:** clothes, embellishments
④ **92ff.:** a speech against "obstinate condolement". Cf. *Twelfth Night*, I. V. 63—69
⑤ **commendable:** (accented on the first syllable) praiseworthy, laudable
⑥ **nature:** human nature
⑦ **bound:** being bound (obliged, committed)
⑧ **term:** period of time
⑨ **obsequious:** dutiful; suitable for funeral rites
⑩ **persever:** (accented on the second syllable) persevere
⑪ **condolement:** grieving, condolence
⑫ **course:** way
⑬ **impious:** undutiful, profane
⑭ **incorrect:** disobedient
⑮ **heaven:** the 1st mention
⑯ **unforified:** weak
⑰ **impatient:** restless, incapable of suffering
⑱ **simple:** foolish, inexperienced
⑲ **unschooled:** childish

As any the most vulgar① thing to sense②,
100　Why should we in our peevish③ opposition
　　　Take it to heart? Fie! 'tis a fault④ to heaven⑤,
　　　A fault against the dead, a fault to nature⑥,
　　　To reason most absurd, whose⑦ common theme⑧
　　　Is death of fathers, and who⑨ still⑩ hath cried,
105　From the first corse⑪ till he⑫ that died to-day,
　　　'This must be so.' We pray you, throw to earth
　　　This unprevailing⑬ woe, and think of us⑭
　　　As of a father; for let the world take note,
　　　You are the most immediate to our throne;⑮
110　And with⑯ no less nobility of love⑰
　　　Than that which⑱ dearest father bears his son,
　　　Do I impart toward you. For⑲ your intent

---

① **vulgar:** common
② **sense:** perception
③ **peevish:** foolish
④ **fault:** offense
⑤ **heaven:** the 2nd mention
⑥ **nature:** natural law
⑦ **whose:** nature's; reason's
⑧ **theme:** topic
⑨ **who:** nature; reason
⑩ **still:** always
⑪ **corse:** corpse. In Judaeo-Christian tradition, the first corpse was that of Abel, who was killed by Cain, his elder brother (*Genesis* 4:11—12), which has been archetypal of sibling slaughter. Its unconscious allusion here simply betrays the speaker's innermost sense of guilt.
⑫ **he:** him
⑬ **unprevailing:** unavailing, futile, useless
⑭ **us:** the royal plural (Claudius refers to himself.)
⑮ **You are ... throne:** You are my heir
⑯ **with:** redundant word
⑰ **no less ... love:** distinguished affection
⑱ **which:** what
⑲ **For:** as for

In going back to school in Wittenberg①,
115　It is most retrograde② to our③ desire;
　　　And we beseech you, bend you④ to remain
　　　Here, in the cheer and comfort of our eye,⑤
　　　Our chiefest courtier, cousin, and our son.
　　　QUEEN
　　　Let not thy mother lose her prayers⑥, Hamlet.
120　I pray thee, stay with us; go not to Wittenberg.
　　　HAMLET
　　　I shall in all my best obey you⑦, madam.

　　　KING
　　　Why, 'tis a loving and a fair reply.
　　　Be as ourself⑧ in Denmark. Madam, come;
　　　This gentle and unforced accord of Hamlet
125　Sits smiling to⑨ my heart;⑩ in grace whereof⑪,
　　　No jocund⑫ health⑬ that Denmark drinks to-day,

---

① **school in Wittenberg:** It was founded in 1502 (so it is anachronistic for Hamlet to go to Wittenberg in the 12th century), which was the cradle of Martin Luther's Reformation. Luther posted his famous *Ninety-Five Theses* on the castle church door in 1517, and Bruno visited Wittenberg in 1586. So it had been a center for revolutionary thoughts in Europe by the end of the 16th century. (As to the question whether Hamlet was at Wittenberg at the time of his father's murder, see A. C. Bradley: *Shakespearean Tragedy*, pp.343—344.)
② **retrograde:** contrary
③ **our:** my
④ **bend you:** change your mind
⑤ **in the cheer ... eye:** He wants to keep Hamlet under control.
⑥ **Let not ... prayers:** Don't let me entreat in vain
⑦ **you:** "You" is more formal than "thee".
⑧ **Be as ourself:** behave as if you were king
⑨ **to:** at
⑩ **Sits ... heart:** personification
⑪ **whereof:** in honor of which
⑫ **jocund:** merry, joyful
⑬ **health:** toast

But the great cannon to the clouds shall tell①,
And the King's rouse② the heavens shall bruit③ again,
Re-speaking④ earthly thunder⑤. Come away.

130 *Exeunt all but HAMLET*

HAMLET

O, that this too too solid⑥ flesh would melt,
Thaw and resolve⑦ itself into a dew!
Or that the Everlasting⑧ had not fixed
His canon⑨ 'gainst self-slaughter!⑩ O God! God!
How weary, stale, flat and unprofitable,
135 Seem to me all the uses⑪ of this world!⑫
Fie⑬ on't! ah fie! 'tis an unweeded⑭ garden⑮,
That grows to seed⑯; things rank⑰ and gross⑱ in nature
Possess it merely⑲. That it should come to this!
But two months dead—nay, not so much, not two!

---

① **tell:** count, announce
② **rouse:** carousal, deep drink
③ **bruit:** report
④ **Re-speaking:** echoing
⑤ **earthly thunder:** cannon; the King's voice
⑥ **solid:** The First Quarto (Q1) reads "sullied", the Second Quarto (Q2) reads "sallied" (assailed), and "solid" is the Folio (F) reading.
⑦ **resolve:** dissolve
⑧ **Everlasting:** God
⑨ **canon:** divine law
⑩ **His ... self-slaughter:** *Exodus* 20.13: "Thou shalt not kill."
⑪ **uses:** doings, customs; enjoyments
⑫ **134—135:** He is sick of the world. (Cf. III. i. 78—90)
⑬ **Fie:** a strong exclamation of shock, reproach or disgust
⑭ **unweeded:** untilled
⑮ **garden:** The garden is a symbol of state or government. (Cf. *Richard II*, III. iv 40—46 & *Henry V*, V. ii. 41—53)
⑯ **grows to seed:** goes to seed, grows shabby
⑰ **things rank:** thick and rampant
⑱ **gross:** luxuriant
⑲ **merely:** entirely

So excellent a king, that was to this[1]
140 Hyperion[2] to a satyr[3], so loving to my mother
That he might not[4] beteem[5] the winds of heaven
Visit her face too roughly. Heaven and earth!
Must I remember? why, she would hang on him,
As if increase of appetite[6] had grown[7]
145 By what it fed on[8], and yet, within a month—
Let me not think on't! Frailty[9], thy name[10] is woman![11]
A little month, or ere[12] those shoes were old
With which she followed my poor father's body,
Like Niobe[13], all tears—why she, even she—O, God! a beast that wants[14]
150 discourse of reason[15],
Would have mourned longer—married with my uncle,
My father's brother, but no more like my father
Than I to Hercules[16]. Within a month,
Ere yet the salt of most unrighteous[17] tears

---

[1] **to this:** compared with the present king
[2] **Hyperion:** Greek sun god
[3] **satyr:** ugly and lustful goat-man.
[4] **might not:** would not; had not the might (strength) to
[5] **beteem:** allow
[6] **appetite:** desire, love. Cf. *Twelfth Night*, II. iv. 104—108: "Orsino: their love may be called appetite / ... / But mine is all as hungry as the sea,/And can digest as much."
[7] **grown:** increased
[8] **By what it fed on:** by being satisfied;
[9] **Frailty:** weakness, inconstancy (cf. *1 Henry IV*, III. iii. 166—168: Falstaff: "I have more flesh than another man, and therefore more frailty.)"
[10] **name:** essence; symbolic representation (Cf. Vico: *New Science*, 433 & 484)
[11] **Fraitty ... woman:** Women are thought to embody frailty or lack of constancy. Cf. Virgil: *Aeneid*. 4.569—570: "Varium et mutabile semper femina."
[12] **ere:** even before
[13] **Niobe:** Queen of Thebes, who lost all her children and herself became a stone.
[14] **wants:** lacks
[15] **discourse of reason:** ability to reason, faculty of reasoning
[16] **Hercules:** a demigod, a symbol of strength and courage
[17] **unrighteous:** not virtuous, insincere

Had left the flushing① in her galled② eyes,
155 She married. O, most wicked speed, to post③
With such dexterity④ to incestuous⑤ sheets!⑥
It is not, nor it cannot⑦ come to good.
But break my heart, for I must hold my tongue.
Enter HORATIO, MARCELLUS, and BERNARDO

160 **HORATIO**

Hail to your lordship!

HAMLET

I am glad to see you well.

Horatio,—or⑧ I do forget myself.⑨

HORATIO

The same, my lord, and your poor servant ever.

HAMLET

Sir, my good friend; I'll change⑩ that name⑪ with you.⑫

---

① **flushing:** redness
② **galled:** irritated, inflamed
③ **post:** rush
④ **dexterity:** skillfulness
⑤ **incestuous:** In Tudor England, it was regarded as incestuous if a widow was married to her husband's brother. Cf. *Leviticus*, 20:21: (Jehovah said to Moses) "If a man takes his brother's wife, it is impurity" etc. Very likely, Claudius would remind Shakespeare's contemporaries of Henry VIII, who divorced his wife Catherine, widow of his brother, in order to marry Ann Boleyn, who gave birth to Elizabeth I.
⑥ **155—156:** Pay attention to the "s" and "ʃ" sounds used here.
⑦ **nor it cannot:** can (an emphatic double negative)
⑧ **or:** unless
⑨ **Horatio, ... myself:** Proverb: A friend is our second self. Cf. Aristotle: *Nicomachean Ethics*, 1170b: "ἕτερος γὰρ αὐτὸς ὁ φίλος ἐστίν" & Zeno: "ἐρωτηθεὶς τίς ἐστι φίλος, ἄλλος, ἔφη, ἐγώ." (Diogenes Laertius: *Lives of Eminent Philosophers*, 7.1.23)
⑩ **change:** exchange
⑪ **name:** i.e. your poor servant
⑫ **I'll change ... you:** We'll call each other "friend".

And what make you from① Wittenberg, Horatio? Marcellus?

MARCELLUS

My good lord—

HAMLET

I am very glad to see you. Good even②, sir.

But what, in faith③, make you from Wittenberg?

HORATIO

A truant④ disposition, good my lord⑤.

HAMLET

I would not hear⑥ your enemy say so,

Nor shall you do mine ear that violence,

To make it truster of⑦ your own report

Against yourself. I know you are no truant.

But what is your affair in Elsinore?

We'll teach you to drink deep⑧ ere you depart.

HORATIO

My lord, I came to see your father's funeral.

HAMLET

I pray thee, do not mock me, fellow-student;

I think it was to see my mother's wedding.

HORATIO

Indeed, my lord, it followed hard upon⑨.

HAMLET

---

① **what make you from:** what are you doing away from
② **even:** evening
③ **in faith:** in truth
④ **truant:** time-wasting
⑤ **good my lord:** a particularly deferential form of address
⑥ **hear:** allow
⑦ **truster of:** one that trusts
⑧ **drink deep:** drink deeply (a school custom)
⑨ **hard upon:** soon after

Thrift, thrift[①], Horatio! the funeral baked meats
180 Did coldly furnish forth the marriage tables.
Would I had met my dearest[②] foe[③] in heaven
Or ever[④] I had seen that day, Horatio!
My father!—methinks[⑤] I see my father.
HORATIO
Where, my lord?
185 **HAMLET**
In my mind's eye, Horatio.
HORATIO
I saw him once; he was a goodly[⑥] king.
HAMLET
He was a man, take him for all in all,
I shall not look upon his like again.
HORATIO
My lord, I think I saw him yesternight[⑦].
190 **HAMLET**
Saw? who?
HORATIO
My lord, the King your father.
HAMLET
The King my father!
HORATIO

---

① **Thrift, thrift:** A. C. Bradley: "This repetition is a habit with Hamlet" (*Shakespearean Tragedy,* p.119), and "a habit of repetition quite as marked by Hamlet's may be found in comic persons, *e.g.* Justice Shallow in *2 Henry IV.*" (p.119, n.1)

② **dearest:** bitterest, direst

③ **dearest foe:** oxymoron. Cf. *Henry V*, V. ii. 202—203: "I love thee cruelly"

④ **ever:** ever before

⑤ **methinks:** I think

⑥ **goodly:** admirable, excellent

⑦ **yesternight:** last night

Season[1] your admiration[2] for awhile
With an attent[3] ear, till I may deliver[4],
Upon the witness of these gentlemen,
195 This marvel to you.

HAMLET
For God's love, let me hear.

HORATIO
Two nights together had these gentlemen,
Marcellus and Bernardo, on their watch,
In the dead vast[5] and middle of the night,
200 Been thus encountered. A figure like your father,
Armed at point[6] exactly, cap-a-pe[7],
Appears[8] before them, and with solemn march
Goes[9] slow[10] and stately by them. Thrice he walked
By their oppressed[11] and fear-surprisèd[12] eyes,
205 Within his truncheon's[13] length; whilst they, distilled[14]
Almost to jelly with the act[15] of fear[16],
Stand[17] dumb and speak[18] not to him. This to me

---

[1] **Season:** moderate
[2] **admiration:** wonder, astonishment
[3] **attent:** attentive
[4] **deliver:** relate, report
[5] **dead vast:** great darkness
[6] **at point:** every point
[7] **cap-a-pe:** from top to toe (French: cap-à-pied)
[8] **Appears:** dramatic present
[9] **Goes:** dramatic present
[10] **slow:** slowly
[11] **oppressed:** overwhelmed
[12] **fear-surprisèd:** terrified
[13] **truncheon's:** mace, staff carried by kings
[14] **distilled:** reduced
[15] **act:** effect; action
[16] **fear:** i.e. fear on them
[17] **stand:** dramatic present
[18] **speak:** dramatic present

In dreadful① secrecy impart they did;
210　And I with them the third night kept the watch;
Where, as they had delivered, both in time,
Form of the thing②, each word made true and good,
The apparition comes③. I knew your father:
These hands are not more like④.

215　**HAMLET**

But where was this?

MARCELLUS

My lord, upon the platform where we watched⑤.

HAMLET

Did you not speak to it?

HORATIO

My lord, I did;
But answer made it none. Yet once methought⑥
220　It lifted up its head and did address
Itself to motion⑦, like as⑧ it would speak;
But even then the morning cock crew loud,
And at the sound it shrunk⑨ in haste away,
And vanished from our sight.

225　**HAMLET**

'Tis very strange.

HORATIO

As I do live, my honored lord, 'tis true;

---

① **dreadful:** laden with dread
② **the thing:** the ghost
③ **comes:** dramatic present
④ **more like:** more like than your father and the ghost
⑤ **we watched:** kept watch
⑥ **methought:** I thought
⑦ **Itself to motion:** begin to make motions
⑧ **like as:** as if
⑨ **shrunk:** shrank

And we did think it writ down in our duty[1]
To let you know of it.

HAMLET

Indeed, indeed, sirs, but this troubles me.
Hold you the watch tonight?

MARCELLUS BERNARDO

230 We do, my lord.

HAMLET

Armed, say you?

MARCELLUS BERNARDO

Armed, my lord.

HAMLET

From top to toe?

MARCELLUS BERNARDO

My lord, from head to foot.

235 **HAMLET**

Then saw you not his face?

HORATIO

O, yes, my lord! he wore his beaver[2] up.

HAMLET

What, looked he frowningly[3]?

HORATIO

A countenance[4] more in sorrow than in anger.

HAMLET

Pale or red?

240 **HORATIO**

Nay, very pale.

HAMLET

---

[1] **writ down in our duty:** required by the loyalty we owe you
[2] **beaver:** mask, helmet's visor
[3] **frowningly:** a sign of sorrow
[4] **countenance:** expression of the face

And fixed his eyes upon you?

HORATIO

Most constantly.

HAMLET

I would I had been there.

HORATIO

It would have much amazed you①.

245 **HAMLET**

Very like②, very like. Stayed it long?

HORATIO

While one with moderate haste might tell③ a hundred.

MARCELLUS BERNARDO

Longer, longer.

HORATIO

Not when I saw't.

HAMLET

His beard was grizzled④—no⑤?

250 **HORATIO**

It was, as I have seen it in his life,
A sable silvered.⑥

HAMLET

I will watch tonight;
Perchance 'twill walk again.

HORATIO

I warrant it will.

---

① **amazed you:** confused your thoughts
② **very like:** likely
③ **tell:** count
④ **grizzled:** gray
⑤ **no:** wasn't it
⑥ **A sable silvered:** black tipped and shot through with silver

255 **HAMLET**

If it assume[1] my noble father's person,
I'll speak to it, though[2] hell itself should gape
And bid me hold my peace[3]. I pray you all,
If you have hitherto concealed this sight,
Let it be tenable[4] in your silence still[5],
260 And[6] whatsoever else shall hap[7] tonight,
Give it an understanding, but no tongue.[8]
I will requite[9] your loves.[10]
So, fare you well.
Upon the platform, 'twixt eleven and twelve,
265 I'll visit you.

All

Our duty to your honor.

HAMLET

Your loves[11], as mine[12] to you. Farewell.

Exeunt all but HAMLET

My father's spirit in arms! All is not well;
I doubt[13] some foul play[14]. Would the night were come!

---

[1] **assume:** take on
[2] **though:** even though
[3] **peace:** be silent
[4] **tenable:** held
[5] **still:** always
[6] **and:** if
[7] **hap:** happen
[8] **Give ... tongue:** Keep mum about this.
[9] **requite:** repay
[10] **loves:** "Love" in Shakespeare's time often took the plural form.
[11] **Your loves:** your loves instead of duty
[12] **mine:** my love
[13] **doubt:** fear, suspect
[14] **foul play:** treacherous action

270 Till then sit still, my soul. Foul deeds will rise①,
Though all the earth o'erwhelm② them, to③ men's eyes.④
Exit

SCENE III. A room in Polonius' house.

Enter LAERTES and OPHELIA

LAERTES
My necessaries⑤ are embarked⑥. Farewell.
And, sister, as⑦ the winds give benefit
And convoy⑧ is assistant⑨, do not sleep,
But let me hear from you.
OPHELIA
5 Do you doubt that?
LAERTES
For⑩ Hamlet and the trifling of his favour⑪,
Hold⑫ it a fashion⑬ and a toy⑭ in blood⑮,

---

① **rise:** be revealed
② **o'verwhlem:** shut
③ **to:** from
④ **270—271:** an epilogue, which is composed of two rhyming lines.
⑤ **necessaries:** personal belongings
⑥ **embarked:** on board ship
⑦ **as:** according as, when
⑧ **convoy:** means of transportation, ships
⑨ **assistant:** available
⑩ **For:** as for, as regards
⑪ **favour:** attention to you
⑫ **Hold:** consider
⑬ **fashion:** temporary enthusiasm
⑭ **toy:** caprice
⑮ **blood:** amorous flirtation, youthful passion (Blood was believed to be the seat of emotions in the Middle Ages.)

A violet in the youth of primy nature[1],
Forward[2], not permanent, sweet, not lasting,
10 The perfume and suppliance[3] of a minute,[4]
No more.

OPHELIA
No more but so[5]?

LAERTES
Think it no more;
For nature crescent[6] does not grow alone
15 In thews and bulk[7], but as this temple[8] waxes[9],
The inward service[10] of the mind and soul
Grows wide withal[11]. Perhaps he loves you now,
And now no soil[12] nor cautel[13] doth besmirch[14]
The virtue of his will[15]; but you must fear,
20 His greatness[16] weighed[17], his will is not his own;
For he himself is subject to his birth.
He may not, as unvalued persons do,
Carve[18] for himself; for on his choice depends

---

[1] **primy nature:** the springtime of life
[2] **Forward:** early, premature; ardent, eager
[3] **suppliance:** supply, pastime
[4] **The perfume ... minute:** that which supplies the sensory pleasure of a moment
[5] **No more but so:** no more than that
[6] **crescent:** growing (post attributive)
[7] **thews and bulk:** sinews and stature, strength and size; physically
[8] **this temple:** the body
[9] **waxes:** grows
[10] **inward service:** inner life
[11] **withal:** with it, at the same time
[12] **soil:** foul thought
[13] **cautel:** craft, deceit
[14] **besmirch:** sully, defile, contaminate
[15] **will:** desire
[16] **greatness:** high rank
[17] **weighed:** considered
[18] **Carve:** choose

The safety and health① of this whole state;②
25 And therefore must his choice be circumscribed③
　　Unto④ the voice⑤ and yielding⑥ of that body⑦
　　Whereof he is the head. Then if he says he loves you,
　　It fits your wisdom so far to believe it⑧
　　As he in his particular act and place⑨
30 May give his saying deed⑩; which is no further
　　Than the main⑪ voice of Denmark goes withal.
　　Then weigh what loss your honor may sustain⑫,
　　If with too credent⑬ ear you list⑭ his songs⑮,
　　Or lose your heart, or your chaste treasure⑯ open
35 To his unmastered⑰ importunity⑱⑲.
　　Fear it, Ophelia, fear it, my dear sister,
　　And keep you in the rear of your affection,⑳

① **The safety and health:** well-being, welfare
② **The safety ... state:** Cf. III. iii. 9—11
③ **circumscribed:** restricted
④ **Unto:** by
⑤ **voice:** vote
⑥ **yielding:** approval
⑦ **that body:** body politic, the state
⑧ **It fits ... it:** you would be wise to believe it only so far
⑨ **his particular act and place:** specific role and position
⑩ **give his saying deed:** put his words of love into action
⑪ **main:** mighty; general
⑫ **sustain:** suffer
⑬ **credent:** gullible; credulous
⑭ **list:** listen to
⑮ **songs:** sweet words
⑯ **chaste treasure:** chastity, maidenly virtue
⑰ **unmastered:** uncontrolled
⑱ **importunity:** emotional pleading, seduction (Some productions and films presume that her relationship with Hamlet is already a sexual one, as can be deduced from the songs she sings in IV. v.)
⑲ Laertes may be inadvertently talking about himself while talking about Hamlet.
⑳ **keep ... affection:** hold yourself back from what affection would lead you to

Out of the shot[1] and danger of desire.[2]
The chariest[3] maid is prodigal enough,
40 If she unmask her beauty to the moon.
Virtue itself 'scapes[4] not calumnious[5] strokes.
The canker[6] galls[7] the infants of the spring[8],
Too oft before their buttons[9] be disclosed[10],
And in the morn[11] and liquid dew of youth
45 Contagious blastments[12] are most imminent[13].
Be wary then; best safety lies in fear.
Youth to itself rebels[14], though none else near[15].

OPHELIA

I shall the effect[16] of this good lesson[17] keep,
As watchman[18] to my heart. But, good my brother,
50 Do not, as some ungracious[19] pastors[20] do,

---

[1] **shot:** range of a bow or gun
[2] **And keep ... desire:** Do not let your love be spoiled by desire.
[3] **chariest:** most careful
[4] **'scapes:** escapes
[5] **calumnious:** slanderous
[6] **canker:** cankerworm
[7] **galls:** gnaws, damages
[8] **the infants of the spring:** early spring flowers
[9] **buttons:** buds
[10] **be disclosed:** are open
[11] **morn:** morning
[12] **Contagious blastments:** withering blights
[13] **most imminent:** immediately threatening
[14] **to itself rebels:** undoes or betray itself
[15] **though none else near:** even though there's no tempter at hand
[16] **effect:** meaning, moral
[17] **lesson:** lecture
[18] **watchman:** guardian
[19] **ungracious:** graceless, ungodly
[20] **pastors:** priests

Show me the steep and thorny way to heaven;
Whiles, like a puffed① and reckless libertine②,
Himself the primrose path③ of dalliance④ treads,
And recks⑤ not his own rede⑥.

LAERTES

55　O, fear me not.⑦
I stay too long. But here my father comes.

Enter POLONIUS

A double blessing⑧ is a double grace⑨,
Occasion⑩ smiles upon a second leave.⑪

POLONIUS

Yet here, Laertes!⑫ aboard, aboard, for shame!
60　The wind sits in the shoulder of your sail,⑬
And you are stayed⑭ for. There⑮—my blessing with thee!
And these few precepts in thy memory
See⑯ thou character⑰. Give thy thoughts no tongue,
Nor any unproportioned⑱ thought his act.

---

① **puffed:** bloated, high-sounding
② **libertine:** sensualist, rake, dandy
③ **primrose path:** flower-strewn road (Cf. *Macbeth*, II. iii. 16—17: "the primrose / way to the everlasting bonfire")
④ **dalliance:** pleasure, love-making
⑤ **recks:** heeds
⑥ **rede:** teaching, advice
⑦ **fear me not:** don't fear for me.
⑧ **A double blessing:** blessing from one's father
⑨ **a double grace:** grace from heaven
⑩ **Occasion:** opportunity
⑪ **Occasion … leave:** Opportunity treats me kindly in granting me a second farewell.
⑫ **Yet here, Laertes:** You haven't left yet?
⑬ **the wind … sail:** you have a following wind
⑭ **stayed:** waited
⑮ **There:** He kisses him.
⑯ **See:** see that
⑰ **character:** (accented on the second syllable) write, inscribe
⑱ **unproportioned:** undisciplined

65　Be thou familiar①, but by no means vulgar②
　　Those friends thou hast, and their adoption③ tried④,
　　Grapple them to thy soul with hoops of steel;
　　But do not dull⑤ thy palm⑥ with entertainment⑦
　　Of each new-hatched⑧, unfledged⑨ comrade. Beware
70　Of entrance to a quarrel, but being in⑩,
　　Bear't⑪ that⑫ the opposed⑬ may beware of thee.
　　Give every man thy ear, but few thy voice;
　　Take each man's censure⑭ but reserve thy judgment.
　　Costly thy habit⑮ as thy purse can buy,
75　But not expressed in fancy⑯, rich, not gaudy⑰;
　　For the apparel oft proclaims the man,⑱
　　And they in France of the best rank and station

---

① **familiar:** friendly
② **vulgar:** indiscriminate
③ **adoption:** friendship
④ **tried:** tested
⑤ **dull:** make callous
⑥ **palm:** hand
⑦ **entertainment:** reception
⑧ **new-hatched:** newly-born
⑨ **unfledged:** untried
⑩ **being in:** once you are involved
⑪ **Bear't:** manage it, conduct the affair
⑫ **that:** so that
⑬ **the opposed:** your opponent
⑭ **censure:** opinion
⑮ **habit:** dress, clothes
⑯ **fancy:** fantastic fashion
⑰ **gaudy:** flashy, ostentatious
⑱ **For ... man:** A man's true nature is often shown by his clothes. Cf. Baldesar Castiglione: "external appearances often bear witness to what is within" (*The Courtier*, II, translated by George Bull, Penguin Books, 1976, p.135)

Are of a most select① and generous② chief③ in that④.

Neither a borrower nor a lender be;

80　For loan oft loses both itself and friend,

And borrowing dulls the edge⑤ of husbandry⑥.

This above all: to thine ownself be true⑦,

And it must follow, as the night the day⑧,

Thou canst not then be false to any man.

85　Farewell. My blessing season this in thee!⑨

LAERTES

Most humbly do I take my leave, my lord.

POLONIUS

The time invites you; go; your servants tend⑩.

LAERTES

Farewell, Ophelia; and remember well

What I have said to you.

OPHELIA

90　'Tis in my memory locked,

And you yourself shall keep the key of it.

LAERTES

Farewell.

Exit

POLONIUS

What is't, Ophelia, he hath said to you?

---

① **select:** refined
② **generous:** noble, graceful
③ **chief:** superior; chiefly
④ **that:** their apparel
⑤ **edge:** blade
⑥ **husbandry:** thrift, good household management
⑦ **true:** truthful, consistent
⑧ **the night the day:** Polonius' pet phrase
⑨ **My blessing ... thee:** Let my blessing make my words acclimatized in you.
⑩ **tend:** attend, are waiting

OPHELIA

So please you, something touching[1] the Lord Hamlet.

POLONIUS

95 Marry[2], well bethought[3]!
'Tis told me, he hath very oft of late[4]
Given private time to you; and you yourself
Have of your audience[5] been most free and bounteous[6].
If it be so, as so 'tis put on me[7],
100 And that in[8] way of caution, I must tell you,
You do not understand yourself[9] so clearly
As it behoves[10] my daughter and your honor[11].
What is between you? Give me up the truth.

OPHELIA

He hath, my lord, of late made many tenders[12]
105 Of his affection[13] to me.

POLONIUS

Affection! pooh! you speak like a green[14] girl,
Unsifted[15] in such perilous circumstance[16].

---

[1] **touching:** about, concerning
[2] **Marry:** By the virgin Marry (a mild oath)
[3] **bethought:** thought of
[4] **very oft of late:** recently
[5] **audience:** interview
[6] **bounteous:** ready (to receive you)
[7] **'tis put on me:** I've been told
[8] **in:** by
[9] **understand yourself:** appreciate your position
[10] **behoves:** becomes, is appropriate for
[11] **honor:** reputation
[12] **tenders:** offers
[13] **affection:** passion (stronger than the modern sense)
[14] **green:** inexperienced
[15] **Unsifted:** untried, untested
[16] **circumstance:** circumstances

Do you believe his tenders, as you call them?

OPHELIA

I do not know, my lord, what I should think.

POLONIUS

110　Marry, I'll teach you! Think yourself a baby;

That you have ta'en① these tenders② for true pay,

Which are not sterling③. Tender④ yourself more dearly⑤,

Or—not to crack the wind⑥ of the poor phrase,

Running it⑦ thus—you'll tender⑧ me a fool.⑨

OPHELIA

115　My lord, he hath importuned⑩ me with love

In honorable fashion⑪.

POLONIUS

Ay, fashion⑫ you may call it; go to⑬, go to.

OPHELIA

And hath given countenance⑭ to his speech, my lord,

With almost all the holy vows of heaven.

POLONIUS

---

① **ta'en:** taken
② **tenders:** currencies (e.g. tender legal)
③ **sterling:** real, lawful, of standard value
④ **Tender:** regard, offer
⑤ **more dearly:** at a higher rate
⑥ **crack the wind:** break the breath
⑦ **Running it:** the word "tender" personified as a horse
⑧ **tender:** regard
⑨ **tender me a fool:** a. make a fool of me; b. present yourself to me as a fool; c. present me with a grandchild
⑩ **importuned:** (accented on the second syllable) solicited persistently
⑪ **fashion:** way
⑫ **fashion:** fad; show (Polonius seizes on the word and twists its meaning)
⑬ **go to:** nonsense (interjection of impatience)
⑭ **countenance:** authority, confirmation

120 Ay, springs① to catch woodcocks②. I do know,
When the blood③ burns④, how prodigal⑤ the soul
Lends the tongue vows. These blazes⑥, daughter,
Giving more light than heat, extinct in both⑦,
Even in their promise, as it is a-making⑧,
125 You must not take⑨ for fire. From this time
Be somewhat scanter⑩ of your maiden presence;
Set your entreatments⑪ at a higher rate
Than a command to parley⑫. For⑬ Lord Hamlet,
Believe so much in⑭ him, that he is young
130 And with a larger tether⑮ may he walk
Than may be given you. In few⑯, Ophelia,
Do not believe his vows; for they are brokers⑰,
Not of that dye⑱ which their investments⑲ show,

---

① **springes:** snares
② **woodcocks:** birds thought stupid and easily captured
③ **blood:** sexual desire
④ **burns:** is aroused
⑤ **prodigal:** prodigally, lavishly
⑥ **blazes:** flashes of rhetoric
⑦ **both:** light and heat
⑧ **a-making:** when it is being made
⑨ **take:** mistake (these blazes)
⑩ **scanter:** less, sparing
⑪ **entreatments:** negotiations (for surrender)
⑫ **a command to parley:** request for a meeting for negotiation (i.e. don't let him see you whenever he wants to)
⑬ **For:** as for
⑭ **in:** of
⑮ **larger tether:** more freedom
⑯ **In few:** in short
⑰ **brokers:** second-hand-clothes dealer; panders, go-betweens in sexual intrigues
⑱ **dye:** color
⑲ **investments:** vestments, clothes

But mere① implorators② of unholy suits③,
135 Breathing④ like sanctified and pious bawds⑤
The better to beguile⑥. This is for all⑦.
I would not, in plain terms, from this time forth,
Have you so slander⑧ any moment⑨ leisure,
As to give words or talk with the Lord Hamlet.
140 Look to't⑩, I charge you. Come your ways⑪.

OPHELIA
I shall obey, my lord.
Exeunt

SCENE IV. The platform.

Enter HAMLET, HORATIO, and MARCELLUS

HAMLET
The air bites shrewdly⑫, it is very cold.

HORATIO

---

① **mere:** out-and-out
② **implorators:** solicitors
③ **unholy suits:** sets of clothes; immoral requests
④ **Breathing:** speaking
⑤ **bawds:** panders
⑥ **beguile:** entice, deceive
⑦ **This is for all:** once and for all
⑧ **slander:** abuse, misuse
⑨ **moment:** moment's
⑩ **to't:** pay attention to this
⑪ **Come your ways:** come along; let's go
⑫ **shrewdly:** keenly, sharply

It is a nipping and an eager① air.
HAMLET
What hour now?
HORATIO
I think it lacks of② twelve.
HAMLET
5   No, it is struck.③
HORATIO
Indeed? I heard it not. Then it draws near the season④
Wherein the spirit held⑤ his wont⑥ to walk.
A flourish of trumpets, and ordnance shot off, within
What does this mean, my lord?
HAMLET
The King doth wake⑦ tonight and takes his rouse⑧,
10   Keeps wassail⑨, and the swaggering up-spring⑩ reels;
And, as he drains⑪ his draughts⑫ of Rhenish⑬ down,
The kettle-drum and trumpet thus bray out⑭
The triumph⑮ of his pledge⑯.
HORATIO

---

①   **eager:** (French: *aigre*) sharp
②   **lacks of:** is just short of, is just before
③   Cf. I. i. 7: "'Tis now struck twelve."
④   **season:** time
⑤   **held:** kept, observed
⑥   **wont:** habit, routine
⑦   **wake:** stay awake, stay up late
⑧   **rouse:** carouses
⑨   **Keeps wassail:** holds a drinking party
⑩   **swaggering up-spring:** a wild German dance
⑪   **drains:** wigs
⑫   **draughts:** glasses
⑬   **Rhenish:** Rhine wine
⑭   **bray out:** make a loud harsh noise
⑮   **triumph:** feat of drinking up at one gulp; public celebration
⑯   **pledge:** toast; promise

Is it a custom?
HAMLET
15　Ay, marry[①], is't;
　　But[②] to my mind, though I am native here
　　And to the manner born[③], it is a custom
　　More honored in the breach than the observance to.[④]
　　This heavy-headed[⑤] revel east and west[⑥]
20　Makes us traduced[⑦] and taxed of[⑧] other nations;
　　They clepe[⑨] us drunkards, and with swinish phrase[⑩]
　　Soil[⑪] our addition[⑫], and indeed it takes[⑬]
　　From our achievements, though performed at height[⑭],
　　The pith and marrow[⑮] of our attribute[⑯].[⑰]
25　So[⑱] oft it chances in[⑲] particular men[⑳],
　　That[㉑] for[㉒] some vicious mole of nature[㉓] in them,

---

① **marry:** by the Virgin Mary (a mild oath)
② **But:** and
③ **to the manner born:** destined by birth to accept this custom
④ **More honored ... to:** more honorable to break than to observe (follow)
⑤ **heavy-headed:** drunken
⑥ **east and west:** universally (modifying "traduced and taxed")
⑦ **traduced:** slandered
⑧ **taxed of:** censured by
⑨ **clepe:** call
⑩ **with swinish phrase:** by calling us pigs
⑪ **Soil:** tarnish
⑫ **addition:** titles of honor, reputation
⑬ **takes:** detracts
⑭ **at height:** outstanding
⑮ **pith and marrow:** essence
⑯ **attribute:** reputation
⑰ **it takes ... attribute:** It detracts reputation from our highest achievements.
⑱ **So:** in the same manner
⑲ **chances in:** happens with
⑳ **particular men:** men of parts
㉑ **That:** who
㉒ **for:** because of
㉓ **vicious mole of nature:** natural serious blemish

As in their birth—wherein they are not guilty,
Since nature cannot choose his① origin—
By the o'ergrowth② of some complexion③,
30 Oft breaking down the pales and forts④ of reason,
Or by some habit that too much o'er-leavens⑤
The form of plausive⑥ manners, that these men,
Carrying, I say, the stamp of one defect,
Being nature's livery⑦, or fortune's star⑧—
35 Their virtues else⑨—be they⑩ as pure as grace,
As infinite as man may undergo⑪—
Shall in the general censure⑫ take corruption⑬
From⑭ that particular fault. The dram⑮ of e'il⑯
Doth all the noble substance often doubt⑰
40 To his own scandal⑱.⑲

HORATIO

---

① **his:** its; their
② **o'ergrowth:** abnormal growth
③ **complexion:** combination of the four humors. Medieval Europeans thought human bodies to be composed of 4 humors: blood, phlegm, choler, melancholy, and that different combinations (too much of any of these fluids) lead to different physical and emotional characters.
④ **pales and forts:** boundaries and fences, limits
⑤ **o'er-leavens:** bloats, radically changes
⑥ **plausive:** pleasing; applauded
⑦ **livery:** uniform; inborn attribute
⑧ **fortune's star:** something determined by fate
⑨ **else:** other; in other respects
⑩ **be they:** even though they are
⑪ **undergo:** sustain
⑫ **general censure:** public opinions
⑬ **corruption:** contagion
⑭ **From:** because of
⑮ **dram:** a very small quantity
⑯ **e'il:** evil
⑰ **doubt:** efface
⑱ **scandal:** disrepute, disgrace
⑲ **The dram … scandal:** The smallest bit of corruption often reduces a person to disgrace, no matter how noble he is.

Look, my lord, it comes!
Enter Ghost
HAMLET
Angels and ministers① of grace② defend us!③
Be thou a spirit of health④ or goblin⑤ damned,
Bring with thee airs from heaven or blasts from hell,
45 Be thy intents wicked or charitable⑥,
Thou comest in such a questionable⑦ shape
That I will speak to thee. I'll call thee Hamlet,
King, father, royal Dane.⑧ O, answer me!
Let me not burst in ignorance; but tell
50 Why thy canonized⑨ bones, hearsèd⑩ in death,
Have burst their cerements⑪, why the sepulchre,
Wherein we saw thee quietly inurned⑫,
Hath oped⑬ his⑭ ponderous and marble jaws,
To cast thee up again. What may⑮ this mean,
55 That thou, dead corse⑯, again in complete steel⑰

---

① **angels and ministers:** angels, saints
② **grace:** God's favor
③ **Angels … us:** Another possible reading: is "angels who minister grace" etc.
④ **health:** salvation
⑤ **goblin:** demon
⑥ **charitable:** benevolent
⑦ **questionable:** question-inviting, problematic
⑧ **King … Dane:** recognition of Name-of-the-Father (Jacques Lacan)
⑨ **Why thy canonized:** (accented on the second syllable) buried with the sacred rites of the Church
⑩ **hearsèd:** enclosed in a hearse or coffin, entombed
⑪ **cerements:** waxed grave-clothes, shrouds
⑫ **inurned:** interred, buried
⑬ **oped:** opened
⑭ **his:** its (the sepulcher's)
⑮ **may:** can
⑯ **corse:** corpse
⑰ **in complete steel:** in full armor

Revisits① thus the glimpses② of the moon,

Making night hideous; and we③ fools of nature④

So horridly⑤ to shake⑥ our disposition⑦

With thoughts beyond the reaches⑧ of our souls⑨?

60 Say, why is this? Wherefore? What should⑩ we do?

Ghost beckons HAMLET

HORATIO

It beckons you to go away with it,

As if it some impartment⑪ did desire

To you alone.

MARCELLUS

Look, with what courteous action

65 It waves⑫ you to a more removèd⑬ ground.

But do not go with it.

HORATIO

No, by no means.

HAMLET

It will not speak; then I will follow it.

HORATIO

Do not, my lord.

---

① **Revisits:** revisitest ("est" is the verbal form of the 2nd person in 16th-century English)
② **glimpses:** pale gleams
③ **we:** make us
④ **fools of nature:** deceived by nature
⑤ **horridly:** horrendously
⑥ **shake:** agitate
⑦ **disposition:** composure; minds
⑧ **reaches:** capacities
⑨ **beyond the reaches of our souls:** beyond our comprehension
⑩ **should:** must
⑪ **impartment:** communication
⑫ **waves:** gestures by waving its hand
⑬ **removèd:** secluded

HAMLET

70　Why, what should be the fear?①

　　I do not set my life in a pin's fee②,

　　And for my soul, what can it③ do to that④,

　　Being a thing immortal as itself?

　　It waves me forth again. I'll follow it.

HORATIO

75　What if it tempt you toward the flood⑤, my lord,

　　Or to the dreadful summit of the cliff

　　That beetles o'er⑥ his base⑦ into the sea,

　　And there assume⑧ some other horrible form,

　　Which might deprive your sovereignty of reason⑨

80　And draw you into madness?⑩ Think of it.

　　The very place⑪ puts toys of desperation⑫,

　　Without more motive, into every brain

　　That looks so many fathoms to the sea

　　And hears it roar beneath.⑬

HAMLET

85　It waves me⑭ still.

　　Go on; I'll follow thee.

---

　　① **what ... fear:** What's there to fear?
　　② **fee:** value
　　③ **it:** the ghost
　　④ **that:** my soul
　　⑤ **flood:** sea
　　⑥ **o'er:** overhangs
　　⑦ **his base:** its bottom
　　⑧ **assume:** subjunctive
　　⑨ **deprive ... reason:** dethrone your reason
　　⑩ **And ... madness:** The first mention of madness, which foreshadows Hamlet's "ecstasy".
　　⑪ **the very place:** i.e. the summit
　　⑫ **toys of desperation:** desperate fancies, irrational impulses
　　⑬ **The very place ... beneath:** It may be the temptation of the devil. (Cf. *Matthew* 4:5 & *Luke* 4:9)
　　⑭ **me:** to me

MARCELLUS

You shall not go, my lord.

HAMLET

Hold off your hands.

HORATIO

Be ruled①, you shall not go.

HAMLET

90 My fate② cries out

And makes each petty artery③ in this body

As hardy as the Nemean lion's④ nerve.⑤

Still am I called⑥. Unhand⑦ me, gentlemen.

By heaven, I'll make a ghost of him that lets⑧ me!

95 I say, away! Go on; I'll follow thee.

Exeunt Ghost and HAMLET

HORATIO

He waxes⑨ desperate with imagination.⑩

MARCELLUS

Let's follow; 'tis not fit thus to obey him.

HORATIO

Have after⑪. To what issue⑫ will this come?

---

① **Be ruled:** be ruled by reason
② **fate:** destiny
③ **artery:** vein; sinew
④ **Nemean lion:** the first of Hercules' Twelve Labors (the 2nd mention)
⑤ **My fate ... nerve:** Cf. *Henry V*, I. ii. 123—124: "you should rouse yourself as did the former lions in your blood."
⑥ **called:** summoned
⑦ **Unhand:** take your hands off
⑧ **lets:** prevents, hinders
⑨ **waxes:** grows
⑩ **He ... imagination:** another foreshadow of Hamlet's madness
⑪ **Have after:** Let us go after him
⑫ **issue:** end

MARCELLUS

Something is rotten in the state of Denmark.①

HORATIO

100 Heaven will direct it.②

MARCELLUS

Nay, let's follow him.

Exeunt

SCENE V. Another part of the platform.

Enter GHOST and HAMLET

HAMLET

Where wilt thou lead me? Speak. I'll go no further.

Ghost③

Mark④ me.

HAMLET

I will.

Ghost

My hour is almost come,⑤

5 When I to sulphurous⑥ and tormenting flames⑦

Must render up myself.

HAMLET

Alas, poor ghost!

Ghost

---

① **Something ... Denmark:** Cf. I. i. 82: "some strange eruption to our state"
② **Heaven ... it:** Horatio's Stoicism is clearly shown here.
③ **Ghost:** The Ghost is often played by an actor who has played Hamlet in the past.
④ **Mark:** pay attention to
⑤ **My hour ... come:** i.e. it is near dawn
⑥ **sulphurous:** reads sulphrous (dissyllabic).
⑦ **tormenting flames:** purgatorial fire

Pity me not, but lend thy serious hearing①
To what I shall unfold②.
HAMLET
10 Speak. I am bound③ to hear.
Ghost
So art thou to revenge, when thou shalt hear.
HAMLET
What?
Ghost
I am thy father's spirit,④
Doomed for a certain term to walk⑤ the night,
15 And for⑥ the day⑦ confined to fast⑧ in fires,
Till the foul crimes done in my days of nature
Are burnt and purged away. But that I am forbid⑨
To tell the secrets of my prison-house⑩,
I could a tale unfold whose lightest word
20 Would harrow up⑪ thy soul, freeze thy young blood,
Make thy two eyes, like stars, start from their spheres⑫,

---

① **lend thy serious hearing:** listen intently
② **unfold:** reveal, narrate
③ **bound:** in duty bound, obliged; destined; ready
④ **I am thy father's spirit:** Cf. Goethe: "The latter spoke with a feeling of melancholy anger rather than of sorrow; but of an anger spiritual, slow and inexhaustible. It was the mistemper of a noble soul, that is severed from all earthly things, and yet devoted to unbounded woe. " (*Wilhelm Meister's Apprenticeship,* Book V, Chapter XI, Bartleby. com, Inc., 2001, p.185.)
⑤ **walk:** patrol
⑥ **for:** during
⑦ **the day:** daytime
⑧ **fast:** go without food
⑨ **But that I am forbid:** if I were not forbidden
⑩ **prison-house:** i.e. the purgatory
⑪ **harrow up:** tear up
⑫ **spheres:** orbits, (fig.) sockets

Thy knotted and combinèd① locks② to part
And each particular hair to stand on end,
Like quills upon the fretful③ porpentine④.
25 But this eternal blazon⑤ must not be
To ears of flesh and blood. List, list, O, list!
If thou didst ever thy dear father love—⑥
HAMLET
O God!
Ghost
Revenge his foul and most unnatural murder.
HAMLET
30 Murder!
Ghost
Murder most foul, as in the best it is;
But this most foul, strange and unnatural.⑦
HAMLET
Haste me to know't⑧, that⑨ I, with wings as swift
As meditation or the thoughts of love,
35 May sweep to my revenge.
Ghost
I find thee apt⑩,
And duller shouldst thou be than the fat⑪ weed

---

① **knotted and combinèd:** combed and wound together
② **locks:** hair
③ **fretful:** irritated
④ **porpentine:** porcupine
⑤ **eternal blazon:** unveiling of the secrets of eternity
⑥ **If thou … love:** Cf. V. v. 363—366: "if thou didst ever hold me in thy heart … tell my story."
⑦ **But … unnatural:** My murder is the worst of all.
⑧ **know't:** know of it
⑨ **that:** so that
⑩ **apt:** ready
⑪ **fat:** thick

That roots itself in ease on Lethe① wharf,
Wouldst thou not stir in this②. Now, Hamlet, hear:
40 'Tis given out③ that, sleeping in my orchard④,
A serpent stung me; so the whole ear of Denmark
Is by a forgèd⑤ process⑥ of my death
Rankly⑦ abused⑧, but know, thou noble youth,
The serpent that did sting⑨ thy father's life
45 Now wears his crown.

HAMLET

O my prophetic⑩ soul! My uncle!

Ghost

Ay, that incestuous, that adulterate⑪ beast,
With witchcraft of his wit⑫, with traitorous gifts,—
O wicked wit and gifts⑬, that have the power
50 So to seduce!—won to his shameful lust
The will⑭ of my most seeming-virtuous queen.⑮
O Hamlet, what a falling-off⑯ was there!
From me, whose love was of that⑰ dignity⑱

---

① **Lethe:** the river of forgetfulness in Hades
② **Wouldst thou not stir in this:** if it could' t move you.
③ **given out:** declared
④ **orchard:** garden
⑤ **forgèd:** false
⑥ **process:** account, report
⑦ **Rankly:** grossly, utterly
⑧ **abused:** deceived
⑨ **sting:** poisoned
⑩ **prophetic:** foreknowing
⑪ **adulterate:** corrupted, adulterous
⑫ **wit:** intellect
⑬ **gifts:** natural gifts
⑭ **will:** sexual desire
⑮ **48—51:** Note the alliteration of labial sounds ("w") . Cf. *Shakespeare's Sonnets* 9
⑯ **falling-off:** degeneration
⑰ **that:** such
⑱ **dignity:** worth

That it went hand in hand even with the vow①
55 I made to her in marriage, and to decline②
Upon a wretch whose natural gifts were poor
To③ those of mine!④
But virtue, as it never will be moved,
Though lewdness court⑤ it in a shape of heaven⑥,
60 So lust⑦, though to a radiant⑧ angel linked,
Will sate⑨ itself in a celestial bed,⑩
And prey on garbage⑪.
But, soft⑫! Methinks⑬ I scent the morning air.
Brief let me be⑭. Sleeping within my orchard,
65 My custom always of⑮ the afternoon,
Upon my secure⑯ hour thy uncle stole,
With juice of cursed hebenon⑰ in a vial⑱,
And in the porches⑲ of my ears did pour

① **even with the vow:** with the very vow
② **decline:** descend, fall back
③ **To:** in comparison to
④ **To those of mine:** Cf. I. ii 139—140
⑤ **court:** woo, pursue
⑥ **in a shape of heaven:** in the form of an angel
⑦ **lust:** will (Gertrude)
⑧ **radiant:** bright
⑨ **sate:** satiate
⑩ 58—62: Virtue, lewdness, and lust are all personified.
⑪ **garbage:** entrails, foul remains (Claudius)
⑫ **soft:** enough; wait
⑬ **methinks:** I think
⑭ The procrastination is characteristic of both father and son. (Cf. Ben Jonson: "would he blotted a thousand") It is said Shakespeare himself played the role, so the verbosity is understandable.
⑮ **of:** during
⑯ **secure:** care-free
⑰ **hebenon:** henbane; ebony (a poison)
⑱ **vial:** small bottle
⑲ **porches:** entrances

The leprous distilment[1], whose effect
70 Holds such an enmity with blood of man
That swift as quicksilver[2] it courses[3] through
The natural gates and alleys of the body,
And with a sudden vigour doth posset[4]
And curd[5], like eager[6] droppings[7] into milk,
75 The thin and wholesome blood; so did it mine;
And a most instant tetter[8] barked[9] about,
Most lazar-like[10], with vile and loathsome crust,
All my smooth body.
Thus was I, sleeping, by a brother's hand
80 Of life, of crown, of queen, at once dispatched[11]:
Cut off even in the blossoms of my sin[12],
Unhouseled[13], disappointed[14], unaneled[15],
No reckoning[16] made, but sent to my account[17]
With all my imperfections on my head.

---

[1] **leprous distilment:** distilment causing leprosy (scales and discoloration of the skin)
[2] **quicksilver:** mercury
[3] **courses:** runs
[4] **posset:** clot, coagulate
[5] **curd:** curdle
[6] **eager:** sour
[7] **droppings:** drops
[8] **tetter:** skin eruption, sores and scabs
[9] **barked:** covered like the bark of a tree
[10] **lazar-like:** like a leper (derived from Lazarus in *Luke*: 16:20)
[11] **dispatched:** deprived
[12] **in the blossoms of my sin:** in the height of my sinful state
[13] **Unhouseled:** without receiving the last sacrament (the Eucharist)
[14] **disappointed:** unprepared spiritually for death, not prepared by confession for eternity
[15] **unaneled:** not anointed, without extreme unction
[16] **reckoning:** confession of sins
[17] **sent to my account:** sent to death to have final judgment

85   O, horrible! O, horrible! most horrible!
If thou hast nature① in thee, bear it not;
Let not the royal bed of Denmark be
A couch for luxury② and damned incest.
But, howsoever thou pursuest this act,
90   Taint not thy mind③, nor let thy soul contrive
Against thy mother aught④. Leave her to heaven⑤
And to those thorns that in her bosom lodge⑥,
To prick and sting her.⑦ Fare thee well at once!
The glow-worm⑧ shows the matin⑨ to be near,
95   And 'gins⑩ to pale his uneffectual⑪ fire.
Adieu⑫, adieu! Hamlet, remember me.
Exit

HAMLET

O all you host of heaven⑬! O earth! what else?
And shall I couple⑭ hell? O, fie⑮! Hold, hold, my heart;

---

  ① **hast nature:** natural feeling, humanity
  ② **luxury:** lust, lechery
  ③ **Taint not thy mind:** Don't let your mind become contaminated
  ④ **aught:** anything
  ⑤ **Leave her to heaven:** Let God to judge and punish her
  ⑥ **those ... lodge:** her conscience
  ⑦ **To prick and sting her:** Here is an example of Shakespeare's appropriation of ancient tragic plot: In Aeschylus' *Oresteia*, Orestes killed his mother to revenge his father, Agamemnon, and was then pursued by the Fates. He fled to Athens, and was declared guiltless by Athena.
  ⑧ **glow-worm:** firebug
  ⑨ **matin:** morning
  ⑩ **'gins:** begins
  ⑪ **uneffectual:** ineffectual
  ⑫ **Adieu:** farewell
  ⑬ **all you host of heaven:** sun, moon and stars
  ⑭ **couple:** link, include
  ⑮ **fie:** an expression of disgust or reproach

And you, my sinews①, grow not instant old②,
100 But bear me stiffly up. Remember thee!
Ay, thou poor ghost, while memory holds a seat
In this distracted globe③. Remember thee!
Yea, from the table④ of my memory⑤
I'll wipe away all trivial⑥ fond⑦ records⑧,
105 All saws⑨ of books, all forms⑩, all pressures⑪ past,
That youth and observation⑫ copied there;⑬
And thy commandment all alone shall live
Within the book and volume of my brain,
Unmixed with baser⑭ matter. Yes, by heaven!
110 O most pernicious woman!
O villain, villain, smiling, damnèd villain!
My tables,—meet⑮ it is I set it down,
That one may smile, and smile, and be a villain;⑯
At least I'm sure it may be so in Denmark.
Writes

---

① **sinews:** tendons, muscles
② **grow not instant old:** don't become feeble as if with sudden aging
③ **this distracted globe:** world; crazy head (with a gesture to his head)
④ **table:** tablet, slate
⑤ **the table ... memory :** Cf. Plato: *Philebus*, 38d—39a. John Locke: *An Essay Concerning Human Understanding*, 1.2.1 & 2.1.2
⑥ **trivial:** meaningless
⑦ **fond:** foolish
⑧ **records:** (accented on the second syllable) recollections
⑨ **saws:** maxims, sayings
⑩ **forms:** ideas, images
⑪ **pressures:** impressions
⑫ **youth and observation:** youthful observation
⑬ **That ... there:** Cf. Augustine: *Confessions*, Book X
⑭ **baser:** less valuable
⑮ **meet:** appropriate
⑯ **one ... villain:** Cf. 3 *Henry VI*, III. ii. 182: "I can smile, and murder whiles I smile". *Julius Caesar*, IV. i. 50—51: "some that smile have in their hearts, I fear, / Millions of mischiefs." *Macbeth*, II. iii. 138: "There's daggers in men's smiles"

115 So, uncle, there you are. Now to my word①;
It is 'Adieu, adieu! remember me.'
I have sworn 't.②

MARCELLUS HORATIO

[*Within*] My lord, my lord,—

MARCELLUS

[*Within*] Lord Hamlet,—

HORATIO

120 [*Within*] Heaven secure③ him!

HAMLET

So be it④!

HORATIO

[*Within*] Hillo, ho, ho, my lord!

HAMLET

Hillo, ho, ho⑤, boy!⑥ Come, bird⑦, come.⑧

Enter HORATIO and MARCELLUS

MARCELLUS

How is't⑨, my noble lord?

HORATIO

125 What news, my lord?

HAMLET

O, wonderful!

---

① **word:** motto
② **I have sworn 't:** A. C. Bradley: The above passage (especially the closing part) reminds one of a place in *Titus Andronicus* IV. i. (*Shakespearean Tragedy,* p.349)
③ **secure:** safeguard, protect
④ **So be it:** Amen
⑤ **ho, ho:** falconer's cry to summon the hawk
⑥ **Hillo ... boy:** Hamlet begins to pretend madness.
⑦ **bird:** lassie
⑧ **Come ... come:** He mocks Marcellus's cry.
⑨ **How is't:** How is it with you (are you all right)

HORATIO

Good my lord, tell it.

HAMLET

No, you'll reveal it.

HORATIO

Not I, my lord, by heaven.

MARCELLUS

130 Nor I, my lord.

HAMLET

How say you① then; would heart of man once② think it?

But you'll be secret?

HORATIO MARCELLUS

Ay, by heaven, my lord.

HAMLET

There's ne'er a villain dwelling in all Denmark

135 But he's③ an arrant④ knave.

HORATIO

There needs no ghost, my lord, come⑤ from the grave

To tell us this.

HAMLET

Why, right; you are i' the right!

And so, without more circumstance⑥ at all,

140 I hold it fit that we shake hands and part,

You, as your business and desire shall point⑦ you;

For every man has business and desire,

---

① **How say you:** what do you say
② **once:** ever
③ **he's:** who is not
④ **arrant:** utter, downright
⑤ **come:** to come
⑥ **circumstance:** elaboration; ceremony
⑦ **point:** direct

Such as it is; and for mine own poor① part,

Look you, I'll go pray②.

HORATIO

145　These are but wild and whirling③ words, my lord.

HAMLET

I'm sorry they offend you, heartily④;

Yes, faith heartily.

HORATIO

There's no offence⑤, my lord.

HAMLET

Yes, by Saint Patrick⑥, but there is, Horatio,

150　And much offence⑦ too. Touching⑧ this vision here,

It is an honest⑨ ghost⑩, that let me tell you.

For⑪ your desire to know what is between us⑫,

O'ermaster 't⑬ as you may. And now, good friends,

As you are friends, scholars and soldiers⑭, ⑮,

155　Give⑯ me one poor request.

HORATIO

What is't, my lord? We will.

---

① **poor:** Hamlet uses this word three times in this scene.
② **pray:** it is anti-climactic
③ **whirling:** excited, extravagant
④ **heartily:** sincerely
⑤ **offence:** cause of displeasure
⑥ **Saint Patrick:** Guardian of Ireland and master of the Purgatory
⑦ **offence:** crime
⑧ **Touching:** concerning
⑨ **honest:** genuine
⑩ **an honest ghost:** no demon in disguise
⑪ **For:** as for
⑫ **what is between us:** what has passed between me and the ghost
⑬ **O'ermaster 't:** overcome your curiosity
⑭ **soldiers:** This word had three syllable.
⑮ **As you ... soldiers:** Cf. III. i. 162: "The courtier's, soldier's, scholar's" etc.
⑯ **Give:** grant

HAMLET

Never make known what you have seen tonight.

HORATIO MARCELLUS

My lord, we will not.

HAMLET

Nay, but swear't.

HORATIO

160 In faith,

My lord, not I.

MARCELLUS

Nor I, my lord, in faith.

HAMLET

Upon my sword.①

MARCELLUS

We have sworn, my lord, already.

HAMLET

165 Indeed, upon my sword, indeed.

Ghost

[*Beneath*] Swear.

HAMLET

Ah, ha, boy! say'st thou so? art thou there,
truepenny②?

Come on—you hear this fellow in the cellarage③—

170 Consent to swear.

HORATIO

Propose the oath, my lord.

HAMLET

Never to speak of this that you have seen,
Swear by my sword.

---

① **Upon my sword:** The sword hilts form a cross.
② **truepenny:** honest fellow
③ **cellarage:** cellars, the stage trap; hell

Ghost

[*Beneath*] Swear.

HAMLET①

175　*Hic et ubique*②? Then we'll shift our ground.③

Come hither, gentlemen,

And lay your hands again upon my sword.

Never to speak of this that you have heard,

Swear by my sword.

Ghost

180　[*Beneath*] Swear.

HAMLET

Well said, old mole! canst work i' the earth so fast?

A worthy pioneer④! Once more remove⑤, good friends.⑥

HORATIO

O day and night, but this is wondrous⑦ strange!

HAMLET

And therefore as a stranger give it welcome.⑧

185　There are more things in heaven and earth, Horatio,

Than are dreamt of in your philosophy. But come;

Here, as before, never, so help you mercy⑨,

How strange or odd soe'er I bear⑩ myself

---

①　Only he hears the ghost.
②　*Hic et ubique*: (Latin) here and everywhere
③　**Then … ground:** In the past, a man taking an oath shifts his ground. (A. C. Bradley: *Shakespearean Tragedy*, p.350)
④　**pioneer:** digger or miner
⑤　**remove:** shift our ground
⑥　Hamlet calls his father's "ghost boy", "fellow", "truepenny", "old mole", "pioneer", in a playful tone to conceal his nervousness.
⑦　**wondrous:** wondrously
⑧　**give it welcome:** Proverb: "Give the stranger welcome."
⑨　**mercy:** God (subject)
⑩　**bear:** behave

(As I perchance[1] hereafter shall think meet[2]
190 To put an antic disposition[3] on),
That you, at such times seeing me, never shall[4],
With arms encumbered[5] thus, or this headshake[6],
Or by pronouncing of some doubtful[7] phrase,
As 'Well, well, we know,' or 'We could[8], an if we would[9],'
195 Or 'If we list[10] to speak,' or 'There be, an if they might,'[11]
Or such[12] ambiguous[13] giving out[14], to note[15]
That you know aught[16] of me—this not to do,
So grace and mercy[17] at your most need help you[18],
Swear.[19]

Ghost

200 [*Beneath*] Swear.

HAMLET

Rest, rest, perturbed spirit!
They swear

---

[1] **perchance:** perhaps
[2] **meet:** see fit
[3] **antic disposition:** grotesque behavior
[4] **That ... shall:** since I may in the future think it fit to act bizarrely
[5] **encumbered:** folded
[6] **headshake:** shaking your heads knowingly
[7] **doubtful:** ambiguous
[8] **could:** could tell
[9] **would:** wanted to
[10] **list:** wished
[11] **There ... might:** there are those (i.e. ourselves) who could explain if they chose to.
[12] **such:** similar
[13] **ambiguous:** double-meaning
[14] **giving out:** pronouncement, utterance
[15] **note:** indicate, disclose
[16] **aught:** anything
[17] **mercy:** God
[18] **at your most need help you:** otherwise you'll answer for it.
[19] **187—199:** "Swear never to note, even through gestures and hints, that you know anything about me, no matter how strangely I act."

So, gentlemen,
With all my love I do commend me① to you;
And what so poor a man as Hamlet is②

205 May do, to express his love and friending③ to you,
God willing④, shall not lack. Let us go in together;
And still your fingers on your lips⑤, I pray.
The time⑥ is out of joint. O cursèd spite⑦,
That ever I was born to set it right!⑧

210 Nay, come, let's go together.
Exeunt

---

① **commend me:** entrust or hand myself over
② Cf. V. ii. 236: "poor Hamlet"
③ **friending:** friendship
④ **God willing:** provided that God is willing
⑤ **still ... lips:** i.e. keep it secret forever
⑥ **time:** age, times
⑦ **cursèd spite:** nuisance
⑧ **O cursèd ... right:** Goethe: "In these words, I imagine, will be found the key to Hamlet's whole procedure. [...] A lovely, pure, noble and most moral nature, without the strength of nerve which forms a hero, sinks beneath a burden which it cannot bear and must not cast away. All duties are holy for him; the present is too hard. Impossibilities have been required of him; not in themselves impossibilities, but such for him." (*Wilhelm Meister's Apprenticeship*, Book IV, Chapter XIII, p.144)

ACT II
SCENE I. A room in Polonius' house.

Enter POLONIUS and REYNALDO

POLONIUS
Give him① this money and these notes②, Reynaldo.
REYNALDO
I will, my lord.
POLONIUS
You shall③ do marvell's④ wisely, good Reynaldo,
Before you visit him, to make inquire⑤
5   Of⑥ his behavior.
REYNALDO
My lord, I did intend it.
POLONIUS
Marry, well said; very well said. Look you, sir,⑦
Inquire me⑧ first what Danskers⑨ are in Paris;
And how, and who, what means⑩, and where they keep⑪,
10 What company, at what expense; and finding⑫

---

① **him:** i.e. Laertes
② **these notes:** this letter
③ **shall:** should be sure to
④ **marvell's:** marvelously
⑤ **make inquire:** ask questions
⑥ **Of:** about
⑦ **Look you, sir:** take care you do this
⑧ **Inquire me:** for me
⑨ **Danskers:** Danes
⑩ **means:** supply of money
⑪ **keep:** live, frequent
⑫ **finding:** if you find

By this encompassment[1] and drift of question[2]
That they do know my son, come you more nearer[3]
Than your particular demands[4] will touch it.
Take you[5], as 'twere, some distant knowledge of him;
15　As thus, 'I know his father and his friends,
And in part him.' Do you mark[6] this, Reynaldo?

REYNALDO

Ay, very well, my lord.

POLONIUS

'And in part him; but' you may say 'not well.
But, if't be he I mean, he's very wild;
20　Addicted so and so'[7], and there put on him[8]
What forgeries[9] you please; marry, none so rank[10]
As may dishonor him; take heed of that;
But, sir, such wanton[11], wild and usual slips[12]
As are companions noted[13] and most known
25　To youth and liberty[14].

REYNALDO

As gaming[15], my lord.

---

① **encompassment:** circling around
② **drift of question:** roundabout questioning
③ **more nearer:** closer (double comparative)
④ **demands:** questions
⑤ **Take you:** assume
⑥ **mark:** notice
⑦ **addicted so and so:** devoted to such and such pursuits
⑧ **put on him:** accuse him of; trick him into believing
⑨ **forgeries:** invented reports
⑩ **rank:** flagrant, offensive
⑪ **wanton:** rebellious
⑫ **wild and usual slips:** wrongdoings
⑬ **noted:** notorious
⑭ **youth and liberty:** the unrestrained behavior of young men
⑮ **gaming:** gambling

POLONIUS

Ay, or drinking, fencing[1], swearing, quarrelling,

Drabbing[2]. You may go so far.

REYNALDO

My lord, that would dishonor him.

POLONIUS

30   'Faith, no[3]; as you may season[4] it in the charge

You must not put another scandal on him,

That he is open to[5] incontinency[6];

That's not my meaning. But breathe his faults so quaintly[7]

That they may seem the taints of liberty[8],

35   The flash and outbreak of a fiery mind,

A savageness[9] in unreclaimed[10] blood,

Of general assault[11].

REYNALDO

But, my good lord,—

POLONIUS

Wherefore should you do this?

REYNALDO

40   Ay, my lord,

I would know that.

---

[1] **fencing:** Fencing schools were regarded by the Elizabethans as a typical resort of the wild youth.
[2] **Drabbing:** whoring
[3] **no:** not necessarily
[4] **season:** temper, modify
[5] **open to:** given to
[6] **incontinency:** excessive indulgence (sexual promiscuity)
[7] **quaintly:** skillfully, cunningly
[8] **taints of liberty:** slight faults of too much freedom
[9] **savageness:** wildness
[10] **unreclaimed:** untamed, undisciplined (usually of hawks)
[11] **Of general assault:** which affects all young men

POLONIUS

Marry, sir, here's my drift①;

And I believe, it is a fetch of warrant②.

You laying these slight sullies③ on my son,

45 As 'twere a thing a little soiled i' the working④,

Mark you, your party⑤ in converse⑥, him you would sound⑦,

Having ever seen⑧ in the prenominate⑨ crimes⑩

The youth you breathe of⑪ guilty, be assured

He closes with you in this consequence;⑫

50 'Good sir,' or so⑬, or 'friend,' or 'gentleman,'

According to the phrase or the addition⑭

Of man and country.

REYNALDO

Very good, my lord.

POLONIUS

And then, sir, does he this—he does—what was I

55 about to say? By the mass, I was about to say something!

Where did I leave?

REYNALDO

At 'closes in the consequence,' at 'friend or so,'

and 'gentleman.'

---

① **drift:** meaning
② **a fetch of warrant:** warrantable strategy, trick that is justified
③ **slight sullies:** stains, blemishes
④ **a thing a little soiled i' the working:** e.g. cloth
⑤ **party:** partner
⑥ **converse:** conversation
⑦ **sound:** detect, probe
⑧ **Having ever seen:** if he has ever seen
⑨ **prenominate:** above-mentioned
⑩ **crimes:** faults
⑪ **breathe of:** speak about
⑫ **He closes … consequence:** then he will be sure to agree with you as follows
⑬ **or so:** or whatever
⑭ **the phrase or the addition:** form of address or title

POLONIUS

At 'closes in the consequence, ' ay, marry;
60 He closes thus: 'I know the gentleman;
I saw him yesterday, or t' other day,
Or then, or then; with such, or such; and, as you say,
There was he gaming; there o'ertook in's① rouse②;
There falling out③ at tennis'; or perchance,
65 'I saw him enter such a house of sale④,'
*Videlicet*⑤, a brothel, or so forth.
See you now—
Your bait of falsehood takes⑥ this carp of truth;⑦
And thus do we of wisdom and of reach⑧,
70 With windlasses and with assays of bias⑨,
By indirections find directions out.
So by my former lecture⑩ and advice,
Shall you my son.⑪ You have⑫ me, have you not?

REYNALDO

My lord, I have.

POLONIUS

75 God be wi' you; fare you well.

REYNALDO

Good my lord!

---

① **'s:** his
② **rouse:** overcome with drunkenness
③ **falling out:** quarreling
④ **a house of sale:** whorehouse
⑤ ***Videlicet:*** that is to say (Latin: "let it be seen")
⑥ **takes:** catches
⑦ **Your … truth:** a fishing metaphor
⑧ **we of wisdom and of reach:** we wise and far-reaching persons
⑨ **with assays of bias:** by roundabout ways
⑩ **lecture:** teaching
⑪ **Shall you my son:** you shall find out my son
⑫ **have:** get, understand

POLONIUS

Observe his inclination① in yourself②.

REYNALDO

I shall, my lord.

POLONIUS

And let him ply③ his music④.

REYNALDO

80 Well, my lord.

POLONIUS

Farewell!

Exit REYNALDO

Enter OPHELIA

How now, Ophelia! what's the matter?

OPHELIA

O, my lord, my lord, I have been so affrighted!

POLONIUS

With what, i' the name of God?

OPHELIA

85 My lord, as I was sewing in my closet⑤,
Lord Hamlet, with his doublet⑥ all unbraced⑦,
No hat upon his head⑧, his stockings fouled⑨,
Ungartered⑩, and down-gyvèd to his ancle⑪,

---

① **inclination:** habits, behaviors
② **in yourself:** with your own eyes
③ **ply:** practice
④ **ply his music:** have his way
⑤ **closet:** boudoir, private chamber (for prayer, reading etc.)
⑥ **doublet:** A short, close-fitting jacket, with or without sleeves, laced to the hose or trousers, worn by men from 14th to 18th century (so it is an anachronism).
⑦ **unbraced:** unfastened.
⑧ **No hat upon his head:** Elizabethans normally wore hats indoors.
⑨ **fouled:** dirty
⑩ **ungartered:** untied
⑪ **down-gyvèd to his ancle:** dangling like fetters round his ankles.

Pale as his shirt; his knees knocking each other;
90 And with a look so[1] piteous in purport[2]
As if he had been loosèd out of hell
To speak of horrors,—he comes[3] before me.

POLONIUS
Mad for thy love?

OPHELIA
My lord, I do not know;
95 But truly, I do fear it.

POLONIUS
What said he?

OPHELIA
He took me by the wrist and held me hard;
Then goes[4] he to the length of all his arm[5];
And, with his other hand thus o'er his brow[6],
100 He falls to such perusal[7] of my face
As[8] he would draw it. Long stayed he so;
At last, a little shaking[9] of mine arm
And thrice his head thus waving up and down,
He raised a sigh so piteous and profound
105 As[10] it did seem to shatter all his bulk[11]
And end his being[12]. That done, he lets me go,

---

[1] **so:** as
[2] **purport:** meaning, implication
[3] **comes:** dramatic present
[4] **goes:** dramatic present
[5] **goes he to the length of all his arm:** then he stepped back an arm's length
[6] **o'er his brow:** forehead
[7] **perusal:** scrutiny
[8] **As:** as if
[9] **a little shaking:** with a little shaking
[10] **As:** that
[11] **bulk:** trunk, body
[12] **being:** existence

And, with his head over his shoulder turned,
He seemed to find his way without his eyes;
For out o' doors he went without their helps,
110 And, to the last, bended① their light② on me.③

POLONIUS
Come, go with me. I will go seek the King.
This is the very ecstasy④ of love,
Whose violent property⑤ fordoes⑥ itself
And leads the will to desperate undertakings
115 As oft as any passion under heaven
That does afflict our natures. I am sorry.⑦
What, have you given him any hard words of late?

OPHELIA
No, my good lord, but, as you did command,
I did repel his letters and denied
120 His⑧ access to me.

POLONIUS
That hath made him mad.
I am sorry that⑨ with better heed and judgment
I had not quoted⑩ him. I feared he did but trifle⑪

---

① **bended:** bent, directed
② **light:** attention
③ Hamlet seems to be sleepwalking. Or, overburdened with a desperate task, he subconsciously assumes madness for relief.
④ **ecstasy:** delirium, madness
⑤ **violent property:** characteristic capacity for violence
⑥ **fordoes:** destroys
⑦ The sentence is unfinished.
⑧ **His:** him
⑨ **I am sorry that:** He picks up the sentence in 116.
⑩ **quoted:** noted, observed
⑪ **trifle:** play with your affection

And meant to wrack[1] thee; but, beshrew[2] my jealousy[3]!
125 By heaven, it is as proper to[4] our age[5]
To cast beyond ourselves in our opinions[6]
As it is common for the younger sort
To lack discretion. Come, go we to the King.
This must be known[7], which, being kept close[8], might move[9]
130 More grief to hide than hate[10] to utter[11] love.[12]
Exeunt

SCENE II. A room in the castle.

Enter KING, QUEEN, ROSENCRANTZ, and GUILDENSTERN, cum aliis[13]

KING
Welcome, dear Rosencrantz and Guildenstern!
Moreover that[14] we much did long to see you,
The need we have to use you did provoke

---

① **wrack:** wreck, ruin
② **beshrew:** damn, curse
③ **jealousy:** suspicion
④ **proper to:** typical of
⑤ **our age:** old men like me
⑥ **To ... opinions:** to be over-prudent
⑦ **known:** reported
⑧ **close:** secret
⑨ **move:** cause, excite
⑩ **hate:** willingness
⑪ **utter:** tell
⑫ **move ... love:** a. "for it, by being kept secret, might cause more grief than our hatred (unwillingness) to utter (tell) it might move (excite) love (in the King and Queen)." b. "It might cause more grief "than move (excite) hate in the King by telling him Hamlet's love for Ophelia." c "This love might cause more grief if hidden than hatred if told about."
⑬ ***cum aliis:*** (Latin) with others
⑭ **Moreover that:** besides the fact that

　　　　Our hasty sending①. Something have you heard
5　Of Hamlet's transformation②; so③ call it,
　　　　Sith④ nor⑤ the exterior nor the inward man
　　　　Resembles that⑥ it was. What it should⑦ be,
　　　　More than his father's death, that thus hath put him
　　　　So much from the understanding of himself,
10　I cannot dream of. I entreat you both,
　　　　That, being of⑧ so young days brought up with him,
　　　　And sith⑨ so ncighbored to⑩ his youth and havior⑪,
　　　　That you vouchsafe your rest⑫ here in our court
　　　　Some little time; so by your companies⑬
15　To draw⑭ him on to pleasures, and to gather,
　　　　So⑮ much as from occasion⑯ you may glean,
　　　　Whether aught to us unknown afflicts him thus,
　　　　That, opened⑰, lies within our remedy⑱.
　　　　QUEEN
　　　　Good gentlemen, he hath much talked of you;

---

① **hasty sending**: sending for you
② **transformation**: euphemism for madness (Cf. 36: "our too much changèd son")
③ **so**: so to
④ **Sith**: since
⑤ **nor**: neither
⑥ **that**: what
⑦ **should**: could
⑧ **being of**: from
⑨ **sith**: ever since
⑩ **neighbored to**: familiar with
⑪ **youth and havior**: youthful behavior (hendiadys)
⑫ **vouchsafe your rest**: agree to stay
⑬ **your companies**: the company of both of you
⑭ **draw**: encourage, attract
⑮ **So**: as
⑯ **occasion**: opportunity
⑰ **opened**: disclosed, revealed
⑱ **lies within our remedy**: can be cured by us

And sure I am two men there are not living
20 To whom he more adheres[1]. If it will please you
To show us so much gentry[2] and good will
As to expend your time with us awhile,
For the supply and profit[3] of our hope,
Your visitation shall receive such thanks
25 As fits a king's remembrance.

ROSENCRANTZ
Both your majesties
Might, by the sovereign power you have of[4] us,
Put your dread pleasures[5] more into command
Than to entreaty.
30 **GUILDENSTERN**
But we both obey,
And here give up ourselves, in the full bent[6]
To lay our service freely at your feet,
To be commanded.

KING
Thanks, Rosencrantz and gentle Guildenstern.

QUEEN
Thanks, Guildenstern and gentle Rosencrantz.
35 And I beseech you instantly to visit
My too much changèd son. Go, some[7] of you,
And bring these gentlemen where Hamlet is.

GUILDENSTERN

---

[1] **more adheres:** is more attached
[2] **gentry:** generosity; courtesy
[3] **supply and profit:** fulfillment and furtherance
[4] **of:** over
[5] **your dread pleasures:** wishes of you as our revered sovereigns
[6] **in the full bent:** to the uttermost (as in bending a bow)
[7] **some:** one

Heavens make our presence and our practices①
40　Pleasant and helpful to him!②

QUEEN

Ay, amen③!

Exeunt ROSENCRANTZ, GUILDENSTERN, and some Attendants
Enter POLONIUS

POLONIUS

The ambassadors from Norway, my good lord,
Are joyfully④ returned.

KING

Thou still⑤ hast been the father⑥ of good news.

45　**POLONIUS**

Have I, my lord? I assure my good liege,
I hold my duty, as I hold my soul,
Both to my God and to my gracious king;
And I do think, or else⑦ this brain of mine
Hunts not the trail of policy⑧ so sure⑨
50　As it hath used to do, that I have found
The very cause of Hamlet's lunacy.

KING

O, speak of that; that do I long to hear.

POLONIUS

Give first admittance to the ambassadors;

---

① **practices**: actions
② **Pleasant and helpful to him**: So they mean well and are unfortunately misunderstood by Hamlet.
③ **amen**: so be it
④ **joyfully**: i.e. bearing a positive report
⑤ **still**: always
⑥ **father**: bearer
⑦ **else**: unless
⑧ **policy**: political cunning
⑨ **sure**: successfully

55　My news shall be the fruit① to that great feast.②
KING
Thyself do grace③ to them, and bring them in.
Exit POLONIUS
He tells me, my dear Gertrude,④ he hath found
The head⑤ and source of all your son's distemper⑥.
QUEEN
I doubt⑦ it is no other but the main⑧;
60　His father's death, and our o'erhasty marriage.⑨
KING
Well, we shall sift⑩ him.
Re-enter POLONIUS, with VOLTEMAND and CORNELIUS
Welcome, my good friends!
Say, Voltemand, what from our brother Norway⑪?
VOLTEMAND
Most fair return⑫ of greetings and desires⑬.
65　Upon our first⑭, he sent out to suppress
His nephew's levies; which to him appeared
To be a preparation 'gainst the Polack⑮;

---

① **fruit:** dessert, the last course
② **My news ... feast:** He purposely postpones the revelation to make it seem more enticing.
③ **grace:** honor
④ **57 ff:** This is their first private conversation. Cf. IV. vii. 16—18: "She's so conjunctive to my life and soul, / That, as the star moves not but in his sphere, / I could not but by her."
⑤ **head:** origin
⑥ **distemper:** mental derangement
⑦ **doubt:** suspect
⑧ **the main:** the chief reason, the central point
⑨ **o'erhasty marriage:** A woman's "prophetic soul"!
⑩ **sift:** question closely (as if through a sieve)
⑪ **brother Norway:** the King of Norway
⑫ **return:** reciprocation
⑬ **desires:** good wishes
⑭ **Upon our first:** as soon as we made known our business
⑮ **the Polack:** Poles

But, better looked into, he truly found
It was against your highness; whereat grieved,
70 That so his sickness, age and impotence①
Was falsely borne in hand②, sends out arrests③
On Fortinbras; which he, in brief, obeys;
Receives rebuke from Norway, and in fine④
Makes vow before his uncle never more
75 To give the assay of arms against⑤ your majesty.
Whereon old Norway, overcome with joy,
Gives him three thousand crowns⑥ in annual fee⑦,
And his commission⑧ to employ those soldiers,
So levied as before, against the Polack;⑨
80 With an entreaty, herein further shown,
[*Gives a paper*]
That it might please you to give quiet pass⑩
Through your dominions⑪ for this enterprise,
On such regards of safety and allowance⑫
As therein are set down.

KING

85 It likes⑬ us well;
And at our more considered⑭ time well read,

---

① **impotence:** feeble health
② **Was falsely borne in hand:** deceived
③ **sends out arrests:** writs of arrest; orders to desist
④ **in fine:** finally
⑤ **give the assay of arms against:** make trial of armed combat, attack
⑥ **three thousand crowns:** land which yielded three thousand crowns
⑦ **fee:** income
⑧ **commission:** authorization
⑨ **against the Polack:** bought obedience
⑩ **quiet pass:** peaceful passage
⑪ **dominions:** territories
⑫ **On such … allowance:** on such conditions as regards public safety and for your approval
⑬ **likes:** pleases
⑭ **considered:** appropriate

Answer, and think upon this business.
Meantime we thank you for your well-took① labor.
Go to your rest; at night② we'll feast together.
90 Most welcome home!
Exeunt VOLTEMAND and CORNELIUS
POLONIUS
This business is well ended.
My liege, and madam, to expostulate③
What majesty should be, what duty is,
Why day is day, night night, and time is time,
95 Were nothing but to waste night, day and time.
Therefore, since brevity is the soul of wit④,
And tediousness⑤ the limbs and outward flourishes⑥,
I will be brief. Your noble son is mad.
Mad call I it; for, to define true madness,
100 What is't but to be nothing else but mad?
But let that go.
QUEEN
More matter⑦, with less art⑧.
POLONIUS
Madam, I swear I use no art at all.
That he is mad, 'tis true: 'tis true 'tis pity;
105 And pity 'tis 'tis true. A foolish figure⑨;
But farewell it, for I will use no art.

---

① **well-took:** well-taken
② **at night:** tonight
③ **expostulate:** discourse upon, dilate at length
④ **wit:** wisdom
⑤ **tediousness:** long-windedness
⑥ **flourishes:** ornaments
⑦ **matter:** substance
⑧ **art:** artfulness
⑨ **figure:** figures of speech, rhetorical device

Mad let us grant him, then. And now remains
That we find out the cause of this effect,
Or rather say, the cause of this defect①,
110　For this effect defective comes by cause.②
Thus it remains, and the remainder thus.③ Perpend④.
I have a daughter—have while she is mine⑤—
Who, in her duty and obedience, mark,
Hath given me this⑥. Now gather, and surmise⑦.
Reads
115　*To the celestial and my soul's idol, the most*
beautified Ophelia,—
That's an ill phrase, a vile phrase; 'beautified' is
a vile phrase. But you shall hear. Thus:
Reads
*In her excellent white bosom, these, & c.*⑧

QUEEN

120　Came this from Hamlet to her?

POLONIUS

Good madam, stay⑨ awhile; I will be faithful⑩.
Reads
*Doubt*⑪ *thou the stars are fire;*
Doubt that the sun doth move;

---

① **defect**: disability
② 109—110: He plays on "effect" and "defect".
③ He plays on "remain" and "remainder"
④ **Perpend**: ponder, consider
⑤ **while she is mine**: before she is married
⑥ **this**: Hamlet's love letter (This is the first of all his three letters read in public during the play.)
⑦ **Now gather, and surmise**: understand what I am about to say and draw your own conclusion
⑧ **& c**: etc (He skips over the formal compliments.)
⑨ **stay**: wait
⑩ **be faithful**: read the entire letter accurately
⑪ **Doubt**: be skeptical about

Doubt[1] *truth to be a liar;*
125 *But never doubt*[2] *I love.*

O dear Ophelia, I am ill at these numbers[3]*;*
I have not art to reckon[4] *my groans; but that*
I love thee best, O most best, believe it. Adieu.
' Thine evermore, most dear lady, whilst
130 *this machine*[5] *is*[6] *to him,*[7] *HAMLET.*
This, in obedience, hath my daughter shown me,
And more above[8], hath his solicitings,
As they fell out[9] by time, by means and place,
All given to mine ear.

KING
135 But how hath she
Received his love?

POLONIUS
What do you think of me?

KING
As of a man faithful and honorable.

POLONIUS
I would fain[10] prove so. But what might[11] you think,

---

[1] ***Doubt***: suspect
[2] ***doubt***: disbelieve
[3] ***numbers:*** verses
[4] ***reckon***: versify
[5] ***machine***: body
[6] ***is***: belongs
[7] ***this machine is to him***: i.e. while he is alive
[8] ***more above***: moreover, besides
[9] ***fell out***: happened, took place
[10] ***fain***: willingly
[11] ***might***: could

140　When I had seen this hot love on the wing①—
　　As I perceived it, I must tell you that,
　　Before my daughter told me—what might you,
　　Or my dear majesty your Queen here, think,
　　If I had played the desk or table-book②,
145　Or given my heart a winking③, mute and dumb,
　　Or looked upon this love with idle sight④;
　　What might you think? No, I went round⑤ to work,
　　And my young mistress thus I did bespeak⑥:
　　'Lord Hamlet is a prince, out of⑦ thy star⑧;
150　This must not be.' And then I precepts⑨ gave her,
　　That she should lock herself from his resort⑩,
　　Admit no messengers, receive no tokens.
　　Which done, she took the fruits⑪ of my advice;
　　And he, repulsed⑫—a short tale to make⑬—
155　Fell into a sadness, then into a fast,
　　Thence to a watch⑭, thence into a weakness,
　　Thence to a lightness⑮, and, by this declension⑯,

---

① **hot love on the wing:** "Hot love" is likened to a flying bird
② **played the desk or table-book:** acted as a passive receiver
③ **given my heart a winking:** deliberately closed my eyes
④ **with idle sight:** seeing it but doing nothing about it
⑤ **round:** straightforwardly
⑥ **bespeak:** address, speak to
⑦ **out of:** outside, beyond
⑧ **star:** sphere, destiny
⑨ **precepts:** instructions
⑩ **resort:** access, reach
⑪ **fruits:** benefits
⑫ **repulsed:** repelled
⑬ **a short tale to make:** in short
⑭ **watch:** sleeplessness
⑮ **lightness:** light-headedness
⑯ **declension:** declining, deterioration

Into the madness wherein now he raves,①
And all we mourn for.

KING

160 Do you think 'tis this?

QUEEN

It may be, very likely.

POLONIUS

Hath there been such a time—I'd fain know that②—
That③ I have positively said 'Tis so,'
When it proved otherwise?

KING

165 Not that I know.

POLONIUS

[*Pointing to his head and shoulder*]
Take this④ from this, if this be otherwise.
If circumstances⑤ lead me, I will find
Where truth is hid⑥, though it were hid indeed
Within the center⑦.

KING

170 How may we try it further?

POLONIUS

You know, sometimes he walks four hours⑧ together⑨

---

① **154—158:** He describes the classic symptoms of love-melancholy. (Cf. *Romeo and Juliet*, I. i. 131—140)
② **I'd fain know that:** a rhetorical pause to engage attention
③ **That:** when
④ **this:** head; office
⑤ **circumstances:** circumstantial (relative) evidence
⑥ **hid:** hidden
⑦ **the center:** the heart of the earth
⑧ **four hours:** several hours ("Four" is a common usage of the time.)
⑨ **together:** at a time

Here in the lobby①.

QUEEN

So he does indeed.

POLONIUS

At such a time I'll loose② my daughter to him.③

175 Be you and I behind an arras④ then;

Mark the encounter. If he love her not

And be not from his reason fall'n thereon⑤,

Let me be no assistant for a state⑥,

But keep a farm and carters⑦.⑧

KING

180 We will try it.

*Enter HAMLET, reading on a book.*⑨

QUEEN

But, look, where sadly the poor wretch⑩ comes reading.

POLONIUS

Away, I do beseech you, both away!

I'll board⑪ him presently⑫.

Exeunt KING, QUEEN, and Attendants

O, give me leave⑬.

---

① **lobby:** anteroom or corridor
② **loose:** (hunting term) set loose
③ **I'll loose … him:** He uses his daughter as a decoy
④ **arras:** tapestry draped from a wall
⑤ **fall'n thereon:** on that account
⑥ **assistant for a state:** councilor with a role in government
⑦ **a farm and carters:** cart-drivers
⑧ **178—179:** Cf. *Henry V,* III. iii. 11—14: "(ma vie! if they march along / unfought withal,) but I will sell my dukedom, / to buy a slobbery and a dirty farm / in that nook-shotten isle of Albion."
⑨ What is he reading for? And what book?
⑩ **poor wretch:** a term of endearment
⑪ **board:** accost (marine metaphor); address
⑫ **presently:** immediately
⑬ **give me leave:** permit me to be alone, excuse me

185 How does① my good Lord Hamlet?

HAMLET

Well, God-a-mercy②.

POLONIUS

Do you know me, my lord?

HAMLET

Excellent well. You are a fishmonger③.

POLONIUS

Not I, my lord.

HAMLET

190 Then I would④ you were so honest a man⑤.

POLONIUS

Honest, my lord?

HAMLET

Ay, sir. To be honest, as this world goes, is to be one man picked out of ten thousand.

POLONIUS

That's very true, my lord.

HAMLET

195 For if the sun breed maggots in a dead dog,⑥ being a god⑦ kissing carrion⑧,—Have you a daughter?

POLONIUS

I have, my lord.

HAMLET

---

① **does:** the third person
② **God-a-mercy:** God have mercy on you (a polite response to a greeting from a social inferior)
③ **a fishmonger:** a fish-seller; one who fishes for information; father who has bred many children; in Elizabethan slang, "a pimp, a toy-boy"
④ **would:** wish
⑤ **so honest a man:** as to be a fishmonger
⑥ Elizabethans believed the sun bred maggots.
⑦ **a god:** the sun god
⑧ **carrion:** dead flesh; sexual corruption

Let her not walk i' the sun.① Conception② is a blessing, but not as your daughter may conceive.③

200 Friend, look to 't.

POLONIUS [*Aside*]

How say you by that④? Still⑤ harping⑥ on my daughter. Yet he knew me not at first; he said I was a fishmonger. He is far gone⑦, far gone! And truly in my youth I suffered much extremity⑧ for

205 love—very near⑨ this. I'll speak to him again. What do you read, my lord?⑩

HAMLET

Words, words, words.

POLONIUS

What is the matter⑪, my lord?

HAMLET

Between who?

POLONIUS

210 I mean, the matter that you read, my lord.

HAMLET

Slanders⑫, sir; for the satirical rogue⑬ says here⑭ that old men have grey beards; that their faces are wrinkled;

---

① **Let ... sun:** lest she conceive to her dishonor (Hamlet puns on "sun" and "son".)
② **Conception:** pregnancy
③ **Conception ... conceive:** He puns on "conceive" and "conception".
④ **How say you by that:** what do you say to that
⑤ **Still:** always
⑥ **harping:** dwelling
⑦ **far gone:** seriously affected
⑧ **much extremity:** inordinate stress, extreme adversity
⑨ **very near:** like
⑩ Gilbert Highet: "The prince was evidently reading Juvenal 10." (*The Anatomy of Satire*, New Jersey: Princeton University Press, 1962, p.266.)
⑪ **the matter:** subject matter (Hamlet changes it to mean "trouble")
⑫ **Slanders:** malicious statements
⑬ **the satirical rogue:** i.e. Erasmus (1466—1536)
⑭ **here:** i.e. *In Praise of Folly* (1511). In fact, Hamlet could not have seen this book.

their eyes purging[1] thick amber and plum-tree gum[2],
that they have a plentiful lack of wit[3], together with
215 most weak hams[4]. All which, sir, though I most powerfully
and potently[5] believe, yet I hold it not honesty[6] to
have it[7] thus set down; for you yourself, sir, should be[8]
old as[9] I am, if like a crab, you could go backward.

POLONIUS

[*Aside*] Though this be madness, yet there is method
220 in 't.[10]—Will you walk out of the air[11], my lord?

HAMLET

Into my grave.

POLONIUS

Indeed, that is out o' the air.

Aside

How pregnant[12] sometimes his replies are! A happiness[13]
that often madness hits on, which reason and sanity
225 could not so prosperously[14] be delivered of[15]. I will
leave him, and suddenly contrive the means of
meeting between him and my daughter.[16]—My honorable

---

① **purging:** shedding, secreting
② **gum:** resin
③ **wit:** understanding
④ **hams:** buttocks and thighs
⑤ **potently:** mightily
⑥ **honesty:** good manners
⑦ **it:** old age
⑧ **should be:** would undoubtedly be
⑨ **old as:** only as old as
⑩ **Though … in 't:** Cf. *King Lear,* IV. vi. 174—175: "O, matter and impertinency mix'd! / Reason in madness!"
⑪ **walk out of the air:** literally, walk indoors
⑫ **pregnant:** full of meaning
⑬ **happiness:** felicity of expression, aptness of phrasing
⑭ **prosperously:** effectively
⑮ **be delivered of:** Cf. "pregnant" in 223
⑯ **I will … daughter:** Cf. 174: "loose my daughter" etc.

lord, I will most humbly take my leave of you.
HAMLET
You cannot, sir, take from me any thing that I will
230 more willingly part withal①—except my life, except my life, except my life.
POLONIUS
Fare you well, my lord.
HAMLET
These tedious old fools!②
Enter ROSENCRANTZ and GUILDENSTERN
POLONIUS
You go to seek the Lord Hamlet; there he is.
ROSENCRANTZ
235 [*To POLONIUS*] God save you, sir!
Exit POLONIUS
GUILDENSTERN
My honored lord!
ROSENCRANTZ
My most dear lord!
HAMLET
My excellent good friends! How dost thou,
Guildenstern? Ah, Rosencrantz! Good lads, how do ye③ both?
ROSENCRANTZ
240 As the indifferent④ children of the earth.⑤
GUILDENSTERN
Happy, in that we are not over-happy;

---

① **withal:** with
② **These tedious old fools:** This line not only reveals Hamlet's aversion to Polonius, as well as his sickness of the world.
③ **ye:** you
④ **indifferent:** ordinary, average
⑤ **the indifferent children of the earth:** the general run of the mortals

On Fortune's cap we are not the very button①.

HAMLET

Nor the soles of her shoe?

ROSENCRANTZ

Neither, my lord.

HAMLET

245 Then you live about her waist, or in the middle of her favours?

GUILDENSTERN

'Faith, her privates② we.

HAMLET

In the secret parts of Fortune? O, most true; she③ is a strumpet④. What's the news?

ROSENCRANTZ

250 None, my lord, but that the world's grown honest.

HAMLET

Then is doomsday near!⑤ But your news is not true. Let me question more in particular. What have you, my good friends, deserved at the hands of Fortune, that she sends you to prison hither?

GUILDENSTERN

Prison, my lord!

HAMLET

255 Denmark's a prison.⑥

---

① **button:** cockade
② **privates:** pun: a. soldiers of the lowest rank; a. private parts; c. intimates
③ **she:** i.e. Goddess of Fortune
④ **strumpet:** prostitute (so none could count on her constant favor)
⑤ **Then ... near:** i.e. Humanity, especially the radical evil in human nature, cannot be changed. Cf. *Matthew* 3:2: "Repent, for the Kingdom of heaven has come near."
⑥ **Denmark's a prison:** Cf. *Richard II,* V. v. 1—2: "I may compare / This prison where I live unto this world"

ROSENCRANTZ

Then is the world one.

HAMLET

A goodly① one; in which there are many confines②,
wards and dungeons③, Denmark being one o' the worst.

ROSENCRANTZ

260 We think not so, my lord.

HAMLET

Why, then, 'tis none to you, for there is nothing
either good or bad, but thinking makes it so.④
To me it is a prison.

ROSENCRANTZ

Why then, your ambition makes it one; 'tis too
265 narrow for your mind.⑤

HAMLET

O God, I could be bounded in a nutshell and count
myself a king of infinite space, were it not that I
have bad dreams.⑥

GUILDENSTERN

Which dreams indeed are ambition, for the very
270 substance of the ambitious is merely the shadow of a dream.⑦

HAMLET

A dream itself is but a shadow.

---

① **goodly:** large, roomy
② **confines:** places of confinement
③ **wards and dungeons:** prison cells
④ **either … so:** Cf. Montaigne: "Good and Evil Depends in Great Measure upon the Opinion We Have of Them" (*The Essays of Montaigne, I.* XL, trans. by Charles Cotton, London: Reeves and Turner, 1877, p.315.)
⑤ **Why … mind:** Spying begins.
⑥ **O God … dreams:** Cf. *The Tempest,* I. ii. 109—110: "Me, poor man—my library was dukedom large enough"
⑦ **the shadow of a dream:** cf. Pindar: "Creatures of a day! What is a man? / What is he not? A dream of a shadow / Is our mortal being." (*Pythian* 8)

ROSENCRANTZ

Truly, and I hold ambition of so airy and light a quality that it is but a shadow's shadow.①

HAMLET

Then are our beggars② bodies③, and our monarchs
275 and outstretched heroes the beggars' shadows.④ Shall we to the court? for, by my fay⑤, I cannot reason.

ROSENCRANTZ GUILDENSTERN

We'll wait upon⑥ you.

HAMLET

No such matter! I will not sort⑦ you with the rest of my servants, for, to speak to you like an honest
280 man, I am most dreadfully attended⑧. But, in the beaten⑨ way of friendship, what make you⑩ at Elsinore?

ROSENCRANTZ

To visit you, my lord; no other occasion⑪.

HAMLET

Beggar that I am, I am even poor in thanks; but I thank you; and sure, dear friends, my thanks are
285 too dear a halfpenny⑫. Were you not sent for? Is it your own inclining⑬? Is it a free visitation? Come,

---

① **a shadow's shadow:** 对观《庄子·齐物论》："方其梦也，不知其梦也。梦之中又占其梦焉，觉而后知其梦也。"《金刚经》："一切有为法，如梦幻光影，如露亦如电，亦作如是观。"
② **our beggars:** those who have no ambitions
③ **bodies:** substance
④ **outstretched heroes the beggars' shadows:** heroes are the oversized shadows of beggars
⑤ **fay:** faith
⑥ **wait upon:** serve, accompany
⑦ **sort:** classify, rank
⑧ **I am most dreadfully attended:** my attendants are a very poor lot
⑨ **beaten:** straight
⑩ **what make you:** what are you doing
⑪ **occasion:** reason
⑫ **too dear a halfpenny:** not worth a halfpenny
⑬ **inclining:** inclination

deal justly① with me. Come, come; nay, speak.
GUILDENSTERN
What should we say, my lord?
HAMLET
Why, any thing, but to the purpose. You were sent
290   for; and there is a kind of confession in your looks
which your modesties② have not craft enough to color③.
I know the good king and queen have sent for you.
ROSENCRANTZ
To what end, my lord?④
HAMLET
That you must teach me. But let me conjure⑤ you by⑥
295   the rights of our fellowship, by the consonancy⑦ of
our youth, by the obligation of our ever-preserved
love, and by what more dear a better proposer⑧ could charge⑨
you withal⑩: be even⑪ and direct with me, whether you were sent for, or no?
ROSENCRANTZ
300   [*Aside to GUILDENSTERN*] What say you?
HAMLET
[*Aside*] Nay, then, I have an eye of⑫ you.—If you
love me, hold not off⑬.

---

① **justly:** honestly
② **modesties:** modest natures
③ **color:** disguise, conceal
④ **To what ... lord:** Cf. 13—18
⑤ **conjure:** entreat, plead with
⑥ **by (294—297):** anaphora
⑦ **consonancy:** harmony, friendship
⑧ **proposer:** speaker
⑨ **charge:** urge, exhort
⑩ **by what ... withal:** by anything more sacred than a better talker might urge in appealing to you
⑪ **even:** frank
⑫ **of:** on
⑬ **not off:** on

GUILDENSTERN

My lord, we were sent for.

HAMLET

I will tell you why, so shall my anticipation[1] prevent[2]
305 your discovery[3], and your secrecy[4] to the King
and queen moult[5] no feather[6]. I have of late[7]—but[8]
wherefore I know not—lost all my mirth, forgone all
custom of exercises[9];[10] and indeed it goes so heavily
with my disposition[11] that this goodly frame[12], the
earth, seems to me a sterile[13] promontory[14], this most
310 excellent canopy, the air[15], look you, this brave[16]
o'erhanging firmament, this majestical roof fretted[17]
with golden fire, why, it[18] appears no other thing to
me than a foul and pestilent congregation of vapours.
What a piece of work[19] is a man! how noble in reason!

---

[1] **anticipation:** saying first
[2] **prevent:** forestall
[3] **discovery:** disclosure
[4] **secrecy:** promise of secrecy
[5] **moult:** (shall) shed
[6] **moult no feather:** retain its luster, sustain no loss
[7] **of late:** recently
[8] **I have ... but:** He may be describing his real feelings while concealing the cause.
[9] **custom of exercises:** customary activities
[10] **I have of late ... exercise:** He is sick of the world: is it true or just "a parade of fashionable melancholy"?
[11] **disposition:** spirits
[12] **frame:** structure
[13] **sterile:** barren
[14] **promontory:** headland; platform
[15] **the air:** the sky
[16] **brave:** splendid
[17] **fretted:** decorated with fretwork (an angular, interlaced design)
[18] **it:** the canopy
[19] **a piece of work:** i.e. creation by God

315　how infinite in faculties①! in form② and moving③ how

express④ and admirable! in action how like an angel!

in apprehension⑤ how like a god! the beauty of the

world! the paragon⑥ of animals! And yet to me

what is this quintessence⑦ of dust? Man delights not me—

320　no, nor woman neither, though by

your smiling you seem to say so.

ROSENCRANTZ

My lord, there was no such stuff in my thoughts.

HAMLET

Why did you laugh then, when I said 'man delights not me'?

ROSENCRANTZ

To think, my lord, if you delight not in man, what

325　lenten⑧ entertainment⑨ the players shall receive from

you. We coted⑩ them on the way; and hither⑪ are they

coming, to offer you service.

HAMLET

He that plays the King shall be welcome; his majesty

shall have tribute⑫ of me; the adventurous knight

330　shall use his foil⑬ and target⑭; the lover shall not sigh gratis⑮;

---

① **faculties:** capacities
② **form:** shape
③ **moving:** motion
④ **express:** exact; well-framed
⑤ **apprehension:** understanding
⑥ **paragon:** supreme example
⑦ **this quintessence:** the 5ᵗʰ element (which would be left if the 4 elements are taken away)
⑧ **lenten:** poor, meager (Lent: 四旬节)
⑨ **entertainment:** reception, welcome
⑩ **coted:** passed
⑪ **hither:** here
⑫ **tribute:** praise, payment
⑬ **foil:** blunted small sword
⑭ **target:** small shield
⑮ **gratis:** for nothing

the humorous man① shall end his part in peace;
the clown shall make those laugh whose
lungs are tickle o' the sear②; and the lady③ shall
say her mind freely, or④ the blank verse shall halt⑤ for't.

335 What players are they?

ROSENCRANTZ
Even⑥ those you were wont⑦ to take delight
in, the tragedians⑧ of the city.⑨

HAMLET
How chances it they travel⑩? Their residence⑪, both
in reputation and profit, was better both ways.

ROSENCRANTZ
340 I think their inhibition⑫ comes by the means of⑬ the late innovation⑭.

HAMLET
Do they hold the same estimation⑮ they did when I was
in the city? Are they so followed⑯?

ROSENCRANTZ
No, indeed, are they not.

---

① **the humorous man:** stock character actor who impersonates a particular humor
② **tickle o' the sear:** quick on the trigger
③ **328—334:** the King, the adventurous knight, the lover, the humorous man, the clown, the lady are all stock figures in Elizabethan plays.
④ **or:** even if
⑤ **halt:** be lame, limp
⑥ **Even:** just
⑦ **wont:** used
⑧ **tragedians:** actors
⑨ **the tragedians of the city:** It alludes to the Lord Admiral's Men, rival of the Lord Chamberlaine's Men, where Shakespeare worked.
⑩ **travel:** tour
⑪ **residence:** staying in the city as a resident company
⑫ **inhibition:** what prevents them from remaining in the city
⑬ **by the means of:** is due to
⑭ **the late innovation:** It refers to a new company of boy actors in Shakespeare's England.
⑮ **estimation:** reputation
⑯ **so followed:** as admired as before

HAMLET

How comes it? Do they grow rusty?

ROSENCRANTZ

345　Nay, their endeavor keeps in the wonted pace①; but there is, sir, an eyrie② of children, little eyases③, that cry out on the top of question④, and are most tyrannically⑤ clapped for't⑥. These are now the fashion, and so berattle⑦ the common stages⑧ (so they

350　call them) that many wearing rapiers⑨ are afraid of goose-quills⑩ and dare scarce come thither⑪.

HAMLET

What, are they children? Who maintains 'em? How are they escoted⑫? Will they pursue⑬ the quality⑭ no longer than they can sing⑮? Will they not say afterwards,

355　if they should grow themselves to common players (as it is most like, if their means are no better) their writers do them wrong, to make them exclaim against their own succession⑯?

---

① **keeps in the wonted pace:** continues as usual
② **eyrie:** aerie, nest
③ **eyases:** hawks
④ **cry out …question:** speak their lines loudly
⑤ **tyrannically:** boisterously
⑥ **cry out … for't:** Cf. III. ii. 1—15
⑦ **berattle:** noisily attack
⑧ **common stages:** public theatres
⑨ **rapiers:** gentlemen (synecdoche)
⑩ **goose-quills:** pens, *i.e.* playwrights for boy actors
⑪ **thither:** there
⑫ **escoted:** supported financially
⑬ **pursue:** follow
⑭ **quality:** skill (i.e. acting profession)
⑮ **no longer … sing:** when their voices change
⑯ **their own succession:** their future selves, what they are going to be

ROSENCRANTZ

'Faith, there has been much to do① on both sides; and
the nation holds it no sin to tarre② them to
controversy. There was, for a while, no money bid
for argument③, unless the poet and the player
went to cuffs④ in the question⑤.⑥

HAMLET

Is't possible?

GUILDENSTERN

O, there has been much throwing about of brains⑦.

HAMLET

Do the boys carry it away⑧?

ROSENCRANTZ

Ay, that they do, my lord; Hercules and his load too.⑨

HAMLET

It is not very strange; for mine uncle is king of
Denmark, and those that would make mows⑩ at him while
my father lived, give twenty, forty, fifty, a hundred ducats
apiece for his picture in little⑪. 'Sblood⑫, there is something
in this more than natural, if philosophy could find it out.

---

① **much to do:** much ado, a great hubbub
② **tarre:** provoke, incite
③ **argument:** play, plot
④ **went to cuffs:** came to blows
⑤ **question:** dialogue
⑥ **There ... question:** There was once a time when no play was salable if it did not take up the quarrel between the children's poets and the adult players.
⑦ **throwing about of brains:** pyrotechnics
⑧ **carry it away:** carry off the victory
⑨ **Hercules and his load:** The boy actors win over the whole world of theatre-goers. "Hercules" refers to the Globe Theatre (1599—1613) used by Shakespeare's theatre. In Greek mythology, Hercules once bore the burden of the globe for Atlas.
⑩ **mows:** mouths, grimaces
⑪ **little:** miniature portrait
⑫ **'Sblood:** God's blood (an oath)

Flourish of trumpets within

GUILDENSTERN

There are the players.

HAMLET

Gentlemen, you are welcome to Elsinore. Your hands[①],
375 come then! The appurtenance[②] of welcome is fashion
and ceremony. Let me comply[③] with you in this garb[④],
lest my extent[⑤] to the players (which, I tell you,
must show fairly outward), should more appear like
entertainment[⑥] than yours. You are welcome. But my
380 uncle-father and aunt-mother are deceived.[⑦]

GUILDENSTERN

In what, my dear lord?

HAMLET

I am but mad north-north-west.[⑧] When the wind
is southerly I know a hawk[⑨] from a handsaw[⑩].[⑪]

Enter POLONIUS

POLONIUS

Well be with you[⑫], gentlemen!

---

① **Your hands:** give me your hands
② **appurtenance:** accessory
③ **comply:** exchange courtesies
④ **in this garb:** in this way
⑤ **extent:** extension of welcome
⑥ **like entertainment:** welcome
⑦ **But ... deceived:** He's being cynic.
⑧ **I am but mad north-north west:** I'm mad only occasionally (when it suits my purpose).
⑨ **hawk:** hack, a type of pickaxe
⑩ **handsaw:** hernshaw (heron).
⑪ **know a hawk from a handsaw:** distinguish between unlike objects
⑫ **Well be with you:** so be it with you, I wish you well

HAMLET

385 Hark you, Guildenstern—and you too—at each ear a
hearer! That great baby you see there① is not yet
out of his swaddling clouts②.

ROSENCRANTZ

Happily③ he's the second time come to them④; for they
say an old man is twice a child.⑤

HAMLET

390 I will prophesy he comes to tell me of the players;
mark⑥ it. You say right, sir; a Monday morning;
'twas⑦ so indeed.

POLONIUS

My lord, I have news to tell you.

HAMLET

My lord, I have news to tell you.

395 When Roscius⑧ was an actor in Rome—

POLONIUS

The actors are come hither, my lord.⑨

HAMLET

Buz, buz!⑩

POLONIUS

Upon my honor—

---

① **there:** Polonius
② **clouts:** clothes
③ **Happily:** perhaps
④ **them:** swaddling clothes
⑤ **an old man is twice a child:** Cf. *King Lear*, I. iii. 20: "Old fools are babes again"
⑥ **mrak:** observe, pay attention to
⑦ **'twas:** it was
⑧ **Roscius:** a famous Roman comic actor in the time of Cicero (Cf. Horace: *Letter to Augustus*, 82)
⑨ **The ... lord:** His news is too late to be new.
⑩ **Buz, buz:** chatter, idle tale (a contemptuous expression)

HAMLET

Then came each actor on his ass①.

POLONIUS

400 The best actors in the world, either for tragedy, comedy, history, pastoral, pastoral-comical, historical-pastoral, tragical-historical, tragical-comical-historical-pastoral, scene individable②, or poem unlimited③.④ Seneca⑤ cannot be too heavy,
405 nor Plautus⑥ too light. For the law of writ⑦ and the liberty, these are the only⑧ men.

HAMLET

O Jephthah, judge of Israel, what a treasure hadst thou!⑨

POLONIUS

What a treasure had he, my lord?

HAMLET

Why,
410 'One fair daughter and no more,
The which⑩ he lovèd passing⑪ well.'

---

① **ass**: suggestive of "arse"
② **scene individable**: one-act show
③ **poem unlimited**: plays not observing the classical unities
④ **The best ... unlimited**: He lists all the theatrical genres prevalent in Elizabethan England.
⑤ **Seneca**: (4 BC—56 AD): Roman writer of declamatory tragedies
⑥ **Plautus**: (254 BC—184 BC): Roman writer of farcical comedies
⑦ **law of writ**: rules of composition (i.e. the classical unities of time and place)
⑧ **only**: best, sole
⑨ **O Jephthah ... thou:** Hamlet quotes a line from a late 16th century ballad about Jephthah's sacrifice of his virgin daughter (Cf. *Judges,* 11: 34—39). And 405, 416, 417, 425, 427 may be quoted from then popular songs.
⑩ **The which**: which, whom
⑪ **passing**: exceedingly, surpassingly

POLONIUS

[*Aside*] Still[1] on my daughter.

HAMLET

Am I not i' the right, old Jephthah?

POLONIUS

If you call me Jephthah, my lord, I have a daughter
415 that I love passing well.

HAMLET

Nay, that follows not.[2]

POLONIUS

What follows, then, my lord?

HAMLET

Why,

'As by lot[3], God wot,'[4]
420 and then, you know,

'It came to pass[5], as most like[6] it was'—

the first row[7] of the pious chanson[8] will show you

more; for look, where my abridgement[9] comes.

Enter four or five Players

You are welcome, masters[10], welcome, all. I am glad to

---

[1] **Still**: always

[2] **Nay, that follows not**: a. Your analogy between yourself and Jephthah is false; b. That isn't the next line in the ballad.

[3] **lot**: chance

[4] **wot**: knows

[5] **came to pass**: happened

[6] **most like**: likely

[7] **row**: stanza

[8] **pious chanson**: religious song, spiritual ballad

[9] **abridgement**: that who cut short my quotation (i.e. the players)

[10] **masters**: gentlemen

425 　see thee well. Welcome, good friends. O, my old friend!
　　　thy face is valenced① since I saw thee last. Com'st
　　　thou to beard② me in Denmark③? What, my young lady
　　　and mistress④! By'r⑤ lady, your ladyship is
　　　nearer to heaven⑥ than when I saw you last, by the altitude
430 　of a chopine⑦. Pray God, your voice, like a piece of uncurrent gold,
　　　be not cracked within the ring.⑧ Masters, you are all welcome.
　　　We'll e'en to't⑨ like French falconers, fly⑩ at any thing
　　　we see.⑪ We'll have a speech straight⑫. Come,
　　　give us a taste of your quality⑬; come, a passionate speech.
　　　First Player
435 　What speech, my lord?
　　　HAMLET
　　　I heard thee speak me⑭ a speech once, but it⑮ was
　　　never acted; or, if it was, not above⑯ once; for the

① **valenced:** fringed (with a beard)
② **beard:** challenge, defy
③ **beard me in Denmark:** Proverb: beard the lion in his den
④ **my young lady and mistress:** the boy who plays a girl
⑤ **By'r:** by our
⑥ **nearer to heaven:** taller; older
⑦ **chopine:** buskin
⑧ **not cracked within the ring:** A gold coin clipped or cracked inside the ring surrounding the sovereign's head was no longer legal tender. (It may suggest a sexual meaning as well.)
⑨ **We'll e'en to't:** we shall just go at it
⑩ **fly:** launch our birds
⑪ **We'll … see:** undertake anything, no matter how difficult
⑫ **straight:** right away
⑬ **quality:** professional skill
⑭ **me:** for me
⑮ **it:** the play containing the speech
⑯ **above:** more than

play, I remember, pleased not the million; 'twas
caviary to the general①; but it was (as I received it,
440 and others, whose judgments in such matters
cried in the top of② mine) an excellent play,
well digested③ in④ the scenes, set down with as much
modesty⑤ as cunning⑥. I remember, one said there
were no sallets⑦ in the lines to make the matter
445 savory⑧, nor no matter in the phrase⑨ that might
indict⑩ the author of affectation; but called it an
honest⑪ method, as wholesome as sweet, and by very
much more handsome than fine⑫. One speech in it I
chiefly loved. 'Twas Aeneas'⑬ tale⑭ to
450 Dido⑮; and thereabout of it⑯ especially, where he speaks of
Priam's⑰ slaughter. If it live in your memory, begin
at this line—let me see, let me see—

---

① **caviary to the general:** something too good to be appreciated by common people
② **in the top of:** with a voice louder than, with more authority than
③ **digested:** organized, arranged
④ **in:** into
⑤ **modesty:** restraint, moderation
⑥ **cunning:** skill
⑦ **sallets:** salads, spicy bits
⑧ **savory:** palatable
⑨ **no matter in the phrase:** nothing in the manner of expression
⑩ **indict:** accuse, charge
⑪ **honest:** in good taste; unpretentious
⑫ **more handsome than fine:** elegant, but not gaudy
⑬ **'Twas Aeneas:** hero of Virgil's *Aeneid*
⑭ **tale:** narration
⑮ **Dido:** the founder and first Queen of Carthage (present-day Tunisia)
⑯ **thereabout of it:** around that part of it
⑰ **Priam:** King of Troy

'The rugged① Pyrrhus②, like the Hyrcanian beast,'③
it is not so; it begins with Pyrrhus:④
455　'The rugged Pyrrhus, he whose sable⑤ arms⑥
Black as his purpose, did the night resemble
When he lay couchèd⑦ in the ominous horse⑧,
Hath now this dread⑨ and black complexion⑩ smeared
With heraldry more dismal⑪; head to foot
460　Now is he total gules⑫; horridly tricked⑬
With blood of fathers, mothers, daughters, sons,
Baked and impasted⑭ with the parching⑮ streets,
That lend a tyrannous⑯ and damnèd light
To their lord's murder⑰. Roasted in wrath and fire,

---

① **rugged:** fierce, savage

② **Pyrrhus:** Achilles' son (also known as Neoptolemus), one of the Greeks concealed in the wooden horses that was pulled into the city of Troy, and he killed Priam. (In Virgil's description, he first kills Priam's son Polites in front of his father as he seeks sanctuary on the altar of Zeus. Priam rebukes Neoptolemus, throwing a spear at him, which misses. Neoptolemus then drags Priam to the altar and there kills him too. See *Aeneid,* Book II)

③ **the Hyrcanian beast:** fierce tigers (Hyrcania: a region in present Iran at the southern end of the Caspian Sea, was famous for its tigers. Cf. *Macbeth,* III. iv. 101; *3 Henry VI,* I. iv. 155)

④ **it begins with Pyrrhus:** The following recitation foreshadows Hamlet's revenge, procrastination, and trick (Trojan horse and the Mousetrap).

⑤ **sable:** black

⑥ **arms:** armor; blazon

⑦ **couchèd:** hidden

⑧ **the ominous horse:** the wooden horse

⑨ **dread:** dreadful

⑩ **black complexion:** general appearances

⑪ **dismal:** grim, dreadful

⑫ **total gules:** red all over

⑬ **gules ... tricked:** decorated (Both "gules" and "tricked" are heraldic terms.)

⑭ **impasted:** coagulated

⑮ **parching:** burning, scorching

⑯ **tyrannous:** savage

⑰ **their lord's murder:** i.e. the murder of Priam

465 And thus o'er-sizèd① with coagulate gore②,
    With eyes like carbuncles③, the hellish Pyrrhus
    Old grandsire④ Priam seeks.'
    So, proceed you.
    POLONIUS
    'Fore⑤ God, my lord, well spoken, with good accent⑥ and
470 good discretion⑦.
    First Player
    'Anon⑧ he finds him
    Striking too short at⑨ Greeks; his antique⑩ sword,
    Rebellious to his arm, lies where it falls,
    Repugnant⑪ to command. Unequal matched,
475 Pyrrhus at Priam drives; in rage strikes wide;
    But with the whiff⑫ and wind⑬ of his fell⑭ sword
    The unnervèd⑮ father falls. Then senseless⑯ Ilium⑰,
    Seeming to feel this blow, with flaming top
    Stoops to his base⑱, and with a hideous crash

---

① **o'er-sizèd:** glazed
② **coagulate gore:** congealed or clotted blood
③ **carbuncles:** brilliant red stones (红榴石)
④ **grandsire:** patriarch
⑤ **'Fore:** before
⑥ **accent:** pronunciation
⑦ **discretion:** judgment, discernment
⑧ **'Anon:** soon
⑨ **Striking too short at:** his sword falling short of
⑩ **antique:** ancient
⑪ **Repugnant:** resisting
⑫ **whiff:** blow
⑬ **wind:** mere disturbance of the air
⑭ **fell:** cruel
⑮ **unnervèd:** enfeebled
⑯ **senseless:** insensible, without human sense
⑰ **Ilium:** another name for Troy (here the fortified battlements of Troy)
⑱ **Stoops to his base:** falls to its foundation

480　Takes prisoner Pyrrhus' ear① For, lo! his sword,
　　　Which was declining② on the milky③ head
　　　Of reverend Priam, seemed i' the air to stick.
　　　So, as a painted④ tyrant, Pyrrhus stood,
　　　And like a neutral to his will and matter⑤
485　Did nothing.⑥
　　　But, as we often see, against⑦ some storm,
　　　A silence in the heavens, the rack⑧ stand still,
　　　The bold winds speechless and the orb⑨ below
　　　As hush⑩ as death, anon the dreadful thunder
490　Doth rend⑪ the region⑫, so, after Pyrrhus' pause,
　　　Arousèd vengeance⑬ sets him new a-work⑭;
　　　And never did the Cyclops'⑮ hammers fall
　　　On Mars's⑯ armor forged for proof eterne⑰,
　　　With less remorse than Pyrrhus' bleeding sword
495　Now falls on Priam.⑱

---

① **Takes prisoner Pyrrhus' ear:** deafen him.
② **declining:** descending
③ **milky:** white
④ **painted:** in a painting; coated with blood
⑤ **like a neutral to his will and matter:** between his purpose and its fulfillment; like one who is unable to act in spite of his desire and duty
⑥ **484—485:** Cf. III. iii. 44—46: Claudius: "like a man to double business bound, / I stand in pause where I shall first begin, / And both neglect."
⑦ **against:** just before
⑧ **rack:** driving clouds
⑨ **the orb:** the earth
⑩ **hush:** silent
⑪ **rend:** tear
⑫ **region:** upper air
⑬ **Arousèd vengeance:** an awakened desire for revenge
⑭ **a-work:** at work
⑮ **Cyclops:** three one-eyed Titans who worked for Vulcan, who forged thunderbolts for Jove, made Achilles' armor in the *Iliad* and Aeneas' armor in the *Aeneid*
⑯ **Mars':** the Roman god of war
⑰ **armor forged for proof eterne:** to stand the test of eternity
⑱ **Now falls on Priam:** Cf. *The Aeneid*, II. 506 ff.

Out, out, thou strumpet①, Fortune!② All you gods,
In general synod③ take away her power;
Break all the spokes④ and fellies⑤ from her wheel⑥
And bowl⑦ the round nave⑧ down the hill of heaven⑨,
500 As low as to the fiends⑩!⑪

POLONIUS

This is too long.

HAMLET

It shall to the barber's, with your beard.
Prithee say on. He's for a jig⑫ or a tale of bawdry⑬, or
he sleeps. Say on; come to Hecuba⑭.

First Player

505 'But who, O, who had seen the mobled⑮ queen—'

HAMLET

'The mobled queen?'

POLONIUS

That's good; 'mobled queen' is good.

---

① **strumpet:** prostitute
② **Out ... Fortune:** Cf. *King Lear,* II. iv. 52: "Fortune, that errant whore"
③ **synod:** council, meeting
④ **spokes:** 车辐
⑤ **fellies:** sections of the wheel's rim
⑥ **her wheel:** symbol of fate or Fortune
⑦ **bowl:** strike
⑧ **round nave:** center of the wheel, hub
⑨ **the hill of heaven:** i.e. Mount Olympus
⑩ **the fiends:** devils in hell
⑪ 498—500: Cf. III. iii. 18—23: "It is a massy wheel, / Fixed on the summit of the highest mount, / To whose huge spokes ten thousand lesser things / Are mortised and adjoined; which, when it falls, / Each small annexment, petty consequence, / Attends the boisterous ruin." *King Lear,* II. iv. 71—72: "when a great wheel runs down a hill"
⑫ **jig:** lively, mocking ballad
⑬ **a tale of bawdry:** a dirty story
⑭ **Hecuba:** Priam's wife, mother of twenty children, including Hector
⑮ **mobled:** muffled

First Player

'Run barefoot up and down, threatening the flames
With bisson rheum①; a clout② upon that head
510 Where late the diadem③ stood, and for a robe,
About her lank and all o'er-teemèd④ loins,
A blanket, in the alarm of fear caught up;
Who⑤ this had seen, with tongue in venom steeped,
'Gainst Fortune's state⑥ would treason have pronounced⑦.
515 But if the gods themselves did see her then
When she saw Pyrrhus make malicious sport
In mincing⑧ with his sword her husband's limbs,
The instant burst of clamor that she made,
Unless things mortal move them not at all,
520 Would have made milch⑨ the burning eyes of heaven,
And passion⑩ in the gods.'

POLONIUS
Look, whe'r⑪ he has not turned⑫ his color and has

---

① **bison rheum:** blinding tears
② **clout:** cloth
③ **diadem:** crown
④ **o'er-teemèd:** shrunken and worn out with childbearing
⑤ **who:** whoever
⑥ **state:** administration
⑦ **would treason have pronounced:** would have uttered treason against Fortune's rule
⑧ **mincing:** cutting into small pieces
⑨ **milch:** milky, wet with tears
⑩ **passion:** strong emotion
⑪ **whe'r:** whether
⑫ **turned:** changed

tears in's① eyes.② Pray you, no more.

HAMLET

'Tis well. I'll have thee speak out the rest soon.
525 Good my lord, will you see the players well
bestowed③? Do you hear, let them be well used④; for
they are the abstract⑤ and brief chronicles of the
time.⑥ After your death you were better⑦ have a bad
epitaph than their ill report while you live.⑧

POLONIUS

530 My lord, I will use⑨ them according to their desert⑩.

HAMLET

God's bodykins⑪, man, much better. Use every man
after⑫ his desert, and who should 'scape⑬ whipping⑭?
Use them after⑮ your own honor and dignity. The less

---

① **in's:** in his
② **Look ... eyes:** Hamlet is sympathetically moved by the grief of Hecuba, who presumably reminds him of his own unfaithful mother. Cf. Goethe: "The person who recites the death of Priam with such feeling, in the first place, makes a deep impression on the Prince himself; he sharpens the conscience of the wavering youth: and, accordingly, this scene becomes a prelude to that other, where, in the second place, the little play produces such effect upon the King." (*Wilhelm Meister's Apprenticeship*, Book IV, Chapter VI, p.174)
③ **bestowed:** lodged, housed
④ **used:** treated
⑤ **abstract:** epitome, summary
⑥ **they are ... time:** Cf. *Richard III*, IV. iv. 28: "brief abstract and record of tedious days"
⑦ **you were better:** it would be better for you to
⑧ **After ... live:** Cf. Thomas Nashe: "If I be evil entreated, let him look that I will rail on him soundly, not for an hour or a day, whilst the injury is fresh in my memory; but in some elaborate polished poem, which I will leave to the world when I am dead, to be a living image to all ages of his beggarly parsimony and ignoble illiberality" (*Invective against Enemies of Poetry*)
⑨ **use:** treat
⑩ **their desert:** what they deserve
⑪ **God's bodykins:** by God's little bodies (an oath)
⑫ **after:** according to
⑬ **'scape:** escape
⑭ **whipping:** the standard punishment for vagabonds (including unlicensed players)
⑮ **after:** according to

they deserve, the more merit is in your bounty①.
535　Take them in.
POLONIUS
Come, sirs.
HAMLET
Follow him, friends. We'll hear a play tomorrow.
Exit POLONIUS with all the Players but the First
Dost thou hear me②, old friend; can you play *The Murder of Gonzago*?
First Player
540　Ay, my lord.
HAMLET
We'll ha't tomorrow night. You could, for a need③, study④ a speech of some dozen or sixteen lines, which I would set down and insert in't,⑤ could you not?
First Player
Ay, my lord.
HAMLET
545　Very well. Follow that lord—and look you mock him not.
Exit First Player
My good friends, I'll leave you till night. You are welcome to Elsinore.
ROSENCRANTZ
Good my lord⑥!

---

① **bounty:** generosity
② **Dost thou hear me:** please listen
③ **for a need:** as required
④ **study:** learn
⑤ **some dozen or sixteen lines:** According to A. C. Bradley, of the "some dozen or sixteen lines" "only six are delivered" (*Shakespearean Tragedy,* p.75).
⑥ **Good my lord:** farewell (a parting formula)

HAMLET

550 Ay, so, God be wi' ye;

Exeunt ROSENCRANTZ and GUILDENSTERN

Now I am alone.[1]

O, what a rogue[2] and peasant slave[3] am I!

Is it not monstrous[4] that this player[5] here,

But[6] in a fiction, in a dream of passion,

555 Could force his soul[7] so to[8] his own conceit[9]

That, from her working[10], all his visage[11] wanned[12],

Tears in his eyes, distraction[13] in's aspect[14],

A broken voice, and his whole function[15] suiting[16]

With forms[17] to[18] his conceit?—and all for nothing[19]![20]

---

[1] 551—609 is Hamlet's second soliloquy in the play. Cf. Goethe: "Hamlet sees himself reproved and put to shame by the player, who feels so deep a sympathy in foreign fictitious woes: and the thought of making an experiment upon the conscience of his stepfather is in consequence suggested to him." (*Wilhelm Meister's Apprenticeship,* Book IV, Chapter VI, p.174)

[2] **rogue:** poor creature
[3] **slave:** villain
[4] **monstrous:** unnatural, strange
[5] **player:** he who feigns passions
[6] **But:** only, merely
[7] **soul:** innermost being
[8] **to:** in accord with
[9] **conceit:** imagination, conception of his part
[10] **her working:** his conceit's activity; his soul's work
[11] **visage:** face
[12] **wanned:** paled
[13] **distraction:** madness
[14] **aspect:** (accented on the second syllable) face
[15] **his whole function:** all his actions and emotions
[16] **suiting:** agrees
[17] **forms:** outward appearances
[18] **to:** in accord with
[19] **and all for nothing:** Cf. 554: "but in a fiction, in a dream of passion"
[20] **553—559:** Cf. Plato: *Ion* 535b—d; Horace: *Epistle to Augustus* 208—213

560　For Hecuba①!②
　　What's Hecuba to him, or he to Hecuba,
　　That he should weep for her? What would he do,
　　Had he the motive and the cue③ for passion
　　That I have? He would drown the stage with tears
565　And cleave④ the general ear⑤ with horrid⑥ speech,
　　Make mad the guilty and appal⑦ the free⑧
　　Confound⑨ the ignorant, and amaze⑩ indeed
　　The very⑪ faculties⑫ of eyes and ears.
　　Yet I,
570　A dull and muddy-mettled⑬ rascal⑭, peak⑮,
　　Like John-a-dreams⑯, unpregnant of⑰ my cause⑱,
　　And can say nothing; no, not even for a king,
　　Upon whose property⑲ and most dear life

---

① **Hecuba:** She is a symbol of grief in Western art and literature
② **For Hecuba:** Cf. Plutarch: *Lives,* Volume One: "[H]e (i.e. Alexander) was ashamed that his citizens should see him, who never pitied any man that he murdered, weep at the sufferings of Hecuba and Andromache." (translated by Arthur Hugh Clough, the Pennsylvania State University, 2003, p.491)
③ **cue:** provocation
④ **cleave:** split
⑤ **the general ear:** the ears of the world
⑥ **horrid:** causing horror
⑦ **appal:** appall, frighten
⑧ **the free:** the innocent
⑨ **Confound:** blast
⑩ **amaze:** stupefy, paralyze, astound
⑪ **very:** proper
⑫ **faculties:** functions
⑬ **muddy-mettle:** poor-spirited
⑭ **rascal:** scoundrel
⑮ **peak:** mope, lament
⑯ **John-a-dreams:** a simple, dreamy character (e.g. John-a-smiles etc.)
⑰ **unpregnant of:** insensible to, unfilled by
⑱ **cause:** duty, revenge
⑲ **property:** kingship or the Kingdom of Denmark

A damned defeat① was made. Am I a coward?②
575　Who calls me villain? breaks my pate③ across?
Plucks off my beard, and blows it in my face?
Tweaks me by the nose? gives me the lie i' the throat④
As deep as to the lungs⑤? Who does me this⑥?
Ha! 'Swounds⑦, I should take it⑧! For it cannot be
580　But I am⑨ pigeon-livered⑩ and lack gall⑪
To make oppression bitter, or ere this⑫
I should have fatted all the region⑬ kites⑭
With this slave's offal⑮. Bloody, bawdy⑯ villain!
Remorseless, treacherous, lecherous, kindless⑰ villain!
585　O, vengeance!
Why, what an ass am I! This is most brave⑱
That I, the son of a dear father murderèd,

---

① **defeat:** destruction
② **Am ... coward:** In one of David Warner's 1965 performance, some audience shouted "Yes!"
③ **pate:** head
④ **gives ... throat:** accuses me of lying; tells me a flagrant lie
⑤ **As ... lungs:** with seeming sincerity
⑥ **does me this:** does this to me
⑦ **'Swounds:** by God's wounds
⑧ **I should take it:** I deserve these insults
⑨ **But I am:** that I am otherwise than; I must surely be
⑩ **pigeon-livered:** chicken-hearted
⑪ **gall:** the supposed source of anger
⑫ **ere this:** before this, otherwise
⑬ **region:** sky
⑭ **region kites:** birds of prey
⑮ **offal:** plucks, guts
⑯ **bawdy:** lewd, immoral
⑰ **kindless:** lacking natural feelings, unnatural
⑱ **brave:** wonderful, admirable,

Prompted① to my revenge by heaven and hell,②
Must like a whore unpack③ my heart with words,
590　And fall a-cursing, like a very drab④,
A scullion⑤! Fie upon't! foh!
About⑥, my brain! I have heard
That guilty creatures⑦ sitting at a play⑧
Have by the very cunning⑨ of the scene⑩
595　Been struck so to the soul that presently⑪
They have proclaimed⑫ their malefactions⑬,⑭
For murder, though it have no tongue, will speak
With most miraculous organ⑮.⑯ I'll have these players
Play something like the murder of my father
600　Before mine uncle. I'll observe his looks;

① **Prompted:** urged
② Cf. IV. v. 136—141: Laertes: "To hell, allegiance! vows, to the blackest devil! / Conscience and grace, to the profoundest pit! / I dare damnation. To this point I stand, / That both the world, I give to negligence, / Let come what comes, only I'll be revenged / Most throughly for my father."
③ **unpack:** unburden, relieve
④ **drab:** prostitute, slut
⑤ **scullion:** kitchen wench
⑥ **About:** turn around; go to work
⑦ **creatures:** people
⑧ **play:** i.e. Anonymous *A Warning for Fair Women,* performed by Shakespeare's Company, includes a reference to the story.
⑨ **cunning:** art, ingenuity
⑩ **scene:** performance
⑪ **presently:** instantly
⑫ **proclaimed:** confessed
⑬ **malefactions:** evil deeds (Shakespeare's own coinage)
⑭ **guilty creatures:** Cf. Thomas Heywood: *An Apology for Actors* (1612): "we prove these exercises to have been the discoverers of many notorious murders long concealed from the eyes of the world." Massinger: *The Roman Actor* (1626), II. i. 653—658: "I once observed / In a tragedy of ours, in which a murder / Was acted to the life, a guilty hearer / Forced by the terror of a wounded conscience / To make discovery of that which torture / Could not wring from him."
⑮ **organ:** instrument
⑯ **With … organ:** Proverbial: Murder will out by itself.

I'll tent[1] him to the quick[2]; if he but blench[3],
I know my course. The spirit that I have seen
May be a devil, and the devil hath power
T' assume a pleasing shape; yea, and perhaps
605 Out of my weakness and my melancholy,
As he is very potent[4] with such spirits[5],
Abuses[6] me to damn me. I'll have grounds[7]
More relative[8] than this[9].[10] The play's the thing[11]
Wherein I'll catch the conscience of the King.
Exit

---

[1] **tent:** probe
[2] **quick:** the most sensitive point
[3] **blench:** flinch, wince
[4] **potent:** influential
[5] **spirits:** moods (melancholy)
[6] **Abuses:** deceives, deludes
[7] **grounds:** proofs
[8] **relative:** relevant, pertinent
[9] **this:** the ghost's story; my suspicions.
[10] **The spirit ... More than this:** Cf. III. iv. 153—154: "This bodiless creation ecstasy / Is very cunning in."
[11] **the thing:** i.e. the mouse-trap

ACT III
SCENE I. A room in the castle.

Enter KING, QUEEN, POLONIUS, OPHELIA, ROSENCRANTZ, and GUILDENSTERN

KING

And can you, by no drift of circumstance①,
Get from him why he puts on② this confusion③,④
Grating⑤ so harshly all his days of quiet
With turbulent and dangerous lunacy?

ROSENCRANTZ

5 He does confess he feels himself distracted⑥;
But from what cause he will by no means speak.

GUILDENSTERN

Nor do we find him forward⑦ to be sounded⑧,
But, with a crafty madness, keeps aloof⑨,
When we would bring him on to some confession
10 Of his true state.

QUEEN

Did he receive you well?

---

① **drift of circumstance:** circumlocution
② **puts on:** assumes
③ **confusion:** mental perturbation
④ **why ... confusion:** why he acts in this distracted way (He suspects that Hamlet is not really mad.)
⑤ **Grating:** disturbing
⑥ **distracted:** perturbed, seriously disturbed
⑦ **forward:** readily disposed, eager
⑧ **sounded:** probed, questioned
⑨ **keeps aloof:** keeps himself at a distance

ROSENCRANTZ

Most like a gentleman.

GUILDENSTERN

But with much forcing of his disposition[1].

ROSENCRANTZ

Niggard[2] of question[3], but of our demands

15 Most free in his reply[4].[5]

QUEEN

Did you assay[6] him?

To any pastime[7]?

ROSENCRANTZ

Madam, it so fell out, that certain players

We o'er-raught[8] on the way. Of these we told him;

20 And there did seem in him a kind of joy

To hear of it. They are about the court,

And, as I think, they have already order[9]

This night to play before him.

POLONIUS

'Tis most true;

25 And he beseeched me to entreat your majesties

To hear and see the matter[10].

KING

With all my heart, and it doth much content[11] me

---

[1] **disposition:** real inclination
[2] **Niggard:** stingy, very sparing
[3] **question:** conversation
[4] **Most free in his reply:** very willingly to fully answer our questions
[5] They kept the secret as is promised.
[6] **assay:** try to attract, tempt; encourage (him) to try
[7] **pastime:** recreation
[8] **o'er-raught:** overtook
[9] **they have already order:** they have already been given the commission
[10] **matter:** performance
[11] **content:** please

To hear him so inclined.

Good gentlemen, give him a further edge①,②

30　And drive his purpose on to③ these delights.④

ROSENCRANTZ

We shall, my lord.

Exeunt ROSENCRANTZ and GUILDENSTERN

KING

Sweet Gertrude, leave us too,

For we have closely⑤ sent for Hamlet hither,

That he, as 'twere⑥ by accident, may here

35　Affront⑦ Ophelia.

Her father and myself, lawful espials⑧,

Will so bestow⑨ ourselves that, seeing unseen,

We may of their encounter frankly judge,

And gather by him, as he is behaved⑩,

40　If 't be the affliction of his love or no⑪

That thus⑫ he suffers for.

QUEEN

I shall obey you.

And for your part, Ophelia, I do wish

---

① **edge:** keenness; push
② **give him a further edge:** sharpen his desire
③ **drive his purpose on to:** encourage intention to take
④ **give ... delights:** Cf. II. ii. 608—609: "The play's the thing / Wherein I'll catch the conscience of the King."
⑤ **closely:** privately; secretly
⑥ **as 'twere:** as if
⑦ **Affront:** meet face to face, confront
⑧ **espials:** espies
⑨ **bestow:** place
⑩ **as he is behaved:** according to his behavior
⑪ **no:** not
⑫ **thus:** in this way

That your good beauties be the happy[1] cause[2]
45 Of Hamlet's wildness. So shall I hope your virtues
Will bring him to his wonted[3] way again,
To both your honors[4].[5]

OPHELIA
Madam, I wish it may[6].

Exit QUEEN

POLONIUS
Ophelia, walk you here. Gracious[7], so please you[8],
50 We will bestow ourselves.

To OPHELIA

Read on this book[9];
That show of such an exercise[10] may colour[11]
Your loneliness[12].[13] We are oft to blame[14] in this—
'Tis too much proved[15]—that with devotion's visage[16]
55 And pious action we do sugar o'er[17]
The devil himself.

---

[1] **happy:** exact; fortuitous
[2] **cause:** reason
[3] **wonted:** usual, normal
[4] **to both your honors:** to the honor of you both, as a double blessing (marriage)
[5] Obviously she has no objection to Ophelia's relationship with Hamlet. Cf. V. i. 238: "I hoped thou shouldst have been my Hamlet's wife"
[6] **I wish it may:** I hope you are right
[7] **Gracious:** Your Gracious (the King)
[8] **so please you:** if it pleases you
[9] **this book:** a prayer book
[10] **such an exercise:** religious exercise, act of private devotion
[11] **colour:** camouflage, justify
[12] **loneliness:** solitariness
[13] **51—53:** A solitary woman with a book used to be a popular symbol of devoutness.
[14] **to blame:** guilty, blameworthy
[15] **too much proved:** too often demonstrated
[16] **devotion's visage:** religious face
[17] **sugar o'er:** disguise ("Devotion's visage" and "sugar over" make a mixed metaphor.)

KING

[*Aside*]① O, 'tis too true! ⁵

How smart② a lash that speech doth give my conscience!

The harlot's cheek, beautied③ with plastering art④,

60 Is not more ugly to the thing that helps it⑤

Than is my deed to⑥ my most painted word.

O heavy burden!⑦

POLONIUS

I hear him coming. Let's withdraw, my lord.

Exeunt KING and POLONIUS

Enter HAMLET

HAMLET⑧

To be, or not to be⑨, that is the question:⑩

65 Whether 'tis nobler in the mind to suffer

The slings⑪ and arrows of outrageous⑫ fortune⑬,

---

① **57 ff.:** These words stab Claudius' conscience and his good self is present. Cf. III. iii. 39 ff
② **smart:** sharp, stinging
③ **beautied:** made beautiful
④ **plastering art:** make-up (Cf. 153—155)
⑤ **it:** her pock-marked cheek
⑥ **to:** compared to
⑦ **O heavy burden:** 57—62 is his first confession of guilt.
⑧ What follows (lines 64—96) is Hamlet's best-known soliloquy. In the First Quarto, the "To be or not to be" soliloquy and the interview with Ophelia precede the arrival of the players and the arrangement for the play-scene. This fact is significant. (A. C. Bradley: *Shakespearean Tragedy*, p.105, note 2) Cf. Ann Thompson & Neil Taylor: "While Hamlet's soliloquies are among the best-known and indeed best-loved features of the play, they seem, on the basis of the three earliest texts, to be movable or even detachable". (*Hamlet,* edited by Ann Thompson & Neil Taylor, London: Arden Shakespeare, 2006, Introduction, p.18)
⑨ **To be, or not to be:** a. whether life in general is worth living; b. whether he should take his own life; c. whether he should act against the King
⑩ **64—66:** Each of the first 3 lines has one more syllable than typical iambic lines.
⑪ **slings:** slingshot
⑫ **outrageous:** atrocious
⑬ **outrageous fortune:** Cf. *King Lear,* IV. vi. 63: "the tyrant's rage"

Or to take arms① against a sea of troubles②,
And by opposing end them? To die, to sleep—
No more③—and by a sleep to say we④ end
70 The heartache and the thousand natural shocks⑤
That flesh is heir to⑥—'tis a consummation⑦
Devoutly to be wished⑧. To die, to sleep—
To sleep, perchance to dream. Ay, there's the rub⑨,
For in that sleep of death what dreams may come
75 When we have shuffled off⑩ this mortal coil⑪
Must give us pause⑫. There's the respect⑬
That makes calamity of so long life⑭.⑮
For who would bear⑯ the whips and scorns of time⑰,
The oppressor's wrong, the proud man's contumely⑱,

---

① **arms:** weapons
② **a sea of troubles:** infinite troubles (sense of futility) Cf. Sophocles: Oedipus Tyrannus, 1527: "κλύδωνα δεινῆς συμφορᾶς" (a stormy sea of troubles)
③ **No more:** exist no more; no more than to sleep
④ **we:** all humanity
⑤ **natural shocks:** battle metaphors
⑥ **That flesh is heir to:** that man are sure to have
⑦ **consummation:** final settlement
⑧ **'tis ... wished:** joy of death, sweet death (Cf. Plato: *Apology* 40c—41a; *Phaedo* 114d—e)
⑨ **rub:** obstacle, impediment (a bowling metaphor) Cf. *King John,* III. iii. 127—130: "even the breath of what I mean to speak / Shall blow ... each little rub, / Out of the path which shall directly lead / Thy foot to England's throne." *Henry V,* II. ii. 198: "But every rub is smoothed on our way." *King Lear,* II. ii. 153—154: "whose disposition ... will not be rubbed nor stopped"
⑩ **shuffled off:** thrown off, cast off
⑪ **mortal coil:** mortal flesh; earthly turmoil
⑫ **give us pause:** cause us to hesitate
⑬ **respect:** regard, consideration
⑭ **long life:** a life
⑮ **makes calamity of so long life**: makes us put up with unhappiness for such a long time (Cf. Sonnet 66: "Tired with all these for restful death I cry.")
⑯ **bear:** endure
⑰ **time:** the world
⑱ **contumely:** insulting or contemptuous treatment

80　The pangs of despised① love, the law's delay,
　　The insolence of office② and the spurns③
　　That patient merit of④ the unworthy⑤ takes,
　　When he himself might his quietus⑥ make⑦
　　With a bare⑧ bodkin⑨? Who would fardels⑩ bear,
85　To grunt and sweat under a weary life⑪, ⑫
　　But that⑬ the dread of something after death,
　　The undiscovered⑭ country⑮, from whose bourn⑯
　　No traveler returns, puzzles⑰ the will
　　And makes us rather bear those ills⑱ we have
90　Than fly to others that we know not of?⑲
　　Thus conscience⑳ does make cowards of us all,
　　And thus the native hue㉑ of resolution

① **despised:** (accented on the first syllable) unrequited
② **insolence of office:** high office
③ **spurns:** rebuffs, rejections
④ **of:** from
⑤ **the unworthy:** despicable people
⑥ **quietus:** complete account, release from debt or life (Latin: *quietus est* = paid off)
⑦ **make:** settle his own account
⑧ **bare:** unsheathed; mere
⑨ **bodkin:** dagger
⑩ **fardels:** burdens, loads
⑪ **a weary life:** like a horse
⑫ **To grunt ... life:** Cf. *Julius Caesar,* I. ii. 60: "groaning underneath this age's yoke"
⑬ **But that:** if nor because
⑭ **undiscovered:** unexplored
⑮ **The undiscovered country:** the Great Beyond, the afterlife
⑯ **bourn:** boundary, frontier
⑰ **puzzles:** bewilders, paralyzes
⑱ **ills:** misfortunes
⑲ **86—90:** Here Hamlet expresses a deep concern for and uncertainty about the after-life.
⑳ **conscience:** reflection on the consequences of action, fear of punishment after death (Those who commit suicide are to be damned in the afterlife. Cf. Dante: *Inferno,* Canto 13)
㉑ **native hue:** natural (ruddy) color or complexion

Is sicklied o'er with the pale cast① of thought②,
And enterprises of great pitch③ and moment④
95 With this regard⑤ their currents turn awry⑥,
And lose the name⑦ of action.—Soft you now!⑧
The fair Ophelia! Nymph⑨, in thy orisons⑩
Be all my sins remembered.

OPHELIA

Good my lord,
100 How does your honor for this many a day⑪?

HAMLET

I humbly⑫ thank you; well, well, well.

OPHELIA

My lord, I have remembrances⑬ of yours,
That I have longèd long to redeliver⑭;
I pray you, now receive them.

HAMLET⑮

105 No, not I.
I never gave you aught⑯.

---

① **cast:** tinge, shade of color
② **thought:** melancholy, contemplation
③ **pitch:** height, scope
④ **moment:** importance
⑤ **with this regard:** on this account
⑥ **turn awry:** lose their momentum and become stagnant
⑦ **name:** essence; honor
⑧ **Soft you now:** Hold! Hush!
⑨ **Nymph:** fairies living in woods or rivers
⑩ **orisons:** prayers
⑪ **this many a day:** these many days
⑫ **humbly:** a gesture of estrangement
⑬ **remembrances:** souvenirs, keepsakes, love-tokens
⑭ **redeliver:** return
⑮ He might have noticed the eavesdroppers.
⑯ **aught:** anything (souvenir)

OPHELIA

My honored lord, you know right well you did;

And, with them, words of so sweet breath composed

As① made the things more rich. Their perfume lost②,

110　Take these again③; for to the noble mind

Rich gifts wax④ poor when givers prove unkind.⑤

There, my lord.⑥

HAMLET

Ha, ha! Are you honest⑦?

OPHELIA

My lord?

HAMLET

115　Are you fair⑧?⑨

OPHELIA

What means your lordship?

HAMLET

That if you be honest and fair, your honesty should admit no discourse⑩ to⑪ your beauty.⑫

---

　① **As:** which

　② **Their perfume lost:** now that their attraction has gone

　③ **again:** back

　④ **wax:** become

　⑤ **Rich ... unkind:** A gift is valued by the mind of the giver.

　⑥ **There, my lord:** 对观《诗·郑风·将仲子》："岂敢爱之？畏我父母。仲可怀也，父母之言亦可畏也。"

　⑦ **honest:** serious; chaste

　⑧ **fair:** beautiful; just

　⑨ **Are you honest ... fair:** Beauty (fairness) and chastity (honesty) were regarded as the most important qualities for women.

　⑩ **discourse:** intercourse

　⑪ **to:** with

　⑫ **That ... beauty:** Beauty is a potential threat to chastity. (The collision between honest and fair was a popular motif in Elizabethan time. Cf. John Donne: *Paradoxes and Problems*, Problem □"Why are the fairest the falsest?")

OPHELIA

Could beauty, my lord, have better commerce① than with honesty?②

HAMLET

Ay, truly, for the power of beauty will sooner transform honesty from what it is to a bawd③ than the force of honesty can translate④ beauty into his⑤ likeness. This was sometime⑥ a paradox⑦, but now the time⑧ gives it proof. I did love you once.

OPHELIA

Indeed, my lord, you made me believe so.

HAMLET

You should not have believed me⑨; for virtue cannot so inoculate⑩ our old stock⑪ but we shall relish⑫ of it.⑬ I loved you not.

OPHELIA

I was the more deceived.

HAMLET

Get thee to a nunnery⑭! Why wouldst thou be a

---

① **commerce:** intercourse, association
② **Could ... honesty:** Aren't there exceptions?
③ **bawd:** madam, brothel-keeper
④ **translate:** transform
⑤ **his:** its
⑥ **sometime:** once, formerly
⑦ **paradox:** absurd statement
⑧ **the time:** the present age
⑨ **You ... me:** Cf. Polonius: "Do not believe his vows" (I. iii. 130)
⑩ **inoculate:** engraft
⑪ **old stock:** nature (original sin)
⑫ **relish:** retain a taste or trace
⑬ **virtue ... it:** Virtue cannot, by grafting, so change our sinful nature that we shall not still have some flavor of it. (Both "inoculate" and "stock" are horticultural terms and biblical allusions. According to Christianity, human's original sin can't be purified except by Jesus Christ's salvation.)
⑭ **nunnery:** convent; brothel

breeder of sinners? I am myself indifferent① honest②; but yet I could accuse me③ of such things that it were better my mother had not borne me④. I am very proud, revengeful,
135　ambitious, with more offences⑤ at my beck⑥ than I have thoughts to put them in⑦, imagination to give them shape⑧, or time to act them in⑨. What should such fellows as I do crawling between earth and heaven? We⑩ are arrant⑪ knaves, all; believe none of us. Go thy ways⑫ to a nunnery.
140　Where's your father?⑬

OPHELIA

At home, my lord.

HAMLET

Let the doors be shut upon him that he may play the fool no where but in's own house.⑭ Farewell.

OPHELIA

O, help him⑮, you sweet heavens!

HAMLET

145　If thou dost marry, I'll give thee this plague⑯ for

---

① **indifferent:** moderately
② **honest:** virtuous
③ **me:** myself
④ **it were better ... me:** indictment against his mother
⑤ **offences:** evil thoughts
⑥ **beck:** beckon (at my hand)
⑦ **put them in:** realize them
⑧ **give them shape:** realize them
⑨ **act them in:** realize them
⑩ **We:** we men
⑪ **arrant:** thoroughgoing
⑫ **Go thy ways:** go away
⑬ **Where's your father:** He has caught sight of Polonius behind the tapestry.
⑭ **Let ... house:** Cf. I. iii. 57ff
⑮ **him:** the mad man
⑯ **plague:** curse

thy dowry: be thou[1] as chaste as ice, as pure as
snow, thou shalt not escape calumny[2]. Get thee to a
nunnery, go, farewell. Or, if thou wilt[3] needs[4]
marry, marry a fool[5]; for wise men know well enough
150 what monsters[6] you[7] make of them. To a nunnery, go,
and quickly too. Farewell.

OPHELIA
O heavenly powers, restore him!

HAMLET[8]
I have heard of your paintings[9] too, well enough.
God hath given you[10] one face, and you make yourselves
155 another. You jig[11], you amble[12], and you lisp[13], and
nick-name[14] God's creatures[15], and make your
wantonness[16] your ignorance[17]. Go to[18],

---

[1] **be thou:** even though you are
[2] **calumny:** slander
[3] **wilt:** will
[4] **needs:** of necessity (as in "must needs")
[5] **fool:** cuckold
[6] **monsters:** cuckolds
[7] **you:** you women
[8] What follows is a famous misogynist speech. Cf. *King Lear*, IV. vi. 118—127: "Down from the waist they are Centaurs, / Though women all above: / But to the girdle do the Gods inherit, / Beneath is all the fiends': there's hell, there's darkness, / there's the sulphurous pit" etc.
[9] **paintings:** making-up, cosmetics
[10] **you:** you women
[11] **jig:** dance sensually
[12] **amble:** walk with a suggestive step
[13] **lisp:** mince one's words
[14] **nick-name:** give affected names to
[15] **You ... God's creatures:** Why does Hamlet find it so offensive? Cf. *Genesis* 2:19—20: "whatever the man called every living creature, that was its name."
[16] **wantonness:** affectation; immorality
[17] **make ... ignorance:** use ignorance as an excuse for foolish or immoral behavior
[18] **Go to:** expression of impatience

I'll[①] no more on't[②]. It hath made me mad[③]. I say we will have
no more marriages. Those that are married already,
all but one[④], shall live. The rest shall keep as they are.
160　To a nunnery, go.
Exit

OPHELIA
O, what a noble mind is here o'erthrown![⑤]
The courtier's, soldier's, scholar's, eye, tongue, sword;
The expectancy and rose[⑥] of the fair state[⑦],
The glass[⑧] of fashion[⑨] and the mould[⑩] of form[⑪][⑫],
165　The observed of all observers[⑬], quite, quite down[⑭]!
And I, of ladies most deject[⑮] and wretched,
That sucked the honey of his music[⑯] vows,
Now see that noble and most sovereign[⑰] reason[⑱],
Like sweet bells jangled[⑲], out of tune and harsh;

---

① **I'll:** I will have
② **on't:** of it
③ **mad:** angry
④ **one:** i.e. Claudius
⑤ **O … o'erthrown:** Cf. V. ii. 378: "Now cracks a noble heart."
⑥ **rose:** (usually of males) symbol of perfection (Cf. *1 Henry IV*, I. iii. 173: [Hotspur describes Richard II as] "that sweet lovely rose")
⑦ **the fair state:** Cf. *Republic*, 527c: "ἐν τῇ καλλιπόλει" etc. It sounds sharply ironic if we remember that, according to Hamlet, "something is rotten in the state of Denmark" (I. iv. 99) and "Denmark's a prison." (II. ii. 256)
⑧ **glass:** mirror, example (Cf. *1 Henry VI*. I. iv. 73: "mirror of all martial men" & *Henry V*, II. Chorus 6: "the mirror of all Christian kings")
⑨ **fashion:** style, properly behavior (Cf. *2 Henry IV*, II. iii. 21—22 & 31—32)
⑩ **mould:** model
⑪ **form:** manly grace, courtly manners
⑫ **The courtier's … form:** Ophelia gives Hamlet some of the attributes of the ideal Renaissance prince.
⑬ **the observed of all ovservers:** the admired object of all eyes
⑭ **down:** destroyed, ruined
⑮ **deject:** dejected, cast down
⑯ **music:** music-like
⑰ **sovereign:** supreme
⑱ **reason:** reason as ruler of the other faculties
⑲ **jangled:** make a harsh sound

170   That unmatched form and feature of blown[1] youth
Blasted with ecstasy[2]. O, woe is me[3]
To have seen what I have seen, see what I see!
Re-enter KING and POLONIUS
KING
Love? His affections[4] do not that way tend;
Nor what he spake[5], though it lacked form[6] a little,
175   Was not like madness. There's something in his soul,
O'er which his melancholy sits on brood;[7]
And I do doubt[8] the hatch[9] and the disclose[10]
Will be some danger;[11] which for to prevent[12],
I have in quick determination
180   Thus set it down[13]: he shall with speed to England,
For the demand of our neglected tribute.
Haply[14] the seas and countries different
With variable[15] objects[16] shall expel
This something-settled[17] matter[18] in his heart,

- [1] **blown:** full-blown
- [2] **Blasted with ecstasy:** blighted by madness
- [3] **woe is me:** it makes me miserable
- [4] **affections:** emotions, passions
- [5] **spake:** spoke
- [6] **form:** method
- [7] **There ... brood:** He feels danger in "all but one shall live" (159).
- [8] **doubt:** fear
- [9] **hatch:** outcome
- [10] **disclose:** disclosure
- [11] **some ... danger:** Cf. 4: "dangerous lunacy"
- [12] **which for to prevent:** in order to prevent which
- [13] **set it down:** made a decision about it
- [14] **Haply:** perhaps
- [15] **variable:** various
- [16] **objects:** sights
- [17] **something-settled:** somewhat fixed
- [18] **matter:** complex, obsession

185 Whereon① his brains still② beating puts him thus
　　 From fashion③ of himself④. What think you on't?
POLONIUS
　　 It shall do well. But yet do I believe
　　 The origin and commencement⑤ of his grief
　　 Sprung⑥ from neglected⑦ love. How now, Ophelia!
190 You need not tell us what Lord Hamlet said;
　　 We heard it all. My lord, do as you please;
　　 But, if you hold⑧ it fit, after the play
　　 Let his queen mother all alone entreat him
　　 To show⑨ his grief⑩. Let her be round⑪ with him;
195 And I'll be placed, so please you, in the ear⑫
　　 Of all their conference⑬. If she find him not⑭,
　　 To England send him, or confine him where
　　 Your wisdom best shall think.⑮
KING
　　 It shall be so.
200 Madness in great ones must not unwatched go.⑯

---

① **Whereon:** on which ("this something-settled matter")
② **still:** constantly
③ **fashion:** the usual way
④ **puts him … himself:** distracts him from his normal self
⑤ **commencement:** beginning, cause
⑥ **Sprung:** sprang
⑦ **neglected:** unrequited
⑧ **hold:** think
⑨ **show:** tell
⑩ **grief:** grievance
⑪ **round:** direct, blunt
⑫ **in the ear:** within the hearing
⑬ **conference:** conversation
⑭ **find him not:** should fail to find out what's wrong with him
⑮ He devises the scheme only to cost his own life. Cf. V. ii. 406—407
⑯ **Madness … go:** Cf. I. iii. 23—24: "on his choice depends / The safety and health of this whole state"; III. iii. 16—18: "The cease of majesty / Dies not alone, but like a gulf doth draw / What's near it with it."

Exeunt

SCENE II. A hall in the castle.

Enter HAMLET and Players

HAMLET
Speak the speech, I pray you, as I pronounced it to you, trippingly[1] on the tongue. But if you mouth[2] it, as many of our[3] players do, I had as lief[4] the town-crier[5] spoke my lines. Nor do not saw the air
5 too much with your hand, thus[6], but use all gently[7]; for in[8] the very torrent, tempest, and, as I may say, whirlwind of your passion, you must acquire and beget[9] a temperance[10] that may give it smoothness. O, it offends me to the soul to hear a robustious[11]
10 periwig-pated[12] fellow tear a passion to tatters, to very rags, to split the ears of the groundlings[13], who for the most part are capable of[14] nothing but

---

[1] **trippingly:** smoothly, lightly, easily
[2] **mouth:** speak in an affected way, declaim
[3] **our:** also "your"
[4] **had as lief:** would rather
[5] **the town-crier:** one who make public announcements by shouting them in the streets
[6] **thus:** with a gesture
[7] **use all gently:** do everything with moderation
[8] **in:** in the midst of
[9] **acquire and beget:** adopt and inculcate
[10] **temperance:** restraint
[11] **robustious:** boisterous, noisy
[12] **periwig-pated:** wearing a wig
[13] **groundlings:** low-class audience
[14] **are capable of:** appreciating

inexplicable dumb shows and noise.① I would have such
a fellow whipped for o'erdoing Termagant②; it out-herods Herod③.
15　Pray you avoid it.
First Player
I warrant④ your honor⑤.
HAMLET⑥
Be not too tame⑦ neither,⑧ but let your own discretion
be your tutor⑨. Suit the action⑩ to the word, the
word to the action; with this special observance, that you o'erstep⑪ not
20　the modesty⑫ of nature⑬. For any thing so overdone is
from⑭ the purpose⑮ of playing⑯, whose end, both at the
first⑰ and now, was and is, to hold, as 'twere, the
mirror⑱ up to nature⑲, to show virtue her own feature⑳,

---

　①　**O, it …noise (8—13):** Cf. John Webster: "should a man present the most sententious tragedy, observing all the critical laws, the breath that comes from the incapable multitude is able to poison it." (*The White Devil, To the Reader*)
　②　**Termagant:** imagined God of the Saracens or Moslems in medieval morality plays
　③　**Herod:** King Herod ruling Israel at the time of Christ, who killed all the children two years old or under (*Matthew*, 2:16). He appeared as a raving tyrant in medieval English miracle plays
　④　**warrant:** promise
　⑤　**your honor:** your lordship
　⑥　Here Shakespeare expresses his own poetics through Hamlet.
　⑦　**tame:** understated, restrained
　⑧　**Be … neither:** 不瘟不火
　⑨　**tutor:** teach you what to do
　⑩　**action:** gesture
　⑪　**o'erstep:** trespass
　⑫　**modesty:** moderation (Cf. II. ii. 443)
　⑬　**nature:** naturalness
　⑭　**from:** away from; opposite to
　⑮　**purpose:** principle
　⑯　**playing:** acting
　⑰　**first:** in early drama
　⑱　**mirror:** true-to-life reflection
　⑲　**nature:** human life
　⑳　**feature:** appearance, form

scorn① her own image, and the very age and body② of
25 the time③ his④ form⑤ and pressure⑥. Now this overdone⑦,
or come tardy off⑧, though it make the unskilful⑨
laugh, cannot but make the judicious grieve; the
censure⑩ of the which one⑪ must in your allowance⑫
o'erweigh a whole theatre of others.⑬ O, there be⑭
30 players that I have seen play, and heard others
praise, and that⑮ highly, not to speak it profanely,
that, neither having the accent of Christians⑯, nor
the gait⑰ of Christian, pagan, nor man, have so
strutted and bellowed that I have thought some of
35 nature's journeymen⑱ had made men and not made them
well, they imitated humanity so abominably.⑲

---

① **scorn:** the scornful person
② **body:** essential reality
③ **time:** times
④ **his:** its
⑤ **form:** shape
⑥ **pressure:** impression
⑦ **Now this overdone:** if this is exaggerated
⑧ **come tardy off:** fallen short of, done inadequately
⑨ **unskillful:** ignorant of acting
⑩ **censure:** opinion
⑪ **the which one:** a single one of them
⑫ **in your allowance:** by your estimation
⑬ **Now ... others:** So Hamlet (Shakespeare) is different from Cicero who, when talking about oratory, holds that "what the multitude approves must win the approval of experts." (*Brutus*) Cf. Plato: *Symposium,* 194b; Horace: *The Art of Poetry*: "[D]on't let them be too youthfully indiscreet in the lines you give them, or crack any filthy or obscene jokes. For such things give offence to those of knightly or freeborn rank and the more substantial citizens; these men don't take kindly to what meets with the approval of the masses ..." (*Classical Literary Criticism,* Penguin, 1981, pp.87—88)
⑭ **be:** are
⑮ **that:** so
⑯ **Christians:** humans
⑰ **gait:** bearing
⑱ **journeymen:** unskilled workmen
⑲ **O ... abominably:** 参见钱锺书《谈艺录·三九》（北京：生活·读书·新知三联书店，2008年，第346页）．

First Player

I hope we have reformed that indifferently① with us②, sir.

HAMLET

O, reform it altogeter. And let those that play

40　your clowns speak no more than is set down for them;③ for there be④ of⑤ them that will themselves laugh, to set on⑥ some quantity⑦ of barren⑧ spectators to laugh too; though, in the mean time, some necessary⑨ question⑩ of the play be then to be considered.

45　That's villanous, and shows a most pitiful ambition in the fool that uses⑪ it. Go, make you ready.

Exeunt Players

Enter POLONIUS, ROSENCRANTZ, and GUILDENSTERN

How now, my lord! Will the King hear this piece of work?

POLONIUS

And the Queen too, and that presently⑫.

HAMLET

Bid the players make haste.

Exit POLONIUS

50　Will you two help to hasten them?

---

① **indifferently:** somewhat, to a moderate extent
② **with us:** in our company
③ **let ... them:** Clowns were allowed to gag it up as occasion rises.
④ **be:** are
⑤ **of:** some of
⑥ **set on:** incite
⑦ **some quantity:** a small number
⑧ **barren:** devoid of judgment, empty-headed
⑨ **necessary:** important
⑩ **question:** issue
⑪ **uses:** practices
⑫ **presently:** immediately

ROSENCRANTZ GUILDENSTERN

We will, my lord.

Exeunt ROSENCRANTZ and GUILDENSTERN

HAMLET

What ho! Horatio!

Enter HORATIO

HORATIO

Here, sweet lord[1], at your service.

HAMLET

Horatio, thou art e'en[2] as just[3] a man
55 As e'er my conversation[4] coped withal[5].

HORATIO

O, my dear lord—

HAMLET

Nay, do not think I flatter;

For what advancement[6] may I hope from thee

That no revenue[7] hast but thy good spirits,

60 To feed and clothe thee? Why should the poor be flattered?

No, let the candied[8] tongue lick absurd[9] pomp,

And crook[10] the pregnant[11] hinges of the knee

Where thrift[12] may follow fawning. Dost thou hear[13]?

---

[1] **sweet lord:** Cf. III. iv. 106: "sweet Hamlet"; V. ii. 378: "sweet prince"
[2] **e'en:** even, exactly
[3] **just:** well-balanced
[4] **conversation:** association
[5] **coped withal:** dealt with
[6] **advancement:** benefits
[7] **revenue:** (accented on the second syllable) income
[8] **candied:** sugared, flattering
[9] **absurd:** (accented on the first syllable) tasteless
[10] **crook:** bend
[11] **pregnant:** supple, ready to bend
[12] **thrift:** profit
[13] **Dost thou hear:** please pay attention to this

Since my dear soul was mistress of her choice①
65　And could of② men distinguish③, her election④
Hath sealed⑤ thee for herself; for thou hast been
As one, in suffering all, that suffers nothing,
A man that fortune's buffets⑥ and rewards
Hast ta'en with equal thanks; and blest are those
70　Whose blood⑦ and judgment are so well commingled⑧,
That they are not a pipe for Fortune's finger
To sound what stop she⑨ please. Give me⑩ that man
That is not passion's slave, and I will wear him
In my heart's core⑪, ay, in my heart of heart,
75　As I do thee.—Something⑫ too much of this. —
There is a play tonight before the King;
One scene⑬ of it comes near the circumstance⑭
Which I have told thee, of my father's death.
I prithee, when thou seest that act afoot⑮,
80　Even with the very comment⑯ of thy soul
Observe mine uncle. If his occulted⑰ guilt

---

① **was mistress of her choice:** has the power of discriminating
② **of:** among
③ **distinguish:** discriminate
④ **election:** choice
⑤ **sealed:** selected, marked for possession
⑥ **buffets:** blows
⑦ **blood:** passion, impulse
⑧ **commingled:** matched
⑨ **she:** Fortune
⑩ **Give me:** I prefer
⑪ **core:** center
⑫ **Something:** somewhat
⑬ **scene:** episode or sequence
⑭ **circumstance:** circumstances
⑮ **afoot:** being performed
⑯ **comment:** observation
⑰ **occulted:** concealed, hidden

Do not itself unkennel[1] in one speech,
It is a damnèd ghost that we have seen,
And my imaginations[2] are as foul[3]
85 As Vulcan's[4] stithy[5]. Give him heedful note[6],
For I mine eyes will rivet to his face,
And after[7] we will both our judgments join
In censure of his seeming[8].

HORATIO
Well, my lord.
90 If he steal aught[9] the whilst[10] this play is playing,
And 'scape[11] detecting[12], I will pay the theft.

HAMLET
They are coming to the play. I must be idle[13].
Get you a place.

Sound a flourish. Enter Trumpets and Kettledrums. Danish march. Enter KING, QUEEN, POLONIUS, OPHELIA, ROSENCRANTZ, GUILDENSTERN, and other Lords attendant, with his Guards carrying torches.

KING
How fares[14] our cousin[15] Hamlet?

---

[1] **unkennel:** come out of its hole, reveal itself (like a dog)
[2] **imaginations:** suspicions
[3] **foul:** offensive, polluted
[4] **Vulcan's:** Roman blacksmith god
[5] **stithy:** smith, forge (stith: anvil)
[6] **note:** attention
[7] **after:** afterwards
[8] **In censure of his seeming:** in passing judgment on his appearance and behavior.
[9] **aught:** anything
[10] **whilst:** while
[11] **'scape:** escapes
[12] **detecting:** being detected
[13] **idle:** foolish and insane
[14] **fares:** goes (but Hamlet takes it to mean "eat")
[15] **cousin:** Cf. I. ii. 64: "my son"

HAMLET

95 Excellent, i' faith; of the chameleon's dish. I eat

the air, promise-crammed①. You cannot feed capons② so.

KING

I have nothing with③ this answer, Hamlet; these words

are not mine④.

HAMLET

No, nor mine now.

To POLONIUS

100 My lord, you played once i' the university, you say?

POLONIUS

That did I, my lord; and was accounted⑤ a good actor.

HAMLET

What did you enact?

POLONIUS

I did enact Julius Caesar; I was killed i' the

Capitol; Brutus killed me.⑥

HAMLET

105 It was a brute⑦ part⑧ of him to kill so capital⑨ a calf⑩

there. Be the players ready?

ROSENCRANTZ

Ay, my lord; they stay upon your patience⑪.

---

① **promise-crammed:** stuffed with promises
② **capons:** chicken
③ **have nothing with:** get nothing out of
④ **are not mine:** have nothing to do with my question
⑤ **accounted:** counted, considered
⑥ **I did ... me:** a topical insertion
⑦ **brute:** pun on Brutus
⑧ **part:** act
⑨ **Capital:** pun on Capitol
⑩ **calf:** fool
⑪ **they stay ... patience:** they are waiting for you to tell them to begin

QUEEN

Come hither, my dear Hamlet, sit by me.

HAMLET

No, good mother, here's metal[1] more attractive[2].

POLONIUS

110 [*To KING*] O, ho! do you mark that?

HAMLET

Lady, shall I lie in your lap?[3]

Lying down at OPHELIA's feet

OPHELIA

No, my lord.

HAMLET

I mean, my head upon your lap?

OPHELIA

Ay, my lord.

HAMLET

115 Do you think I meant country[4] matters[5]?

OPHELIA

I think nothing, my lord.

HAMLET

That's a fair thought to lie between maids' legs[6].

OPHELIA

What is, my lord?

HAMLET

Nothing.[7]

---

[1] **metal:** magnet
[2] **metal more attractive:** i.e. Ophelia
[3] **Lady ... lap:** Cf. Pietà (a motif in the miracle play)
[4] **country:** pun on cant
[5] **country matters:** uncouth behavior, sexual activities
[6] **lie ... legs:** have sex
[7] **Nothing:** "Thing" could be a euphemism for a man's penis; alternatively "nothing" could refer to a woman's vagina.

OPHELIA

120　You are merry①, my lord.

HAMLET

Who, I?

OPHELIA

Ay, my lord.

HAMLET

O God, your only② jig-maker③. What should a man do but be merry? For, look you, how cheerfully my

125　mother looks, and④ my father died within 's⑤ two hours.

OPHELIA

Nay, 'tis twice two months, my lord.⑥

HAMLET

So long? Nay then, let the devil wear black⑦, for I'll have a suit of sables. O heavens! die two months ago, and not forgotten yet?⑧ Then there's hope a great man's

130　memory may outlive his life half a year. But, by'r⑨ lady⑩, he must build churches, then, or else⑪ shall he suffer not thinking on⑫, with⑬ the hobby-horse, whose epitaph⑭ is

---

① **merry:** mad
② **only:** best
③ **jig-maker:** comedian, song and dance man (Hamlet bitterly casts himself as the clown)
④ **and:** that, too, when
⑤ **within's:** these
⑥ **Nay … lord:** Cf. "but two months dead" etc. (A. C. Bradley: *Shakespearean Tragedy*, p.105)
⑦ **black:** mourning clothes
⑧ **die … yet:** a cynic tone
⑨ **by'r:** by our
⑩ **lady:** the Virgin Mary
⑪ **else:** otherwise
⑫ **thinking on:** being thought about
⑬ **with:** along with
⑭ **epitaph:** catchphrase

'For, O, for, O, the hobby-horse[1] is forgot.'

Hautboys[2] play. The dumb-show enters.

Enter a King and a Queen very lovingly; the Queen embracing him, and he her. She kneels, and makes show of protestation[3] unto him. He takes her up and declines his head upon her neck. He lays him down upon a bank of flowers. She, seeing him asleep, leaves him. Anon comes in a fellow, takes off his crown, kisses it, and pours poison in the sleeper's ears, and leaves him. The Queen returns; finds the King dead, and makes passionate action[4]. The poisoner with some three or four come in again, seem to lament with her. The dead body is carried away. The poisoner wooes the Queen with gifts. She seems harsh awhile but in the end accepts his love.

Exeunt

OPHELIA

What means this, my lord?

HAMLET

135   Marry, this is miching[5] mallecho[6]; it means mischief.

OPHELIA

Belike[7] this show imports the argument[8] of the play.

Enter Prologue

HAMLET

We shall know by this fellow. The players[9] cannot keep counsel[10]; they'll tell all.

---

[1] **hobby-horse:** a character in morris dances (Puritans thought it to be a symbol of forgetfulness.)
[2] ***Hautboys:*** oboes
[3] ***protestation:*** love and faith
[4] ***action:*** gestures
[5] **miching:** (dialect) skulking
[6] **mallecho:** (Spanish: *malhecho*) secret misdeed
[7] **Belike:** perhaps
[8] **argument:** plot, synopsis
[9] **players:** i.e. Claudius
[10] **keep counsel:** keep a secret

OPHELIA

Will he tell us what this show meant?

HAMLET

140　Ay, or any show that you'll show① him. Be not you②

ashamed to show, he'll not shame to tell you what it means.

OPHELIA

You are naught③, you are naught. I'll mark④ the play.

Prologue

For us, and for our tragedy,

Here stooping⑤ to your clemency⑥,

145　We beg your hearing patiently.

Exit

HAMLET

Is this a prologue, or the posy of a ring⑦?

OPHELIA

'Tis brief, my lord.

HAMLET

As woman's love.

*Enter two Players, King and Queen*⑧

Player King⑨

*Full thirty times hath Phoebus' cart*⑩ *gone round*

---

① **show:** coquet with (Hamlet puns on the word.)
② **Be not you:** if you are not
③ **naught:** naughty, indecent
④ **mark:** watch, attend to
⑤ **stooping:** bowing
⑥ **clemency:** mercy, generosity
⑦ **posy of a ring:** motto inscribed inside a ring
⑧ Now begins the play within the play.
⑨ **Player King:** According to A. C. Bradley, the opening of the Player-King's speech recalls Greene's *Alphonsus King of Aragon*, IV. 33 ff. (*Shakespearean Tragedy*, p.346, n2). Evidently his speech is a parody of the high-flown and artificial style of the then classical drama.
⑩ **Phoebus' cart:** the chariot of the sun-god (the sun)

150 *Neptune's salt wash*[1] *and Tellus'*[2] *orbèd ground*[3],
    And thirty dozen moons with borrowed sheen[4]
    About the world have times twelve thirties been,
    Since love our hearts and Hymen[5] *did our hands*
    Unite commutual[6] *in most sacred bands*[7].[8]

Player Queen

155 *So many journeys may the sun and moon*
    Make us again count o'er ere love be done!
    But, woe is me, you are so sick of late,
    So far from cheer and from your former state,
    That I distrust[9] *you. Yet, though I distrust,*
160 *Discomfort you, my lord, it nothing*[10] *must;*[11]
    For women's fear and love holds quantity[12];
    In neither aught[13], *or in extremity*[14].
    Now, what my love is, proof[15] *hath made you know;*
    And as my love is sized, my fear is so:[16]
165 *Where love is great, the littlest doubts are fear;*
    Where little fears grow great, great love grows there.

---

[1] **salt wash:** oceans
[2] **Tellus:** Roman Goddess of the earth
[3] **orbèd ground:** the earth
[4] **sheen:** light
[5] **Hymen:** the god of marriage
[6] **commutual:** together
[7] **bands:** bonds
[8] **149-154:** We've been married for thirty years.
[9] **distrust:** fear for, worry about
[10] **nothing:** in no way
[11] **it nothing must:** it must not discomfort you at all
[12] **holds quantity:** are in proportion to each other, match in amount
[13] **In neither aught:** either there is no fear or love at all
[14] **in extremity:** when she loves, she also fears
[15] **proof:** experience
[16] **And ... so:** and my fear is as great as my love

Player King

'Faith, I must leave thee, love, and shortly too;
My operant① powers② their functions leave③ to do④.
And thou shalt live in this fair world behind,
170 Honored, beloved; and haply one as kind
For husband shalt thou—

Player Queen

O, confound⑤ the rest!⑥
Such love must needs be treason in my breast.
In second husband let me be accurst!
175 None wed the second but who killed the first.⑦

HAMLET

[*Aside*] Wormwood⑧, wormwood.

Player Queen

The instances⑨ that second marriage move⑩
Are base respects⑪ of thrift⑫, but none of love.
A second time I kill my husband dead,
180 When second husband kisses me in bed.

Player King

I do believe you think what now you speak;
But what we do determine oft we break.

---

① **operant:** operating
② **operant powers:** vital forces
③ **leave:** cease
④ **do:** function
⑤ **confound:** destroy
⑥ **O ... rest:** May God destroy what you are about to say!
⑦ **169—175 & 177—180:** these lines seem to be Hamlet's insertion.
⑧ **Wormwood:** a bitter herb (for Claudius)
⑨ **instances:** causes
⑩ **move:** motives; prompt
⑪ **respects:** considerations
⑫ **thrift:** worldly profit

Purpose is but the slave to memory[1],
Of violent birth[2], *but poor validity*[3];[4]
185 *Which*[5] *now, like fruit unripe, sticks on the tree;*
But fall, unshaken, when they mellow be.
Most necessary 'tis that we forget
To pay ourselves what to ourselves is debt.[6]
What to ourselves in passion we propose,
190 *The passion ending, doth the purpose lose.*
The violence of either grief or joy
Their own enactures[7] *with themselves destroy.*[8]
Where[9] *joy most revels, grief doth most lament;*
Grief joys, joy grieves[10], *on slender accident*[11].
195 *This world is not for aye*[12], *nor 'tis not strange*
That even our loves should with our fortunes change;
For 'tis a question left us yet to prove[13],
Whether love lead[14] *fortune, or else fortune love.*
The great man down[15], *you mark his favourite*[16] *flies;*
200 *The poor advanced makes friends of enemies.*

---

[1] **Purpose ... memory:** purposes are easily forgotten
[2] **Of ... birth:** robust to begin with
[3] **validity:** vigor, strength
[4] **poor validity:** i.e. They would be forgotten.
[5] **Which:** i.e. purpose
[6] **we ... debt:** a. We conveniently forget the promises we make to ourselves. b. It is essential that we forget the debts we owe to ourselves.
[7] **enactures:** actions, enactments
[8] **191—192:** Violent grief and joy destroy themselves in the very act of manifesting or fulfilling themselves.
[9] **Where:** in persons in whom
[10] **Grief ... grieves:** grief turns into joy, and joy turns into grief
[11] **slender accident:** the slightest occasion
[12] **for aye:** for ever
[13] **prove:** resolve, answer
[14] **lead:** dominates
[15] **down:** disgraced
[16] **favourite:** favored supporter

And hitherto doth love on fortune tend;
For who① not needs② shall never lack a friend,
And who in want a hollow friend doth try③,
Directly seasons④ him⑤ his enemy.
205 But, orderly to end where I begun⑥,
Our wills and fates do so contrary⑦ run
That our devices⑧ still⑨ are overthrown⑩;
Our thoughts are ours, their ends none of our own.⑪
So think thou wilt no second husband wed;
210 But die thy thoughts⑫ when thy first lord is dead.

Player Queen⑬

Nor⑭ earth to me give food, nor heaven light!
Sport⑮ and repose lock from me day and night!
To desperation turn my trust and hope!
An anchor's cheer⑯ in prison be my scope⑰!
215 Each opposite⑱ that blanks⑲ the face of joy

---

① **who:** those who, whoever
② **not needs:** has no need
③ **try:** test (his friendship)
④ **seasons:** ripens
⑤ **seasons him:** turns him into
⑥ **begun:** began
⑦ **contrary:** accented on the second syllable
⑧ **devices:** plans
⑨ **still:** always
⑩ **overthrown:** frustrated
⑪ **Our ... own:** Proverbial: Man proposes, God disposes.
⑫ **die thy thoughts:** your thoughts will die
⑬ **211—218:** She takes an oath (Hamlet's insertion).
⑭ **Nor:** neither
⑮ **Sport:** recreation, entertainment
⑯ **anchor's cheer:** hermit's diet
⑰ **scope:** portion, limit
⑱ **opposite:** obstacle
⑲ **blanks:** makes pale

Meet what I would have well and it destroy[1]!
Both here and hence[2] pursue me lasting strife[3],
If, once a widow, ever I be wife!

HAMLET
If she should break it now![4]

Player King
220 'Tis deeply sworn. Sweet, leave me here awhile;
My spirits grow dull, and fain[5] I would beguile
The tedious day with sleep.

Sleeps

Player Queen
Sleep rock[6] thy brain,
And never come mischance between us twain!

Exit

HAMLET
225 Madam, how like you this play?

QUEEN
The lady protests too much[7], methinks.

HAMLET
O, but she'll keep her word.

KING
Have you heard the argument[8]? Is there no offence in 't?

---

[1] **Meet ... destroy:** encounter and destroy everything I want to go well
[2] **here and hence:** in the next world
[3] **pursue me lasting strife:** let lasting strife pursue me
[4] **If ... now:** It would be particularly shocking if she were to break her vow after these emphatic words.
[5] **fain:** willingly
[6] **rock:** soothe, dull
[7] **protests too much:** makes too many protestations
[8] **argument:** plot

HAMLET

No, no, they do but jest, poison① in jest; no offence② i' the world.

KING

230　What do you call the play?

HAMLET

'The Mousetrap.'③ Marry, how? Tropically④.
This play is the image of a murder done in Vienna. Gonzago is
the duke's name, his wife, Baptista.⑤ You shall see anon
'tis a knavish piece of work, but what o' that? Your majesty

235　and we that have free⑥ souls, it touches us not.⑦
let the galled⑧ jade⑨ wince, our withers⑩ are unwrung⑪.⑫

Enter LUCIANUS

This is one Lucianus, nephew to the King⑬.

OPHELIA

You are as good as a chorus, my lord.

HAMLET

I could interpret between you and your love, if I

---

① **poison:** Cf. 176: "wormwood" (the first mention)

② **offence:** crime

③ **'The Mousetrap':** a medieval symbolism. In the right panel of Robert Campin's Mérode Altarpiece (1415—1428), Saint Joseph, who was a carpenter, is constructing a mouse trap symbolizing Christ's trapping and defeat of the devil, a metaphor used three times by Saint Augustine (Sermon 130: "The cross of the Lord was the devil's mousetrap; the bait by which he was caught was the Lord's death.") that can be traced back to *The Battle of Frogs and Mice* (11.110—121).

④ **Tropically:** pun on trope-trap: trapically (as a trap); figuratively (as a trope)

⑤ **Gonzago ... Baptista:** The historical Francesco Maria I della Rovere, Duke of Urbino, who died in October 1538, was reputedly murdered by having poison poured in his ears at the instigation of a kinsman of the Duchess, one Luigi Gonzago.

⑥ **free:** innocent, guiltless

⑦ **Your ... not:** Cf. II. ii. 601: "I'll tent him to the quick."

⑧ **galled:** sore, chafed

⑨ **jade:** nag, old horse

⑩ **withers:** ridge between the horses' shoulders 马肩胛骨

⑪ **unwrung:** not chafed

⑫ **let ... unwrung:** Let guilty people flinch, but we have clear consciences.

⑬ **nephew to the King:** It is double-edged

240 could see the puppets[1] dallying[2].[3]

OPHELIA

You are keen[4], my lord, you are keen.

HAMLET

It would cost you a groaning to take off[5] my edge[6].

OPHELIA

Still better[7], and worse.[8]

HAMLET

So[9] you mistake your husbands.[10] Begin, murderer; pox[11],
245 leave thy damnable faces[12], and begin!
Come, 'the croaking raven doth bellow for revenge.'[13]

LUCIANUS[14]

Thoughts black, hands apt, drugs fit, and time agreeing;

---

   [1] **puppets:** a puppet show; you and your love ("Puppets" has a sexual meaning, related to the use of "poop" for the vagina)
   [2] **dallying:** making love
   [3] **I ... dallying:** I could play the role of narrator at a puppet show in which you and your lover are shown making love.
   [4] **keen:** sharp; penetrating
   [5] **take off:** blunt
   [6] **edge:** sexual desire
   [7] **better:** keener
   [8] **better, and worse:** more witty and more offensive
   [9] **So:** in the same way
   [10] **mistake your husbands:** take other men as husband (Christian marriage oath: "for better or for worse"); mistake me
   [11] **pox:** a pox on you!
   [12] **damnable faces:** execrable grimaces
   [13] **the croaking ... revenge:** a mockery of a line in the anonymous *The True Tragedy of Richard III* (c.1591): "The screeching raven sits croaking for revenge. / Whole herds of beasts come bellowing for revenge."
   [14] Some commentators have suggested the following lines (247—253) are the ones inserted by Hamlet.

Confederate[①] *season*[②], *else*[③] *no creature seeing*[④];
Thou[⑤] *mixture rank*[⑥], *of midnight weeds collected*[⑦],
250 *With Hecate's*[⑧] *ban*[⑨] *thrice blasted, thrice infected,*
Thy natural magic and dire property[⑩],
On wholesome life usurp[⑪] *immediately.*
Pours the poison into the sleeper's ears

HAMLET
He poisons him i' the garden for's estate[⑫]. His
255 name's Gonzago. The story is extant, and writ[⑬] in
choice Italian. You shall see anon[⑭] how the murderer
gets the love of Gonzago's wife.

OPHELIA
The King rises.

HAMLET
What, frighted[⑮] with false fire[⑯]!

QUEEN
How fares my lord?

---

① **Confederate:** co-conspiring
② **Confederate season:** time being my ally
③ **else:** otherwise, besides
④ **no creature seeing:** no one present at witness
⑤ **Thou:** apostrophe
⑥ **rank:** malign (post attributive)
⑦ **of midnight weeds collected:** concocted from weeds gathered at midnight
⑧ **Hecate:** Greek goddess of witchcraft (Cf. Hesiod: *Theogony*, 405 ff.)
⑨ **ban:** curse; bane (poison)
⑩ **dire property:** evil power or capacity
⑪ **usurp:** supplants
⑫ **estate:** wealth, property
⑬ **writ:** written
⑭ **anon:** soon
⑮ **frighted:** frightened
⑯ **false fire:** gun firing blanks (i.e. mere show)

POLONIUS

260 Give o'er[1] the play.

KING

Give me some light! Away!

All

Lights, lights, lights!

Exeunt all but HAMLET and HORATIO

HAMLET

Why, let the strucken[2] deer[3] go weep,[4]

The hart[5] ungalled[6] play;

265 For some must watch[7], while some must sleep:

So runs the world away.[8]

Would not this[9], sir, and a forest of feathers[10]—if

the rest of my fortunes turn Turk with[11] me—with two

Provincial[12] roses[13] on my razed[14] shoes, get me a

270 fellowship[15] in a cry[16] of players, sir?

---

① **Give o 'er:** give up, abandon
② **strucken:** *stricken, wounded*
③ **the strucken deer:** *Claudius*
④ **Why … weep:** The weeping deer is a complex iconographical image involving death, healing and religion as well as melancholy. (Cf. *As You Like It,* II. ii. 36—43)
⑤ **hart:** *male deer (esp. over 5 years old)*
⑥ **ungalled:** *unhurt*
⑦ **watch:** *stay awake*
⑧ **So runs the world away:** *Thus the world runs its way; / This is the way of the world.*
⑨ **this:** *my contribution to the play*
⑩ **feathers:** *plumes worn by actors*
⑪ **turn Turk with:** *turn against, betray*
⑫ **Provincial:** *of Provence*
⑬ **roses:** *large rosettes worn by actors*
⑭ **razed:** *fashionably slashed, patterned*
⑮ **fellowship:** *share, partnership*
⑯ **cry:** *pack (hounds)*

HORATIO

Half a share.①

HAMLET

A whole one, I.

For thou dost know, O Damon② dear,

This realm dismantled③ was

275 Of Jove④ himself; and now reigns here

A very, very—pajock⑤.

HORATIO

You might have rhymed⑥.

HAMLET

O good Horatio, I'll take the ghost's word for a

thousand pound. Didst⑦ perceive?

HORATIO

280 Very well, my lord.

HAMLET

Upon the talk of the poisoning?

HORATIO

I did very well note him.

HAMLET

Ah, ha! Come, some music! come, the recorders⑧!

For if the King like not the comedy,

285 Why then, belike⑨, he likes it not, perdy⑩.

---

① **Half a share:** His response to Hamlet's elation is muted. (In Shakespeare's time, third-class players could only get half a share.)

② **Damon:** in Greek legend famous for his devoted friendship for Pythias

③ **dismantled:** deprived, stripped

④ **Jove:** an allusion to old Hamlet

⑤ **pajock:** peacock, a reputed lecherous and cruel bird, referring to Claudius

⑥ **rhymed:** used "ass" instead of "pajock"

⑦ **Didst:** did you

⑧ **recorders:** flutes or wooden pipes

⑨ **belike:** perhaps

⑩ **perdy:** par Dieu (by God)

Come, some music!

Re-enter ROSENCRANTZ and GUILDENSTERN

GUILDENSTERN

Good my lord[1], vouchsafe[2] me a word with you.

HAMLET

Sir, a whole history[3].

GUILDENSTERN

The King, sir—

HAMLET

290 Ay, sir, what of him?

GUILDENSTERN

Is in his retirement[4] marvellous[5] distempered[6].

HAMLET

With drink, sir?

GUILDENSTERN

No, my lord, rather with choler[7].

HAMLET

Your wisdom should[8] show itself more richer[9] to
295 signify[10] this to his doctor; for, for me to put him
to his purgation[11] would perhaps plunge him into far
more choler[12].

---

[1] **Good my lord:** His mode of address is carefully reverential
[2] **vouchsafe:** grant, condescend to give
[3] **history:** story
[4] **retirement:** withdrawal to his private chamber
[5] **marvellous:** marvelously
[6] **distempered:** out of sorts physically (e.g. drunk), upset
[7] **choler:** bile, anger
[8] **should:** would surely
[9] **more richer:** much more rich or resourceful (double comparative)
[10] **signify:** communicate
[11] **purgation:** cleansing (of guilt or sin)
[12] **choler:** anger (then he twists meaning into biliousness)

GUILDENSTERN

Good my lord, put your discourse into some frame① and start② not so wildly from my affair③.

HAMLET

300 I am tame④, sir. Pronounce⑤.

GUILDENSTERN

The Queen, your mother, in most great affliction⑥ of spirit, hath sent me to you.

HAMLET

You are welcome.

GUILDENSTERN

Nay, good my lord, this courtesy is not of the right
305 breed⑦. If it shall please you to make me a wholesome⑧ answer, I will do your mother's commandment; if not, your pardon⑨ and my return shall be the end of my business.

HAMLET

Sir, I cannot.

GUILDENSTERN

310 What, my lord?

HAMLET

Make⑩ you a wholesome answer; my wit's⑪ diseased. But, sir, such answer as I can make, you shall command;

---

① **frame:** order
② **start:** shy away
③ **affair:** business
④ **tame:** calm, subdued
⑤ **Pronounce:** speak it
⑥ **affliction:** distress
⑦ **breed:** kind; breeding in manners
⑧ **wholesome:** sane, rational
⑨ **pardon:** permission to leave
⑩ **Make:** I can not make
⑪ **wit:** brain, intelligence

or, rather, as you say, my mother①. Therefore no
more, but to the matter②! My mother, you say—
ROSENCRANTZ
315 Then thus she says: your behavior hath struck her
into amazement and admiration③.
HAMLET
O wonderful son, that can so astonish a mother! But
is there no sequel at the heels of this
mother's admiration? Impart.
ROSENCRANTZ
320 She desires to speak with you in her closet④, ere you
go to bed.
HAMLET
We⑤ shall obey, were she ten times our mother⑥. Have
you any further trade⑦ with us?
ROSENCRANTZ
My lord, you once did love me.⑧
HAMLET
325 So I do still, by these pickers and stealers⑨.
ROSENCRANTZ
Good my lord, what is your cause of distemper⑩?
You do, surely, bar the door upon your own liberty, if

---

① **my mother:** it is my mother who is commanding
② **the matter:** the subject
③ **admiration:** wonder, astonishment
④ **closet:** private room
⑤ **We:** the royal "we" (a deliberate distancing tactic)
⑥ **ten times our mother:** i.e. by her remarriage
⑦ **trade:** business
⑧ **My lord ... me:** Cf. III. i. 125 & 129
⑨ **by ... stealers:** by these ten fingers (The phrase is borrowed from catechism, where one is told to "keep hands from picking and stealing".)
⑩ **your cause of distemper:** the cause of your disorder of mind

you deny your griefs to your friend.①
HAMLET
Sir, I lack advancement②③.
ROSENCRANTZ
330　How can that be, when you have the voice of the King himself for your succession in Denmark?④
HAMLET
Ay, but sir, '*While the grass grows*'⑤—the proverb is something⑥ musty⑦.
Re-enter Players with recorders
O, the recorders! Let me see one. To withdraw⑧ with
335　you—why do you go about⑨ to recover the wind of me⑩, as if you would drive me into a toil⑪?
GUILDENSTERN
O, my lord, if my duty be too bold⑫, my love is too unmannerly⑬.
HAMLET
I do not well understand that. Will you play upon
340　this pipe?
GUILDENSTERN
My lord, I cannot.

---

① **You do ... friend:** You will be put into prison if you go on like this. (Is it a threat or a friendly advice?)
② **advancement:** promotion
③ **Sir ... advancement:** Hamlet still "denies his griefs to his friend".
④ **when ... Denmark:** when the King himself has said you are to succeed him on the throne
⑤ *While the grass grows*: The rest of the proverb reads "the horse starves."
⑥ **something:** somewhat
⑦ **musty:** stale (so it need not be quoted in full)
⑧ **withdraw:** be private
⑨ **go about:** try
⑩ **recover the wind of me:** get to the windward side of me
⑪ **toil:** net or trap
⑫ **if my duty be too bold:** if I'm too bold in carrying out my duty
⑬ **my love is too unmannerly:** it is because my love has overcome my manners

HAMLET

I pray you.

GUILDENSTERN

Believe me, I cannot.

HAMLET

I do beseech you.

GUILDENSTERN

345 I know no touch of it①, my lord.

HAMLET

'Tis as easy as lying. Govern these ventages② with your lingers and thumb, give it breath with your mouth, and it will discourse most eloquent music. Look you, these are the stops③.

GUILDENSTERN

350 But these④ cannot I command to any utterance⑤ of harmony. I have not the skill.

HAMLET

Why, look you now, how unworthy⑥ a thing you make of me! You would play upon me; you would seem to know my stops; you would pluck out the heart of my
355 mystery⑦; you would sound⑧ me from my lowest note to the top of my compass⑨; and there is much music, excellent voice, in this little organ⑩; yet cannot you make it

---

① **I know ... it:** I don't have the skill to play it
② **ventages:** openings, holes
③ **stops:** openings, holes
④ **these:** stops
⑤ **utterance:** sound
⑥ **unworthy:** contemptible
⑦ **mystery:** secret; skill at a craft or trade
⑧ **sound:** play on; explore (my) depths, measure; test
⑨ **compass:** range, scope
⑩ **organ:** instrument (the recorder)

speak. 'Sblood①, do you think I am easier to be played on than a pipe? Call me what instrument you will, though
360 you can fret me②, you cannot play upon me.

Enter POLONIUS

God bless you, sir!③

POLONIUS

My lord, the Queen would speak with you, and presently.

HAMLET

Do you see yonder cloud that's almost in shape of a camel?

POLONIUS

365 By the mass, and 'tis like a camel, indeed.

HAMLET

Methinks it is like a weasel.

POLONIUS

It is backed like a weasel.④

HAMLET

Or like a whale?

POLONIUS

Very like a whale.⑤

HAMLET

370 Then I will come to my mother by and by⑥.

---

① **'Sblood:** by God's blood
② **fret me:** manipulate my frets (small wooden bar that hold strings tight); irritate me
③ **God ... sir:** He bids goodbye to their friendship.
④ **It ... weasel:** Its back is like that of a weasel.
⑤ **Very ... whale:** Cf. *Antony and Cleopatra*, IV. xiv. 3—11: "Sometime we see a cloud that's dragonish; / A vapour sometime like a bear or lion, / A tower'd citadel, a pendent rock, / A forked mountain, or blue promontory / With trees upon't that nod unto the world / And mock our eyes with air. Thou hast seen these signs; / They are black vesper's pageants. / ... / That which is now a horse, even with a thought / The rack dislimns, and makes it indistinct, / As water is in water."
⑥ **by and by:** soon, right away

They fool me① to the top of my bent②. I will come by and by.

POLONIUS

I will say so.

HAMLET

By and by is easily said.

Exit POLONIUS

Leave me, friends.

Exeunt all but HAMLET

375 'Tis now the very witching time③ of night,
When churchyards yawn④ and hell itself breathes⑤ out⑥
Contagion⑦ to this world. Now could I drink hot blood,
And do such bitter business as the day
Would quake to look on⑧. Soft!⑨ now to my mother!
380 O heart, lose not thy nature⑩; let not ever
The soul of Nero⑪ enter this firm⑫ bosom.
Let me be cruel, not unnatural;
I will speak daggers to her, but use none.
My tongue and soul in this⑬ be hypocrites—

---

① **fool me:** indulge my folly
② **to the top of my bent:** to the uttermost
③ **witching time:** hour appropriate for witchcraft
④ **yawn:** open wide
⑤ **breathes:** Q2 reads: "break"
⑥ **breathes out:** release
⑦ **Contagion:** pestilence, poison
⑧ **such bitter … on:** i.e. matricide
⑨ **Soft:** Be quiet!
⑩ **thy nature:** natural love of one's mother
⑪ **Nero:** Roman tyrant, noted for his cruelty, who killed his mother Agrippina. She murdered her husband, the emperor Claudius, so that her son by a previous marriage, Nero, would become emperor.
⑫ **firm:** resolved (against doing violence)
⑬ **in this:** in this regard

385　How in my words soever① she be shent②,
　　To give them seals③ never, my soul, consent!④
　　Exit

SCENE III. A room in the castle.

Enter KING, ROSENCRANTZ, and GUILDENSTERN

KING

　　I like him not⑤, nor stands⑥ it safe with us
　　To let his madness range⑦. Therefore prepare you;
　　I your commission⑧ will forthwith dispatch⑨,
　　And he⑩ to England shall along⑪ with you.
5　The terms of our estate⑫ may not endure
　　Hazard so dangerous as doth hourly grow
　　Out of his lunacies.

GUILDENSTERN

　　We will ourselves provide⑬.
　　Most holy and religious fear⑭ it is

---

① **soever:** however
② **shent:** (past participle of "shend") reproved
③ **seals:** validate, put into action
④ **How … consent:** However much she may be shamed by my words, my soul will never consent to authorize putting them into action.
⑤ **I like him not:** I don't like the way he is acting
⑥ **stands:** considers
⑦ **range:** go rampant, run freely
⑧ **commission:** a sealed letter
⑨ **dispatch:** draw up, prepare promptly
⑩ **He:** Hamlet
⑪ **along:** go along
⑫ **The terms of our estate:** my position as king
⑬ **ourselves provide:** equip ourselves, make ourselves ready
⑭ **fear:** concern

10 To keep those many many bodies safe
     That live and feed upon your majesty.[1]
     ROSENCRANTZ
     The single and peculiar[2] life is bound[3],
     With all the strength and armor of the mind,
     To keep itself from noyance[4]; but much more
15 That spirit[5] upon whose weal[6] depend and rest
     The lives of many. The cease[7] of majesty[8]
     Dies not alone; but, like a gulf[9], doth draw[10]
     What's near it with it.[11] It is a massy[12] wheel,
     Fixed on the summit of the highest mount,
20 To whose huge spokes ten thousand lesser things
     Are mortised[13] and adjoined; which, when it falls,
     Each small annexment[14], petty consequence[15],
     Attends[16] the boisterous[17] ruin[18].[19] Never alone
     Did the King sigh, but with a general groan[20].

---

[1] **That ... majesty:** Cf. I. iii. 23—24: "on his choice depends / The safety and health of this whole state"
[2] **single and peculiar:** individual, private
[3] **bound:** obliged
[4] **noyance:** annoyance, injury, harm
[5] **That spirit:** i.e. the King
[6] **weal:** welfare, well-being
[7] **The cease:** cessation, decease, death
[8] **majesty:** royalty
[9] **gulf:** whirlpool
[10] **draw:** attract, pull in
[11] **What's near it with it:** a foreboding of his own fate
[12] **massy:** massive
[13] **mortised:** securely fastened
[14] **annexment:** annex, addition
[15] **petty consequence:** trivial thing connected with it
[16] **Attends:** accompanies
[17] **boisterous:** tumultuous
[18] **ruin:** downfall
[19] **It is a massy wheel ... ruin:** Cf. II. ii. 496—500
[20] **a general groan:** everyone's sorrow

KING

25 Arm you①, I pray you, to② this speedy③ voyage;
For we will fetters put upon this fear④,
Which now goes too free-footed⑤.⑥

ROSENCRANTZ GUILDENSTERN

We will haste us.

Exeunt ROSENCRANTZ and GUILDENSTERN

Enter POLONIUS

POLONIUS

My lord, he's going to his mother's closet⑦.
30 Behind the arras⑧ I'll convey⑨ myself,
To hear the process⑩; and warrant⑪ she'll tax him home⑫;
And, as you said, and wisely was it said,⑬
'Tis meet⑭ that some more audience than a mother,
Since nature makes them partial, should o'erhear
35 The speech, of vantage⑮. Fare you well, my liege.
I'll call upon you ere you go to bed,
And tell you what I know.

KING

Thanks, dear my lord.

---

① **Arm you:** equip yourselves
② **to:** for
③ **speedy:** imminent, hastily planned
④ **fear:** danger
⑤ **free-footed:** swiftly
⑥ 26—27: Note the alliteration of the "f" sound.
⑦ **closet:** private chamber
⑧ **arras:** wall-hanging
⑨ **convey:** place, remove
⑩ **process:** proceedings
⑪ **warrant:** guarantee
⑫ **tax him home:** scold him thoroughly
⑬ **as … said:** In fact it was he himself who said it (III. i. 194—196).
⑭ **meet:** appropriate
⑮ **of vantage:** in addition; from the vantage point of concealment

Exit POLONIUS

O, my offence is rank①, it smells to heaven;
40 It hath the primal eldest curse② upon't,
A brother's murder③. Pray can I not,
Though inclination be as sharp as will.
My stronger guilt defeats my strong intent;
And, like a man to double business bound④,
45 I stand in pause where I shall first begin,
And both neglect. What if⑤ this cursèd hand
Were thicker than itself with brother's blood?
Is there not rain enough in the sweet heavens
To wash it white as snow?⑥ Whereto serves mercy⑦
50 But to confront the visage⑧ of offence⑨?⑩
And what's in prayer⑪ but this two-fold force⑫,
To be forestallèd⑬ ere we come to fall⑭,

---

① **rank:** offensive, foul-smelling
② **the primal eldest curse:** curse of Cain, who slew his brother Abel and was condemned to a life of "a fugitive and vagabond" (*Genesis* 4: 11—12).
③ **A brother's murder:** the murder of a brother (he does not mention incest)
④ **to double business bound:** obliged to take two tasks at once
⑤ **what if:** even if
⑥ **Is ... snow:** *Psalms* 51:7: "wash me, and I shall be whiter than snow"; *Macbeth*, II. ii. 59—60: "Will all great Neptune's ocean wash this blood / Clean from my hand?"
⑦ **mercy:** God's mercy
⑧ **visage:** face
⑨ **offence:** crime, sin, guilt
⑩ **where to ... offence:** What is the function of mercy if it does not confront guilt? / What purpose does mercy serve except to defend the sinner in the face of his offense? (The promise of the *New Testament* is that the mercy, in the person of Christ, will, at the Last Judgment, oppose itself to the face of the offended Deity, and thus secure forgiveness of our sins.)
⑪ **what's in prayer:** what is the use of prayer
⑫ **this two-fold force:** two-fold force of prayer (i.e. we not be "led into temptation" and that we be "forgiven our trespasses")
⑬ **forestallèd:** prevented
⑭ **fall:** do wrong

Or pardoned① being down②? Then I'll look up;
My fault is past③. But, O, what form of prayer
55 Can serve my turn? 'Forgive me my foul murder'?
That cannot be, since I am still possessed
Of those effects④ for which I did the murder,
My crown, mine own ambition⑤ and my Queen⑥.
May one be pardoned and retain⑦ the offence⑧?
60 In the corrupted currents⑨ of this world
Offence's gilded⑩ hand may shove by⑪ justice,
And oft 'tis seen the wicked prize itself
Buys out the law. But 'tis not so above⑫:
There is no shuffling⑬; there the action⑭ lies
65 In his⑮ true nature⑯; and we ourselves compelled,
Even to the teeth and forehead⑰ of our faults,
To give in evidence.⑱ What then? What rests⑲?

---

① **pardoned**: to be pardoned
② **being down**: when we have done wrong
③ **past**: already committed (so let bygones be bygones)
④ **effects**: benefits
⑤ **ambition**: achievement of my ambition
⑥ 56—58: Cf. *Henry VIII*, II. ii. 15—16: "It seems the marriage with his brother's wife / Has crept too near his conscience."
⑦ **retain**: keep
⑧ **offence**: gains of sin
⑨ **currents**: courses, ways
⑩ **gilded**: covered with gold
⑪ **shove by**: elbow aside, evade
⑫ **so above**: in heaven
⑬ **shuffling**: sharp practice, trickery
⑭ **action**: the case
⑮ **his**: its
⑯ **true nature**: is judged by the true facts
⑰ **teeth and forehead**: every detail
⑱ **there … evidence**: In God's court, the legal action must be brought in accord with the facts; and we are even forced to testify against ourselves / we are forced to present evidence of the worst of our sins.
⑲ **rests**: remains, is left

Try what repentance can[1]. What can it not?
Yet what can it when one can not repent?
70 O wretched state! O bosom black as death!
O limèd[2] soul, that, struggling to be free,
Art more engaged[3]! Help, angels! Make assay[4]!
Bow, stubborn knees; and, heart with strings of steel,
Be soft as sinews of the newborn babe!
75 All may be well.

He kneels.

Enter HAMLET

HAMLET
Now might I do it pat[5], now he is praying;
And now I'll do't. And so he goes to heaven,
And so am I revenged. That would be scanned[6].
A villain kills my father, and for that,
80 I, his sole son, do this same villain send
To heaven.
O, this is hire and salary[7], not revenge.
He took my father grossly[8], full of bread[9],
With all his crimes broad blown[10], as flush[11] as May;[12]

---

[1] **can:** can achieve
[2] **limèd:** snared (lime: a sticky substance)
[3] **engaged:** entangled
[4] **assay:** attempt, try
[5] **pat:** conveniently; at the right moment
[6] **would be scanned:** needs to be considered
[7] **hire and salary:** something Claudius should pay me for
[8] **grossly:** in a gross condition
[9] **full of bread:** in a state of sensual satiety; in the full enjoyment of the earthly pleasures (Cf. *Ezekiel* 16:49: "Pride, fullness of bread, and abundance of idleness.")
[10] **broad blown:** in full bloom
[11] **flush:** lusty
[12] **With all ... May:** Cf. I. v. 82: "unhouseled, disappointed, unaneled" etc.

85 And how his① audit② stands, who knows save heaven?
But in our circumstance and course of thought③,
'Tis heavy with him④. And am I then revenged,
To take him in the purging of his soul,
When he is fit and seasoned⑤ for his passage⑥?
90 No.
Up⑦, sword; and know thou a more horrid hent⑧⑨.
When he is drunk asleep, or in his rage,
Or in the incestuous pleasure of his bed;
At gaming, swearing, or about some act
95 That has no relish⑩ of salvation in't⑪
Then trip⑫ him, that his heels may kick at heaven⑬,
And that his soul may be as damned and black
As hell, whereto it goes. My mother stays⑭.
This physic⑮ but prolongs thy sickly days.

Exit

KING

100 [*Rising*] My words fly up, my thoughts remain below;

---

① **his:** old Hamlet's
② **audit:** final account
③ **in ... thought:** in our circumstantial thought
④ **'Tis heavy with him:** i.e. his spirit is in a serious state
⑤ **seasoned:** prepared
⑥ **passage:** passing to the next world
⑦ **Up:** back to sheath
⑧ **hent:** occasion, opportunity
⑨ **know ... hent:** wait for a more horrible occasion
⑩ **relish:** hint, trace
⑪ **That ... in't:** when his death will involve his damnation
⑫ **trip:** cause (him) to stumble and fall
⑬ **his ... heaven:** he may plunge headlong into hell
⑭ **stays:** awaits, is waiting
⑮ **physic:** medicine (his prayer)

Words without thoughts never to heaven go.[1]

Exit

SCENE IV. The Queen's closet.

Enter QUEEN and POLONIUS

POLONIUS
He will come straight[2]. Look you lay home to him[3].
Tell him his pranks[4] have been too broad[5] to bear with[6],
And that your grace hath screened and stood between
Much heat[7] and him. I'll silence me even here.
5 Pray you, be round[8] with him.

HAMLET
[*Within*] Mother, mother, mother!

QUEEN
I'll warrant[9] you,
Fear me not.[10] Withdraw, I hear him coming.

POLONIUS hides behind the arras
Enter HAMLET

---

[1] **Words ... go:** in response to "All may be well" (and Hamlet has lost the chance to take his revenge)
[2] **straight:** immediately
[3] **lay home to him:** reprove him thoroughly
[4] **pranks:** reprehensible actions
[5] **broad:** excessive, unrestrained
[6] **bear with:** tolerate
[7] **heat:** anger on the King's part
[8] **round:** forthright, blunt
[9] **warrant:** be bound to
[10] **Fear me not:** Don't doubt me (that I'll spare him).

HAMLET

Now, mother, what's the matter?

QUEEN①

10　Hamlet, thou hast thy father② much offended.

HAMLET

Mother, you have my father much offended.

QUEEN

Come, come, you answer with an idle③ tongue.

HAMLET

Go, go, you question with a wicked tongue.

QUEEN

Why, how now, Hamlet!

HAMLET

15　What's the matter now?

QUEEN

Have you forgot④ me⑤?

HAMLET

No, by the rood⑥, not so!

You are the Queen, your husband's brother's wife,

And (would⑦ it were not so!) you are my mother.

QUEEN

20　Nay, then, I'll set those to you that can speak⑧.

HAMLET

Come, come, and sit you down; you shall not budge⑨!

---

① **10—13:** a stichomythia (i.e. alternate lines)
② **thy father:** i.e. Claudius
③ **idle:** foolish, senseless
④ **forgot:** forgotten
⑤ **me:** who I am
⑥ **rood:** crucifix, Christ's cross
⑦ **would:** I wish
⑧ **speak:** speak more forcefully
⑨ **budge:** move

You go not till I set you up a glass①
Where you may see the inmost part of you.

QUEEN

What wilt thou do? Thou wilt not murder me?
25 Help, help, ho!

POLONIUS

[*Behind*] What, ho! help, help, help!

HAMLET

[*Draws*] How now, a rat? Dead for a ducat, dead!②

Makes a pass through the arras and kills POLONIUS.

POLONIUS

[*Behind*] O, I am slain!

QUEEN

O me, what hast thou done?

HAMLET

30 Nay, I know not. Is it the King?

QUEEN

O, what a rash and bloody deed is this!

HAMLET

A bloody deed—almost as bad, good mother,
As③ kill a king and marry with his brother.④

QUEEN

As kill a king?

HAMLET

35 Ay, lady, 'twas my word.⑤

Lifts up the arras and sees POLONIUS

---

① **glass:** mirror
② **Dead ... dead:** I'll wager a ducat that he is dead.
③ **As:** as to
④ **As ... brother:** a moment of revelation!
⑤ **Ay ... word:** Philip Edwards: "It is extraordinary that neither of them takes up this all-important matter again. Gertrude does not press for an explanation; Hamlet does not question further the Queen's involvement." (*Hamlet,* Introduction, p.133)

Thou wretched, rash, intruding fool, farewell!
I took thee for thy better①. Take thy fortune②;
Thou find'st to be too busy③ is some danger.④
Leave wringing of your hands. Peace, sit you down,
40　And let me wring your heart; for so I shall
If it⑤ be made of penetrable stuff⑥,
If damnèd custom⑦ have not brazed⑧ it so
That it is proof⑨ and bulwark⑩ against sense⑪.

QUEEN

What have I done, that thou darest wag thy tongue⑫
45　In noise so rude against me?

HAMLET

Such an act⑬
That blurs⑭ the grace and blush⑮ of modesty⑯,
Calls virtue hypocrite, takes off the rose⑰
From the fair forehead of an innocent love
50　And sets a blister⑱ there, makes marriage vows

---

① **thy better:** i.e. Claudius
② **Take thy fortune:** accept your fate
③ **busy:** interfering
④ **Thou ... danger:** What a cold-blooded prince! Here we find something demonic in Hamlet. (V. i. 259: "have I something in me dangerous" etc.)
⑤ **it:** your heart
⑥ **If ... stuff:** if it has still retained any sensitivity to emotion
⑦ **damnèd custom:** cursed habit, habitual wickedness
⑧ **brazed:** hardened, as if plated with brass
⑨ **proof:** armor, impenetrable
⑩ **bulwark:** armored and fortified
⑪ **sense:** natural or proper feeling (i.e. guilt)
⑫ **wag thy tongue:** scold
⑬ **Such an act:** it is such an act
⑭ **blurs:** disfigures
⑮ **blush:** rosy color
⑯ **modesty:** a modest woman
⑰ **rose:** symbol of true love
⑱ **blister:** mark of a brand (e.g. scarlet letter)

As false as dicers' oaths①. O, such a deed②
As from the body③ of contraction④ plucks
The very soul, and sweet religion makes⑤
A rhapsody⑥ of words! Heaven's face doth glow⑦
55 Over this solidity and compound mass⑧,
With tristful⑨ visage⑩, as against⑪ the doom⑫,
Is thought-sick⑬ at the act.⑭

QUEEN

Ay me, what act,
That roars so loud, and thunders in the index⑮?

HAMLET

60 Look here, upon this picture, and on this,
The counterfeit presentment⑯ of two brothers.
See, what a grace was seated on this brow,
Hyperion's curls⑰; the front⑱ of Jove⑲ himself,
An eye like Mars⑳, to threaten and command,

---

① **dicers' oaths:** the rash promises of gamblers
② **such a deed:** it is such a deed
③ **body:** substance
④ **contraction:** a marriage contract
⑤ **sweet religion makes:** such a deed makes sweet religion (into)
⑥ **rhapsody:** jumble
⑦ **glow:** flush with anger
⑧ **this ... mass:** the earth
⑨ **tristful:** sad
⑩ **visage:** face
⑪ **against:** in face of
⑫ **doom:** Doomsday, Judgment Day
⑬ **thought-sick:** sick at heart
⑭ **as against ... act:** The world is sick at Gertrude's act as if at the approach of Judgment Day.
⑮ **index:** prologue, introductory remarks
⑯ **counterfeit presentment:** representation in portraits
⑰ **Hyperion's curls:** golden tresses
⑱ **front:** brow, forehead
⑲ **Jove:** Jupiter (Zeus), the King of the gods
⑳ **An eye like Mars:** dominating glare

65   A station① like the herald Mercury②
     New lighted③ on a heaven-kissing④ hill,
     A combination⑤ and a form indeed,
     Where every god did seem to set his seal⑥,
     To give the world assurance of a man.
70   This was your husband. Look you now, what follows.⑦
     Here is your husband, like a mildewed⑧ ear⑨,
     Blasting⑩ his wholesome brother. Have you eyes?
     Could you on this fair mountain leave⑪ to feed,
     And batten on⑫ this moor⑬? Ha! Have you eyes?
75   You cannot call it love, for at your age
     The heyday⑭ in the blood⑮ is tame, it's humble
     And waits upon⑯ the judgment; and what judgment
     Would step from this to this? Sense⑰, sure, you have,
     Else⑱ could you not have motion; but sure that sense
80   Is apoplexed⑲; for madness would not err⑳,

---

① **station:** stance, standing posture
② **Mercury:** Hermes, messenger of gods
③ **New lighted:** newly alighted
④ **heaven-kissing:** sky-scratching
⑤ **combination:** physical features
⑥ **set his seal:** place his mark of approval or ownership
⑦ **Look you now, what follows:** a sharp contrast
⑧ **mildewed:** blighted
⑨ **ear:** ear of wheat
⑩ **Blasting:** destroying
⑪ **leave:** cease
⑫ **batten on:** feed on, grow fat on
⑬ **moor:** barren land
⑭ **heyday:** high-day, excitement
⑮ **blood:** passion, lust
⑯ **waits upon:** defer to
⑰ **sense:** feeling, basic comprehension
⑱ **Else:** otherwise
⑲ **apoplexed:** paralyzed
⑳ **madness would not err:** even a mad person would not make this mistake

Nor sense① to ecstasy② was ne'er so thralled③
But it reserved some quantity of choice④
To serve in such a difference⑤. What devil was't
That thus hath cozened⑥ you at hoodman-blind⑦?
85 Eyes without feeling, feeling without sight,
Ears without hands or eyes, smelling sans⑧ all⑨,
Or but a sickly part of one true sense
Could not so mope⑩.
O shame! where is thy blush? Rebellious hell⑪,
90 If thou canst mutine⑫ in a matron's bones,
To flaming youth let virtue⑬ be as wax⑭
And melt in her own fire⑮. Proclaim no shame
When the compulsive⑯ ardor⑰ gives the charge⑱,
Since frost⑲ itself as actively⑳ doth burn

---

① **sense:** sensibility
② **ecstasy:** madness
③ **thralled:** enthralled, enslaved
④ **quantity of choice:** power to choose
⑤ **To ... difference:** to enable you to choose where the difference was so big
⑥ **cozened:** deceived
⑦ **hoodman-blind:** blind man's buff (i.e. you must have been blind-folded when you chose Claudius)
⑧ **sans:** without
⑨ **all:** the other senses
⑩ **so mope:** be so stupefied, behave in such an aimless way
⑪ **Rebellious hell:** the evil impulse in human nature
⑫ **mutine:** incite mutiny, rebel
⑬ **virtue:** chastity
⑭ **wax:** like the wax in a burning candle
⑮ **fire:** lust
⑯ **compulsive:** compelling
⑰ **ardor:** youthful passion
⑱ **charge:** (signal for) attack
⑲ **frost:** age
⑳ **actively:** vigorously

95 And reason panders① will②.③

QUEEN

O Hamlet, speak no more!

Thou turn'st mine eyes into my very soul,

And there I see such black and grainèd④ spots

As will not leave their tinct⑤.

HAMLET

100 Nay⑥, but to live

In the rank⑦ sweat of an enseamèd⑧ bed,

Stewed⑨ in corruption, honeying⑩ and making love

Over the nasty sty⑪!

QUEEN

O, speak to me no more;

105 These words like daggers enter in mine ears.⑫

No more, sweet Hamlet!

HAMLET

A murderer and a villain!

A slave that is not twentieth part the tithe⑬

---

① **panders:** forgives; satisfies

② **will:** passion

③ **proclaim no shame ... reason panders will:** Don't call it shameful when youthful passion acts impetuously, since the frost of age is itself aflame and reason is like a pander for desire instead of controlling it.

④ **grainèd:** ingrained, fast dyed

⑤ **tinct:** color, stain

⑥ **Nay:** let me go on

⑦ **rank:** offensive, excessive

⑧ **enseamèd:** greasy, defiled with seam (hog fat) or semen

⑨ **stewed:** smothered, steeped

⑩ **honeying:** calling each other "honey"

⑪ **nasty sty:** pig-sty

⑫ **These ... ears:** His words take effect as expected. (Cf. III. ii. 383: "I will speak daggers to her" etc.)

⑬ **tithe:** one tenth (of income)

Of your precedent① lord; a vice② of③ kings④;
110 A cutpurse⑤ of the empire and the rule⑥,
That from a shelf the precious diadem stole
And put it in his pocket!

QUEEN
No more!

HAMLET
A king of shreds and patches⑦

Enter Ghost

115 Save me,⑧ and hover o'er me with your wings,
You heavenly guards! What would⑨ your gracious figure?

QUEEN
Alas, he's mad!⑩

HAMLET
Do you not come your tardy⑪ son to chide,
That, lapsed in time and passion⑫, lets go by
120 The important⑬ acting⑭ of your dread command?
O, say!

Ghost
Do not forget. This visitation

---

① **precedent:** former
② **vice:** the Devil's servant in morality plays, later evolved into the Elizabethan fool
③ **of:** among
④ **a vice of kings:** a buffoon of a king
⑤ **cutpurse:** thief
⑥ **rule:** kingdom
⑦ **shreds and patches:** ragged patchwork (king of shreds and patches: clown, vice)
⑧ **Save me:** He appeals to angels for protection.
⑨ **would:** wish
⑩ **Alas ... mad:** She does not see the ghost.
⑪ **tardy:** late, procrastinating
⑫ **lapsed in time and passion:** having let the time slip by and passion cool
⑬ **important:** importunate, urgent
⑭ **acting:** execution

Is but to whet① thy almost blunted purpose.
But look, amazement on thy mother sits②.
125 O, step between③ her and her fighting soul!④
Conceit⑤ in weakest bodies strongest works.
Speak to her, Hamlet.

HAMLET
How is it with you, lady?

QUEEN
Alas, how is't with you,
130 That you do bend⑥ your eye on vacancy⑦
And with the incorporal⑧ air do hold discourse⑨?
Forth at your eyes your spirits wildly peep,
And, as the sleeping soldiers in the alarm⑩,
Your bedded⑪ hair, like life in excrements⑫,
135 Starts up, and stands on end. O gentle son,
Upon the heat and flame of thy distemper
Sprinkle cool patience. Whereon do you look?

HAMLET
On him, on him! Look you, how pale he glares!
His form and cause conjoined⑬, preaching to stones,
140 Would make them capable⑭. [*To the Ghost*] Do not look upon me,

---

① **whet:** sharpen
② **amazement ... sits:** your mother is greatly shocked
③ **step between:** intervene in
④ **step ... soul:** pacify her
⑤ **conceit:** imagination
⑥ **bend:** focus, direct
⑦ **vacancy:** empty space
⑧ **imcorporal:** immaterial, incorporeal
⑨ **hold discourse:** converse
⑩ **in the alarm:** waked by the call to arms
⑪ **bedded:** matted, lying flat
⑫ **life in excrements:** lifeless outgrowths (e.g. hair and nails)
⑬ **conjoined:** united
⑭ **capable:** capable of some form of response, responsive

Lest with this piteous action you convert[1]
My stern effects[2]. Then what I have to do
Will want[3] true color[4]—tears perchance for blood.

QUEEN

To whom do you speak this?

HAMLET

145 Do you see nothing there?

QUEEN

Nothing at all; yet all that is I see.[5]

HAMLET

Nor did you nothing hear?

QUEEN

No, nothing but ourselves.

HAMLET

Why, look you there! Look how it steals away!
150 My father, in his habit[6] as he lived![7]
Look, where he goes, even now, out at the portal[8]!

Exit Ghost

QUEEN

This is the very[9] coinage[10] of your brain.
This bodiless creation[11] ecstasy[12]

---

[1] **convert:** turn me away from
[2] **effects:** purposes
[3] **want:** lack
[4] **true color:** (its) true character (Cf. III. i. 92: "the native hue of resolution")
[5] **Nothing ... see:** Why she doesn't see the ghost: a. it is the will of the ghost (he determines to whom he appears); b. she's guilty.
[6] **habit:** dress
[7] **in his ... lived:** in the clothes he wore when he was alive
[8] **portal:** doorway
[9] **very:** mere
[10] **coinage:** invention
[11] **This bodiless creation:** manufacture of fantasies
[12] **ecstasy:** madness

Is very cunning in.①

HAMLET

155　Ecstasy!
My pulse, as yours, doth temperately② keep time,
And makes as healthful music. It is not madness
That I have uttered. Bring me to the test,
And I the matter will reword③, which madness
160　Would gambol from④. Mother, for love of grace⑤,
Lay not that flattering unction⑥ to your soul⑦
That not your trespass but my madness speaks.
It will but skin and film⑧ the ulcerous place⑨,
Whilst rank corruption, mining⑩ all within,
165　Infects unseen. Confess yourself to heaven,
Repent what's past, avoid what is to come⑪,
And do not spread the compost⑫ on the weeds,
To make them ranker⑬. Forgive me this my virtue,
For in the fatness⑭ of these pursy⑮ times
170　Virtue itself of vice must pardon beg,

---

① **This bodiless … cunning in:** Madness is skillful in this invisible creation.
② **temperately:** regularly
③ **reword:** repeat word by word
④ **gambol from:** (of horses) shy away
⑤ **love of grace:** God's grace
⑥ **flattering unction:** healing ointment, soothing salve
⑦ **Lay … soul:** Don't falsely comfort yourself by saying
⑧ **skin and film:** cover thinly, scab over
⑨ **ulcerous place:** rotten soul
⑩ **mining:** undermining
⑪ **what is to come:** i.e. future sin
⑫ **compost:** fertilizer
⑬ **ranker:** more luxuriant
⑭ **fatness:** grossness
⑮ **pursy:** fat, panting

Yea, curb[1] and woo for leave[2] to do him good.
QUEEN
O Hamlet, thou hast cleft my heart in twain![3]
HAMLET
O, throw away the worser[4] part of it,
And live the purer with the other half.
175 Good night—but go not to mine uncle's bed.
Assume a virtue if you have it not.
That monster, custom, who all sense[5] doth eat[6],[7]
Of habits devil[8], is angel[9] yet in this,
That to the use[10] of actions fair and good
180 He likewise gives a frock or livery[11],
That aptly[12] is put on[13],[14] Refrain tonight,
And that shall lend a kind of easiness
To the next abstinence; the next more easy;
For use[15] almost can change the stamp of nature,[16]
185 And either [...][17] the devil or throw him out

---

[1] **curb:** bow low
[2] **leave:** permission
[3] **O ... twain:** Cf. 105: "These words like daggers enter in mine ears."
[4] **worser:** worse
[5] **sense:** sensitivity (to wicked practices)
[6] **eat:** destroy, consume
[7] **That ... eat:** Proverbial: Custom makes sin no sin.
[8] **devil:** evil
[9] **angel:** angelic
[10] **use:** habit, practice
[11] **frock or livery:** coat or uniform
[12] **aptly:** easily
[13] **aptly put on:** fits well
[14] **That monster ... put on:** customs make bad ways acceptable and lead to the adaptation of good ways
[15] **use:** habit
[16] **use ... nature:** Habit is another nature.
[17] **[...]:** a lacuna, presumably "shame" or "master"

With wondrous① potency②. Once more, good night,
And when you are desirous③ to be blest,
I'll blessing beg④ of you. For⑤ this same lord⑥,
I do repent; but heaven hath pleased it so⑦
190 To punish me with this⑧ and this with me⑨,
That I must be their⑩ scourge and minister⑪.
I will bestow⑫ him, and will answer⑬ well
The death I gave him. So again, good night.
I must be cruel only to be kind.
195 Thus bad⑭ begins and worse remains behind⑮.
One word more, good lady.
QUEEN
What shall I do?
HAMLET
Not this, by no means, that I bid you do:⑯
Let the bloat⑰ king tempt you again to bed,
200 Pinch wanton⑱ on your cheek, call you his mouse⑲,

---

① **wondrous:** remarkable
② **potency:** power
③ **are desirous:** want
④ **beg:** beg blessing
⑤ **For:** as for
⑥ **this same lord:** i.e. Polonius
⑦ **heaven hath pleased it so:** such is heaven's pleasure
⑧ **this:** presumably the killing of Polonius
⑨ **this with me:** punish this with me
⑩ **their:** heaven's
⑪ **scourge and minister:** punishment and agent
⑫ **bestow:** remove, dispose of
⑬ **answer:** answer for
⑭ **bad:** the killing of Polonius
⑮ **remains behind:** is yet to come
⑯ **Not this … you do:** Don't do the following things
⑰ **bloat:** fat, bloated with drinking
⑱ **wanton:** amorously
⑲ **mouse:** term of endearment

And let him, for a pair of reechy[1] kisses
Or paddling[2] in your neck with his damned fingers,
Make you to ravel[3] all this matter out
That I essentially[4] am not in madness,
205 But mad in craft[5]. 'Twere good you let him know,
For who that's but a queen, fair, sober, wise[6],
Would from a paddock[7], from a bat, a gib[8],
Such dear[9] concernings[10] hide? Who would do so?
No, in despite of sense and secrecy[11],
210 Unpeg[12] the basket[13] on the house's top,
Let the birds fly, and like the famous ape,[14]
To try conclusions[15], in the basket creep,
And break your own neck down[16].[17]

QUEEN
Be thou assured, if words be made of breath
215 And breath of life, I have no life to breathe
What thou hast said to me.

---

[1] **reechy:** reeking, foul-smelling
[2] **paddling:** stroking
[3] **ravel:** unravel
[4] **essentially:** really
[5] **craft:** cunning
[6] **fair, sober, wise:** post attributive
[7] **paddock:** toad
[8] **gib:** tomcat (Claudius)
[9] **dear:** valuable, important
[10] **concernings:** matters
[11] **sense and secrecy:** your promise of sense and secrecy
[12] **unpeg:** unfasten
[13] **basket:** cage
[14] **like the famous ape:** The story Hamlet alludes to is lost.
[15] **try conclusions:** make an experiment
[16] **down:** by the fall; utterly
[17] **break ... down:** you'll be killed if you leak the information.

HAMLET

I must to England, you know that?

QUEEN

Alack[①],

I had forgot! 'Tis so concluded on[②].

HAMLET

220 There's letters sealed;[③] and my two schoolfellows,

Whom I will trust as I will adders fanged,

They bear the mandate[④];[⑤] they must sweep my way[⑥],

And marshal[⑦] me to knavery[⑧]. Let it[⑨] work;

For 'tis the sport to have the enginer[⑩]

225 Hoist[⑪] with his own petard[⑫]; and 't shall go hard

But I will[⑬] delve[⑭] one yard below their mines,

And blow them at[⑮] the moon. O, 'tis most sweet,

When in one line two crafts[⑯] directly meet[⑰].

This man[⑱] shall set me packing[⑲].

---

① **Alack:** alas
② **concluded on:** decided
③ **letters sealed:** perhaps taken from Polonius' pocket
④ **mandate:** order
⑤ **220—222:** How could Hamlet have known it?
⑥ **sweep my way:** prepare the way for me
⑦ **marshal:** lead
⑧ **knavery:** trick (intended for me)
⑨ **it:** the plot
⑩ **enginer:** engineer, maker of military devices
⑪ **Hoist:** hoisted, blown up
⑫ **petard:** bomb, landmine
⑬ **'t shall go hard But I will:** it will be hard luck if I do not; with any luck, I will
⑭ **delve:** dig
⑮ **at:** to
⑯ **crafts:** schemes
⑰ **directly meet:** meet head-on
⑱ **This man:** Polonius
⑲ **packing:** leaving at once; carrying off a burden (Polonius' body); plotting

230 I'll lug[1] the guts[2] into the neighbor room.
　　Mother, good night. Indeed this counselor[3]
　　Is now most still, most secret and most grave,
　　Who was in life a foolish prating[4] knave.[5]
　　Come, sir[6], to draw toward an end with you[7].
235 Good night, mother.
　　Exeunt [HAMLET tugging in POLONIUS]

① **lug:** pull, tug
② **the guts:** the body
③ **this counselor:** Polonius
④ **prating:** chattering
⑤ **Who ... knave:** Cf. II. ii. 233: "These tedious old fools!"
⑥ **Sir:** ie. Polonius
⑦ **draw ... you:** make an end of my business with you; drag you towards your grave

ACT IV
SCENE I. A room in the castle.

Enter KING, QUEEN, ROSENCRANTZ, and GUILDENSTERN

KING

There's matter① in these sighs, these profound② syllable heaves③
You must translate④; 'tis fit we understand them.
Where is your son?

QUEEN

Bestow this place on us⑤ a little while.

Exeunt ROSENCRANTZ and GUILDENSTERN

5 Ah, my good lord, what have I seen tonight!

KING

What, Gertrude? How does Hamlet?

QUEEN

Mad as the sea and wind, when both contend
Which is the mightier. In his lawless⑥ fit⑦,
Behind the arras hearing something stir,
10 Whips out his rapier, cries, 'A rat, a rat!'
And, in this brainish apprehension⑧, kills⑨
The unseen⑩ good old man.

---

① **matter:** meaning, significance
② **profound:** accented on the first
③ **profound syllable heaves:** heavings of the breast, sob
④ **translate:** interpret
⑤ **Bestow this place on us:** leave us alone
⑥ **lawless:** unruly
⑦ **fit:** attack of epilepsy
⑧ **brainish apprehension:** brain-sick fancy
⑨ **kills:** whips, cries, kills (dramatic present)
⑩ **unseen:** hidden

KING

O heavy[1] deed!

It had been so with us, had we[2] been there.

15 His liberty is full of threats to all—

To you yourself, to us, to every one.

Alas, how shall this bloody deed be answered[3]?

It will be laid to us[4], whose providence[5]

Should have kept short[6], restrained and out of haunt[7],

20 This mad young man. But so much was our love,

We would not[8] understand what was most fit,

But, like the owner of a foul disease,

To keep it from divulging[9], let it feed

Even on the pith[10] of life. Where is he gone?

QUEEN

25 To draw apart the body he hath killed,

O'er whom his very madness, like some ore[11]

Among a mineral[12] of metals base[13],

Shows itself pure: he weeps for what is done.[14]

KING

O Gertrude, come away!

---

[1] **heavy:** grievous, dreadful
[2] **we, us:** the royal plural
[3] **answered:** accounted for, explained
[4] **laid to us:** blamed on me, charged against me
[5] **providence:** foresight, forethought
[6] **kept short:** closely reined
[7] **out of haunt:** away from others
[8] **would not:** chose not to
[9] **divulging:** being made known, coming to light
[10] **pith:** essence
[11] **ore:** deposit or vein of gold (i.e. reason)
[12] **mineral:** mine
[13] **metals base:** passion, madness
[14] **25—28:** She is trying to protect Hamlet.

30　　The sun no sooner shall the mountains touch,①
　　　But we will ship him hence; and this vile deed
　　　We must with all our majesty② and skill
　　　Both countenance③ and excuse④. Ho, Guildenstern!
　　　Enter ROSENCRANTZ and GUILDENSTERN
　　　Friends both, go join you with some further aid⑤.
35　　Hamlet in madness hath Polonius slain,
　　　And from his mother's closet hath he dragged him.
　　　Go seek him out, speak fair⑥, and bring the body
　　　Into the chapel. I pray you, haste in this.
　　　Exeunt ROSENCRANTZ and GUILDENSTERN
　　　Come, Gertrude, we'll call up our wisest friends
40　　And let them know, both what we mean to do
　　　And what's untimely done […]⑦.
　　　Whose whisper⑧ o'er the world's diameter⑨,
　　　As level as⑩ the cannon to his blank⑪,
　　　Transports his poisoned shot, may miss our name⑫
45　　And hit the woundless⑬ air. O, come away!
　　　My soul is full of discord and dismay.
　　　Exeunt

---

① **The sun ... touch:** as soon as dawn breaks
② **majesty:** royal authority
③ **countenance:** face out, approve
④ **excuse:** offer justification
⑤ **go ... aid:** find others to help you
⑥ **speak fair:** address him courteously
⑦ **[…]:** a lacuna (Edward Capell suggested "so haply slander")
⑧ **Whose whisper:** the rumor of which deed
⑨ **o'er the world's diameter:** throughout the world
⑩ **As level as:** as well-aimed as
⑪ **blank:** target
⑫ **miss our name:** avoid hurting my reputation
⑬ **woundless:** invulnerable

SCENE II. Another room in the castle.

Enter HAMLET

HAMLET
Safely stowed①.
GENTLEMEN
[*Within*] Hamlet! Lord Hamlet!
HAMLET
What noise? Who calls on Hamlet?
O, here they come.
Enter ROSENCRANTZ and GUILDENSTERN
ROSENCRANTZ
5 What have you done, my lord, with the dead body?
HAMLET
Compounded② it with dust, whereto 'tis kin.③
ROSENCRANTZ
Tell us where 'tis, that④ we may take it thence
And bear it to the chapel.
HAMLET
Do not believe it.
ROSENCRANTZ
10 Believe what?
HAMLET
That I can keep your counsel⑤ and not mine own.

---

① **stowed:** put away; hidden
② **Compounded:** mixed, combined
③ **Compounded … kin:** Cf. *Genesis* 3:19: "You are dust, and to dust you shall return."
④ **that:** so that
⑤ **counsel:** secret (that you are agents for the King)

Besides, to be demanded of① a sponge, what replication② should be made by the son of a king?

ROSENCRANTZ

Take you me for a sponge, my lord?

HAMLET

15 Ay, sir, that soaks up the King's countenance③, his rewards, his authorities. But such officers do the King best service in the end. He keeps them, like an ape④, in the corner of his jaw⑤, first mouthed, to be last swallowed. When he needs what you have
20 gleaned⑥, it is but squeezing you, and, sponge, you shall be dry again.

ROSENCRANTZ

I understand you not, my lord.

HAMLET

I am glad of it: a knavish⑦ speech sleeps in a foolish ear⑧.

ROSENCRANTZ

25 My lord, you must tell us where the body is and go with us to the King.

HAMLET

The body is with⑨ the King, but the King is not with the body. The King is a thing—

---

① **demanded of:** questioned by
② **replication:** reply
③ **countenance:** favorable looks
④ **an ape:** as an ape does
⑤ **the corner of his jaw:** cheek pouch
⑥ **gleaned:** collected, gathered
⑦ **knavish:** wicked
⑧ **sleeps ... foolish ear:** is not understood by a foolish person
⑨ **with:** supports, follows

GUILDENSTERN

A thing, my lord!

HAMLET

30 Of nothing.[1] Bring me to him. Hide fox, and all after.[2]

Exeunt

SCENE III. Another room in the castle.

Enter KING, attended

KING

I have sent to seek him and to find the body.
How dangerous is it that this man goes loose![3]
Yet must not we put the strong law on him[4].
He's loved of[5] the distracted[6] multitude[7],
5 Who like not in their judgment, but their eyes;[8]
And where 'tis so, the offender's scourge[9] is weighed[10],
But never the offence[11]. To bear all[12] smooth and even,
This sudden sending him away must seem
Deliberate pause[13]. Diseases desperate grown

---

[1] **Of nothing:** Cf. *Psalms* 144: 4: "They (*i.e.* mortals) are like a breath; their days are like a passing shadow."
[2] **Hide fox, and all after:** people say this in playing hide-and-seek.
[3] **How ... loose:** Cf. III. i. 200: "Madness in great ones must not unwatched go."
[4] **put the strong law on him:** punish him to the full extent of the law
[5] **of:** by
[6] **distracted:** confused
[7] **multitude:** populace, mass
[8] **Who like ... eyes:** who approve by appearance rather than judgment
[9] **scourge:** punishment
[10] **weighed:** taken seriously
[11] **offence:** crime
[12] **bear all:** manage everything
[13] **Deliberate pause:** the result of careful thought; deliberate suspension of judgment

10 By desperate appliance① are relieved,②
Or not at all.
Enter ROSENCRANTZ
How now! What hath befallen③?
ROSENCRANTZ
Where the dead body is bestowed, my lord,
We cannot get from him.
KING
15 But where is he?
ROSENCRANTZ
Without④, my lord; guarded, to know your pleasure.
KING
Bring him before us.
ROSENCRANTZ
Ho, Guildenstern! Bring in my lord.
Enter HAMLET and GUILDENSTERN
KING
Now, Hamlet, where's Polonius?
HAMLET
20 At supper.⑤
KING
At supper? Where?
HAMLET
Not where he eats, but where he is eaten. A certain

---

① **appliance:** application, remedies
② **By desperate ... relieved:** A desperate disease must have a desperate cure.
③ **befallen:** happened
④ **Without:** outside
⑤ **At supper:** dead (Cf. *Revelation* 19:9: "Blessed are those who are invited to the marriage supper of the Lamb.")

convocation of politic[1] worms[2] are e'en[3] at him. Your worm is your only emperor for diet[4]. We fat[5] all
25 creatures else to fat us, and we fat ourselves for maggots. Your fat king and your lean beggar is but variable service[6]—two dishes, but to one table. That's the end.

KING

Alas, alas!

HAMLET

30 A man may fish with the worm that hath eat[7] of a king, and eat of the fish that hath fed of[8] that worm.

KING

What dost thou mean by this?

HAMLET

Nothing but to show you how a king may go a progress[9] through the guts of a beggar.

KING

35 Where is Polonius?

HAMLET

In heaven. Send hither to see. If your messenger find him not there, seek him i' the other place[10] yourself.[11]

---

[1] **politic:** shrewd, scheming
[2] **A certain ... worms:** Perhaps a reference to the Diet (council) of Worms (a German city), a meeting of high church officials summoned in 1521 by Holy Roman Emperor Charles V to question and condemn Martin Luther.
[3] **e'en:** even now
[4] **Your ... diet:** for even an emperor is food for worms
[5] **fat:** fatten
[6] **variable service:** various courses, two ways of serving the same food
[7] **eat:** eaten
[8] **of:** on
[9] **progress:** royal journey
[10] **the other place:** hell
[11] **seek ... yourself:** "You go to hell!" is understood.

But indeed, if you find him not within this month, you
shall① nose② him as you go up the stairs into the lobby③.
KING
40 Go seek him there.
To some Attendants
HAMLET
He will stay④ till ye come⑤.
Exeunt Attendants
KING
Hamlet, this deed, for thine especial safety—
Which we do tender⑥ as we dearly⑦ grieve
For that which thou hast done—must send thee hence
45 With fiery quickness. Therefore prepare thyself.
The bark⑧ is ready and the wind at help⑨,
The associates tend⑩, and every thing is bent⑪
For England.
HAMLET
For England?⑫
KING
50 Ay, Hamlet.
HAMLET
Good.

---

① **shall:** must
② **nose:** smell
③ **lobby:** anteroom, corridor
④ **stay:** wait
⑤ **come:** die
⑥ **tender:** care for, value highly
⑦ **dearly:** highly; deeply
⑧ **bark:** vessel, sailing ship
⑨ **help:** favorable
⑩ **tend:** attend you, wait for you
⑪ **bent:** prepared
⑫ **For England:** He is presumably expressing sardonic knowingness rather than surprise.

KING

So is it, if thou knew'st our purposes.

HAMLET

I see a cherub[1] that sees them[2]. But come, for England!
Farewell, dear mother.

KING

55 Thy loving father, Hamlet.

HAMLET

My mother! Father and mother is man and wife,
man and wife is one flesh, and so, my mother.
Come, for England!

Exit

KING

Follow him at foot[3]; tempt[4] him with speed aboard;
60 Delay it not. I'll have him hence tonight.
Away! for every thing is sealed and done
That else leans[5] on the affair. Pray you, make haste.

Exeunt ROSENCRANTZ and GUILDENSTERN

And England[6], if my love thou hold'st at aught[7]—
As my great power thereof may give thee sense[8],
65 Since yet thy cicatrice[9] looks raw and red
After the Danish sword, and thy free[10] awe[11]

---

[1] **cherub:** angel (of love) believed to see and know all
[2] **them:** purposes
[3] **at foot:** at his heels, closely
[4] **tempt:** coax, encourage
[5] **leans:** hinges, depends
[6] **England:** King of England
[7] **hold'st at aught:** consider to be of any value
[8] **give thee sense:** make you realize the importance of my love
[9] **cicatrice:** scar, wound
[10] **free:** freely given
[11] **awe:** voluntary submission

Pays homage to us—thou mayst not coldly set①
Our sovereign process②, which imports at full③,
By letters congruing④ to that effect,
70 The present⑤ death of Hamlet.⑥ Do it, England;
For like the hectic⑦ in my blood he rages,
And thou must cure me. Till I know 'tis done,
Howe'er⑧ my haps⑨, my joys were ne'er begun.
Exit

SCENE IV. A plain in Denmark.

Enter FORTINBRAS with his Army over the stage.

PRINCE FORTINBRAS
Go, captain, from me greet the Danish king.
Tell him that, by his license⑩, Fortinbras
Craves the conveyance⑪ of⑫ a promised march
Over⑬ his kingdom. You know the rendezvous⑭.

---

① **coldly set:** regard indifferently, ignore
② **Our sovereign process:** my royal command
③ **imports at full:** fully portends
④ **congruing:** conforming, agreeing
⑤ **present:** instant, immediate
⑥ 63—70: Cf. *The Iliad*, 6.167—170: Bellerophon's story
⑦ **hectic:** fever
⑧ **Howe'er:** however good, whatever
⑨ **haps:** fortunes
⑩ **license:** permission
⑪ **conveyance:** escort
⑫ **of:** during
⑬ **Over:** through
⑭ **the rendezvous:** where we have arranged to meet

5   If that[1] his majesty would aught with us[2],
     We shall express our duty[3] in his eye[4];
     And let him know so[5].

CAPTAIN

I will do't, my lord.

PRINCE FORTINBRAS

Go softly[6] on.

Exeunt all but the Captain.

Enter HAMLET, ROSENCRANTZ, GUILDENSTERN, and others

HAMLET

10   Good sir, whose powers[7] are these?

CAPTAIN

They are of Norway, sir.

HAMLET

How purposed[8], sir, I pray you?

CAPTAIN

Against some part of Poland.

HAMLET

Who commands them, sir?

CAPTAIN

15   The nephew to old Norway, Fortinbras.

HAMLET

Goes it[9] against the main[10] of Poland, sir,

---

[1] **If that:** if
[2] **would aught with us:** wishes anything with me (he uses the royal plural)
[3] **express our duty:** pay our respects
[4] **eye:** presence
[5] **so:** this
[6] **softly:** quietly, slowly
[7] **powers:** forces
[8] **purposed:** what is the purpose
[9] **it:** the troop
[10] **main:** mainland, major part

Or for some frontier[1]?

CAPTAIN

Truly to speak, and with no addition[2],
We go to gain a little patch of ground
20   That hath in it no profit but the name[3].
To pay five ducats, five, I would not farm it;[4]
Nor will it yield to Norway or the Pole[5]
A ranker[6] rate, should it be sold in fee[7].

HAMLET

Why, then the Polack[8] never will defend it.

CAPTAIN

25   Yes, it is already garrisoned.

HAMLET

Two thousand souls and twenty thousand ducats
Will not debate[9] the question of this straw[10].
This is the imposthume[11] of much wealth and peace,
That inward breaks, and shows no cause without[12]
30   Why the man dies.[13] I humbly thank you, sir.

CAPTAIN

God be wi' you, sir.

Exit

---

① **frontier:** border
② **addition** (four syllables): added details, exaggeration
③ **the name:** fame; the mere name of conquest
④ **To ... it:** I would not pay five ducats to rent it
⑤ **the Pole:** King of Poland
⑥ **ranker:** higher
⑦ **in fee:** outright, as a freehold
⑧ **the Polack:** King of Pole
⑨ **debate:** decide, settle
⑩ **straw:** trifle
⑪ **imposthume:** abscess
⑫ **without:** on the outside
⑬ **This is ... the man dies:** i.e. too much wealth and peace lead to war.

ROSENCRANTZ

Wilt please you go, my lord?

HAMLET

I'll be with you straight①. Go a little before.

*Exeunt all but HAMLET.*②

How all occasions③ do inform against④ me,

35 And spur my dull⑤ revenge! What is a man,

If his chief good⑥ and market⑦ of his time⑧

Be but to sleep and feed? A beast, no more.

Sure He⑨ that made us with such large discourse⑩,

Looking before and after⑪, gave us not

40 That capability and god-like reason

To fust⑫ in us unused.⑬ Now, whether it be

Bestial oblivion⑭, or some craven⑮ scruple⑯

Of⑰ thinking too precisely⑱ on the event⑲—

---

① **straight:** immediately
② The following soliloquy is absent not only from the First Quarto but also from the Folio. It exhibits very strikingly his inability to understand why he has delayed so long. (A. C. Bradley: *Shakespearean Tragedy,* p.112 & p.113)
③ **occasions:** occurrences, circumstances
④ **inform against:** accuse, denounce
⑤ **dull:** sluggish
⑥ **good:** welfare
⑦ **market:** profit
⑧ **of his time:** that he sells his time for
⑨ **He:** God
⑩ **large discourse:** great power of reasoning
⑪ **Looking before and after:** that looks into the past and the future
⑫ **fust:** grow stale, decay
⑬ **What is a man …used :** Human beings are different from animals because they are capable of remembering the past and thinking about the future.
⑭ **Bestial oblivion:** forgetfulness characteristic of animals
⑮ **craven:** cowardly
⑯ **scruple:** hesitation
⑰ **Of:** that results from, caused by
⑱ **precisely:** carefully
⑲ **the event:** the outcome

A thought which, quartered①, hath but one part wisdom
45　And ever three parts coward—I do not know
Why yet I live to say 'This thing's to do②,'
Sith③ I have cause and will and strength and means
To do't. Examples gross④ as earth exhort me.
Witness this army of such mass⑤ and charge⑥
50　Led by a delicate and tender prince,⑦
Whose spirit with divine ambition puffed⑧
Makes mouths⑨ at the invisible⑩ event⑪,
Exposing what is mortal and unsure
To all that fortune, death and danger dare,
55　Even for an egg-shell⑫. Rightly to be great
Is not to stir⑬ without great argument⑭,
But greatly to find quarrel in a straw
When honor's at the stake⑮.⑯ How stand I then,
That have a father killed, a mother stained⑰,
60　Excitements⑱ of my reason and my blood,

---

① **quartered**: divide into four parts
② **to do**: to be done
③ **Sith**: since
④ **gross**: large; obvious, evident
⑤ **mass**: size
⑥ **charge**: expense
⑦ **a delicate and tender prince**: Cf. I. i. 109—110: "young Fortinbras, / of unimproved mettle, hot and full" etc.
⑧ **puffed**: swelled, inflated
⑨ **mouths**: mocks
⑩ **invisible**: unforeseeable
⑪ **event**: result, outcome
⑫ **egg-shell**: a small patch of land (Cf. Lucian: *Icaromenippus*, 18: "Then I looked at the Peloponnese, my eyes fell on the Cynurian district, and the thought occurred that it was for this little plot, no broader than an Egyptian lentil, that all those Argives and Spartans fell in a single day.")
⑬ **stir**: take up arms
⑭ **argument**: matter of contention, cause for resentment
⑮ **at the stake**: at risk
⑯ **Rightly … stake**: "The truly great man will stir when his honor is being challenged."
⑰ **stained**: dishonored
⑱ **Excitements**: motives to incite

And let all sleep, while to my shame I see
The imminent death of twenty thousand men
That for a fantasy① and trick② of③ fame④
Go to their graves like beds, fight for a plot⑤
65 Whereon the numbers⑥ cannot try the cause⑦,
Which is not tomb enough and continent⑧
To hide⑨ the slain⑩? O, from this time forth
My thoughts be bloody or be nothing worth!
Exit

SCENE V. Elsinore. A room in the castle.

Enter QUEEN, HORATIO, and a Gentleman

QUEEN
I will not speak with her.
GENTLEMAN
She is importunate⑪, indeed distract⑫.
Her mood⑬ will need⑭ be pitied.

---

① **fantasy:** illusion, fanciful notion
② **trick:** imposture
③ **of:** regarding
④ **fame:** honor
⑤ **plot:** piece of land
⑥ **numbers:** soldiers
⑦ **cannot try the cause:** haven't the room to fight
⑧ **continent:** container
⑨ **hide:** hold, provide burial space for
⑩ **slain:** dead soldiers
⑪ **importunate:** persistent in her demands
⑫ **distract:** insane, distraught
⑬ **mood:** state of mind
⑭ **will need:** must necessarily

QUEEN
What would she have?[1]
GENTLEMAN
5　She speaks much of her father, says she hears
　　There's tricks[2] i' the world[3], and hems[4], and beats her heart,
　　Spurns enviously[5] at straws[6], speaks things in doubt[7]
　　That carry but half sense. Her speech is nothing[8],
　　Yet the unshapèd use of it[9] doth move[10]
10　The hearers to collection[11]. They aim[12] at it,
　　And botch the words up[13] fit to[14] their own thoughts[15];
　　Which[16], as her winks and nods and gestures yield[17] them,
　　Indeed would make one think there might be thought,
　　Though nothing sure, yet much unhappily[18].[19]
HORATIO
15　'Twere good[20] she were spoken with, for she may strew[21]

---

① **What would she have:** what does she want
② **tricks:** plots, deceptions
③ **There's tricks i' the world:** Cf. III. i. 163: "the fair state"
④ **hems:** makes inarticulate sounds; clears her throat
⑤ **Spurns enviously:** takes offense angrily; reacts suspiciously
⑥ **straws:** trifles, trivial things
⑦ **in doubt:** equivocally, ambiguously
⑧ **nothing:** nonsense
⑨ **the unshapèd use of it:** the formlessness of her speech
⑩ **move:** cause
⑪ **collection:** find coherence, infer conclusions
⑫ **aim:** guess, conjecture ("yawn" in Q2: gape with surprise)
⑬ **botch ... up:** patch together
⑭ **fit to:** to match
⑮ **thoughts:** sense; guesses
⑯ **Which:** her words
⑰ **yield:** render, deliver
⑱ **unhappily:** awkwardly
⑲ **Though ... unhappily:** Ophelia's madness is parallel to Hamlet's, only Hamlet feigns madness, whereas Ophelia is mad indeed.
⑳ **'Twere good:** It'd be good if
㉑ **strew:** spread

Dangerous conjectures in ill-breeding① minds②.

QUEEN

Let her come in.

Exit HORATIO

[*Aside*] To my sick soul (as sin's true nature is③),
Each toy④ seems prologue⑤ to some great amiss⑥.
20 So full of artless jealousy⑦ is guilt,
It spills⑧ itself in fearing to be spilt⑨.⑩

Enter OPHELIA distracted

OPHELIA

Where is the beauteous majesty of Denmark?

QUEEN

How now, Ophelia!

OPHELIA [*Sings*]⑪

How should I your true love know
25 *From another one?*
By his cockle hat and staff,
And his sandal shoon⑫.⑬

---

① **ill-breeding:** fomenting evil
② **ill-breeding minds:** minds prone to evil thoughts
③ **sin's true nature is:** Sin in its true nature is a disease of the soul
④ **toy:** trifle
⑤ **prologue:** prelude
⑥ **amiss:** calamity, disaster, misfortune
⑦ **artless jealousy:** unskilled apprehension, clumsy unreasonable suspicion
⑧ **spills:** destroys
⑨ **spilt:** divulged
⑩ **20—21:** Guilt produces such paranoia that it betrays itself by its very own fear of betrayal.
⑪ What she sings is a version of a popular ballad much quoted elsewhere.
⑫ **shoon:** shoes
⑬ **By ... shoon:** The cockle hat (hat decorated with a cockle shell), the staff and the sandals denoted a pilgrim returning from the shrine of St. James at Compostella in Spanish Galicia. Medieval poets often compared girls to saints, and her wooers to pilgrims.

QUEEN

Alas, sweet lady, what imports① this song?

OPHELIA

Say you②? Nay, pray you, mark③.

[*Sings*]

30 He is dead and gone, lady,

He is dead and gone;

At his head a grass-green turf,

At his heels a stone.

O ho!④

QUEEN

35 Nay, but Ophelia—

OPHELIA

Pray you, mark.

[*Sings*]

White his shroud as the mountain snow—

Enter KING

QUEEN

Alas, look here, my lord.

OPHELIA [*Sings*]

Larded⑤ with sweet flowers

40 Which bewept to the grave⑥ did not go

With true-love showers.⑦

KING

How do you, pretty lady?

---

① **imports**: signifies, means
② **Say you**: what did you say
③ **mark**: pay attention
④ **O ho**: a conventional representation of a sigh or groan
⑤ **Larded**: strewn, decorated (culinary term)
⑥ **grave**: Q2 reads "ground"
⑦ **40—41**: No true love tears had been shed over the flowers which went to the grave.

OPHELIA

Well, God 'ild[1] you! They say the owl was a baker's daughter.[2] Lord, we know what we are, but know not what we may be.[3] God be at your table!

KING

Conceit[4] upon[5] her father.

OPHELIA

Pray you, let's have no words of this, but when they ask you what it means, say you this:

[*Sings*]

To-morrow is Saint Valentine's day,
All in the morning betime[6],
And I a maid at your window,
To be your Valentine[7].
Then up he rose, and donned[8] his clo'es[9],
And dupped[10] the chamber-door;
Let in the maid, that out a maid
Never departed more.[11]

KING

---

[1] **God 'ild:** yield; reward
[2] **the owl ... daughter:** Here is a story of transformation: a baker's daughter refused bread to Jesus, who turned her into an owl.
[3] **we know ... be:** Cf. I. v. 185—186: "There are more things in heaven and earth, Horatio, / Than are dreamt of in your philosophy."
[4] **conceit:** thinking, fantasies
[5] **upon:** about
[6] **betime:** early
[7] **Valentine:** lover
[8] **donned:** put on, dressed
[9] **clo'es:** clothes
[10] **dupped:** opened
[11] **49—56:** The song alludes to the ancient custom that the first girl a man sees on Valentine's Day is to be his true lover.

Pretty Ophelia!①

OPHELIA

Indeed, without an oath, I'll make an end on't②:

*Sings*③

By Gis④ and by Saint Charity,

60　Alack, and fie for shame!

Young men will do't, if they come to't⑤;

By Cock⑥, they are to blame.

Quoth she, before you tumbled⑦ me,

You promised me to wed.

65　So would I ha' done, by yonder sun,

An⑧ thou hadst not come to my bed.

KING

How long hath she been thus?

OPHELIA

I hope all will be well. We must be patient, but I cannot choose but weep⑨ to think they should lay him⑩ i' the

70　cold ground. My brother shall know of it. And so I thank you for your good counsel. Come, my coach! Good night, ladies. Good night, sweet ladies⑪. Good night, good night.

Exit

---

　① **Pretty Ophelia:** Here Claudius shows his humanity (Cf. 73—84: "poor Ophelia" etc.; 207: "I must commune with your grief")

　② **on't:** of it

　③ What follows is a story about an abandoned girl.

　④ **Gis:** Jesus

　⑤ **do't, if they come to 't:** have sex when opportunity offers

　⑥ **Cock:** God; penis

　⑦ **tumbled:** had sex with, fucked

　⑧ **An:** if

　⑨ **cannot choose but weep:** can not help weeping

　⑩ **him:** i.e. Polonius

　⑪ **ladies:** Are there other ladies? Why does Ophelia only address them?

KING

Follow her close①; give her good watch, I pray you.

Exit HORATIO

O, this is the poison of deep grief②. It springs
75 All from her father's death. O Gertrude, Gertrude,③
When sorrows come, they come not single spies
But in battalions④.⑤ First, her father slain;
Next, your son gone, and he most violent author⑥
Of his own just⑦ remove⑧; the people muddied⑨,
80 Thick⑩ and unwholesome in their thoughts and whispers
For⑪ good Polonius' death, and we have done but greenly⑫
In hugger-mugger⑬ to inter⑭ him; poor Ophelia
Divided from herself and her fair judgment⑮,
Without the which⑯ we are pictures or mere beasts;
85 Last, and as much containing⑰ as all these,
Her brother is in secret come from France,

---

① **close:** secretly
② **poison of deep grief:** So Ophelia dies metaphorically of poison, as old Hamlet, the Queen, the King, Laertes and Hamlet die literally by it.
③ **O Gertrude, Gertrude:** Cf. 92: "O my dear Gertrude"
④ **battalions:** large armies
⑤ **When ... battalions:** Cf. IV. vii. 177: "One woe doth tread upon another's heel."
⑥ **anthor:** cause, executor
⑦ **just:** justified, deserved
⑧ **remove:** removal
⑨ **muddied:** confused, stirred up
⑩ **Thick:** stupid
⑪ **For:** because of
⑫ **greenly:** foolishly
⑬ **hugger-mugger:** secretly and hastily
⑭ **inter:** bury
⑮ **Divided ... judgment:** driven mad
⑯ **the which:** which (judgment, reason)
⑰ **containing:** comprising, importing

Feeds on his wonder①, keeps himself in clouds②
And wants not buzzers③ to infect his ear
With pestilent speeches of his father's death,
90 Wherein necessity, of matter④ beggared,⑤
Will nothing stick⑥ our person to arraign⑦
In ear and ear⑧. O my dear Gertrude, this⑨,
Like to a murdering piece⑩, in many places
Gives me superfluous death⑪.

A noise within

QUEEN

95 Alack, what noise is this?

KING

Where are my Switzers⑫? Let them guard the door.

Enter a Messenger.

What is the matter?

Gentleman

Save yourself, my lord.
The ocean, overpeering⑬ of his list⑭,
100 Eats not⑮ the flats⑯ with more impetuous haste

---

① **Feeds on his wonder:** finds food (for revenge) in these amazing events
② **clouds:** conjecture, suspicion
③ **wants not buzzers:** lacks no gossipers
④ **matter:** substantial evidence
⑤ **Wherein necessity, of matter beggared:** driven by necessity for lacking facts
⑥ **Will nothing stick:** will in no way refuse, will not scruple
⑦ **our person to arraign:** to accuse me
⑧ **In ear and ear:** one ear after another, in every ear
⑨ **this:** all of these things
⑩ **murdering piece:** small cannon scattering grapeshot when fired 霰弹炮
⑪ **Gives me superfluous death:** kills me over and over (as if shot by a murdering piece)
⑫ **Switzers:** Swiss guards (mercenary soldiers)
⑬ **overpeering:** looking over its shore; overflowing
⑭ **list:** shores, limits
⑮ **Eats not:** doesn't consume (submerge)
⑯ **flats:** low-lying land, beach

Than young Laertes, in a riotous① head②,
O'erbears③ your officers. The rabble④ call him 'lord',
And, as⑤ the world were now but to begin,
Antiquity forgot⑥, custom not known⑦,
105 The ratifiers and props of every word,⑧
They cry 'Choose we, Laertes shall be king!'
Caps, hands, and tongues, applaud it to the clouds,
'Laertes shall be king, Laertes king!'⑨

QUEEN
How cheerfully on the false trail⑩ they cry⑪!
110 O, this is counter⑫, you false Danish dogs!⑬

KING
The doors are broke⑭.

Noise within

Enter LAERTES, armed; Danes following

LAERTES
Where is this king? Sirs, stand you all without.

Danes
No, let's come in.

---

① **riotous:** rebellious
② **head:** armed band
③ **O'erbears:** overpowers
④ **rabble:** the *hoi polloi*
⑤ **as:** as if
⑥ **forgot:** forgotten
⑦ **not known:** forgotten
⑧ **The ratifiers ... word:** assuming the right to ratify and support any suggestion
⑨ **Laertes shall be king, Laertes king!:** a familiar scene of riot and rebellion: now Denmark is headed for a civil war. Who's to blame?
⑩ **trail:** scent
⑪ **cry:** bark (like hunting dogs)
⑫ **counter:** the wrong direction
⑬ **you false Danish dogs:** Her curse bespeaks a foreign consort.
⑭ **broken:** broken

LAERTES

I pray you, give me leave①.

Danes

115 We will, we will.

Exeunt his Followers.

LAERTES

I thank you. Keep② the door. O thou vile③ king,

Give me my father!

QUEEN

Calmly, good Laertes.

LAERTES

That drop of blood that's calm proclaims me bastard,

120 Cries cuckold④ to my father, brands the harlot⑤

Even here, between⑥ the chaste unsmirchèd⑦ brow

Of my true⑧ mother.⑨

KING

What is the cause, Laertes,

That thy rebellion looks so giant-like⑩?

125 Let him go, Gertrude. Do not fear⑪ our person.

There's such divinity doth hedge⑫ a king,

That treason can but peep to⑬ what it would,

---

① **give me leave:** leave me alone with the King
② **keep:** guard
③ **vile:** wicked
④ **cuckold:** betrayed husband
⑤ **harlot:** prostitute
⑥ **between:** in the middle of
⑦ **unsmirchèd:** unstained, unsullied
⑧ **true:** faithful, chaste
⑨ **the chaste ... mother:** His words must tent Gertrude to the quick.
⑩ **giant-like:** huge
⑪ **fear:** fear for
⑫ **hedge:** defend, protect
⑬ **peep to:** look at from a distance

Acts[1] little of his[2] will[3].[4] Tell me, Laertes,
Why thou art thus incensed. Let him go, Gertrude.
130 Speak, man.
LAERTES
Where is my father?
KING
Dead.
QUEEN
But not by him!
KING
Let him demand his fill.
LAERTES
135 How came he dead? I'll not be juggled with[5].
To hell, allegiance[6]! Vows, to the blackest devil!
Conscience and grace[7], to the profoundest pit[8]!
I dare damnation. To this point I stand[9],
That both the worlds[10] I give to negligence[11],[12]
140 Let come what comes, only I'll be revenged
Most thoroughly for my father.
KING
Who shall stay[13] you?

---

[1] **Acts:** is able to perform
[2] **his:** its
[3] **will:** desires
[4] **126—128:** Cf. *Richard II,* III. ii. 54—62: "The breath of worldly men cannot depose / The deputy elected by the Lord" etc.
[5] **juggled with:** trifled with, manipulated, cheated
[6] **allegiance:** both to God and King
[7] **Conscience and grace:** regard for God's laws
[8] **the profoundest pit:** hell
[9] **To this point I stand:** I am firm in this resolve
[10] **both the worlds:** this world and the next
[11] **give to negligence:** disregard
[12] **both ... negligence:** Cf. Hamlet: "To be, or not to be, that is the question."
[13] **stay:** hinder, prevent

LAERTES

My will, not all the world①!

And for② my means, I'll husband③ them so well,

They shall go far with little.

KING

Good Laertes,

If you desire to know the certainty

Of your dear father's death, is't writ in④ your revenge,

That, swoopstake⑤, you will draw⑥ both friend and foe,

150 Winner and loser?⑦

LAERTES

None but his enemies.⑧

KING

Will you know them then?

LAERTES

To his good friends thus wide I'll ope⑨ my arms;

And like the kind life-rendering pelican,⑩

155 Repast⑪ them with my blood.

KING

Why, now you speak

Like a good child and a true gentleman.⑫

---

① **My will, not all the world:** It is my will, not all the world that shall stay me.
② **for:** as for
③ **husband:** entrench, use economically
④ **writ in:** required by
⑤ **swoopstake:** as in a sweepstake
⑥ **draw:** Q1: draw at (= draw your sword on)
⑦ **is't ... loser:** Do you expect to revenge indiscriminately?
⑧ **None but his enemies:** I'll be revenged upon none but his enemies.
⑨ **ope:** open
⑩ **the kind life-rendering pelican:** The mother pelican was thought to feed her young with her own blood taken from her breast with her beak. Cf. *King Lear*, III. iv. 75 & *Richard II*, II. i. 126.
⑪ **Repast:** feed
⑫ **Like ... gentleman:** Now the King speaks like a loving parent and a true friend.

That I am guiltless of your father's death,
And am most sensibly① in grief for it,
160 It shall as level② to your judgment pierce
As day does to your eye.

Danes
[*Within*] Let her come in.

LAERTES
How now? What noise is that?
Enter OPHELIA
O heat, dry up my brains! Tears seven③ times salt,
165 Burn out the sense and virtue④ of mine eye!
By heaven, thy madness shall be paid by weight
Till our scale turn the beam⑤. O rose of May!
Dear maid, kind sister, sweet Ophelia!
O heavens! is't possible a young maid's wits
170 Should be as mortal⑥ as an old man's life?
Nature is fine⑦ in⑧ love, and where 'tis fine⑨,
It sends some precious instance⑩ of itself⑪
After the thing it loves.⑫

OPHELIA [*Sings*]
They bore him barefaced⑬ on the bier⑭;

---

① **sensibly:** feelingly, intensely
② **level:** clear, plain
③ **seven:** many
④ **virtue:** faculty, power
⑤ **paid ... beam:** avenged (he asserts the Senecan view that revenge has to outdo the original crime.)
⑥ **mortal:** short-lived
⑦ **fine:** refined
⑧ **in:** by
⑨ **fine:** refined
⑩ **instance:** sample, proof
⑪ **precious ... itself:** its refined nature
⑫ **172—173:** Ophelia's nature has sent her wits after her father in proof of love.
⑬ ***They bore him barefaced*:** i.e. There is no coffin or that the coffin is open.
⑭ **bier:** stretcher or litter on which a corpse is carried

175　*Hey non nonny, nonny, hey nonny;*
　　And in his grave rained many a tear.
　　*Fare you well, my dove*①*!*

LAERTES

Hadst thou thy wits② and didst persuade revenge,
It could not move③ thus.

OPHELIA

180　You must sing 'a-down a-down', An④ you, 'Call him
　　a-down-a'.⑤ O, how the wheel⑥ becomes⑦ it! It is the
　　false steward⑧ that stole his master's daughter⑨.

LAERTES

This nothing's more than matter⑩.

OPHELIA

There's rosemary⑪, that's for remembrance. Pray you,
185　love, remember. And there is pansies⑫, that's for thoughts.

LAERTES

A document⑬ in madness! Thoughts and remembrance fitted⑭.

---

① **my dove:** She is perhaps mistaking Laertes for Hamlet.
② **Hadst thou thy wits:** even if you had your wits
③ **move:** move me
④ **An:** if
⑤ **You ... a-down-a:** Both are refrains in a song.
⑥ **the wheel:** the tune of the ballad; the wheel of fortune; the spinning wheel
⑦ **becomes:** fits
⑧ **steward:** Presumably she refers to Hamlet.
⑨ **daughter:** Presumably she refers to herself.
⑩ **This ... matter:** this nonsense is more moving than sensible speech
⑪ **rosemary:** 迷迭香
⑫ **pansies:** 三色堇 (French: *pensées*)
⑬ **document:** object lesson, instruction
⑭ **fitted:** put together appropriately; would be fitting for me

OPHELIA

There's fennel① for you, and columbines②. There's rue③ for you, and here's some for me. We may call it herb-grace o'Sundays④. O you must wear your rue with a difference⑤! There's a daisy⑥.
190 I would give you some violets⑦, but they withered all when my father died. They say he made a good end.

Sings

For bonny⑧ sweet Robin is all my joy.

LAERTES

Thought⑨ and affliction, passion⑩, hell itself,
She turns to favor⑪ and to prettiness.

OPHELIA [*Sings*]
195 *And will he not come again?*
And will he not come again?
No, no, he is dead;
Go to thy deathbed;
He never will come again.
200 *His beard was as white as snow,*
All flaxen⑫ was his poll⑬.⑭
He is gone, he is gone,

---

① **fennel:** symbol of flattery and deceit
② **columbines:** symbol of disloyalty
③ **rue:** symbol of sorrow or repentance
④ **o'Sundays:** on Sundays
⑤ **with a difference:** (heraldic term) for a variation of arms to distinguish one branch of family from another; for a different reason
⑥ **daisy:** symbol of dissembling
⑦ **violets:** symbol of faithfulness
⑧ **bonny:** stout
⑨ **Thought:** melancholy, sorrow
⑩ **passion:** suffering, grief
⑪ **favor:** charm, attractiveness
⑫ **flaxen:** pale-yellow
⑬ **poll:** head
⑭ **201:** His hair is as white as flax.

205 And we cast away moan.①

God 'a'② mercy on his soul!

And of all Christian souls, I pray God. God be wi' ye.

Exit

LAERTES

Do you see this, O God?

KING

Laertes, I must commune③ with④ your grief,

Or⑤ you deny me right⑥. Go but apart⑦,

Make choice of whom⑧ your wisest friends you will,

210 If by direct or by collateral⑨ hand

They find us⑩ touched⑪, we will our kingdom give,

Our crown, our life, and all that we call ours,

To you in satisfaction⑫; but if not,

Be you content to lend your patience to us,

215 And we shall jointly labor with your soul

To give it due content.

LAERTES

Let this be so.

His means of death, his obscure⑬ funeral—

---

① ***we cast away moan***: we waste (or throw away) our mourning
② ***'a'***: have
③ ***commune***: accented on the first syllable
④ ***commune with***: participate in; converse with
⑤ ***Or***: unless
⑥ 207—208: I have an undeniable right to talk to you in your grief
⑦ ***Go but apart***: Let us discuss this privately somewhere else
⑧ ***of whom***: which of
⑨ ***collateral***: indirect
⑩ ***us***: the royal plural
⑪ ***touched***: implicated in the crime
⑫ ***satisfaction***: payment, reparation
⑬ ***obscure***: accented on the first syllable

220　No trophy①, sword, nor hatchment② o'er his bones,
　　　No noble rite nor formal ostentation③—
　　　Cry④ to be heard, as 'twere from heaven to earth,
　　　That⑤ I must call't in question⑥.
　　KING
　　So you shall;
　　And where the offence is let the great axe⑦ fall.
225　I pray you, go with me.
　　Exeunt

SCENE VI. Another room in the castle.

Enter HORATIO with an Attendant

HORATIO
What⑧ are they that would speak with me?
Servant
Sailors, sir. They say they have letters for you.
HORATIO
Let them come in.
Exit Attendant
I do not know from what part of the world
5　I should be greeted, if not from Lord Hamlet.

---

　　① **trophy:** memorial
　　② **hatchment:** a panel bearing the arms (blazon) of the dead and then hung over the tomb
　　③ **ostentation:** ceremony (Cf. I. v. 82—83: "Unhouseled, disappointed, unaneled, / No reckoning made")
　　④ **Cry:** demand
　　⑤ **That:** so that
　　⑥ **call't in question:** demand an explanation
　　⑦ **the great axe:** implement of execution, the axe of vengeance
　　⑧ **what:** what sort of men

Enter Sailors

First Sailor

God bless you, sir.

HORATIO

Let him bless thee too.

First Sailor

He shall, sir, an't please him①. There's a letter for
you, sir. It comes from the ambassador② that was bound
for England—if your name be Horatio, as I am let to know③ it is.

HORATIO [*Reads*]④

Horatio, when thou shalt have
overlooked⑤ this, give these fellows some means⑥ to the King.
They have letters for him. Ere we were two days old⑦
at sea, a pirate⑧ of very warlike appointment⑨ gave us
chase. Finding ourselves too slow of sail, we put on
a compelled⑩ valor⑪, and in the grapple⑫ I boarded them.
On the instant they got clear of⑬ our ship; so I alone
became their prisoner. They have dealt with me like
thieves of mercy⑭, but they knew what they did. I am to

---

① **an't please him:** if he like (subjunctive)
② **the ambassador:** i.e. Hamlet (It is likely he has concealed his identity from the sailors.)
③ **let to know:** informed
④ This is the second of the three letters of Hamlet. (The first letter is to his lover Ophelia, the second to his friend Horatio, and the third to his enemy Claudius.)
⑤ **overlooked:** read over
⑥ **means:** means of access, help in approaching
⑦ **were two days old:** had spent two days
⑧ **pirate:** pirate ship
⑨ **appointment:** equipment
⑩ **compelled:** compelled by necessity
⑪ **a compelled valor:** plucked up courage under compulsion
⑫ **in the grapple:** when the two ships were grappled
⑬ **got clear of:** run away from
⑭ **thieves of mercy:** merciful pirates

20　do a good turn[1] for them. Let the King have the letters
　　I have sent, and repair[2] thou to me with as much speed
　　as thou wouldst fly[3] death. I have words to speak in
　　thine ear will[4] make thee dumb; yet are they[5] much too
　　light[6] for the bore[7] of the matter[8]. These good fellows
25　will bring thee where I am[9]. Rosencrantz and
　　Guildenstern hold their course for England. Of them I have
　　much to tell thee. Farewell.
　　He that thou knowest thine[10], HAMLET.
　　Come, I will make you way[11] for these your letters;
30　And do't the speedier that you may direct me
　　To him from whom you brought them.
　　Exeunt

SCENE VII. Another room in the castle.

Enter KING and LAERTES

KING
Now must your conscience my acquaintance[12] seal[13],[14]

---

[1]　**turn:** favor
[2]　**repair:** come
[3]　**fly:** flee
[4]　**will:** which will
[5]　**they:** my words
[6]　**light:** trivial
[7]　**bore:** caliber, importance
[8]　**matter:** subject (Hamlet compares his words to small bullets in a large canon.)
[9]　**where I am:** He is hiding in a secret place.
[10]　**thine:** to be yours
[11]　**way:** means of access, admittance
[12]　**my acquaintance:** verdict of acquittal
[13]　**seal:** confirm
[14]　**my acquaintance seal:** acknowledge my innocence

And you must put me in your heart for friend,
Sith① you have heard, and with a knowing② ear,
That he which③ hath your noble father slain
5 Pursued my life④.
LAERTES
It well appears. But tell me
Why you proceeded not⑤ against these feats⑥,
So crimeful⑦ and so capital⑧ in nature,
As by your safety, wisdom, all things else,
10 You mainly⑨ were stirred up⑩.
KING
O, for two special reasons,
Which may to you perhaps seem much unsinewed⑪,
But yet to me they are strong. The Queen his mother
Lives almost by his looks, and for⑫ myself—
15 My virtue or my plague, be it either which⑬—
She's so conjunctive to⑭ my life and soul,
That, as the star⑮ moves not but in his sphere,

---

① **Sith:** since
② **knowing:** understanding
③ **which:** who
④ **Pursued my life:** tried to kill me
⑤ **proceeded not:** do not take on legal proceedings
⑥ **feats:** deeds
⑦ **crimeful:** criminal
⑧ **capital:** punishable by death, very serious, deadly
⑨ **mainly:** greatly, mightily
⑩ **stirred up:** incited (to take action)
⑪ **unsinewed:** weak
⑫ **for:** as for
⑬ **be it either which:** whichever of the two you may call it
⑭ **conjunctive to:** closely joined to
⑮ **star:** planet

I could not[1] but by her[2]. The other motive[3]
Why to a public count[4] I might[5] not go,
20 Is the great love the general gender[6] bear him;
Who, dipping all his faults in their affection,
Would[7] like the spring that turneth wood to stone,
Convert his gyves[8] to graces[9], so that my arrows,
Too slightly timbered[10] for so loud a wind[11],
25 Would have reverted to my bow again,
And not where I had aimed them.

LAERTES
And so have I a noble father lost,
A sister driven into desperate terms[12],[13]
Whose worth, if praises may go back again[14],
30 Stood challenger on mount of[15] all the age[16]
For her perfections[17]. But my revenge will come.

KING
Break not your sleeps[18] for that. You must not think

---

[1] **could not:** i.e. could not move
[2] **by her:** in her sphere
[3] **motive:** reason
[4] **count:** judgment, accounting
[5] **might:** could
[6] **general gender:** common sort (of people)
[7] **Would:** Q2: work (operate)
[8] **gyves:** fetters; faults
[9] **graces:** honors
[10] **timbered:** shafted
[11] **so loud a wind:** such a fierce opposition
[12] **terms:** condition, circumstances
[13] **And so ... terms:** Cf. IV. iv. 58—59: Hamlet: "How stand I then, / That have a father killed, a mother stained" etc.
[14] **if praises may go back again:** if I may praise her for what she was like before
[15] **on mount of:** on top of
[16] **all the age:** the entire age
[17] **whose ... perfections:** whose worth challenged all the age to equal her excellence
[18] **Break not your sleeps:** do not lose any sleep (i.e. do not worry)

That we① are made of stuff so flat and dull②

That we can let our beard be shook③ with④ danger⑤

35　And think it pastime⑥. You shortly shall hear more⑦.

I loved your father, and we love ourself⑧,

And that, I hope, will teach you to imagine—

Enter a Messenger with letters

How now! What news?

Messenger⑨

Letters, my lord, from Hamlet:

40　This to your majesty, this to the Queen.

KING

From Hamlet! Who brought them?

Messenger

Sailors, my lord, they say. I saw them not.

They were given me by Claudio⑩. He received them

Of⑪ him that brought them⑫.

KING

45　Laertes, you shall hear them. Leave us.

Exit Messenger

*Reads*⑬

---

　　① **we:** the royal plural
　　② **flat and dull:** inert and slow
　　③ **shook:** shaken, plucked
　　④ **with:** by
　　⑤ **we … shook:** Cf. II. ii. 576: Hamlet: "Plucks off my beard and blows it in my face" etc.
　　⑥ **pastime:** harmless sport
　　⑦ **more:** i.e. Hamlet's death
　　⑧ **ourself:** the royal plural
　　⑨ In 18th and 19th century theatrical traditions the messenger was Bernardo.
　　⑩ **Claudio:** Who is this person? It seems to indicate Shakespeare did not actively think of the King as Claudius.
　　⑪ **Of:** from
　　⑫ **them:** the sailors
　　⑬ **Reads:** This is the 3rd and last letter of Hamlet, which implies revenge.

High and mighty, you shall know I am set naked[1] *on your*
kingdom. Tomorrow shall I beg leave[2] *to see your kingly eyes,*
when I shall (first asking your pardon[3] *thereunto*[4]*) recount*
the occasion[5] *of my sudden and more strange*[6] *return. HAMLET.*

50 What should this mean? Are all the rest[7] come back?
Or is it some abuse[8] and no such thing?

LAERTES

Know you the hand[9]?

KING

'Tis Hamlet's character. 'Naked'—
And in a postscript here, he says 'alone.'[10]
55 Can you advise[11] me?

LAERTES

I'm lost in[12] it, my lord. But let him come!
It warms[13] the very sickness in my heart,
That I shall live and tell him to his teeth
'Thus didest[14] thou.'

KING

60 If it be so, Laertes—
As how should it be so? how otherwise?—
Will you be ruled by me?

---

① **naked**: defenseless, unarmed
② **leave**: permission
③ **pardon**: permission
④ **thereunto**: for it
⑤ **occasion**: circumstances, reason
⑥ **more strange**: even more strange than sudden
⑦ **all the rest**: the two escorts
⑧ **abuse**: trick, deception
⑨ **hand**: character
⑩ **alone**: It suggests a duel.
⑪ **advise**: explain it to
⑫ **lost in**: baffled by
⑬ **warms**: does good to
⑭ **didest**: diest?

LAERTES

Ay, my lord,

So① you will not o'errule me to a peace②.

KING

65 To thine own peace. If he be now returned,

As③ checking at④ his voyage, and that⑤ he means

No more to undertake it, I will work him

To an exploit⑥, now ripe in my device⑦,

Under the which⑧ he shall not choose but fall;

70 And for his death no wind of blame shall breathe,

But even his mother shall uncharge⑨ the practise⑩

And call it accident.⑪

LAERTES

My lord, I will be ruled,

The rather if you could devise it so

75 That I might be the organ⑫.

KING CLAUDIUS

It falls right⑬.

You have been talked of since your travel much,

And that in Hamlet's hearing, for a quality⑭

---

① **So:** so long as, provided that
② **o'errule me to a peace:** compel me to agree to peace
③ **As:** as a result of; inasmuch as
④ **checking at:** deviating or swerving from, giving up
⑤ **that:** if
⑥ **exploit:** adventurous action, risk
⑦ **device:** devising, planning
⑧ **the which:** which
⑨ **uncharge:** acquit
⑩ **practise:** plotting
⑪ **But ... accident:** Even his mother shall not blame his death on our plot.
⑫ **organ:** agent, instrument
⑬ **It falls right:** that will fit excellently
⑭ **quality:** accomplishment

Wherein they say you shine. Your sum of parts[1]
80 Did not together pluck such envy from him
As did that one, and that, in my regard,
Of the unworthiest siege[2].

LAERTES
What part is that, my lord?

KING CLAUDIUS
A very[3] riband[4] in the cap of youth,
85 Yet needful too, for youth no less becomes[5]
The light and careless livery[6] that it wears
Than settled age[7] his sables[8] and his weeds[9],
Importing[10] health[11] and graveness[12]. Two months since[13],
Here was a gentleman of Normandy.
90 I've seen myself, and served[14] against, the French,
And they can[15] well[16] on horseback, but this gallant[17]
Had witchcraft in't. He grew unto his seat,
And to such wondrous doing[18] brought his horse,

---

[1] **Your sum of parts:** all of your accomplishments
[2] **siege:** seat, rank
[3] **very:** mere
[4] **riband:** ribbon, decoration
[5] **becomes:** suits, befits
[6] **livery:** uniform
[7] **Than settled age:** than settled age becomes
[8] **sables:** furs
[9] **weeds:** formal clothes, dignified attire
[10] **Importing:** indicating, signifying
[11] **health:** prosperity
[12] **graveness:** dignity
[13] **since:** ago
[14] **served:** was in military action
[15] **can:** can do
[16] **can well:** are skillful
[17] **gallant:** daring or spirited man
[18] **doing:** performance

As① he had been incorpsed② and demi-natured③
95　With the brave④ beast⑤. So far he topped⑥ my thought⑦
That I in forgery⑧ of shapes and tricks⑨,
Come⑩ short of⑪ what he did⑫.
LAERTES
A Norman was't?
KING CLAUDIUS
A Norman.
LAERTES
100　Upon my life, Lamond.
KING CLAUDIUS
The very same.
LAERTES
I know him well. He is the brooch⑬ indeed
And gem of all the nation.
KING CLAUDIUS
He made confession of you⑭,
105　And gave you such a masterly report
For art and exercise⑮ in your defence⑯,

---

① **As:** as if
② **incorpsed:** made one body with it
③ **demi-natured:** sharing the nature
④ **brave:** noble
⑤ **With the brave beast:** as if he were a centaur
⑥ **topped:** exceeded, surpassed
⑦ **thought:** expectation, imagination
⑧ **forgery:** (my) imagination
⑨ **tricks:** his feats (horsemanship)
⑩ **Come:** fall
⑪ **Come short of:** cannot compare with
⑫ **what he did:** his actual performance
⑬ **brooch:** broach (ornament)
⑭ **made confession of you:** acknowledged your ability
⑮ **art and exercise:** skillful practice (hendiadys)
⑯ **defence:** fencing

And for your rapier① most especially,
That he cried out 'twould be a sight② indeed,
If one could match you. The 'scrimers③ of their nation,
110 He swore, had④ neither motion⑤, guard, nor eye⑥,
If you opposed them. Sir, this report of his
Did Hamlet so envenom⑦ with his envy
That he could nothing do but wish and beg
Your sudden coming o'er, to play⑧ with him.
115 Now, out of this—
LAERTES
What out of this, my lord?
KING
Laertes, was your father dear to you?
Or are you like the painting of a sorrow,
A face without a heart?⑨
LAERTES
120 Why ask you this?
KING
Not that⑩ I think you did not love your father,
But that I know love is begun by time,
And that I see, in passages of proof⑪,
Time qualifies⑫ the spark and fire of it.

---

① **rapier:** a fashionable weapon for dueling around 1600
② **sight:** spectacle
③ **'scrimers:** skilled fencers (French *escrimeurs*)
④ **had:** would have
⑤ **motion:** movement
⑥ **eye:** faculty of visual perception
⑦ **envenom:** embitter
⑧ **play:** fence
⑨ **117—119:** a clever suspension
⑩ **that:** because
⑪ **in passages of proof:** by proven instances; from experiences which put this to test
⑫ **qualifies:** diminishes, reduces

125 There lives within the very flame of love
　　　A kind of wick or snuff① that will abate② it,
　　　And nothing is at a like③ goodness still;④
　　　For goodness, growing to a plurisy⑤,
　　　Dies in his own too much⑥. That⑦ we would⑧ do
130 We should do when we would; for this 'would'⑨ changes
　　　And hath abatements⑩ and delays as many
　　　As there are tongues⑪, are hands⑫, are accidents;
　　　And then this 'should' is like a spendthrift⑬ sigh,
　　　That hurts by easing.⑭ But, to the quick⑮ o' the ulcer!
135 Hamlet comes back. What would you undertake,
　　　To show yourself your father's son in deed⑯
　　　More than in words?⑰

LAERTES

To cut his throat i' the church!

KING

No place, indeed, should murder sanctuarize⑱;

---

① **a kind of wick or snuff:** charred wick that dims the candle's flame
② **abate:** dull, blunt
③ **a like:** the same
④ **And ... still:** and nothing remains always at the same level of perfection
⑤ **plurisy:** excess (of humors), plethora
⑥ **his own too much:** its own excess
⑦ **That:** what
⑧ **would:** wish to
⑨ **would:** will to act
⑩ **abatements:** reductions
⑪ **tongues:** words
⑫ **hands:** actions
⑬ **spendthrift:** wasteful
⑭ **a spendthrift ... easing:** According to old notions of medicine, a sigh eases distress but draws blood away from the heart.
⑮ **the quick:** most sensitive part, the main point (Cf. II. ii. 601: "I'll tent him to the quick.")
⑯ **in deed:** in fact, in action
⑰ **More than in words:** in deed (Cf. II. ii. 589: "must like a whore unpack my heart with words" etc.)
⑱ **murder sanctuarize:** protect a murderer (Hamlet) from punishment

140　Revenge should have no bounds. But, good Laertes,
　　　Will you do this? Keep close① within your chamber②.
　　　Hamlet returned shall know you are come home.
　　　We'll put on③ those④ shall praise your excellence
　　　And set a double varnish on the fame⑤.
145　The Frenchman gave you, bring you in fine⑥ together
　　　And wager⑦ on your heads. He, being remiss⑧,
　　　Most generous⑨ and free from all contriving⑩,
　　　Will not peruse⑪ the foils⑫, so that, with ease,
　　　Or with a little shuffling⑬, you may choose
150　A sword unbated⑭, and in a pass of practice⑮
　　　Requite⑯ him for your father.

LAERTES

I will do't!
And for that purpose I'll anoint my sword.
I bought an unction⑰ of⑱ a mountebank⑲,

---

① **close:** secret
② **chamber:** heart
③ **put on:** organize, incite
④ **those:** those who
⑤ **fame:** reputation
⑥ **in fine:** finally
⑦ **wager:** bet
⑧ **remiss:** careless, negligent
⑨ **generous:** noble-minded
⑩ **contriving:** scheming, deception
⑪ **peruse:** scrutinize, examine
⑫ **foils:** light swords used for fencing
⑬ **shuffling:** sleight of hand (i.e. mixing up the swords)
⑭ **unbated:** not blunted
⑮ **pass of practice:** (treacherous) thrust
⑯ **Requite:** kill
⑰ **unction:** ointment
⑱ **of:** from
⑲ **mountebank:** quack doctor

155　So mortal① that, but dip a knife in it,
　　　Where it draws blood no cataplasm② so rare,
　　　Collected from③ all simples④ that have virtue⑤
　　　Under the moon⑥, can save the thing from death
　　　That is but scratched withal. I'll touch my point
160　With this contagion⑦, that⑧, if I gall⑨ him slightly,
　　　It may be death.
　　　KING
　　　Let's further think of this,
　　　Weigh what convenience both of time and means
　　　May fit⑩ us to our shape⑪. If this should fail,
165　And that⑫ our drift⑬ look⑭ through our bad performance⑮,
　　　'Twere better not assayed⑯. Therefore this project
　　　Should have a back⑰ or second⑱ that might hold⑲
　　　If this should blast⑳ in proof㉑. Soft㉒, let me see.

---

① **mortal:** deadly
② **cataplasm:** poultice
③ **Collected from:** composed of
④ **simples:** herbs
⑤ **virtue:** power
⑥ **Under the moon:** collected at midnight and therefore most powerful; anywhere on earth
⑦ **contagion:** poison that infects the blood
⑧ **that:** so that
⑨ **gall:** scratch, graze, hurt by rubbing
⑩ **fit:** adapt
⑪ **shape:** role, purpose
⑫ **that:** if
⑬ **drift:** intention
⑭ **look:** be exposed
⑮ **bad performance:** failed attempt
⑯ **assayed:** attempted
⑰ **back:** backing, back-up
⑱ **second:** second string
⑲ **hold:** prove effective
⑳ **blast:** blow up, fail
㉑ **in proof:** in the testing, when tested
㉒ **Soft:** wait a moment

We'll make a solemn① wager on your cunning②—I ha't!
170 When in your motion you are hot and dry—
As③ make your bouts more violent to that end—
And that he calls for drink, I'll have prepared him
A chalice④ for the nonce⑤, whereon but sipping,
If he by chance escape your venomed stuck⑥,
175 Our purpose may hold⑦ there.—But stay, what noise?
Enter QUEEN
How now, sweet queen?

QUEEN

One woe doth tread upon another's heel,⑧
So fast they follow. Your sister's drowned, Laertes.

LAERTES

Drowned! O, where?

QUEEN

180 There is a willow⑨ grows aslant⑩ a brook
That shows⑪ his⑫ hoar⑬ leaves in the glassy stream.
Therewith fantastic⑭ garlands⑮ did she come

---

① **solemn:** formal
② **cunning:** skills
③ **As:** as to
④ **chalice:** large cup, goblet
⑤ **for the nonce:** for the particular occasion
⑥ **stuck:** (fencing) thrust
⑦ **hold:** succeed
⑧ **One ... heel:** Cf. IV. v. 76—77: "When sorrows come, they come not single spies / But in battalions."
⑨ **willow:** symbolic of unrequited love
⑩ **aslant:** bending over
⑪ **shows:** reflects
⑫ **his:** its
⑬ **hoar:** grey, silvery
⑭ **fantastic:** elaborate
⑮ **garlands:** flower rings

Of crow-flowers, nettles, daisies, and long purples①
That liberal② shepherds give a grosser name③,
185　But our cold④ maids do "dead men's fingers" call them.
There on the pendent⑤ boughs her coronet weeds⑥
Clamb'ring to hang, an envious⑦ sliver⑧ broke,
When down her weedy trophies⑨ and herself
Fell in the weeping brook.⑩ Her clothes spread wide,
190　And mermaid-like awhile they bore her up,
Which time⑪ she chanted snatches⑫ of old lauds⑬,
As one incapable of⑭ her own distress,
Or like a creature native and endued⑮
Unto that element⑯. But long it could not be
195　Till that her garments, heavy with their drink,
Pulled the poor wretch⑰ from her melodious lay⑱
To muddy death.

LAERTES

Alas, then she is drowned?

---

　　① **long purples:** early purple orchids
　　② **liberal:** lewd, free-speaking, plainspoken
　　③ **a grosser name:** i.e. bull's pizzle, dogstones, fool's ballocks etc., which are named after their testicle-shaped tubers
　　④ **cold:** chaste
　　⑤ **pendent:** overhanging
　　⑥ **coronet weeds:** crown of wild flowers
　　⑦ **envious:** malicious
　　⑧ **sliver:** branch
　　⑨ **her weedy trophies:** her garlands (coronet weeds)
　　⑩ **in the weeping brook:** In her account Ophelia's death is an accident rather than suicide.
　　⑪ **which time:** during which time, while
　　⑫ **snatches:** brief extracts, fragments
　　⑬ **lauds:** hymns (Are they ditties or songs of mourning as she sings in IV. v.?)
　　⑭ **incapable of:** insensible to
　　⑮ **endued:** habituated, naturally adapted
　　⑯ **that element:** i.e. water
　　⑰ **wretch:** creature (term used to express pity and affection)
　　⑱ **melodious lay:** song

QUEEN
Drowned, drowned.
LAERTES
200 Too much of water hast thou, poor Ophelia,
And therefore I forbid my tears. But yet
It is our trick①; nature② her custom holds,③
Let shame say what it will. When these④ are gone⑤,
The woman⑥ will be out⑦. Adieu, my lord.
205 I have a speech of fire that fain would⑧ blaze,
But that this folly⑨ douts⑩ it.
Exit
KING
Let's follow, Gertrude.
How much I had to do to calm his rage!
Now fear I this⑪ will give it start again.
210 Therefore let's follow.
Exeunt

---

① **our trick:** the normal reflex of human beings
② **nature:** human nature
③ **nature her custom holds:** nature holds her custom
④ **these:** tears
⑤ **gone:** shed
⑥ **The woman:** this feminine weakness (I. II. 146: "Frailty, thy name is woman!" *King John*, IV. i. 35—36: "I must be brief, lest resolution drop / Out at mine eyes in tender womanish tears." *Henry V*, IV. vi. 30—32: "But I had not so much of man in me, / And all my mother came into mine eyes / And gave me up to tears." *Henry VIII*, III. ii. 429—431: "I did not think to shed a tear / In all my miseries; but thou hast forced me, / Out of thy honest truth, to play the woman.")
⑦ **be out:** exhausted (I'll be a man again)
⑧ **fain would:** is eager to
⑨ **folly:** foolish impulse (of weeping)
⑩ **douts:** extinguishes
⑪ **this:** i.e. Ophelia's death

ACT V
SCENE I. A churchyard.①

Enter two Clowns, with spades and pickaxes

First Clown

Is she to be buried in Christian burial② that
willfully seeks her own salvation③?

Second Clown

I tell thee she is; therefore make her grave
straight④. The crowner⑤ hath sat on her⑥ and finds it⑦
5 Christian burial.⑧

First Clown

How can that be, unless she drowned herself in her
own defense⑨?

Second Clown

Why, 'tis found so.

First Clown

It must be *se offendendo*⑩; it cannot be else⑪. For here

---

① According to A. C. Bradley, this scene, which is a comic relief, as well as Hamlet's mockery of Osric, "could hardly be defended on purely dramatic grounds". (*Shakespearean Tragedy*, p.47)

② **Christian burial:** i.e. interment in consecrated ground

③ **willfully seeks her own salvation:** commits suicide

④ **straight:** straightaway, immediately

⑤ **crowner:** coroner

⑥ **sat on her:** judged her case

⑦ **finds it:** adjudicates her worthy of

⑧ **The crowner ... burial:** Suicides were buried at crossroads, but Ophelia, a lady of the court, was allowed a Christian burial.

⑨ **own defense:** Self-defense can excuse murder.

⑩ *se offendendo*: He had meant to say "*se defendendo*" (Latin: in self-defense)

⑪ **else:** otherwise

10   lies the point: if I drown myself wittingly[1], it argues
an act; and an act hath three branches—it is to act, to
do, to perform.[2] Argal[3], she drowned herself wittingly[4].
Second Clown
Nay, but hear you, Goodman[5] Delver[6]—
First Clown
Give me leave[7]. Here lies the water; good. Here
15   stands the man; good. If the man go to this water,
and drown himself, it is, will he nill he[8], he
goes; mark[9] you that. But if the water come to him
and drown him, he drowns not himself. Argal, he that
is not guilty of his own death shortens not his own life.
Second Clown
20   But is this law?
First Clown
Ay, marry, is't—crowner's quest law[10].
Second Clown
Will you ha' the truth on't[11]? If this had not been
a gentlewoman, she should have been buried out o'[12]
Christian burial.

---

[1]   **wittingly:** knowingly, deliberately
[2]   **three ... perform:** It alludes to the famous suicide of Sir James Hales in 1554.
[3]   **Argal:** He had meant to say "ergo" (Latin: therefore)
[4]   **wittingly:** knowingly
[5]   **Goodman:** It could be used to address someone of lower social status.
[6]   **Delver:** digger
[7]   **Give me leave:** Let me go on
[8]   **will he nill he:** willy-nilly, whether wished or not
[9]   **mark:** take note, remember
[10]   **crowner's quest law:** coroner's inquest law
[11]   **on't:** of it
[12]   **o':** of

First Clown

25　Why, there thou say'st!① And the more pity
　　that great folk should have count'nance② in this
　　world to drown or hang themselves more than
　　their even-Christian③. Come, my spade. There is
　　no ancient④ gentleman but gardeners, ditchers, and
30　grave-makers. They hold up⑤ Adam's profession.

Second Clown

　　Was he a gentleman?

First Clown

　　He was the first that ever bore arms⑥.

Second Clown

　　Why, he had none.

First Clown

　　What, art⑦ a heathen? How dost thou understand
35　the Scripture⑧? The Scripture says Adam digged⑨.
　　Could he dig without arms? I'll put another
　　question to thee. If thou answerest me not
　　to the purpose⑩, confess thyself⑪—

Second Clown

　　Go to⑫!

---

① **there thou say'st:** you said it correctly; you've made a good point
② **count'nance:** countenance, legal approval
③ **even-Christian:** fellow Christians
④ **ancient:** venerable
⑤ **hold up:** keep up, maintain
⑥ **arms:** part of human body; spade; a coat of arms (the mark of a gentleman), blazon (heraldic insignia)
⑦ **art:** are you
⑧ **Scripture:** Bible
⑨ **digged:** dug
⑩ **to the purpose:** correctly
⑪ **confess thyself:** i.e. and be hanged
⑫ **Go to:** go away, shut up, enough

First Clown

40 What is he that builds stronger than either the mason, the shipwright, or the carpenter?

Second Clown

The gallows-maker; for that frame[1] outlives a thousand tenants.

First Clown

I like thy wit well, in good faith. The gallows
45 does well[2]. But how does it well? It does well to those that do ill. Now, thou dost ill to say the gallows is built stronger than the church. Argal, the gallows may do well to thee[3]. To't[4], come.

Second Clown

Who builds stronger than a mason, a shipwright, or
50 a carpenter?

First Clown

Ay, tell me that, and unyoke.[5]

Second Clown

Marry[6], now I can tell.

First Clown

To't[7].

Second Clown

Mass[8], I cannot tell.

Enter HAMLET and HORATIO afar off

---

[1] **frame:** structure
[2] **does well:** serves well; makes a good answer
[3] **do well to thee:** serve its purpose by hanging you
[4] **To't:** tell me the answer, try it again
[5] **unyoke:** quit (as a farmer does when he unyokes his team of oxen), put an end to your labor
[6] **Marry:** by Mary
[7] **To't:** get on with it
[8] **Mass:** by the mass

First Clown

55　Cudgel thy brains no more about it, for your dull
　　ass will not mend his pace with beating. And, when
　　you are asked this question next①, say 'a grave-maker'.
　　The houses that he makes last till doomsday. Go, get
　　thee to Yaughan②; fetch me a stoup③ of liquor.
　　Exit Second Clown
　　*He digs and sings*④

60　In youth, when I did love, did love,
　　Methought it was very sweet
　　To contract⑤—O—the time—for—ah—my behove⑥,
　　O, methought there was nothing meet⑦.

HAMLET

　　Has this fellow no feeling⑧ of his business, that he
65　sings in grave-making?

HORATIO

　　Custom hath made it in him a property of easiness⑨ ⑩.

HAMLET

　　'Tis e'en so. The hand of little employment⑪ hath

---

① **next:** next time
② **Yaughan:** an unusual spelling of "Johan" (probably a real name)
③ **stoup:** large mug, jug
④ **60—63:** What he sings is a popular song written by Lord Vaux, printed in Richard Tottel's *Miscellany* (1577), entitled "The Aged Lover Renounceth Love".
⑤ **contract:** shorten; pass
⑥ **behove:** behoof, benefit; pleasure
⑦ **meet:** fit, becoming, appropriate
⑧ **feeling:** fear
⑨ **a property of easiness:** a matter of indifference
⑩ **66:** Habit makes it easy for him.
⑪ **of little employment:** not frequently used

the daintier sense[1].

First Clown [*Sings*]

But age with his stealing steps
70 Hath clawed[2] me in his clutch,
And hath shipped[3] me intil[4] the land[5],
As if I had never been such.

Throws up a skull

HAMLET

That skull had a tongue in it, and could sing once.
How the knave jowls[6] it to the ground, as if it were
75 Cain's jaw-bone[7], that did the first murder! It might be the
pate[8] of a politician[9], which this ass now o'er-reaches[10],
one[11] that would[12] circumvent[13] God, might it not?

HORATIO

It might, my lord.

HAMLET

Or of a courtier, which could say 'Good morrow,
80 sweet lord! How dost thou[14], good lord?' This might be
my lord such-a-one, that praised my lord such-a-one's horse,
when he meant to beg it, might it not?

---

[1] **hath the daintier sense:** is more sensitive
[2] **clawed:** (combination of clutch and caught) seized
[3] **shipped:** transported
[4] **intil:** into
[5] **the land:** land of death
[6] **jowls:** hurls (with a pun on "jawl")
[7] **Cain's jaw-bone:** Traditionally Cain was thought to have killed Abel with the jawbone of an ass.
[8] **pate:** head
[9] **politician:** schemer
[10] **o'er-reaches:** gets the better of
[11] **one:** Cain
[12] **would:** wished to
[13] **circumvent:** get around
[14] **How dost thou:** how are you

HORATIO

Ay, my lord.

HAMLET

Why, e'en so! And now my Lady Worm's①, chapless②,
85 and knocked about the mazzard③ with a sexton's spade.
Here's fine revolution④, if we had the trick⑤ to see't.
Did these bones cost no more the breeding⑥ but to play at
loggets⑦ with 'em? Mine⑧ ache⑨ to think on't.

First Clown [*Sings*]

A pick-axe, and a spade, a spade,
*For and*⑩ *a shrouding sheet;*
*O, a pit of clay for to be made*⑪
90 *For such a guest*⑫ *is meet.*
[*Throws up another skull*]

HAMLET

There's another. Why may not that be the skull
of a lawyer? Where be his quiddities⑬ now, his quillets⑭,
95 his cases, his tenures⑮, and his tricks⑯? Why does he suffer

---

① **my Lady Worm's:** skull
② **chapless:** jawless
③ **mazzard:** head (a slang term)
④ **revolution:** wheel of fortune, alteration or reversal
⑤ **trick:** skill, knack
⑥ **breeding:** in the breeding
⑦ **loggets:** loggats
⑧ **Mine:** my heart
⑨ **ache:** aches
⑩ *For and*: and
⑪ *a pit of clay for to be made*: for a pit of clay to be made
⑫ **guest:** tenant
⑬ **quiddities:** hair-splitting definitions
⑭ **quillets:** quibbles, legal subtleties
⑮ **tenures:** property titles, holdings
⑯ **tricks:** law-tricks

this rude knave now to knock him about the sconce[1] with
a dirty shovel, and will not tell[2] him of his action[3] of battery[4]?
Hum! This fellow might be in's time a great buyer of land,
with his statutes[5], his recognizances[6], his fines[7], his
100 double vouchers[8], his recoveries[9]. Is this the fine[10] of his
fines, and the recovery[11] of his recoveries, to have his fine[12]
pate full of fine[13] dirt? Will his vouchers vouch him no
more of his purchases, and double ones too, than the
length and breadth of a pair of indentures[14]? The very
105 conveyances[15] of his lands will scarcely[16] lie in this box[17];
and must the inheritor[18] himself have no more, ha?[19]

HORATIO
Not a jot[20] more, my lord.

HAMLET
Is not parchment made of sheepskins?

---

[1] **sconce:** head
[2] **tell:** suit
[3] **action:** law-suit
[4] **battery:** physical assault, attack
[5] **statutes:** securities for debts or mortgages
[6] **recognizances:** legal documents acknowledging debts
[7] **fines:** legal process to transfer an estate
[8] **double vouchers:** guarantors of title
[9] **recoveries:** suits for obtaining possession
[10] **fine:** finality, finis
[11] **recovery:** gain
[12] **fine:** nice
[13] **fine:** very small
[14] **indentures:** contracts, legal agreements in duplication on a single sheet
[15] **conveyances:** title deeds
[16] **scarcely:** hardly
[17] **box:** coffin
[18] **inheritor:** owner
[19] **The very ... ha:** Cf. Horace: *Epistle to Florus*, 167—179
[20] **jot:** bit

HORATIO

Ay, my lord, and of calveskins too.

HAMLET

110 They① are sheep and calves② which seek out assurance③ in that. I will speak to this fellow. Whose grave's this, sirrah④?

First Clown

Mine, sir.

Sings

O, a pit of clay for to be made

115 For such a guest is meet.

HAMLET

I think it be thine, indeed; for thou liest in't.⑤

First Clown

You lie out on't⑥, sir, and therefore it is not yours. For my part, I do not lie in't, and yet it is mine.

HAMLET

Thou dost lie in't, to be in't and say it is thine.

120 'Tis for the dead, not for the quick⑦; therefore thou liest.

First Clown

'Tis a quick⑧ lie, sir; 'twill away⑨ again from me to you.⑩

HAMLET

---

① **They:** buyer of land
② **sheep and calves:** fools, subhuman
③ **assurance:** assurance of possession
④ **sirrah:** title used when addressing to inferiors
⑤ **116 & 119—120:** Hamlet makes a pun on "lie".
⑥ **on't:** outside of it
⑦ **quick:** living
⑧ **quick:** quick-moving
⑨ **'twill away:** jump away
⑩ **'twill … you:** I can quickly put it back onto you.

What man dost thou dig it for?

First Clown

125　For no man, sir.

HAMLET

What woman, then?

First Clown

For none neither.

HAMLET

Who is to be buried in't?

First Clown

One that was a woman, sir; but, rest her soul①, she's dead.②

HAMLET

130　How absolute③ the knave④ is! We must speak by the
card⑤, or equivocation⑥ will undo us. By the Lord,
Horatio, these three⑦ years I have taken a note of it:
the age is grown so picked⑧ that the toe of the peasant
comes so near the heel of the courtier he galls his kibe⑨.⑩

135　How long hast thou been a grave-maker?

First Clown

Of all the days i' the year, I came to't that day
that⑪ our last king Hamlet overcame Fortinbras.⑫

---

① **rest her soul:** may her soul rest
② **she's dead:** Ironically, Hamlet does not know she is Ophelia.
③ **absolute:** precise, strict
④ **knave:** rogue
⑤ **speak by the card:** speak exactly to the point (card: a sailor's chart or compass)
⑥ **equivocation:** quibbling, ambiguity
⑦ **three:** several
⑧ **picked:** refined, affected
⑨ **kibe:** the courtier's sore heel
⑩ **these three ... his kibe:** The present age has become so affected that peasants walk on the very heels of courtiers.
⑪ **that:** when
⑫ **Of ... Fortinbras:** Cf. I. i. 94—109

HAMLET

How long is that since?

First Clown

Cannot you tell that? Every fool can tell that. It
140　was the very day that young Hamlet was born—he
that① is mad, and sent into England.

HAMLET

Ay, marry, why was he sent into England?

First Clown

Why, because he was mad. He shall recover his wits
there. Or if he do not, it's no great matter there.

HAMLET
145　Why?

First Clown

'Twill② not be seen③ in him there. There the
men are as mad as he.

HAMLET

How came he mad?

First Clown

Very strangely, they say.

HAMLET
150　How strangely?

First Clown

Faith, e'en with losing his wits.

HAMLET

Upon what ground④?

First Clown

Why, here in Denmark. I have been sexton here, man

---

① **that:** who
② **'Twill:** madness will
③ **seen:** noticed
④ **ground:** reason; earth

and boy, thirty years.
HAMLET
155 How long will a man lie i' the earth ere① he rot?
First Clown
I' faith, if he be not rotten before he die—as we have many pocky② corses③ nowadays that will scarce④ hold⑤ the laying in⑥—he⑦ will last you some eight year or nine year. A tanner will last you nine year.
HAMLET
160 Why he more than another?
First Clown
Why, sir, his hide⑧ is so tanned with his trade that he will keep out water a great while; and your water is a sore⑨ decayer of your whoreson⑩ dead body. Here's a skull now: this skull has lien⑪ i' the earth
165 three and twenty years.
HAMLET
Whose was it?
First Clown
A whoreson mad fellow's it was. Whose do you think it was?
HAMLET
Nay, I know not.

---

① **ere:** before
② **pocky:** suffering from the "pox" (syphilis, venereal disease)
③ **corses:** corpses
④ **scarce:** scarcely
⑤ **hold:** endure, remain unrotten
⑥ **laying in:** lying in
⑦ **he:** a healthy corpse
⑧ **hide:** skin
⑨ **sore:** grievous
⑩ **whoreson:** son of bitch, here "vile"
⑪ **lien:** lain

First Clown

A pestilence① on him for a mad rogue! He poured a
170　flagon of Rhenish② on my head once. This same
skull, sir, was Yorick's skull, the King's jester.

HAMLET

This?

First Clown

E'en that③.

HAMLET

Let me see.

Takes the skull

175　Alas, poor Yorick! I knew him, Horatio.
A fellow of infinite jest, of most excellent fancy④.
He hath borne me on his back a thousand times.⑤
And now, how abhorred⑥ in my imagination it is⑦!
My gorge⑧ rims⑨ at it. Here hung those lips that I
180　have kissed I know not how oft. Where be your gibes⑩
now? your gambols⑪? your songs? your flashes⑫ of
merriment⑬, that were wont to⑭ set the table on a roar?

---

① **pestilence:** plague
② **Rhenish:** Rhine wine
③ **E'en that:** exactly
④ **fancy:** invention; fantasies
⑤ **He ... times:** Obviously Yorick used to be Hamlet's closest friend in childhood.
⑥ **abhorred:** filled with horror
⑦ **in my imagination it is:** when I think of it
⑧ **gorge:** stomach
⑨ **rims:** rises
⑩ **gibes:** wisecracks
⑪ **gambols:** playful tricks
⑫ **flashes:** sudden show of wit
⑬ **merriment:** gaiety
⑭ **were wont to:** used to

Not one now to mock your own grinning①? Quite chapfallen②?
Now get you to my lady's③ chamber, and tell her, let
185 her paint an inch thick, to this favor④ she must come.
Make her laugh at that. Prithee, Horatio, tell me one thing.
HORATIO
What's that, my lord?
HAMLET
Dost thou think Alexander⑤ looked o' this fashion⑥
i' the earth?
HORATIO
190 E'en so⑦.
HAMLET
And smelt so? Pah!
Puts down the skull
HORATIO
E'en so, my lord.
HAMLET
To what base uses we may return, Horatio! Why
may not imagination trace the noble dust of Alexander
195 till he find it stopping a bunghole⑧?
HORATIO
'Twere to consider too curiously⑨ to consider so.
HAMLET
No, faith, not a jot; but to follow him thither

---

① **grinning:** skull (e.g. grinning death)
② **chapfallen:** jawless; dejected
③ **my lady's:** the Queen's
④ **favor:** facial appearance
⑤ **Alxander:** Alexander the Great
⑥ **o' this fashion:** in this way
⑦ **E'en so:** exactly
⑧ **bunghole:** hole in a beer barrel
⑨ **curiously:** fancifully, elaborately

with modesty① enough, and likelihood to lead it②, as
thus: Alexander died, Alexander was buried,
200　Alexander returneth into dust; the dust is earth; of
earth we make loam③; and why of that loam, whereto
he was converted, might they not stop a beer barrel?
*Imperious④ Caesar, dead and turned to clay,
Might stop a hole to keep the wind away.*
205　*O, that that earth⑤ which kept the world in awe
Should patch⑥ a wall to expel the winter flaw⑦!*
But soft⑧! but soft! aside! Here comes the King—
Enter KING, QUEEN, LAERTES, and a coffin, with Priests and Lords attendant
The Queen, the courtiers. Who is this they follow?
And with such maimèd⑨ rites? This doth betoken⑩
210　The corse⑪ they follow did with desp'rate hand
Fordo⑫ it⑬ own life. 'Twas of some estate⑭.
Couch⑮ we awhile, and mark⑯.
Retires with HORATIO

---

① **with modesty**: without exaggeration (modesty: moderation)
② **it**: imagination
③ **loam**: soil consisting of sand and clay
④ *Imperious*: majestic, imperial
⑤ *that earth*: Caesar, his body
⑥ **patch**: cover
⑦ *winter flaw*: squall, gust of wind; shower of rain
⑧ **soft**: be silent
⑨ **maimèd**: impaired, curtailed
⑩ **betoken**: indicate
⑪ **corse**: corpse
⑫ **Fordo**: destroy
⑬ **it**: its
⑭ **some estate**: considerable rank
⑮ **Couch**: hide
⑯ **mark**: observe

LAERTES

What ceremony else①?

HAMLET

That is Laertes,
215 A very noble youth. Mark.

LAERTES

What ceremony else?

First Priest

Her obsequies② have been as far enlarged③
As we have warrantry④. Her death was doubtful⑤;
And, but that⑥ great⑦ command o'ersways⑧ the order⑨,
220 She should in ground unsanctified⑩ have lodged⑪
Till the last trumpet⑫. For⑬ charitable prayers,
Shards⑭, flints and pebbles should be thrown on her.
Yet here she is allowed her virgin crants⑮,
Her maiden strewments⑯ and the bringing⑰ home⑱
225 Of bell and burial⑲.

---

① **else:** further
② **obsequies:** (accented on the first syllable) funeral rites
③ **enlarged:** extended, prolonged
④ **warrantry:** authority
⑤ **doubtful:** suspicious
⑥ **but that:** if not
⑦ **great:** the King's
⑧ **o'ersways:** prevails over, overrides
⑨ **the order:** the normal proceeding; the rule of the church
⑩ **unsanctified:** unhallowed
⑪ **lodged:** been buried
⑫ **trumpet:** the Judgment Day, the end of the world
⑬ **For:** instead of
⑭ **Shards:** broken pieces of pottery
⑮ **crants:** garlands (German "kranz": crown)
⑯ **strewments:** flowers strewn on the grave
⑰ **the bringing:** being brought
⑱ **home:** to the grave, her last resting place
⑲ **Of bell and burial:** with bell-ringing and burial rites

LAERTES

Must there no more be done?

First Priest

No more be done.

We should profane the service of the dead

To sing a requiem① and such rest② to her

230　As to peace-parted souls③.

LAERTES

Lay her i' the earth.

And from her fair and unpolluted flesh

May violets④ spring! I tell thee, churlish⑤ priest,

A ministering angel shall my sister be

235　When thou liest howling⑥.

HAMLET

What, the fair Ophelia!

QUEEN

Sweets⑦ to the sweet⑧! Farewell.

Scatters flowers

I hoped thou shouldst have been my Hamlet's wife;⑨

I thought thy bride-bed to have decked, sweet maid,

240　And not have strewed thy grave.⑩

---

① **requiem:** funeral song
② **such rest:** to pray for such rest
③ **peace-parted souls:** souls departed in peace, those who have died a natural death
④ **violets:** youthful love (cf. I. iii. 8); loss or death of love (cf. IV. v. 190—191)
⑤ **churlish:** surly, villainous
⑥ **howling:** wailing in hell
⑦ **sweets:** flowers
⑧ **sweet:** maiden
⑨ **I hoped ... wife:** Cf. III. i. 43—47
⑩ **thy bride-bed ... thy grave:** Cf. *Romeo and Juliet*, IV. v. 89: "Our bridal flowers served for a buried corpse."

LAERTES

O, treble woe①

Fall ten times treble on that cursèd head②,

Whose wicked deed③ thy most ingenious sense④

Deprived thee of! Hold off the earth⑤ awhile⑥,

245 Till I have caught her once more in mine arms.

*Leaps into the grave*⑦

Now pile your dust upon the quick⑧ and dead,

Till of this flat⑨ a mountain you have made,

To o'ertop⑩ old Pelion, or the skyish⑪ head

Of blue Olympus.⑫.

HAMLET

250 [*Advancing*] What is he whose grief

Bears such an emphasis⑬, whose phrase of sorrow

Conjures⑭ the wandering stars⑮ and makes them stand⑯

Like wonder-wounded⑰ hearers? This is I,

---

① **treble woe:** let treble woe
② **that cursèd head:** i.e. *Hamlet*
③ **wicked deed:** the murder of Polonius
④ **ingenious sense:** intelligence, rationality
⑤ **Hold off the earth:** hold off from filling the grave with earth
⑥ **awhile:** for a while
⑦ ***Leaps into the grave***: an archetypal scene suggestive of "a fatal struggle in the upper world" (Northrop Frye: *Anatomy of Criticism*, Princeton: Princeton University Press, 1957, p.140.)
⑧ **quick:** living
⑨ **flat:** level ground
⑩ **o'ertop:** rise higher than
⑪ **skyish:** close to the sky
⑫ **Pelion, Olympus:** According to Greek legend, Pelion was the home of the centaurs, especially Chiron. In mythology, two giants tried to reach heaven to make war on the gods by piling Pelion on the neighboring peak Ossa to scale Olympus, and they were slain by Apollo
⑬ **Bears such an emphasis:** is expressed in such forceful language
⑭ **Conjures:** puts a spell on
⑮ **stars:** planets
⑯ **stand:** stand still
⑰ **wonder-wounded:** struck with wonder, awe-stricken

Hamlet the Dane①.

Leaps into the grave

LAERTES

255 The devil take thy soul!

Grappling with him

HAMLET

Thou pray'st not well.

I prithee, take thy fingers from my throat,

For though I am not splenitive② and rash③,

Yet have I something in me dangerous,

260 Which let thy wisdom④ fear. Hold off thy hand!

KING

Pluck them asunder⑤.

QUEEN

Hamlet, Hamlet!

All

Gentlemen!

HORATIO

Good my lord, be quiet⑥.

Attendants part them, and they leave the grave.

HAMLET

265 Why, I will fight with him upon this theme⑦

Until my eyelids will no longer wag⑧.⑨

---

① **the Dane:** King of Denmark
② **splenitive:** splenetic (spleen was seen as the seat of various emotions ranging from anger and melancholy and mirth)
③ **rash:** quick-tempered
④ **wisdom:** wiseness, better judgment
⑤ **asunder:** apart
⑥ **be quiet:** calm down
⑦ **this theme:** i.e. love (Cf. 268: "I loved Ophelia.")
⑧ **wag:** move
⑨ **Until ... wag:** until I have no life at all.

QUEEN

O my son, what theme?

HAMLET

I loved Ophelia. Forty thousand brothers
Could not with all their quantity[1] of love
270 Make up my sum. What wilt thou do for her?

KING

O, he is mad, Laertes!

QUEEN

For love of God, forbear[2] him.

HAMLET

'Swounds[3], show me what thou'lt[4] do.
Woo't[5] weep? woo't fight? woo't fast? woo't tear thyself?
275 Woo't drink up eisel[6], eat a crocodile?
I'll do't. Dost thou come here to whine?
To outface[7] me with leaping in her grave?
Be buried quick[8] with her, and so will I.
And if thou prate[9] of mountains, let them throw
280 Millions of acres[10] on us, till our ground[11],
Singeing[12] his pate[13] against the burning zone[14],[15]

---

[1] **quantity:** small bit
[2] **forbear:** bear with, tolerate
[3] **'Swounds:** by God's wounds (a powerful oath)
[4] **thou'lt:** thou wouldst (i.e. you'll)
[5] **Woo't:** wouldst thou (i.e. will you)
[6] **eisel:** vinegar; the name of a river (Yssel?)
[7] **outface:** overcome, defeat
[8] **quick:** alive
[9] **prate:** brag, boast
[10] **Millions of acres:** large quantities of land
[11] **our ground:** the ground on top of us
[12] **Singeing:** scorching
[13] **his pate:** its head
[14] **the burning zone:** the sun
[15] **281:** scorching its top by touching the sun's orbit

Make Ossa like a wart①! Nay, an thou'lt mouth②,
I'll rant③ as well as thou.

QUEEN

This is mere④ madness;
285 And thus awhile the fit⑤ will work on him.
Anon, as patient⑥ as the female dove,
When that⑦ her golden couplets⑧ are disclosed⑨,
His silence will sit drooping⑩.

HAMLET

Hear you, sir!
290 What is the reason that you use⑪ me thus?⑫
I loved you ever. But it is no matter.
Let Hercules himself do what he may⑬,
The cat will mew, and dog will have his day.
Exit

KING

I pray thee⑭, good Horatio⑮, wait upon⑯ him.⑰
Exit HORATIO

---

① **Make ... wart:** to dwarf Ossa
② **an thou'lt mouth:** if you want to shout
③ **rant:** roar
④ **mere:** sheer, utter
⑤ **fit:** sudden attack or burst
⑥ **patient:** calm
⑦ **When that:** when
⑧ **golden couplets:** two young birds covered with yellow down
⑨ **disclosed:** hatched
⑩ **His ... drooping:** he will be quiet and contemplative
⑪ **use:** treat
⑫ **What ... thus:** It seems that Hamlet does not think him guilty of the death of Polonius and Ophelia.
⑬ **what he may:** i.e. revenge
⑭ **thee:** He uses more familiar "you / your" to Laertes.
⑮ **good Horatio:** Hamlet also calls him "good Horatio".
⑯ **upon:** accompany
⑰ **I ... him:** (Cf. IV. v. 73: "Follow her close; give her good watch, I pray you.")

To LAERTES

295 Strengthen your patience in[1] our last night's speech.
We'll put the matter to the present push[2].—
Good Gertrude, set some watch over your son.[3]—
This grave shall have a living monument[4].
An hour of quiet[5] shortly shall we see;
300 Till then in patience our proceeding be.
Exeunt

SCENE II. A hall in the castle.

Enter HAMLET and HORATIO

HAMLET

So much for this, sir. Now shall you see the other[6].
You do remember all the circumstance[7]?

HORATIO

Remember it, my lord![8]

HAMLET

Sir, in my heart there was a kind of fighting
5 That would not let me sleep. Methought[9] I lay

---

[1] **in:** by thinking of
[2] **to the present push:** into immediate action
[3] **set ... son:** an watching eye imagery (Cf. III. i. 36—37: "Her father and myself, lawful espials, / Will so bestow ourselves that, seeing unseen"; III. i. 200: "Madness in great ones must not unwatched go.")
[4] **living monument:** enduring memorial (perhaps he implies Hamlet shall be sacrificed as an offering to Ophelia's memory)
[5] **quiet:** peace
[6] **the other:** the rest of the story
[7] **circumstance:** circumstances
[8] **Remember ... lord:** How could I forget it?
[9] **Methought:** it seemed to me

Worse than the mutines① in the bilboes②. Rashly—
And praised be rashness for it: let us know③,
Our indiscretion④ sometimes serves us well
When our deep plots do pall⑤;⑥ and that should learn⑦ us
10 There's a divinity⑧ that shapes our ends⑨,
Rough-hew them how we will—⑩

HORATIO

That is most certain.

HAMLET

Up from my cabin,
My sea-gown⑪ scarfed⑫ about me, in the dark
15 Groped I to find out them⑬; had my desire,
Fingered⑭ their packet, and in fine⑮ withdrew
To mine own room again, making so bold,
My fears forgetting manners, to⑯ unseal
Their grand commission; where I found, Horatio—
20 O royal knavery!—an exact command,

---

① **mutines:** mutineers
② **bilboes:** shackles, iron fetters for shackling disorderly sailors
③ **know:** recognize as a fact
④ **indiscretion:** rashness, action committed without premeditation
⑤ **pall:** lose strength, fail
⑥ **Our indiscretion … do pall:** Cf. III. i. 92—97: "the native hue of resolution / Is sicklied o'er with the pale cast of thought" etc.
⑦ **learn:** teach
⑧ **divinity:** providence
⑨ **end:** the outcome of our plans, destinations
⑩ **Rough … will:** no matter how roughly we ourselves shape them (Cf. 216—217: "There's a special / providence in / the fall of a sparrow".)
⑪ **sea-gown:** seaman's coat
⑫ **scarfed:** wrapped
⑬ **them:** Rosencrantz and Guildenstern
⑭ **Fingered:** laid hold on, pilfered
⑮ **fine:** finally
⑯ **to:** as to

Larded① with many several② sorts of reasons
Importing③ Denmark's health④ and England's too,
With, ho! such bugs⑤ and goblins⑥ in my life⑦,⑧
That, on the supervise⑨, no leisure bated⑩,
25 No, not to stay⑪ the grinding of the axe,
My head should be struck off.

HORATIO

Is't possible?

HAMLET

Here's the commission; read it at more leisure.
But wilt thou hear me how I did proceed?

HORATIO

30 I beseech you.

HAMLET

Being thus benetted⑫ round with villanies,
Ere I could make a prologue⑬ to my brains⑭,
They had begun the play. I sat me down⑮,
Devised a new commission, wrote it fair⑯.

---

① **Larded:** garnished, ornamented
② **several:** separate, different
③ **Importing:** signifying, relating to
④ **health:** welfare
⑤ **bugs:** bugbears, ghosts
⑥ **goblins:** causes of alarm
⑦ **in my life:** if I were allowed to live
⑧ **23:** i. e. my existence is described as so dangerous
⑨ **supervise:** perusal
⑩ **no leisure bated:** with no time wasted
⑪ **stay:** await
⑫ **benetteed:** meshed, caught in a net
⑬ **prologue:** outline of the forthcoming action
⑭ **to my brains:** instinctively and immediately
⑮ **I sat me down:** my brains began to work
⑯ **fair:** in good handwriting

35　I once did hold it, as our statists① do,
　　A baseness② to write fair and labored much
　　How to forget that learning; but, sir, now
　　It did me yeoman's③ service④. Wilt thou know
　　The effect⑤ of what I wrote?
HORATIO
40　Ay, good my lord.
HAMLET
　　An earnest conjuration⑥ from the King,
　　As England was his faithful tributary⑦,
　　As love between them like the palm⑧ might flourish,
　　As peace should still⑨ her wheaten garland⑩ wear
45　And stand a comma⑪ 'tween their amities,
　　And many such-like 'Ases'⑫ of great charge⑬,
　　That, on the view and knowing of these contents,
　　Without debatement⑭ further, more or less,
　　He should the bearers put to sudden death,
50　Not shriving time⑮ allowed.

---

① **statists:** statesmen (who didn't write themselves)
② **A baseness:** something beneath me, a lower-class skill
③ **yeoman's:** loyal; substantial
④ **yeoman's service:** i.e. humble but excellent service
⑤ **effect:** purport, substance
⑥ **conjuration:** call, request
⑦ **tributary:** payer of tribute, country paying tribute
⑧ **palm:** symbol of prosperity
⑨ **still:** always
⑩ **wheaten garland:** a symbol of peace and prosperity
⑪ **comma:** a connecting link
⑫ **Ases:** Hamlet parodies official language and puns on "asses"
⑬ **great charge:** significance, weight
⑭ **debatement:** debate
⑮ **shriving time:** time for confession

HORATIO

How was this sealed?

HAMLET

Why, even in that was heaven ordinant[1].
I had my father's[2] signet[3] in my purse,
Which was the model[4] of that Danish seal;
55 Folded the writ[5] up in form of the other,
Subscribed[6] it, gave't the impression[7], placed it safely,
The changeling[8] never known. Now, the next day
Was our sea-fight; and what to this was sequent[9]
Thou know'st already.

HORATIO

60 So Guildenstern and Rosencrantz go to't[10].

HAMLET

Why, man, they did make love to this employment!
They are not near my conscience. Their defeat[11]
Does by their own insinuation[12] grow.[13]
'Tis dangerous when the baser[14] nature comes

---

[1] **ordinant:** providential, working to control events
[2] **my father's:** the only one mention of father by Hamlet in Act V, and his last mention too
[3] **signet:** small seal
[4] **model:** likeness, replica
[5] **writ:** commission
[6] **Subscribed:** signed
[7] **gave't the impression:** sealed it with the signet on wax
[8] **changeling:** a dwarf or imp left by the fairies in place of a human baby they have stolen; substitution
[9] **sequent:** subsequent
[10] **to't:** to their deaths
[11] **defeat:** destruction
[12] **insinuation:** involvement
[13] **Does ... grow:** they asked for it
[14] **baser:** inferior

65　Between the pass① and fell② incensèd points③
　　Of mighty opposites④.⑤

HORATIO

Why, what a king is this!⑥

HAMLET

Does it not, think'st thee, stand me now upon⑦—
He that hath killed my King and whored my mother,
70　Popped in between the election and my hopes,
　　Thrown out his angle⑧ for my proper⑨ life,
　　And with such cozenage⑩—is't not perfect conscience⑪
　　To quit⑫ him with this arm? And is't not to be damned
　　To let this canker of our nature⑬ come
75　In⑭ further evil?

HORATIO⑮

It must be shortly known to him⑯ from England
What is the issue⑰ of the business there.

---

① **pass:** thrust
② **fell:** fierce, deadly
③ **incensèd points:** sword-fighting
④ **opposites:** opponents
⑤ **Of ... opposites:** Cf. III. iii. 16—18: "The cease of majesty / Dies not alone; but like a gulf doth draw/ What's near it with it."
⑥ **Why ... this:** It is a very strange comment. What does Horatio mean at all?
⑦ **Does it not stand me now upon:** is it not now incumbent on me
⑧ **angle:** fishing hook
⑨ **proper:** own
⑩ **cozenage:** trickery, deception (pun on cousin)
⑪ **conscience:** isn't it morally justifiable (Cf. 62: "They are not near my conscience.")
⑫ **quit:** requite, repay
⑬ **nature:** humanity
⑭ **In:** into
⑮ It is noteworthy that Horatio does not respond but shifts the topic thereupon.
⑯ **him:** Claudius
⑰ **issue:** outcome

HAMLET

It will be short. The interim[1] is mine,

And a man's life's no more than to say 'One.'

80 But I am very sorry, good Horatio,

That to Laertes I forgot myself;

For by the image of my cause[2] I see

The portraiture[3] of his. I'll court his favors.

But, sure, the bravery[4] of his grief did put me

85 Into a towering passion[5].

HORATIO

Peace! Who comes here?

Enter OSRIC, a courtier

OSRIC

Your lordship is right welcome back to Denmark.

HAMLET

I humbly thank you, sir. [*Aside to Horatio*] Dost know this waterfly[6]?

HORATIO [*Aside to Hamlet*]

No, my good lord.

HAMLET

90 Thy state[7] is the more gracious[8],

for 'tis a vice to know him. He hath much land,

and fertile. Let a beast be lord of beasts, and his

---

[1] **interim:** interval
[2] **cause:** revenge
[3] **portraiture:** portrait
[4] **bravery:** pretentious display, boastful showiness
[5] **did ... passion:** did pique my jealousy
[6] **waterfly:** worthless creature who flits over the surface of life
[7] **state:** condition
[8] **gracious:** free from sin, virtuous

crib① shall stand at the King's mess②.③ 'Tis a chough④;
but, as I say, spacious in the possession of dirt⑤.

OSRIC

95　Sweet lord, if your lordship were at leisure, I
should impart a thing⑥ to you from his majesty.

HAMLET

I will receive it, sir, with all diligence⑦ of
spirit. Put your bonnet⑧ to his⑨ right use,
'tis for the head.⑩

OSRIC

100　I thank your lordship, it is very hot.

HAMLET

No, believe me, 'tis very cold; the wind is
northerly.

OSRIC

It is indifferent⑪ cold, my lord, indeed.

HAMLET

But yet methinks it is very sultry and hot for my
105　complexion⑫.

OSRIC

Exceedingly, my lord; it is very sultry, as 'twere—

---

① **crib:** manger
② **mess:** table
③ 92—93: If a man, however bestial he is, has enough money, he will be welcome at the King's table.
④ **chough:** crow or jackdaw (both birds can be trained to talk)
⑤ **dirt:** land
⑥ **a thing:** something
⑦ **diligence:** attentiveness
⑧ **bonnet:** hat
⑨ **his:** its
⑩ **Put ... head:** put it on your head
⑪ **indifferent:** somewhat
⑫ **complexion:** temperament, bodily constitution

I cannot tell how. But my lord, his majesty bade me
signify to you that he has laid a great wager on your head.
Sir, this is the matter—
HAMLET
110 I beseech you, remember[1].
HAMLET moves him to put on his hat
OSRIC
Nay, good my lord, for mine ease[2], in good faith.
Sir, here is newly come to court Laertes—believe
me, an absolute[3] gentleman, full of most excellent
differences[4] of very soft society[5] and great showing[6].
115 Indeed, to speak feelingly of him, he is the card[7] or
calendar[8] of gentry[9], for you shall find in him the
continent[10] of what[11] part[12] a gentleman would see.
HAMLET[13]
Sir, his definement[14] suffers no perdition[15] in you[16],
though I know to divide him inventorially[17] would

---

[1] **remember:** i.e. remember to put your hat on
[2] **for mine ease:** a polite protestation
[3] **absolute:** perfect
[4] **excellent differences:** unique accomplishments
[5] **of very soft society:** agreeable company; gentle and courteous manners
[6] **great showing:** impressive appearance
[7] **card:** chart, index
[8] **calendar:** model, example
[9] **gentry:** gentility, courtly manners
[10] **continent:** container, possessor
[11] **what:** whatever
[12] **part:** the qualities
[13] He purposely parodies Osric's affected style of speech.
[14] **definement:** definition, description
[15] **perdition:** loss
[16] **you:** by your words
[17] **inventorially:** inventory or list them

120　dozy① the arithmetic of memory②, and yet but yaw③ neither④, in respect of⑤ his quick sail⑥. But, in the verity⑦ of extolment⑧, I take him to be a soul of great article⑨, and his infusion⑩ of such dearth⑪ and rareness, as, to make true diction⑫ of him⑬, his semblable⑭
125　is his mirror⑮, and who else would trace⑯ him, his umbrage⑰, nothing more.

OSRIC

Your lordship speaks most infallibly⑱ of him.

HAMLET

The concernancy⑲, sir? Why do we wrap the gentleman in our more rawer breath⑳?㉑

OSRIC

130　Sir?

---

① **dozy:** dizzy, confuse
② **the arithmetic of memory:** the ability of memory to calculate
③ **yaw:** steer off in the wake of a fast boat, fall short of
④ **neither:** after all
⑤ **in respect of:** in comparison with
⑥ **sail:** sailing
⑦ **verity:** truth
⑧ **extolment:** praise, eulogy
⑨ **soul of great article:** genius (he continues the language of the inventory)
⑩ **infusion:** natural endowments
⑪ **dearth:** dearness
⑫ **diction:** description
⑬ **to make true diction:** to speak truly of him
⑭ **semblable:** like, match
⑮ **mirror:** mirror image
⑯ **trace:** follow, emulate
⑰ **his umbrage:** is his shadow
⑱ **infallibly:** truthfully
⑲ **concernancy:** relevance
⑳ **in our more rawer breath:** in cruder words (words too crude to do him justice)
㉑ **Why ... breath:** Why are we talking about him?

HORATIO

[*Aside to Hamlet*] Is't not possible[1] to understand
in another tongue[2]?
You will do't[3], sir, really.

HAMLET

What imports the nomination[4] of this gentleman?

OSRIC

135   Of Laertes?

HORATIO

[*Aside*] His purse is empty already; all's golden
words are spent.

HAMLET

Of him, sir.

OSRIC

I know you are not ignorant—

HAMLET

140   I would you did, sir; yet, in faith, if you did,
it would not much approve[5] me.[6] Well, sir?

OSRIC

You are not ignorant of what excellence Laertes is—

HAMLET

I dare not confess that, lest I should compare with
him in excellence; but to know a man well were[7] to
145   know himself.

---

[1] **Is't not possible:** i.e. possible for Osric
[2] **another tongue:** another manner of speech
[3] **do't:** outdo Osric in affectation of language; manage it (i.e. speak more plainly)
[4] **nomination:** naming, mention
[5] **approve:** commend
[6] **it ... me:** it wouldn't do me any good
[7] **were:** is

OSRIC

I mean, sir, for his weapon; but in the imputation①
laid on him by them②, in his meed③ he's unfellowed④.

HAMLET

What's his weapon?

OSRIC

Rapier and dagger.

HAMLET

150　That's two of his weapons—but well.

OSRIC

The King, sir, hath wagered with him six Barbary⑤
horses, against the which⑥ he has imponed⑦, as I
take it, six French rapiers and poniards⑧, with their
assigns⑨, as⑩ girdle⑪, hangers⑫, and so⑬. Three of
155　the carriages⑭, in faith, are very dear to fancy⑮,
very responsive⑯ to the hilts, most delicate carriages,
and of very liberal conceit⑰.

---

① **imputation:** reputation
② **them:** those who know his merit
③ **meed:** merit
④ **unfellowed:** unmatched, without equal
⑤ **Barbary:** barbarian (i.e. Arabian)
⑥ **the which:** which
⑦ **imponed:** staked, wagered
⑧ **poniards:** daggers
⑨ **assigns:** accessories
⑩ **as:** such as
⑪ **girdle:** sword-belt
⑫ **hangers:** attaching straps
⑬ **so:** so on
⑭ **carriages:** loops of sword belts (but Hamlet interprets it as wheeled supports for cannons)
⑮ **dear to fancy:** tastefully designed
⑯ **very responsive:** well matched
⑰ **liberal conceit:** ingenious design

HAMLET

What call you the carriages?

HORATIO

[*Aside to Hamlet*] I knew you must be edified① by the margent② ere you had done.③

OSRIC

160 The carriages, sir, are the hangers.

HAMLET

The phrase would be more germane④ to the matter
if we could carry cannon by our sides. I would it might
be hangers till then. But on⑤! Six Barbary horses
against six French swords, their assigns, and three
165 liberal-conceited carriages: that's the French bet
against the Danish. Why is this imponed⑥, as you call it?

OSRIC

The King, sir, hath laid⑦ that, in a dozen passes⑧
between yourself and him, he shall not exceed you
three hits. He hath laid on twelve for nine, and it
170 would come to immediate trial if your lordship
would vouchsafe the answer⑨.

HAMLET

How if I answer no?

---

① **edified:** instructed
② **margent:** a marginal note
③ **I knew ... done:** I knew you would ask him this question.
④ **germane:** relevant
⑤ **on:** continue, go ahead
⑥ **imponed:** staked
⑦ **laid:** wagered
⑧ **passes:** exchanges, rounds, bouts
⑨ **vouchsafe the answer:** agree to accept the challenge (but Hamlet takes "answer" to mean "make a reply")

OSRIC

I mean, my lord, the opposition of your person[①] in trial.

HAMLET

Sir, I will walk here in the hall. If it please his
175 majesty, 'tis the breathing time of day with me[②]. Let
the foils be brought, the gentleman willing, and the
King hold his purpose, I will win for him an[③] I can.
If not, I will gain nothing but my shame and the odd hits[④].

OSRIC

Shall I redeliver you[⑤] e'en so?

HAMLET

180 To this effect, sir, after what flourish[⑥] your nature will[⑦].

OSRIC

I commend[⑧] my duty[⑨] to your lordship.

HAMLET

Yours, yours.

Exit OSRIC

He does well to commend[⑩] it himself. There are no
tongues else for's turn[⑪].

HORATIO

185 This lapwing[⑫] runs away with the shell on his head.

---

① **person:** presence
② **the breathing … me:** my daily time for exercise
③ **an:** if
④ **the odd hits:** any hits I may make
⑤ **redeliver you:** report back your message
⑥ **after what flourish:** in whatever elaborate style
⑦ **will:** wishes, intends
⑧ **commend:** offer (but Hamlet takes it to mean "praise")
⑨ **duty:** services
⑩ **commend:** praise
⑪ **for's turn:** for his purpose (i.e. to praise him)
⑫ **lapwing:** plover, newly hatched chicken

HAMLET

He did comply with[1] his dug[2] before he sucked it.
Thus has he—and many more of the same bevy[3] that
I know the drossy[4] age dotes on—only got the tune[5]
of the time[6] and out of an habit of encounter[7], a kind
of yesty collection[8], which carries them through and
through the most fond and winnowed[9] opinions[10];
and do but blow them to their trial, the bubbles are out.[11]

Enter a Lord

LORD

My lord, his majesty commended him[12] to you by young
Osric, who brings back to him that you attend him in
the hall. He sends to know if your pleasure hold to
play[13] with Laertes, or that[14] you will take longer time.

HAMLET

I am constant to my purposes; they[15] follow[16] the King's

---

[1] **comply with:** pay compliments to
[2] **his dug:** his mother's nipple
[3] **bevy:** company
[4] **drossy:** dressy, worthless
[5] **tune:** manner of speaking
[6] **only ... time:** captured only the fashionable style of the day
[7] **out of ... encounter:** from frequent social intercourse
[8] **yesty collection:** frothy mess
[9] **fond and winnowed:** sifted and refined
[10] **which ... opinions:** their elegant manners gain for them the complete approval of the most discriminating
[11] **do but ...out:** if you blow on them (Osric and his like) to see if there is any worth, they will collapse like bubbles
[12] **commended him:** sent his commendations or greetings
[13] **play:** fence
[14] **that:** if
[15] **they:** my purposes
[16] **follow:** obey, agree with

pleasure. If his fitness① speaks②, mine is ready;③ now or whensoever, provided I be so④ able as now.

LORD

The King and queen and all are coming down.

HAMLET

In happy time⑤.

LORD

The Queen desires you to use some gentle entertainment to⑥ Laertes before you fall to play.

HAMLET

She well instructs me.

Exit Lord

HORATIO

You will lose this wager, my lord.

HAMLET

I do not think so. Since he went into France, I have been in continual practice⑦; I shall win at the odds⑧. But thou wouldst not think how ill all's here about my heart. But it is no matter.

HORATIO

Nay, good my lord—

HAMLET

It is but foolery⑨, but it is such a kind of

---

① **fitness:** convenience
② **speaks:** suits
③ **If … ready:** if the King is ready, so am I
④ **so:** as
⑤ **In happy time:** opportunely (i.e. I'm glad to hear it)
⑥ **use … to:** greet with cordial courtesy, receive in a friendly way
⑦ **Since … practice:** Hamlet here contradicts his earlier claim that he has "forgone all / custom of exercises" (II. ii. 307—308).
⑧ **at the odds:** with the odds (advantage) allowed me
⑨ **foolery:** foolishness

gaingiving[1] as would perhaps trouble a woman.[2]
HORATIO
If your mind dislike any thing, obey it. I will
forestall their repair[3] hither, and say you are
215 not fit.
HAMLET
Not a whit[4], we defy augury[5]. There's a special
providence in the fall of a sparrow[6]. If it be now,
'tis not to come; if it be not to come, it will be
now; if it be not now, yet it will come.[7] The
220 readiness is all[8]. Since no man has aught of what he
leaves[9], what is't to leave[10] betimes[11]?
Enter KING, QUEEN, LAERTES, and Lords, with other Attendants with foils and gauntlets. A table and flagons of wine on it.
KING
Come, Hamlet, come, and take this hand from me.
He puts Laertes' hand into Hamlet's.
HAMLET
[*To Laertes*] Give me your pardon, sir. I have done you wrong;

---

[1] **gaingiving:** against giving, misgiving
[2] **It is but ... a woman:** He now has an ominous premonition.
[3] **repair:** coming
[4] **Not a whit:** not at all
[5] **augury:** omen
[6] **a special ... sparrow:** Cf. *Matthew* 10.29—31
[7] **If it be now ... yet it will come:** Cf. Epicurus: *A Letter to Menoikeos*
[8] **is all:** is the only important matter (Cf. *Henry V,* IV. iii. 71: "All things are ready, if our minds be so." *Julius Caesar,* II. ii. 35—37: "It seems to me most strange that men should fear; / Seeing that death, a necessary end, / Will come when it will come." *King Lear,* V. ii. 9—11: "Men must endure/Their going hence, even as their coming hither. / Ripeness is all.") Harold Bloom interprets this line as meaning: "personality is all, once personality has purged itself into a second birth." (*Shakespeare: The Invention of the Human,* New York: Riverhead Books, 1998, p.428)
[9] **no man ... leaves:** no man knows anything about what he leaves behind
[10] **leave:** die
[11] **betimes:** early

But pardon't, as you are a gentleman.
225　This presence① knows,
And you must needs② have heard, how I am punished
With sore③ distraction④. What I have done,
That might your nature⑤, honor and exception⑥
Roughly⑦ awake⑧, I here proclaim was madness.
230　Was't Hamlet wronged⑨ Laertes? Never Hamlet.
If Hamlet from himself be⑩ ta'en away,
And when he's not himself does wrong Laertes,
Then Hamlet does it not, Hamlet denies it.
Who does it, then? His madness. If't be so,
235　Hamlet is of the faction⑪ that is wronged;
His madness is poor Hamlet's enemy.⑫
Sir, in this audience,
Let my disclaiming from⑬ a purposed⑭ evil⑮
Free me so far in your most generous thoughts
240　That I have⑯ shot mine arrow o'er the house

---

① **This presence:** this royal audience, the whole court
② **needs:** necessarily
③ **sore:** severe, serious
④ **distraction:** madness
⑤ **nature:** filial love
⑥ **exception:** dissatisfaction, objection
⑦ **Roughly:** harshly
⑧ **awake:** arouse
⑨ **wronged:** who wronged
⑩ **be:** is
⑪ **faction:** party
⑫ **His ... enemy:** Cf. Samuel Johnson: "Of the feigned madness of Hamlet there appears no adequate cause, for he does nothing which he might not have done with the reputation of sanity. He plays the madman most, when he treats Ophelia with so much rudeness, which seems to be useless and wanton cruelty." (*On Shakespeare*)
⑬ **disclaiming from:** denial of
⑭ **purposed:** intended
⑮ **purposed evil:** deliberate evil intention
⑯ **That I have:** as if I had, as to imagine I have

And hurt my brother①.
LAERTES②
I am satisfied in nature③,
Whose motive④ in this case should stir me most
To my revenge. But in my terms⑤ of honor⑥
245 I stand aloof and will⑦ no reconcilement⑧,
Till by some elder masters⑨ of known honor,
I have a voice⑩ and precedent⑪ of peace⑫,
To keep my name⑬ ungored⑭.⑮ But till that time
I do receive your offered love like love
250 And will not wrong it.
HAMLET
I embrace it freely,
And will this brother's wager frankly⑯ play.
Give us the foils. Come on.
LAERTES
Come, one for me.

---

① **my brother:** Cf. 82—83: "by the image of my cause I see / The portraiture of his."
② **242—250:** As Hamlet glosses over his past fault (227—241) , Laertes dissimulates about his planned revenge.
③ **in nature:** in terms of my natural affections for my father and my sister
④ **Whose motive:** the motivation of which
⑤ **terms:** circumstances
⑥ **honor:** sense of honor
⑦ **will:** wish for, desire
⑧ **reconcilement:** reconciliation
⑨ **masters:** experts in these matters
⑩ **voice:** opinion
⑪ **precedent:** previous example
⑫ **peace:** reconciliation
⑬ **name:** reputation
⑭ **ungored:** unstained
⑮ **245—248:** " I will accept no reconciliation until experts in those questions give a decision that may serve as a precedent for making peace, thus freeing my reputation from a charge of dishonor."
⑯ **frankly:** freely, willingly

HAMLET

255 I'll be your foil①, Laertes. In mine ignorance
Your skill shall, like a star i'② the darkest night,
Stick fiery off③ indeed.

LAERTES

You mock me, sir.

HAMLET

No, by this hand.

KING

260 Give them the foils, young Osric. Cousin Hamlet,
You know the wager?

HAMLET

Very well, my lord.
Your grace has laid the odds o' the weaker side.

KING

I do not fear it; I have seen you both.
265 But since he is bettered④, we have therefore odds⑤.

LAERTES

This is too heavy, let me see another.⑥

HAMLET

This likes⑦ me well. These foils have all a⑧ length?

Prepare to play

OSRIC

Ay, my good lord.

---

① **foil:** setting or background, a person used to set off another
② **i':** in contrast to
③ **Stick fiery off:** stand out brilliantly
④ **is bettered:** has improved
⑤ **But ... odds:** that Laertes must make three more hits to win (9 in 12 passes)
⑥ **This ... another:** He selects the sharpened, poisoned rapier.
⑦ **likes:** pleases
⑧ **all a:** the same

KING

Set me the stoups[1] of wine upon that table.
270 If Hamlet give the first or second hit
Or quit[2] in answer of the third exchange[3],
Let all the battlements[4] their ordnance[5] fire;
The King shall drink to Hamlet's better breath[6],
And in the cup an union[7] shall he throw,
275 Richer than that which four successive kings
In Denmark's crown have worn. Give me the cups,
And let the kettle[8] to the trumpet speak,
The trumpet to the cannoneer without[9],
The cannons to the heavens, the heavens to earth,
280 'Now the King drinks to Hamlet.' Come, begin.
And you, the judges, bear a wary eye.

HAMLET

Come on, sir.

LAERTES

Come, my lord.

They play

HAMLET

One.[10]

LAERTES

285 No.

---

[1] **stoups:** big goblets, flagons
[2] **quit:** repay
[3] **quit ... exchange:** requite Laertes for earlier hits by scoring the third hit
[4] **battlements:** soldiers
[5] **ordnance:** cannon
[6] **breath:** health; improved performance
[7] **union:** large pearl
[8] **kettle:** kettledrum
[9] **without:** outside
[10] **One:** Hamlet claims one hit.

HAMLET

Judgment!

OSRIC

A hit, a very palpable① hit.

LAERTES

Well, again!

KING

Stay②, give me drink. Hamlet, this pearl is thine.③

290 Here's to thy health.④

Drum; trumpets sound; a piece goes off within

Give him the cup.

HAMLET

I'll play this bout first; set it by awhile. Come.

They play

Another hit. What say you?

LAERTES

A touch, a touch. I do confess.

KING

295 Our son⑤ shall⑥ win.

QUEEN

He's fat⑦, and scant of⑧ breath.

Here, Hamlet, take my napkin⑨, rub thy brows.

The Queen carouses⑩ to thy fortune, Hamlet.

---

① **palpable:** tangible, definite
② **Stay:** wait a moment
③ **Hamlet, the pearl is thine:** The pearl either contains the poison or identifies Hamlet's cup.
④ **Here's to thy health:** Claudius drinks first to dissipate (if any) suspicion.
⑤ **Our son:** Mock endearment: he is feeling uneasy now.
⑥ **shall:** will surely
⑦ **fat:** sweaty
⑧ **scant of:** out of
⑨ **napkin:** handkerchief
⑩ **carouses:** drinks a toast

She Lifts the Cup.

HAMLET

Good madam!

KING

300 Gertrude, do not drink.

QUEEN

I will, my lord; I pray you pardon me.①

She Drinks.

KING

[*Aside*] It is the poisoned cup; it is too late.

HAMLET

I dare not drink yet, madam; by and by②.

QUEEN

Come, let me wipe thy face.

LAERTES

305 My lord, I'll hit him now.

KING

I do not think't.

LAERTES

[*Aside*] And yet 'tis almost 'gainst my conscience.

HAMLET

Come, for the third, Laertes! You but dally③.

I pray you, pass④ with your best violence⑤.

310 I am afeard⑥ you make a wanton of me⑦.

---

① **I will … me:** This is a significant answer. Perhaps she has sensed or seen through the trick and therefore drinks the poison deliberately.

② **by and by:** soon, before long

③ **dally:** dodge

④ **pass:** thrust

⑤ **best violence:** utmost strength

⑥ **afeard:** afraid

⑦ **make a wanton of me:** treat me as a spoiled child.

LAERTES

Say you so? Come on.

They play.

OSRIC

Nothing, neither way①.

LAERTES

Have at you now!②

LAERTES wounds HAMLET; then in scuffling, they change rapiers, and HAMLET wounds LAERTES

KING

Part them! They are incensed③.

HAMLET

315   Nay, come! again!

The Queen falls.

OSRIC

Look to the Queen there, ho!

HORATIO

They bleed on both sides. How is it, my lord?

OSRIC

How is't, Laertes?

LAERTES

Why, as a woodcock④ to mine own springe⑤, Osric.

320   I am justly killed with mine own treachery.

HAMLET

How does the Queen?

---

① **neither way:** no advantage on either side
② **Have at you now:** He sneaks upon Hamlet for a surprise attack.
③ **incensed:** irritated
④ **woodcock:** bird stupid and easy to catch
⑤ **to mine own springe:** caught in my own trap

KING

She swoons[1] to see them bleed.

QUEEN

No, no, the drink, the drink! O my dear Hamlet!

The drink, the drink! I am poisoned.[2]

Dies.

HAMLET

325　O villany! Ho! Let the door be locked.

Treachery[3]! Seek it[4] out.

LAERTES

It is here, Hamlet. Hamlet, thou art slain;

No med'cine in the world can do thee good.

In thee there is not half an hour of life.

330　The treacherous instrument is in thy hand,

Unbated[5] and envenomed[6]. The foul practice[7]

Hath turned itself[8] on me. Lo, here I lie,

Never to rise again. Thy mother's poisoned.

I can[9] no more. The King, the King's to blame[10].

HAMLET

335　The point envenomed too!

Then, venom, to thy work.

Hurts the King

ALL

Treason! treason!

---

[1]　**swoons:** faints
[2]　**323—324:** She reveals the King's plot to her son just before her death.
[3]　**Treachery:** treason
[4]　**it:** the murderer
[5]　**Unbated:** sharp
[6]　**envenomed:** poisoned
[7]　**practice:** plot, trick
[8]　**itself:** redounded
[9]　**can:** can say or do
[10]　**the King's to blame:** the King is the real murderer

KING

O, yet defend me, friends! I am but hurt.

HAMLET

Here, thou incestuous, murderous, damnèd Dane,

340 Drink off this potion! Is thy union① here?

Forces him to drink the poison.

Follow my mother.

KING dies.

LAERTES

He is justly served.

It is a poison tempered② by himself.

Exchange forgiveness with me, noble Hamlet.

345 Mine③ and my father's death come not upon thee④,

Nor thine⑤ on me.

Dies.

HAMLET

Heaven make thee free of⑥ it⑦!⑧ I follow thee.

I am dead, Horatio. Wretched⑨ queen, adieu!

You that look pale and tremble at this chance⑩,⑪

350 That are but mutes⑫ or audience to this act⑬,

---

① **union:** pearl; marriage and death
② **tempered:** mixed, compounded
③ **Mine:** my death
④ **come not upon thee:** be not charges against you (at the Last Judgment)
⑤ **thine:** your death
⑥ **of:** from
⑦ **it:** the guilt
⑧ **Heaven ... it:** Hamlet forgives Laertes, too.
⑨ **Wretched:** unhappy, poor
⑩ **chance:** mischance; what has happened
⑪ **You that ... chance:** Cf. Aristotle: "Tragedy represents ... incidents that cause fear and pity". (*Poetics*, 1452a)
⑫ **mutes:** walk-on parts, actors without speaking parts
⑬ **act:** section, performance

Had I but time—as[1] this fell[2] sergeant[3], Death,
Is strict[4] in his arrest—O, I could tell you—
But let it be. Horatio, I am dead;
Thou livest; report me and my cause aright[5]
355 To the unsatisfied[6].

HORATIO
Never believe it.[7]
I am more an antique Roman[8] than a Dane.
Here's yet some liquor left.
He picks up the cup.

HAMLET
As thou'rt[9] a man,
360 Give me the cup. Let go![10] By heaven, I'll have't.
O good Horatio, what a wounded name[11],
Things standing thus unknown, shall live behind me!
If thou didst ever hold me in thy heart,
Absent thee from[12] felicity[13] awhile,
365 And in this harsh world draw thy breath in pain,
To tell my story.
March afar off, and shot within.

---

[1] **as:** because; whereas
[2] **fell:** fierce, cruel
[3] **sergeant:** officer
[4] **strict:** precise, rigorous
[5] **report ... aright:** give an accurate account of my story
[6] **the unsatisfied:** those ignorant of the truth and perplexed; those who demand an explanation
[7] **Never believe it:** No way!
[8] **antique Roman:** The noble Romans committed suicide for their friends, e.g. Cato and Brutus.
[9] **thou'rt:** you are
[10] **Let go:** He snatches the cup from Horatio's hand.
[11] **wounded name:** damaged reputation (i.e. treason)
[12] **Absent thee from:** keep yourself from
[13] **felicity:** the happiness of death

What warlike noise is this?
OSRIC
Young Fortinbras, with conquest① come from Poland,
To the ambassadors of England gives②
370 This warlike volley③.
HAMLET
O, I die, Horatio!
The potent poison quite o'er-crows④ my spirit⑤.
I cannot live to hear the news from England,
But I do prophesy the election lights⑥
375 On Fortinbras. He has my dying voice⑦.⑧
So tell him, with the occurrents⑨, more and less⑩,
Which have solicited⑪. The rest is silence.⑫
Dies.
HORATIO
Now cracks a noble heart.⑬ Good night, sweet prince,

---

① **conquest:** victorious ceremony
② **gives:** has shot off
③ **volley:** a volley of gunfire (to salute the ambassadors of England)
④ **o'er-crows:** triumphs over, overpowers
⑤ **spirit:** vitality, life
⑥ **lights:** alights, falls
⑦ **voice:** vote
⑧ 374—375: Dying Hamlet voices a new political order by appointing Fortinbras as King of Denmark, so his death "results in tragic resurrection, in the sense that he has died while saving the kingdom for mankind". Although he had not been "put on" (421) and failed to "have proved most royally" (422), Hamlet is nevertheless the Prince (Latin: *princeps*, "first man, first citizen") of New Denmark. (John Doebler: *The Play within the Play: The Muscipula Diaboli in Hamlet*, in *Shakespeare Quarterly*, Vol. 23, No. 2, 1972)
⑨ **occurrents:** occurrences
⑩ **more and less:** (all the events) major and minor
⑪ **solicited:** brought on (this tragedy); incited (me to give him my support)
⑫ **The rest is silence:** Samuel Weber:"[T]he defiant silence of the tragic hero constitute an act that announces a radical break with the vicious circle of guilt and atonement rather than a confirmation of its ineluctability." (*Benjamin's -abilities*, Harvard University Press, 2008, p.151.)
⑬ **Now cracks a noble heart:** Cf. I. ii. 158: "break my heart"; III. i 161: "what a noble mind is here o'erthrown!"

And flights[1] of angels sing thee to thy rest![2]
380 Why does the drum come hither?

March within.

Enter FORTINBRAS and English Ambassadors, with Drum, Colors, and Attendants.

PRINCE FORTINBRAS
Where is this sight?

HORATIO
What is it you would see?
If aught of woe or wonder[3], cease your search.

PRINCE FORTINBRAS
This quarry[4] cries on[5] havoc[6].[7] O proud Death,
385 What feast is toward[8] in thine eternal cell
That thou so many princes at a shot
So bloodily hast struck?

FIRST AMBASSADOR
The sight is dismal[9],
And our affairs from England come too late.
390 The ears are senseless that should give us hearing
To tell him[10] his commandment is fulfilled,
That Rosencrantz and Guildenstern are dead.
Where should we have our thanks?

---

① **flights:** flying companies
② **And ... rest:** This line suggests Hamlet's salvation or the reconciliation between man and God.
③ **wonder:** calamity
④ **quarry:** pile of dead bodies
⑤ **on:** out
⑥ **havoc:** the old battle cry for "No quarter"
⑦ **This quarry ... havoc:** This pile of dead bodies proclaims that there has been a massacre.
⑧ **toward:** going forward, in preparation
⑨ **dismal:** dreadful, disastrous (with a stronger meaning than the modern use)
⑩ **him:** i.e. Claudius

HORATIO

Not from his① mouth,
395　Had it the ability of life to thank you.
　　He never gave commandment for their death.
　　But since, so jump② upon③ this bloody question④,
　　You from the Polack wars, and you from England,
　　Are here arrived, give order that these bodies
400　High on a stage⑤ be placèd to the view,
　　And let me speak to the yet unknowing world⑥
　　How these things came about. So shall you hear
　　Of carnal⑦, bloody, and unnatural acts;
　　Of accidental judgments⑧, casual⑨ slaughters;
405　Of deaths put on⑩ by cunning⑪ and forced⑫ cause;
　　And, in this upshot⑬, purposes mistook⑭
　　Fall'n on the inventors' heads. All this can I
　　Truly deliver⑮ ⑯.

---

① **his:** the King's
② **jump:** exactly, timely
③ **upon:** right upon the heels of
④ **question:** event
⑤ **stage:** platform
⑥ **394—401:** a choric epilogue
⑦ **carnal:** sensual, incestuous
⑧ **accidental judgements:** Judgments of God brought about by accident
⑨ **casual:** occurring by chance
⑩ **put on:** instigated
⑪ **cunning:** plot
⑫ **forced:** strained, exaggerated
⑬ **upshot:** consequence, conclusion
⑭ **purposes mistook:** of mistaken purposes
⑮ **deliver:** report, tell.
⑯ **All ... deliver:** Cf. Hannah Arendt: "[O]nly the spectator occupies a position that enables him to see the whole ... The spectator is impartial by definition—no part is assigned him." (*Lectures on Kant's Political Philosophy,* Chicago: The University of Chicago Press, 1992, p.63) "Judgment is retrospective and is pronounced by the bystander or onlooker ... Correspondingly, only the political spectator, removed from the action, can render disinterested judgment on the human significance of events unfolding in the political world." (id., p.131)

PRINCE FORTINBRAS

Let us haste to hear it,

410 And call the noblest to the audience.

For[1] me, with sorrow I embrace my fortune[2].[3]

I have some rights of memory[4] in this kingdom,

Which now to claim my vantage[5] doth invite me[6].

HORATIO

Of that I shall have also cause to speak,

415 And from his mouth whose voice[7] will draw on[8] more[9].

But let this same[10] be presently[11] performed,

Even while men's minds are wild[12], lest more mischance

On[13] plots and errors happen[14].

PRINCE FORTINBRAS

Let four captains

420 Bear Hamlet like a soldier to the stage;[15]

For he was likely, had he been put on[16],

To have proved most royally; and for his passage[17]

The soldiers' music and the rites of war

---

[1] **For:** as for
[2] **fortune:** good luck
[3] **with sorrow ... my fortune:** Cf. I. ii. 10—14: "with a defeated joy" etc.
[4] **rights of memory:** rights remembered, unforgotten rights
[5] **vantage:** advantageous position
[6] **Which ... me:** which my presence here at this advantageous time invites me to claim. Cf. V. i. 86—87: "Here's fine revolution, if we had the trick to / see't."
[7] **voice:** vote
[8] **draw on:** attract the approval of
[9] **more:** more voices or votes
[10] **this same:** the aforesaid
[11] **presently:** immediately
[12] **wild:** excited, disturbed
[13] **On:** on account of
[14] **On ... happen:** happen as a result of plots and errors
[15] **Bear ... stage:** Hamlet is to be given a proper funeral ceremony.
[16] **put on:** put to the test, given the opportunity to rule as king
[17] **passage:** passing, death

Speak① loudly for him.

425 Take up the bodies. Such a sight as this

Becomes② the field③, but here shows much amiss④.

Go, bid the soldiers shoot.

*Exeunt marching; after the which a peal of ordinance is shot off.*⑤

---

① **Speak:** let … speak
② **Becomes:** befits, is appropriate to
③ **field:** battlefield
④ **shows much amiss:** is most out of place
⑤ ***shot off***: The play ends with a burial and, as it were, a lustration ceremony. (Cf. IV. v. 103: "as the world were now but to begin")

哈姆雷特的问题

1. 悲　剧

《哈姆雷特》一名《丹麦王子哈姆雷特的悲剧》（*The Tragedy of Hamlet, Prince of Denmark*），我们就从标题中的"悲剧"谈起。

"悲剧"意味着什么呢？《哈姆雷特》剧终时，莎士比亚借剧中人Horatio之口现身说法（V. ii. 402—407）：

> 你会听到
> 肉欲、血腥和违反伦常的行为，
> 偶然的决断和意外的屠戮，
> 诡诈与胁迫引致的死亡，
> 以及最后的作法自毙。

在这里，他对全剧内容做了简要回顾，也仿佛给"悲剧"下了一个定义。作者的看法自然值得重视，但正如我们经常看到的那样，作者本人对自己作品的解释或认识不一定是最准确的（有时甚至是不准确的）[①]；"肉欲、血腥和违反伦常的行为，偶然的决断和

[①] 即如伽达默尔所说："创造某个作品的艺术家并不是这个作品的理想解释者。艺术家作为解释者，并不比普通的接受者有更大的权威性。就他反思他自己的作品而言，他就是他自己的读者。他作为反思者所具有的看法并不具有权威性。"参见《真理与方法》，洪汉鼎译，上海：上海译文出版社，1992年，第249—250页。

意外的屠戮，诡诈与胁迫引致的死亡"固然是悲剧中常见的主题情节，但是这些东西显然不足以概括悲剧——无论是一般悲剧还是这个悲剧——的本质。

亚里士多德在《诗学》中将悲剧界定为"对一个严肃、完整、有一定长度的行动的摹仿"（第6章）①。此处说的"摹仿"（mimesis）具有"再现"的意思，因此我们可以说《哈姆雷特》再现了哈姆雷特王子的复仇行为。不过这个定义偏于形式，并不足以说明悲剧的本质。亚里士多德本人做过一些补充说明，指出悲剧表现高贵者因自身过错（hamartia，或译"偏差""罪过"）致使命运发生逆转，从而引发怜悯与恐惧的效果（《诗学》第13章）②。以《哈姆雷特》为例，哈姆雷特王子由于遭受陷害和内心惶惑而"延宕"复仇行动，致使包括自身在内总共八人③丧生，这一结局不禁令人产生"怜悯与恐惧"的感受（Cf. V. ii. 349:"You that look pale and tremble at this chance" *etc.*）。不过，哈姆雷特是否犯有"过错"呢？如果他犯了"过错"，这又是怎样的"过错"呢？显然，我们需要重新审度"过错"的含义才能回答上述问题。黑格尔认为恶就是"存在对于应当的非适合性"④：对于理想状态的"应当"来说，现实的"存在"必然总是有所欠缺、不够完美；在这个意义上讲，存在即罪过⑤，——这个略显笼统的说法或许就是最终的答案。

不同于亚里士多德关注悲剧形式的做法，黑格尔主要探讨了

---

① 亚里士多德：《诗学》，陈中梅译，北京：商务印书馆，1996年，第63页。
② 同上书，第97页。
③ 此八人是：Polonius, Ophelia, Rosencrantz, Guildenstern, Gertrude, Laertes, Claudius以及Hamlet本人。
④ 黑格尔：《哲学科学全书纲要》第391节，薛华译，上海：上海人民出版社，2002年，第288页。
⑤ 叔本华举西班牙剧作家卡尔德隆（Calderón, 1600—1681）的诗句"人的最大罪恶就是他诞生了"为例，指出悲剧的真正意义在于深刻地认识到悲剧主人公所赎的不是他个人特有的罪，而是人类的原罪即生存本身之罪（参见叔本华：《作为意志与表象的世界》，石冲白译，北京：商务印书馆，1982年，第352页）。关于"存在即罪过"这个问题，德国社会学家舍勒（M. Scheler）曾有专文讨论，读者可参看他的《论悲剧性现象》一文（载刘小枫主编：《人类困境中的审美精神》，上海：东方出版中心，1994年，特别是第307、309页）。

"悲剧性"或曰悲剧的精神。在他看来，悲剧表现为片面正义——悲剧人物之间的冲突、破裂以及永恒正义的调停、胜出。如其在《美学》中所说："基本的悲剧性"产生于"对立的双方各有他那一方面的辩护理由，而同时每一方拿来作为自己所坚持的那种目的和性格的真正内容的，却只能是把同样有辩护理由的对方否定掉或破坏掉"；同时"随着这种个别特殊性的毁灭，永恒正义就把伦理的实体和统一恢复过来了"。[①]他在《法哲学原理》中也说：

> 这些人物（按：即悲剧人物）作为具有同等权利的各种不同伦理力量在彼此对立中出现，它们由于某种不幸而发生冲突；又因为其结果是这些人物由于跟伦理性的东西相对立而获有罪责。于是在这种情况下产生了双方的法与不法，从而真正的伦理理念，经过纯化并克服了这种片面性之后，就在我们心目中得到调和。[②]

他在《哲学史讲演录》中谈到苏格拉底时也指出："在真正悲剧性的事件中，必须有两个合法的、伦理的力量相互冲突"[③]，"两方面都是无罪的，但是这个无罪却是有罪的，并且因为它的罪过而受到惩罚"；"一个伟大的人会是有罪的，他担负起伟大的冲突"而执行了"精神的更高的原则"；"这个新的原则是与以往的原则矛盾的，是以破坏的姿态出现的；因此英雄们是以暴力强制的姿态出现，是损害法律的"；结果他们"作为个人，都各自没落了；但是这个原则却贯彻了"。[④]

黑格尔的观点对后世影响深远（例如尼采的悲剧理论虽然另辟

---

① 黑格尔：《美学》第三卷（下册），朱光潜译，北京：商务印书馆，1981年，第286、287页。
② 黑格尔：《法哲学原理》，范扬、张企泰译，北京：商务印书馆，1961年，第157页注2。
③ 黑格尔：《哲学史讲演录》（第二卷），贺麟、王太庆译，北京：商务印书馆，1960年，第44页。
④ 同上书，第106—107页。

蹊径，但是也遵循了"冲突—和解"的思路①），特别是他的"片面正义"说，构成了"hamartia"与舍勒所谓"积极价值"②的一个中间环节。仍以《哈姆雷特》为例，哈姆雷特对Claudius有杀父之仇、夺国之恨，他的举动自然不乏正义性；Polonius逢君之恶自以为忠、Laertius为复亲仇不择手段亦有其"片面正义"在；甚至Claudius弑兄篡位在很大程度上也是出于对Gertrude的炽热爱情（Cf. IV. vii. 15—18）。他后来派人刺探、设计谋害哈姆雷特也是为了保全自身，从他本人的立场来看也是正当的；何况他因看戏而良心发现（III. i. 58—62），痛苦地忏悔了自己的罪孽（III. iii. 39—75），后来看到Ophelia的疯态心生恻隐，叮嘱Horatio看护好她（IV. v. 57 & 73），亦见其天良未泯、善念犹存③。存在固然是罪过，但同时"存在即合理"④：这一存在的吊诡构成了悲剧性的环中之义。

悲剧既是一种特定的文学样式（tragedy），也是一种风格、意蕴或精神；前者是特定历史文化条件下的产物（因此有"悲剧已经消亡"之说），而后者普遍存在于人类社会，甚至可以说是"宇宙本身的一种基本要素"⑤。中文将"tragedy"译为"悲剧"在一定程

---

① 不过对立双方不是各执一偏的伦理，而是"日神精神"与"酒神精神"，它们最终也在"兄弟联盟"中取得了和解："狄奥尼索斯讲的是阿波罗的语言，而阿波罗终于也讲起了狄奥尼索斯的语言"（尼采：《悲剧的诞生》第21节，孙周兴译，北京：商务印书馆，2012年，第159页）。尼采后来在《看哪这人！》中说他的这本书"散发着令人讨厌的黑格尔气息"（尼采：《权力意志》，张念东、凌素心译，北京：商务印书馆，1991年，第50页），可见他的观点确实受到了黑格尔的影响。

② 舍勒指出："悲剧性始终是以价值和价值关系为支点和基础的"；"悲剧性首先是相当高的积极价值的载体（如处于同一婚姻、同一家庭或同一国家的若干贤德高位者）之间爆发的矛盾；悲剧性是在积极价值及其载体内部起支配作用的'冲突'"；"毁灭更高积极价值的力量本身来源于积极价值的载体，当同样高的价值'天生注定'一般相互消耗、相互扬弃时，悲剧性现象便最为粹而不杂、轮廓鲜明"（《论悲剧性现象》，《人类困境中的审美精神》，第292页、第293—294页、第298页）。

③ Cf. A. C. Bradley: *Shakespearean Tragedy*, London: The Macmillan Press Ltd., 1974, pp.138—139.

④ 参见黑格尔：《精神现象学》（下卷）贺麟、王玖兴译，北京：商务印书馆，1979年，第86页；《法哲学原理》，序言第11页；《哲学史讲演录》（第一卷），第39页；《小逻辑》，贺麟译，北京：商务印书馆，1980年，第43、296页。

⑤ 舍勒：《论悲剧性现象》，《人类困境中的审美精神》，第289、299页。

度上混淆了这两者，于是一度产生"中国有无悲剧"的讨论。事实上，前一种意义上的悲剧起源于原始宗教祭礼，确切讲是古希腊酒神节（Dionysia）中的献祭仪式（dithyramb→tragoidia→tragedy，原意为"山羊歌"，盖以山羊为祭品而得名），译为"牺牲剧"似乎更为贴近悲剧的本质。

献祭是一种宗教行为，或者说是人神之间的一种交往模式。根据"经济人"（homo economicus）的理论假设[①]，献祭也是一种原始的商业交换行为，其目的是奉献牺牲向神换取利好的结果（"do ut des"），而牺牲则是赎买福报的代价与手段。悲剧就是这种交往模式的艺术再现，尽管有所变形：在古希腊悲剧中，茫茫天道（亦即"命运"）成为人的归宿或终极目的，而悲剧英雄（如索福克勒斯笔下的俄狄浦斯王）则是人类向命运祭献上的牺牲。这是一种原始的目的论生命哲学，它在悲剧形式中得到了最初表达，并且构成了希腊悲剧的精神内核与伦理支点。

在这个意义上，"目的论"与"戏剧性"实乃一枚硬币的两面。古希腊人把宇宙视为一出起承转合丝丝入扣的戏剧，"命运"就是它的结局或曰终极目的，其中每一角色、对白、事件均为这一目的而存在，都是它的必要环节和有意味的组成部分。中世纪神学也承袭了这一隐喻思维，只不过把"命运"换成了"上帝"，作为牺牲的悲剧英雄也变成了耶稣基督。这一点最终由德国古典哲学发挥为"历史具有长期合目的性"（康德）、"世界历史是精神的舞台"（黑格尔）等哲学理念[②]。至此，目的论和戏剧性几乎可以等量齐观了。

不过，哲学往往把终极目的视为"善"或者是"美"，而古希

[①] 这一理论假设一切人都具有趋利避害的理性，这种理性以利益最大化为目标与决策原则，做出最有利的决定，并且不受文化、感情、习俗、道德、信仰等非理性因素的影响。

[②] 基督教神学认为上帝编导了世界—历史，但在德国古典哲学体系中上帝变成了目的理性。如黑格尔提出目的是"真实的东西"与"事物的灵魂"，即"概念"或曰"自在自为的本质"；世界历史就是以"精神"为目的而必然展开的实现过程（参见黑格尔：《哲学史讲演录》（第一卷），第355页、第370—373页）。

腊悲剧中的"命运"却意谓无情的必然性。如哲学家怀特海（A. N. Whitehead）所说，古希腊悲剧诗人把命运视为无偏无党、不以人的意志为转移的"自然秩序"，后世的科学精神即由此开出：

> 悲剧的本质不是不幸，而是事物无情活动的严肃性。但这种命运的必然性，只有通过人生中真实的不幸遭遇才能说明。因为只有通过这些剧情才能说明逃避是无用的。这种无情的必然性充满了科学的思想。物理的定律就等于人生命运的律令。①

如其所说，则命运乃是一种外在的目的，它横亘于人类之前（或之外），壁立千仞而无法企越，表现为绝对的否定力量：你必须／必然付出牺牲，但是你的牺牲或许并无意义！

临对这样一种冥茫难测的命运，人类无法不感到惶惑甚至愤懑。他们最初只是抱怨命运不公，诘问"天命反侧，何罚何佑"（《楚辞·天问》），并未怀疑上苍的存在，如基督教《旧约》中的约伯自怨自艾之余仍不忘申明"我知道我的救赎主活着"（*Job* 19:25）。但是到后来，人类对上苍的存在也产生了怀疑，如司马迁有一段著名的议论：

> 或曰"天道无亲，常与善人"。若伯夷、叔齐，可谓善人者非邪？积仁絜行如此而饿死！且七十子之徒，仲尼独荐颜渊为好学。然回也屡空，糟糠不厌，而卒蚤夭。天之报施善人，其何如哉？盗蹠日杀不辜，肝人之肉，暴戾恣睢，聚党数千人横行天下，竟以寿终。是遵何德哉？此其尤大彰明较著者也。若至近世，操行不轨，专犯忌讳，而终身逸乐，富厚累世不绝。或择地而蹈之，时然后出言，行不由径，非公正不发愤，而遇祸灾者，不可胜数也。余甚惑焉，傥所谓天道，是邪非

---

① 怀特海：《科学与近代世界》，何钦译，北京：商务印书馆，1959年，第10页。

邪？（《史记·伯夷叔齐列传》）

司马迁之问"是邪非邪？"和哈姆雷特的问题"To be, or not to be?"一样，对终极目的表示出极大的怀疑，其锋芒直指天道或永恒正义的存在。太史公本人没有明言，但是后人替他说出了答案，这就是："天地无心，万物同途"（刘琨：《答卢谌》），"吾固知苍苍之无信，莫莫之无神"（柳宗元：《祭吕衡州温文》）！

不过细想之下，问难其实预肯了信从，质疑者往往正是因为相信——而且是过于相信——才比常人更加激愤。老子断言"天地不仁，以万物为刍狗"（《老子》第五章）就要冷静得多。当然，这种哲人式的冷静还不等于绝望；绝望的人是不会发问的，因为他已经全然麻木而浑无所谓了。这时悲剧变成反讽，一切都沉入了虚无。例如《红楼梦》第五十四回，王熙凤在贾府的元宵夜宴上讲了这样一个诡异的笑话：

> 凤姐儿想了一想，笑道："一家子也是过正月半，合家赏灯吃酒，真真的热闹非常，祖婆婆、太婆婆、婆婆、媳妇、孙子媳妇、重孙子媳妇、亲孙子、侄孙子、重孙子、灰孙子、滴滴搭搭的孙子、孙女儿、外孙女儿、姨表孙女儿、姑表孙女儿，……嗳哟哟，真好热闹！"众人听他说着，已经笑了，都说："听数贫嘴，又不知编派那一个呢。"尤氏笑道："你要招我，我可撕你的嘴。"凤姐儿起身拍手笑道："人家费力说，你们混，我就不说了。"贾母笑道："你说你说，底下怎么样？"凤姐儿想了一想，笑道："底下就团团的坐了一屋子，吃了一夜酒就散了。"众人见他正言厉色的说了，别无他话，都怔怔的还等下话，只觉冰冷无味。①

"真真的热闹非常"，然而"吃了一夜酒就散了"，这乃是《红楼

---

① 曹雪芹、高鹗：《红楼梦》，北京：人民文学出版社，1982年，第765页。

梦》全书的点睛之笔：人生不过是一个"冰冷无味"的"笑话"罢了！这个笑话惊心动魄，而作者竟让书中人无意间以笑语出之，更觉耐人寻味。

《哈姆雷特》正处在悲剧转向反讽的临界点上。以往的悲剧英雄都对自身选择的合理性与正义性深信不疑，而哈姆雷特对此却具有充分的自省意识；他在刹那间得窥世界的无情本质而质疑命运的终极目的，并就此产生了一种形而上的、对于存在本身的失望：如果人类的牺牲不能促成永恒正义的显现，那么——"To be, or not to be?"基督教悲剧英雄约伯最终蒙受了双倍神恩（*Job* 42:10），但哈姆雷特并不需要这种莫名其妙的恩典；作为一国储君和被害人的独子，他无法超然置身局外（Cf. I. v. 208—209: "The time is out of joint. O cursèd spite / That ever I was born to set it right!"），而作为清醒的思想者，他也不可能自欺欺人或麻木不仁（Cf. V. ii. 4—5: "Sir, in my heart there was a kind of fighting / That would not let me sleep."）。于是，留给他的就有痛苦的自觉和自觉的痛苦了。

不过痛苦是生物的特权，正是在痛苦中我们感受到了自己的主体性[①]。"我痛故我在"：器官产生病变时才会使人注意到它们的存在；同理，生命中出现了痛苦才会让我们感到自身存在的真实，并对之进行反思，如托尔斯泰笔下的安娜那样追问"我在哪里？我在做什么？为什么？"个体由于痛苦而发现了小我，并有可能以此为契机进一步冲破小我，站在类族或大我的立场上重新审度命运。这时他或许会发现：个体意志在命运的轰击下凝然持存，不仅拓展了生存的厚度与深度，甚且把命运收回自身而成为生命的内在目的。这一内在目的即是个体生命的真实存在；这时，存在不再是否定的悲剧，而是成为肯定的喜剧。

《哈姆雷特》全剧以葬礼告终，但剧终时分的殷殷炮声暗示了

[①] 黑格尔：《逻辑学》（下卷），杨一之译，北京：商务印书馆，1976年，第467页。《历史哲学》，王造时译，上海：上海书店出版社，1999年，第200页。

新生的开始:哈姆雷特死了,但是他的意志却借助他的敌手和镜像人物 Fortinbras 得到了实现（V. ii. 411—413）;同时,他的精神生命也在见证人与后死者的记忆与传述中（V. ii. 401—415）得到了延续①。这个结尾是意味深长的。

---

① Hannah Arendt: *Lectures on Kant's Political Philosophy*, Chicago: The University of Chicago Press, 1992, p.63 & 131.

2. 比 兴

《红楼梦》第六回"贾宝玉初试云雨情,刘姥姥一进荣国府",作者旁白曰:

> 按荣府中一宅人合算起来,人口虽不多,从上至下也有三四百丁;虽事不多,一天也有一二十件,竟如乱麻一般,并无个头绪可作纲领。正寻思从那一件事自那一个人写起方妙,恰好忽从千里之外,芥荳之微,小小一个人家,因与荣府略有些瓜葛,这日正往荣府中来,因此便就此一家说来,倒还是头绪。①

按"合抱之木,生于毫末",由小民细事而敷陈一大故事,洵乃大家手笔。莎氏亦深谙此道,故以Bernado与Fransisco发端开场。Bernado与Fransisco职属王宫戍卫,与王子之挚友Horatio一党同袍,哈姆雷特友视之而未寄腹心,正是刘姥姥一流人物。作者借彼演绎剧情,自可间而不离,以"零度写作"姿态悠然道来而渐入佳境。

非独如此,西方悲剧素有"歌队"之传统,作者以二三角色代

---

① 曹雪芹、高鹗:《红楼梦》,北京:人民文学出版社,1982年,第99页。

表大众或理想人格,述评甚且介入剧中人事①,实一己之化身而兼护符者也②。Horatio亦是一歌队人物,然其职能非限于此(后节当详论之);Bernado与Fransisco(包括Marcellus)则专属开场歌队,——古希腊悲剧《阿伽门农》开场之"守望人"及进场之歌队即为其典型,——作者借此补叙必要之背景情节,并点染全剧之基调与底色。补叙之例,如Bernado向Horatio讲述鬼魂前两次显灵经过(I. i. 39—49 & 72—79)③,Marcellus与Horatio一问一答,交代先王与挪威老王交兵本末(73—74 & 93—109)并挪威王子复仇犯境(109—121)、举国匆忙备战之事(83—92)。点染之例,如Bernado与Fransisco换岗时之对白(10—12):

> Fran. For this relief much thanks. 'Tis bitter cold,
> And I am sick at heart.
> Ber. Have you had quiet guard?
> Fran. Not a mouse stirring.

寥寥数语,凛冽之气沦肤浃髓,而全剧之肃杀氛围底定矣。寒天旷野子夜(49:"the bell then beating one"),故曰"bitter cold";军事倥偬(88—91),孤身执勤,且接连两夜均于此刻邂逅幽魂,自是"sick at heart";怵惕以待,偏生万籁俱寂,更觉诡秘无端。有论者剖析造型艺术之特点,要在选择高潮即将到来前"最具生发性之刹那"④;"not a mouse stirring"云云,悬扼反衬"山雨欲来风满楼"之势,正中"于无声处听惊雷"之谓也。

---

① 或谓中国戏曲(如京剧昆曲)以丑角交通台上台下,庶几近之,然多为科诨发挥,似不得以"歌队"目之(弋阳腔如川剧中之"帮腔"则另当别论)。
② Leo Strauss: *Persecution and the Art of Writing*, Chicago: The University of Chicago Press, 1988, p.24.
③ 老哈姆雷特的鬼魂出现共五次:前两次系虚写,第三次向Horatio显现(I. i. 50—63),第四次出现向哈姆雷特讲述被害内幕(I. iv. 41— v. 200),第五次出现督促哈姆雷特尽快复仇(III. iv. 115—143)。
④ 莱辛:《拉奥孔》,朱光潜译,北京:人民文学出版社,1979年,第18、83页。

又，此处笔法与所谓"比兴"颇多契合，宜细加玩味。"比兴"为中国诗学一大关目，二者并称而有分，自《周礼·春官·大师》以降，意见猬集。《文心》作者综合平章，曰"起情故兴体以立，附理故比体以生"，又称"比则蓄愤以斥言，兴则环譬以记讽"（《文心雕龙·比兴》）；唐孔颖达则截断众流，以为"比之隐者谓之兴，兴之显者谓之比，比之与兴，深浅为异耳"（《左传·文公七年》），一扫"美刺"陈说；宋人李仲蒙谓"索物以托情谓之比，情附物也；触物以起情谓之兴，物动情也"（《困学纪闻·诗》），别立胜义；今人叶嘉莹氏因心（情意）物（形象）关系立论，以"由心及物"者为"比"（如"飘飘何所似，天地一沙鸥"），"由物及心"者为"兴"（如"树欲静而风不止，子欲养而亲不待"）[①]，其说亦庶几乎！

更而言之，则比兴不外意象譬喻，即今人所谓"symbol"、"metaphor"之类。唐孔颖达云"凡喻皆取其象""兴必取象"（《毛诗正义》疏）；南宋陈骙称"《易》之有象，以尽其意，《诗》之有比，以达其情，文之作也，可无喻乎"（《文则·丙》）；清章学诚谓"《易》象"与"《诗》之比兴"互为表里，"深于比兴"即"深于取象"（《文史通义·内篇·易教下》）。近世以降，学者采撷西学，于"比兴"新有发明。如朱自清撰《赋比兴通释》一文，以为后世"比兴"连称，而"兴"实则"譬喻"或"比体"之"比"[②]。朱氏所谓"兴"，闻一多名之曰"隐"，以为"隐"者《易》之象、《诗》之兴，即西人所谓意象、象征之类[③]。

即以《哈姆雷特》之开场而论，子夜之意境固无论矣；"'Tis bitter cold"者，《哈姆雷特》全剧之起兴也，隐寓隆冬末世之意

[①] 叶嘉莹：《"比兴"之说与"诗可以兴"》，《中国词学的现代观》，长沙：岳麓书社，1990年，第89页。

[②] 朱自清：《诗言志辨》，上海：古籍出版社，1956年，第83页。

[③] 闻一多：《说鱼》，《神话与诗》，上海：古籍出版社，1956年，第117—119页。

象；"sick at heart"，兴而兼比者也；征象疾入膏肓之情境，二者与后文之"Something is rotten in the state of Denmark"（I. iv. 99），"in my heart there was a kind of fighting / That would not let me sleep"（V. ii. 4—5），"thou wouldst not / think how ill all's here / about my heart"（id, 190—191）反复映照，并遥领后文"O, that this too too solid flesh"（I. ii. 130—159）与"To be, or not to be"（III. i. 64—96）等著名独白。中世纪诗人但丁谓文章涵具多意（polysemous），最上为秘密义①（后世现象学文论家所谓"形上品性"②），"'Tis bitter cold"与"sick at heart"参差是已。

不宁唯是，《哈姆雷特》之开场于后文仿佛anagoge，二者潜相呼应，适为一"双重视域"（double vision）。有论者弗莱谓基督教《圣经》之"真实本义"实为隐喻，即《新约》与《旧约》互文，其细节后前照应而不可一味托实，如《马可福音》一章六节云施洗者约翰衣驼毛、腰皮带而取食蝗虫野蜜（"Now John was clothed with camel's hair, with a leather belt around his waist"），即对应《列王记·下》一章八节中以利亚（Elijah）之形容（"A hairy man, with a leather belt around his waist"）③。按此说前人多有道及，第所用术语不同耳（中世纪之神学家固无论矣，十七世纪哲人帕斯卡尔即说约瑟乃耶稣基督之象征，二人事迹往往暗合云④）。

请以此言《哈姆雷特》开场与后文之互文关系。Horatio羽林流亚而有学者之目（Cf. I. i. 52: "Thou art a scholar; speak to it, Horatio"），对观Ophelia谓哈姆雷特兼美廷臣、战士、学者（III. i. 162: "The courtier's, scholar's, soldier's, eye, tongue, sword"）语，二

---

① Michael Caesar (ed.): *Dante: The Critical Heritage*, London: Routledge, 1995, pp.93—94.
② Roman Ingarden: *The Literary Work of Art: An Investigation on the Borderlines of Ontology, Logic, and Theory of Literature*, Evanston: Northwestern University Press, 1973, pp.291—292.
③ Northrop Frye: *The Double Vision*, Toronto: University of Toronto Press, 1991, p.69 & 71.
④ 参见帕斯卡尔：《思想录》第768节，何兆武译，北京：商务印书馆，1985年，第383—384页。

者殆形之与影乎；Ophelia目之为"邦国之华"（III. i. 163—165），其风华可想而知，唯命运"坎陷"，竟无从展示耳（Cf. I. iii. 20—21: "his will is not his own, / For he himself is subject to his birth"; V. ii. 421—422: "he was likely, had he been put on, / To have proved most royally"）。

其次，开场始自凌晨子时前，而终于拂晓鸡鸣。子夜者，往日将逝未逝，来日象而未形之混沌瞬间也①；而《哈姆雷特》始于老王逝世下葬、新主登基新婚，此时阴谋肆逞而真相隐沦，亦可谓文本时间（text-time）之子夜时分矣②。幽魂出没往来，或即剧中黑暗势力（V. ii. 66: "mighty opposites"）之象征；而金鸡一唱，阴氛为之廓清，剧中台下咸得宽舒，岂非Fortinbras之隐喻化身？《哈姆雷特》最后，善恶贤愚同归于尽，然终不至"白茫茫大地真干净"者，以有Fortinbras收拾残局故；其人血气方刚、好勇斗狠（Cf. I. i. 97—98 &IV. iv. 50—55），但以偶然际遇，革旧鼎新（V. ii. 419 ff.），直是变形之"机关神"（deus ex machina）矣。"雄鸡一唱天下白"（I. i. 181—182: "But look, the morn, in russet mantle clad, / Walks o'er the dew of yon high eastern hill."）；晓鸡体象阳明，此处铺陈其祛邪本领，更引基督降生传说渲染祥和气象（I. i. 165—170 & 173—179），虽不无枝蔓，良有以也。

---

① 方以智曰："溯天地未分前，则位亥子之间；不得已而状之图之，实十二时皆子午、无子午也。"（《东西均·三徵》）是则混沌在在皆有，无时不然也。

② 四幕五场中Laertes率兵为父复仇，信使来报，中有"天地若将新开，往旧废弃"（IV. v. 103—104: "as the world were now but to begin,/ Antiquity forgot"）等语。斯言也，可与"To be, or not to be"及"we know what we are, but know not what we may be"（IV. v. 44—45）相互发明，实为全剧文眼。另见Twelfth Night, V. i. 225: "A natural perspective, that is and is not"按二剧皆作于1600年，正值世纪献替，莎氏之创作心境可以想见，故一年之中数致意焉。

3. 自杀

有生之属,莫不趋生避死;独人类不然,而有自杀之举。禽兽亦有自杀者,如丧偶之天鹅、获捕之山魈、搁浅之海鲸,所在多有;然观其所为,皆似出于本能,而人之自杀不无理智考虑,其动机、方式与后果亦洋洋不一。谓自杀为人类特有之行为,不亦宜乎?

虽然,人之向生本能(biophilia)异常顽强,适足抗衡人类之"死亡本能"①,于是有种种禁忌戢戮。如哈姆雷特既痛父王之遽然去世,复慊母后之率尔再嫁,心碎气结(I. ii. 158),因萌轻生之念(130—131)。其所以踌躇再三者,基督教有禁杀之令②(132—133),且不知死后毕竟何如也(III. i. 74 & 86—90)。噫,从容赴死亦难矣哉!

初,个人乃宗族或宗教共同体之一员,身为公共资产,本人无权处置,故自杀者难辞其咎。亚里士多德于《伦理学》十章末申说此意,即以自杀违背"正理"(δικαιοσύνη),在城邦为"不义",

---

① 弗洛伊德以为生物均有渴望恢复初始状态之"惰性"倾向,此即所谓"死亡本能"。参见Sigmund Freud: *Beyond the Pleasure Principle*, trans. by C. J. M. Hubback, The International Psycho-Analytical Press, 1922, pp. 29—48;弗洛伊德:《超越唯乐原则》,《弗洛伊德后期著作选》,林尘等译,上海:上海译文出版社,1986年,第41—42页。

② 基督教"十诫"第六条:"不可杀生"(*Exodus* 20: 13)。

故足耻而当惩云云（1138a）。西塞罗亦云舍生者逃避天职①。基督教以为上帝造人，故生命属于上帝，而自杀悖逆神意，死后将堕地狱②，声色愈厉矣。中国之例，如《论语·泰伯》篇载：

> 曾子有疾，召门弟子曰："启予足！启予手！《诗》云：战战兢兢，如临深渊，如履薄冰。而今而后，吾知免夫！小子！"

所谓"身体发肤，受之父母，不敢毁伤，孝之始也"（《孝经·开宗明义章》），个人理当为家族全生保命，"慎终追远"、死而后已，故自杀为不孝之大者③。中西合璧，于是有所谓"自绝于人民"之妙论。——"人民"者，教主而兼家长之谓也，"其义则丘窃取之矣"。

西欧中世纪后，权威崩落解散，而个体意识贲张奋扬。我身既为我有，则其取舍在我；于是自杀之禁稍去，而"吾丧我"之风渐长。典型之例如英国，十六世纪时厌世者逐年增长④，文学作品中涉及自杀者蔚成风习。1580—1620年四十年间，英伦演剧百余部，其中可见两百余自杀事件；以莎剧而论，涉及自杀者即达五十二种之多⑤。如《哈姆雷特》一剧，王子恋人Ophelia与王后Gertrude即分以

---

① 西塞罗：《国家篇 法律篇》，沈叔平、苏力译，北京：商务印书馆，1999年，第129—130页。

② 如"中世纪最后一位诗人"但丁将自杀者安置于地狱第七层第二环，并借彼埃尔·德拉·维涅鬼魂之口谴责自杀为"不正义之事"，颇能代表当时西方社会对自杀之看法（参看《神曲·地狱篇》第13章，田德望译，北京：人民文学出版社，1990年，第92页）。

③ 如《史记·吕太后本纪》载："赵王恢之徙王赵，心怀不乐。太后以吕产女为赵王后，王后从官皆诸吕，擅权，微伺赵王，赵王不得自恣。王有所爱姬，王后使人酖杀之。王悲，六月即自杀。太后闻之，以为王用妇人弃宗庙礼，废其嗣。"——"弃宗庙礼"者，宗族之罪人也。

④ 1500—1509年61例，1510—1519年108例，1520—1529年216例，1530—1539年343例，1540—1549年499例，1550—1559年714例，1560—1569年798例，1570—1579年940例，1580—1589年923例，1590—1599年801例。参见乔治·米诺瓦：《自杀的历史》，李佶等译，北京：经济日报出版社，2003年，第66—67页、124页。

⑤ 《自杀的历史》，第96、117、119页。

投水饮鸩而亡①。按《哈》剧作于1600年前后，时值文艺复兴末期，"巨人"豪情黯然摧剥，而悲凉之雾渐布人心。如哈姆雷特既以半神（Hercules）自况（V. i. 292—293），复以此而自嘲（I. ii. 151—153），且以有身为苦，不乐在世（II. ii. 229—231），进而憎恶人类全体（id, 318—319）；凡此种种，皆其征也。

如斯厌世情结，或可以"出位之思"形容之。当日钱锺书先生拈出此语②，表彰超越之神思（transcendent imagination）；究其源，则根诸《周易》，非仅思维方式之谓也。《坤·文言传》："君子黄中通理，正位居体"，《鼎·象传》："君子以正位凝命"，它如"当位""得位"之例，不一而足。对观《中庸》"致中和，天地位焉，万物育焉"一语，可知"位"者，各得性命之正之谓也；否则为"失位""不当位"，庄生所谓"使人喜怒失位，居处无常，思虑不自得，中道不成章，于是乎天下始乔诘卓鸷，而后有盗跖曾史之行"（《庄子·在宥》）是也。性命不得其正，故有出位之思焉，如"辟世辟地""乘桴浮海"（《论语·宪问》《公冶长》）之类；诉诸歌咏，则有云游羁旅飘零之主题意象。"逝将去女，适彼乐土"（《诗·魏风·硕鼠》）之歌已肇其端；屈子忠信被谗，亦有"怀信侘傺，忽乎吾将行兮"（《涉江》）、"悲时俗之迫阨兮，愿轻举而远游"（《远游》）之叹。至于《古诗十九首》，更发"人生天地间，忽如远行客""人生寄一世，奄

---

① Ophelia之死因，由掘墓人所说可见端倪（V. i. 1—2 & 218—221: "Is she to be buried in Christian burial that / she willfully seeks her own salvation?"，"Her death was doubtful;/ And, but that great command o'ersways the order,/ She should in ground unsanctified have lodged/ Till the last trumpet." 基督教仪规定自杀者不得礼葬，故云）。Gertrude因疑酒中下毒，故为爱子揩汗（V. ii. 297—298），复与Claudius从容致歉（id., 301），诀别之后，毅然饮下；由是观之，其必死之心可知矣。——《哈》剧中自杀者皆为女性，此或"Frailty, thy name is woman!"（I. ii. 146）一语之反讽乎？

② 钱氏早年记游雪窦，即有"乃知水与山，思各出其位"之句。《管锥编》中曾多处提点，如第二册论"法自然"云："……格物则知物理之宜，素位本分也。若夫因水而悟人之宜弱其志，因谷而悟人之宜虚其心，因物态而悟人事，此出位之异想、旁通之歧径，于词章为'寓言'，于名学为'比论'，可以晓喻，不能证实，勿足供思辨之依据也。"（中华书局，1979年，第434—435页）

忽若飘尘""人生忽如寄"之哀音，俨然以在世为出位矣。

老氏洞明此意，等观生死，而云"出生入死"（《老子》五十章）；漆园深达斯旨，以死为反真①，乃曰"劳我以生，息我以死"（《庄子·大宗师》）。是生者，死之出位也；死者，生之归止也②。人生离乱颠荡，则不免望死如归，而以有生为憾。《诗·小雅·苕之华》："知我如此，不如无生"，《大雅·桑柔》："我生不辰，逢天僤怒"，即其先声③；哈姆雷特曰"The time is out of joint. O cursèd spite, / That ever I was born to set it right!"（Ⅰ. v. 208—209），又云"it were better my / mother had not borne me"（Ⅲ. i. 134—135），亦"不辰""无生"之叹也。

生命有肉体生命与精神生命之别，而古人尤重后者。孔子不云乎："志士仁人，无求生以害仁，有杀身以成仁"（《论语·卫灵公》）。孟子由是倡言"舍生取义"，曰：

> 生亦我所欲也，义亦我所欲也；二者不可得兼，舍生而取义者也。生亦我所欲，所欲有甚于生者，故不为苟得也；死亦我所恶，所恶有甚于死者，故患有所不辟也。如使人之所欲莫甚于生，则凡可以得生者，何不用也？使人之所恶莫甚于死者，则凡可以辟患者，何不为也？由是则生而有不用也，由是则可以辟患而有不为也，是故所欲有甚于生者，所恶有甚于死者。非独贤者有是心也，人皆有之，贤者能勿丧耳。（《孟子·

---

① 顾炎武《日知录》卷第十八"破题用庄子"条引《说文》徐氏系传曰："真"从"匕"，"匕即化也"，"反人为亡，从目从匕"；"以生为寄，以死为归，于是有真人、真君、真宰之名"（《日知录集释》，长沙：岳麓书社，1994年，第659页）。西人以"死"为"生"之铁槛，人于临死之刹那方克体会生命之真，故"生"为"死"变现之隐喻，斯亦"反真"之意也（Richard Shiff: *Art and Life,* in Sheldon Sacks (ed.): *On Metaphor*, Chicago: The University of Chicago Press, 1980, pp.106—107）。

② 如《世说》载"白首同归"之谶（《仇隙》），《红楼》有"虎兕相逢大梦归"（第五回元春判词）之悬记，京剧《洪羊洞》（前身为杂剧《昊天塔》又名"三星归位"）（其中杨六郎及部将焦赞、孟良均毕命乎此，故名），皆资取证焉。

③ 《管锥编》卷一"毛诗正义·正月"（中华书局，1979年，第146—147页）及卷五（第143—144页、第274页）列举甚详，读者可以参看。

告子上》)

吕氏亦称:"辱莫大于不义,故不义,迫生也。而迫生非独不义也,故曰迫生不若死。"(《吕氏春秋·仲春纪·贵生》)汉儒韩婴则云:"为夫义之不立,名之不显,则士耻之,故杀身以遂其行。"(《韩诗外传卷一·第八章》)由是观之,自杀或即"成仁"之一途,未可厚非也矣。宋儒究极性命之学,视"尽性"重于"全归",如《论语·卫灵公》中"志士仁人,无求生以害仁,有杀身以成仁"一句,程子以为"有杀身以成仁者,只是成就一个是而已",朱子注曰:

> 志士,有志之士。仁人,则成德之人也。理当死而求生,则于其心有不安矣,是害其心之德也。当死而死,则心安而德全矣。①

"是"也者,"德"也,"理"也;"成是"义同"全德",乃理之当然;既当理,则大患有所不辞焉。

设若中西哲人晤言一室,交相辩驳,则必有可观者也。西土哲人云:惟理性有权自由立法,而得理之大全者,其唯神乎?凡人生皆不得全,故无权自裁也明矣!康德因"责任"之"普遍命令"与"自在目的"立论,力陈自杀之非②;黑格尔以死或由乎"自然原因",或出诸"伦理理念",故个人无权弃让生命③云

---

① 朱熹:《四书章句集注》,北京:中华书局,1983年,第163页。
② 康德断言:"以通过情感促使生命的提高为职责的自然竟然把毁灭生命作为自己的规律,这是自相矛盾的,从而也就不能作为自然而存在";"有理性的本性作为自在目的而实存着",因此人不是工具,"在任何时候都必须在他的一切行动中,把他当作自在目的看待,从而他无权处置代表他人身的人,摧残他、毁灭他、戕害他。"参见《道德形而上学原理》,苗力田译,上海:上海人民出版社,2002年,第39页、第47—48页。
③ 黑格尔《法哲学原理》(商务印书馆,第157页):"外界活动的包罗万象的总和,即生命,不是同人格相对的外在东西,因为人格就是这一人格自身,它是直接的。放弃或牺牲生命不是这个人格的定在,而是正相反。所以一般说来,我没有任何权利放弃生命,享有这种权利的只有伦理理念,因为这种理念自在地吞没这个直接的单一人格,而且是对人格的现实权利";"因此,说人具有支配其生命的权利,那是矛盾的,因为这等于说人有凌驾于其自身之上的权利了。所以……他不能对自己做出判断。"

云。中土哲人则曰：不然。大论近是，惜有一间未达。西方伦理之学，蔽于人而昧于天：康德之"理性"介乎本体、现象之间①，然偏重现象（"命"）一边，以本体为不得已之假设，于是天人毕竟睽隔，人而不得其仁矣；黑格尔之"伦理理念"，殆同亚里士多德之"正理"，亦外乎人（"命"）而与人对，既断"性"、"命"为两撅，而"仁"不得其全也无论矣。然"仁"有二格，一曰"小体"，一曰"大体"；"从其大体为大人，从其小体为小人"（《孟子·告子上》）。"从其大体为大人"即是"明明德"（《大学》）②，"明明德"即是"尽性"，"尽性"即是"践形"（《孟子·尽心上》），"践形"即是"成仁"。成仁之人，恒以"大体"（"伦理理念"）裁制"小体"（发布"普遍命令"），"从心所欲不逾矩"（《论语·为政》）、"无可无不可"（《论语·微子》），而况自杀乎！

于是佛陀合十赞叹："是则善终，后世亦善！"③论辩至此，论题已非"人可否自杀"，而一变为"内在而超越之我是否可能"。如其然，则吾人有自决之权；否则"代大匠斫者，希有不伤其手矣"（《老子》七十四章），终不免康德"僭越"之讥也。或问："人皆可以为尧舜"，其然？岂其然乎？答曰："可以为，未必能也；虽不能，无害可以为"（《荀子·性恶》）；"仁远乎哉？我欲仁，斯仁至矣"（《论语·述而》），"积善成德，而神明自得，圣心备焉"（《荀子·劝学》）；本体即工夫，工夫即

---

① 参看康德：《未来形而上学导论》，庞景仁译，北京：商务印书馆，1978年，第147页前后。
② 《四书章句集注》，第3页。
③ 参见《杂阿含经》卷四十七："跋迦梨白佛：……世尊！我身苦痛，极难堪忍，欲求刀自杀，不乐苦生。佛告跋迦梨：我今问汝，随意答我，云何，跋迦梨？色是常耶？为非常耶？跋迦梨答言：无常，世尊。复问：若无常，是苦耶？答言：是苦，世尊。复问：跋迦梨，若无常、苦者，是变易法，于中宁有可贪、可欲不？跋迦梨白佛：不也，世尊，受、想、行、识亦如是说。佛告跋迦梨：若于彼身无可贪、可欲者，是则善终，后世亦善。"（《大正新修大藏经》第2卷，东京：大正一切经刊行会，昭和三年，第347页）标点为笔者试加。

本体，真积力久，则道德本体朗然呈现，迥非惚恍窈冥之虚设也。第"仁之难成久矣"（《礼记·表记》），贤如颜回者，"其心三月不违仁，其余则日月至焉而已"（《论语·雍也》），况中人及以下之人哉！文中子曰："杀身而成仁者，其中人之行欤"（《中说·事君篇》），非人情也。故曰"慷慨杀身者易，从容就义者为难"（《二程遗书·明道先生语一》）云云。

然"义"义难知，自杀一念发动，或者理消欲长，则求仁而失仁矣。哈姆雷特所以踌躇沉吟者，无乃在诸？彼大叹美Horatio之为人，曰（III. ii. 54—72）：

> 在我结交的人当中，
> 霍拉旭，你是最中正通达的，
> ……
> 你浑若无事地忍受一切苦楚，
> 对命运的苛待和优遇都一视同仁；
> 这样的人是有福的，
> 他的情感和理智调理得十分停当，
> 命运无法随意排遣他。

聆斯言，其志意昭然可知矣。所谓"仁者不忧"（《论语·子罕》），Horatio自性贞定，故能八风不动，居易顺化如此。哈姆雷特则不然：既视六合为囹圄（II. ii. 256—259: "Ham. Denmark's a prison. Ros. Then is the world one. / Ham. A goodly one; in which there are many confines, / wards, and dungeons, Denmark being one o' the worst."），形无所遁（266—268: "O God, I could be bounded in a nutshell and / count / myself a king of infinite space, were it not that I / have bad dreams."），复以方寸作战场，忧心难寐（V. ii. 4—5: "in my heart there was a kind of fighting / That would not let me sleep"），愤世嫉俗并自伤自怜（III. i. 137—138: "What should such fellows as I do / crawling between earth and heaven?"; V. i. 193: "To what base uses we may return"; IV. v. 44—45: "we know what we are, but know not / what we may be."），真实心不可得（III. ii. 72—75: "Give me that man / That is not passion's slave, and I will wear him / In my heart's core, ay, in my heart of heart, / As I do thee."），彷徨无所依归（III. i. 64: "To be, or not to be, that is the question"），欲自尽解脱而不能不生（II. ii. 229—231: "You cannot, sir, take from me anything that I will /more willingly part withal-except my life, except my life, except / my life."），忍死待命而已（V. ii. 217—220: "If it be now, / 'tis not to come', if it be not to come, it will be now; if it be not now, yet it will come'. The readiness is all"），至弥留之际，欲有说而终于无言（V. ii. 351—353: "Had I but time ... O, I could tell you-/ But let it be." 377: "The rest is silence."），悲哉！

4. 恋父情结与死者神化

哈姆雷特曾向朋友这样说起自己的父亲:"He was a man, take him for all in all / I shall not look upon his like again"(I. ii. 187—188)。他怀念去世不久的父亲,认为他是"杰出的君王",和现任国王Claudius比起来,一个是天神,一个是妖魔(I. ii. 139—140:"So excellent a king, that was to this / Hyperion to a satyr"; III. iv. 114:"A king of shreds and patches!"),二者完全不可同日而语(III. iv. 108—109:"A slave that is not twentieth part the tithe / Of your precedent lord")。后来他在训斥母后时更强调了这一巨大反差(III. iv. 60—69)——在他眼中,父亲简直就是神的化身:

> 你看这一个眉宇间是何等高贵:
> 太阳神的鬈发,天帝的额头,
> 眼睛如同战神那样威慑人心、君临一切,
> 仪态好似刚刚降临在高山之巅的神使。
> 这真是一个完美的形象,
> 每一个神灵仿佛都在此留下了他的标记。

日神的鬈发,战神的眼睛,天帝的额头,天使的仪态……父亲的形象在死后被神化了。如果说开场时王宫卫兵的口令"Long live the King!"（Ⅰ.i.4）反讽了"The King is dead"这一事实，那么反过来讲，恰恰是"死亡"这一事实使"不朽"成为可能；换句话说，正是生者的缺席，导致了死者的神化。

死后被神化，这是一种由来已久、屡见不鲜的人类现象，在神话和宗教中表现得尤其明显。基督教《新约》中记述耶稣死后第三天的复活、显现和升天（*Luke* 24:36—51）就是一个典型的例子。中国历史上孔子的"变形"也是一例①。唐代史学家刘知几曾经感叹"儒教传授，既欲神其事，故谈过其实"（《史通·惑经》），其实何独《春秋》、儒门为然？一切宗教莫不热衷于制造神话。教主本人的言行也许尽人情而合物理，但身后往往遭到弟子不近情理的圣化，如谓佛五体放光、耶稣在海面上行走之类，莫不如此（与后世造神运动相比，此又不过小巫耳）。

真实、本来的缺失往往带来"完型"冲动，即发扬想象来"光荣化"虚拟的对象。王充曾说"述事者好高古而下今，贵所闻而贱所见"（《论衡·齐世篇》），这与耶稣所说的"先知在他乡受到

---

① 如《论语》记载孔子死后被人毁谤，子贡对此进行了反驳：叔孙武叔语大夫于朝，曰："子贡贤于仲尼。"子服景伯以告子贡。子贡曰："譬之宫墙，赐之墙也及肩，窥见室家之好。夫子之墙数仞，不得其门而入，不见宗庙之美，百官之富。得其门者或寡矣。夫子之云，不亦宜乎！"（《论语·子张》）叔孙武叔毁仲尼。子贡曰："无以为也！仲尼不可毁也。他人之贤者，丘陵也，犹可逾也；仲尼，日月也，无得而逾焉。人虽欲自绝，其何伤于日月乎？多见其不知量也。"（同上）陈子禽谓子贡曰："子为恭也，仲尼岂贤于子乎？"子贡曰："君子一言以为知，一言以为不知，言不可不慎也！夫子之不可及也，犹天之不可阶而升也。夫子之得邦家者，所谓立之斯立，道之斯行，绥之斯来，动之斯和。其生也荣，其死也哀，如之何其可及也？"（同上）子贡认为孔子非凡人所能窥测，而是像"日月""天"一样高不可攀，这直接启动了孔子身后的神化工程。《孟子·公孙丑上》中也记述了宰我、子贡、有若的类似赞词：宰我、子贡、有若，智足以知圣人，汙不至阿其所好。宰我曰："以予观于夫子，贤于尧、舜远矣。"子贡曰："见其礼而知其政，闻其乐而知其德，由百世之后，等百世之王，莫之能违也。自生民以来，未有夫子也。"有若曰："岂惟民哉！麒麟之于走兽，凤凰之于飞鸟，泰山之于丘垤，河海之于行潦，类也。圣人之于民，亦类也。出于其类，拔乎其萃，自生民以来，未有盛于孔子也。"宰我认为孔子超过了尧、舜这些孔子本人所仰慕的圣人，子贡进一步指出孔子是史无前例的伟人，而有若更是断言孔子是超越时空的人类最高楷模。弟子们的颂扬层层加码、越拔越高，在后世甚至神化到了可笑的地步（例如后世谶纬之学宣称孔子有"海口、牛唇、虎掌、龟脊"等异相，几不成人类矣）。

敬仰"（*Matthew* 3:57）是一个意思。"他乡"可以这样来理解：人类以在世为本乡，死是生的缺失与超绝，故身后为绝对的他乡，这样死者对于生者来说就是幽远他乡的先知了。这是一种典型的乌托邦想象。德国学者卡尔·曼海姆指出：如果一种思想状况与它所处的现实状况不相一致，那么这种"超越思想环境的思想"就是乌托邦；同时乌托邦与人类的欲望有关，"当想象力不能在现实中取得满足时，它便寻求躲避于用愿望建成的象牙塔"①。这种欲望归根结底是一种本能的、内在的"生"（*to be*）的冲动：我在（*That I be*）！为此，我必须肯定自我，证明我之所"是"，即自身合目的、自在自为的"善"。恋父与神化死者无疑来自这种冲动，只是它投射到了不在场的、外在于我的客体，并且通过这个客体折射、释放了主体的这种冲动。

在特殊情况下，这种冲动亦可能投向主体自身：一方面，主体继续保持为"我"，另一方面则异化出一个"他我"，作为投射对象的"我"，也就是客体化了的、处于某个不同时空的主体。这两种主体之间的时空距离可以很短，也可以很长。例如，小说《围城》中讲到李梅亭、方鸿渐与赵辛楣赴三闾大学任教，中途困在某县城，李梅亭和旅社附近的风尘女子搭讪，后者答应通过关系让他们搭上军车，李梅亭自鸣得意，他——

> 回身向赵方二人得意地把头转个圈儿，一言不发，望着他们。二人钦佩他异想天开，真有本领。李先生恨不能身外化身，拍着自己肩膀，说："老李，真有你！"

这里的"身外化身"即属于前一种情形。至于后一种情形，则往往表现为摆老资格、吹嘘"当年勇"等等。荷马史诗《伊利亚特》中的老将奈斯托耳（Nestor）就是一个典型的例子。为了鼓励大家

---

① 卡尔·曼海姆：《意识形态与乌托邦》，黎鸣、李书崇译，北京：商务印书馆，2000年，第196页、第209—210页。

迎战赫克托耳（Hector），他回忆起少年时会战猛将厄柔萨利昂（Ereuthalion）的情形：

> "厄柔萨利昂叫嚷着要和我们中最勇敢的人拼斗，但他们全都吓得战战兢兢，不敢和他交手。只有我，磨炼出来的勇气其时催促我和他拼斗，以大无畏的气概，虽说论年龄，我是最年轻的一个。我和他绞杀扑打，帕拉丝·雅典娜把荣誉送入我的手中。在被我杀死的人中，他是最高大、最强健的一个，……但愿我现在年轻力壮，和当年一样，浑身有使不完的力气！这样，顷刻之间，头盔闪亮的赫克托耳即会找到匹敌的对手！"①

这种场景出现过不止一次。回忆起当年，他真是"浑身有使不完的力气"！奈斯托耳的口头禅是"听从我的劝导吧，我曾同比你们更好的人交往过"，"其后我再也没有、将来也不会再见到那样的人杰"，"生活在今天的凡人全都不是他们的对手"②——这可以说是一种社会退化论的观点，用鲁迅笔下人物"九斤老太"的话讲就是："一代不如一代！"

在人类历史上，这种"九斤老太情结"曾以各种面目出现过。如古希腊人认为人类世界先后产生过每况愈下的五个种族：黄金种族、白银种族、黄铜种族、英雄种族与黑铁种族③；古罗马人认为人类社会先后经历了黄金时代、白银时代、黄铜时代与黑铁时代，其中每一代都比上一代更加堕落④。中国古人也有类似的想法，例如道家认为人类社会就是道德不断"下衰"的过程（《庄子·缮性》），而儒家也总是感叹世风日下、人心不古而称美三代之治。

---

① 荷马：《伊利亚特》，陈中梅译，广州：花城出版社，1994年，第157页。
② 同上书，第11页。
③ 赫西俄德：《工作与时日 神谱》，张竹明、蒋平译，北京：商务印书馆，1991年，第4—7页。
④ 奥维德：《变形记》第1章，杨周翰译，北京：人民文学出版社，1984年，第3—5页。

无论是儒家还是道家，他们的共同之处在于用时间上的居前关系隐喻了逻辑上的优先关系，即以虚拟历史作为经验事实来论证道德本体的存在（例如以黄帝或尧舜禹等上古圣王肯定人性本善、可善与应善）；换言之，他们通过认同这一道德本体而使自身精神生命取得了认同。

因此，这种怀旧情绪说到底是自我的张扬，或者说源于自恋的本能冲动。当哈姆雷特讲"这三年来时代变得真是精致，山野村夫的脚丫子紧跟着朝廷贵人的足踝，连脚上的冻疮都擦破了"（V. i. 132—134），其中就流露出一丝微妙的自恋情绪。他也说人是"造化的玩物"（I. iv. 57），悲叹自己蠢伏在天地之间无所作为（III. i. 137—138），但其内心深处却未尝不以海格力斯那样的神武英雄自期（Cf. V. i. 292: "Let Hercules himself do what he may"）。的确，如果不是出于牢不可拔的自恋或者说"我执"，他又何必如此感到失落和沉痛呢？

不过，和他周围的人比起来，哈姆雷特终究是一个清醒的自觉者。在自我认识的冷静鉴照之下，顽强的自恋本能不得不采取一种隐晦的表现方式，转向与"我"最为相似的客体——父亲，把父亲的记忆作为"我"的替身而流连礼赞。对父亲的虚幻记忆满足了自我的生存冲动（will to be）。老王的鬼魂诉说了被害真相后，与儿子依依道别："Adieu, adieu! Remember me"（I. v. 96）；听到此言，哈姆雷特不禁热血沸腾（I. v. 102—109）：

> 记住你？是的，我要从我的记忆的书版上
> 拭去一切琐碎愚蠢的记录、
> 一切书本上的格言、
> 一切陈言套语、
> 一切旧日印象，
> 凡是少年时代的阅历都统统删除，
> 在我的脑海中只有你的指示，

不留下任何次等材料。

在这个时刻，"我"与"父亲"的认同上升到顶峰而完全合一；在"我"的灵魂中，除了对父亲的记忆之外，一切都黯然消失了。"记住我"，这个焦虑的呼喊与其说是来自死去的"父亲"，不如说它发自"我"的内心："That I be!"的自恋冲动在现实王国中幻化出一个记忆的乌托邦，渴望不朽的"记忆"取代了经验和反思，以"操心"的面目出现而居有了"此在"的王座，直至生命的最后一刻（V. ii. 351—352 & 363—366）：

> 我没有时间了（死神是无情的）
> 否则可以告诉你们……
> ……
> 如果你真心爱我，
> 请暂时放弃天国的喜乐，
> 在严苛的人间艰难存活，
> 把我的故事讲给世人。①

---

① 斯多葛哲人教导说："朋友，请你等待神的召唤吧。当他发出信号，要免除你的义务的时候，你再离开去见他吧。不过目前，请你暂时在这个地方忍耐一下吧，神派你到哪儿你就在哪暂时生活吧。……等着吧，不要违反理性地离去。"（《爱比克泰德论说集》，王文华译，北京：商务印书馆，2009年，第60—61页）哈姆雷特的临终遗言，与之如出一辙。——不过，他要求知交好友（后者仿佛是他在尘世的替身）"把我的故事讲给世人"，可见其"到底意难平"了！

5. 庭训和话语—权力

新王加冕典礼既成，Laertes准备返回法国。临行前，他的父亲Polonius长篇大论地教导了儿子一番，告诫他不要轻易表露自己的想法，凡事须三思而行（I. iii. 63—64），交友要慎重（65—69），避免和人冲突，但一旦发生争执就不能让人小觑（69—71），多听别人讲，自己少表态（72—73），甚至扯到穿戴要大方得体（74—77），不要向人借钱，更不要借钱给别人（78—80），最后强调对自己和他人都须忠实，不要自欺欺人（81—83），这才意犹未尽地收住了话头。

这老儿好不啰唆！性急的读者也许干脆跳过直接去看下一场了——我们和哈姆雷特还等着从老王鬼魂的口中了解事情的真相呢。然而且慢，这可是西方文学中少见的一篇"庭训"妙文，它为我们了解当时欧洲家庭的权力结构提供了生动的例证。

也许是农耕文明重视经验传承的缘故，中国古人似乎格外喜欢训诫子孙。早在《逸周书》中就记录了周文王对太子发的教导："汝敬之哉！民物多变，民何向非利？利维生痛，痛维生乐，乐维生礼，礼维生义，义维生仁。"（《文儆解》）这大约是现存文献中中国最古老的家训和教子书了。更著名的例子是孔子对儿子孔鲤的"庭训"①。口头的"庭训"写成文字,即是家训、家书或诫子书一类的作品。在中国,这类作品自汉末以来盛行于世,差不多构成了某种"亚文类"②。这类作品不但数量众多,而且至亲骨肉之间私相授受,绝少虚言浮辞而多见真情实感。古人云"修辞立其诚"(《易·文言传》),不诚不真固不足为家书矣。也正因如此,家书不好写,写得好更不容易。例如三国时就流传"汝无自誉,观汝作家书!"③的谚语,时至一千四百多年后黄宗羲仍然感叹"至文不过家书写"(《南雷诗历·与唐翼修广文论文》)。原因何在?《孟子·离娄上》中曾专门谈到这个问题:

> 公孙丑曰:"君子之不教子,何也?"孟子曰:"势不行也。教者必以正。以正不行,继之以怒。继之以怒,则反夷矣。夫子教我以正,夫子未出于正也,则是父子相夷也。父子相夷,则恶矣。古者易子而教之。父子之间不责善,责善则离,离则不祥莫大焉。"

孟子的担忧不无道理。《大学》论"齐家"曰:"君子有诸己

---

① 《论语·季氏》:陈亢问于伯鱼曰:"子亦有异闻乎?"对曰:"未也。尝独立,鲤趋而过庭,曰:'学《诗》乎?'对曰:'未也。''不学《诗》,无以言。'鲤退而学《诗》。他日又独立,鲤趋而过庭,曰:'学《礼》乎?'对曰:'未也。''不学《礼》,无以立。'鲤退而学《礼》。闻斯二者。"陈亢退而喜曰:"问一得三,闻《诗》,闻《礼》,又闻君子之远其子也。"

② 南宋学者王应麟在《困学纪闻·评文》中曾列举了最著名的几种:《艺文类聚》鉴诫类,多格言法语。……姚信《诫子》曰:"古人行善者,非名之务,非人之为,险易不亏,始终如一。"诸葛武侯《诫子》曰:"非学无以广才,非志无以成学。"颜延之《庭语》曰:"性明者欲简,嗜繁者气昏。"……司马德操《诫子》曰:"论德则吾薄,说居则吾贫。勿以薄而志不仕,贫而行不高。"王修《诫子》曰:"时过不可还,若年大不可少也。言思乃出,行详乃动。"羊祜《诫子》曰:"恭为德首,谨为行基。无传不经之谈,无听毁誉之语。"徐勉《与子书》曰:"见贤思齐,不宜忽略以弃日。非徒弃日,乃是弃身。"此外如刘备的《敕后主词》、嵇康的《家诫》、陶渊明的《与子俨等疏》等等,也都是著名的篇什。号称笼罩群言、体大虑周的《文心雕龙》仅在《诏策》一篇论"戒"中提到"汉太祖之敕太子,东方朔之戒子,亦顾命之作也。及马援以下,各贻家戒"云云,未免有遗珠之憾。

③ 语见《典论·太子篇序》:"里语曰:'汝无自誉,观汝作家书!'言其难也。"引自《丛书集成新编》第80册,台湾,新文丰出版公司,1985年,第55页。

而后求诸人，无诸己而后非诸人；所藏乎身不恕，而能喻诸人者，未之有也。"所谓言传身教，身不教则言不传，而父子之间身教更胜于言传。如果父亲本人不能实践他所鼓吹的信条，甚至言行相悖，那么再堂皇正大的说教也难以让人信服，甚至适得其反，致使父子"责善"、"相夷"而"贼恩"①。在这个意义上讲，"立德"（诚有是德）是"立言"的前提与目的，否则"美言不信"，难免有"巧言乱德"之虞了。

我们再来看Polonius的"庭训"。他老人家教训儿子多听少说，自己却絮叨不已（Cf. III. iv. 233: "a foolish prating knave"），甚至在君王前也多嘴饶舌，如他向国王禀报哈姆雷特发疯时说（II. ii. 92—101）：

> 王上，王后，详细解说什么是王者的尊严、
> 什么是臣子的职分，
> 白昼何以为白昼，黑夜何以为黑夜，时间何以为时间，
> 这只会浪费日夜和时间；
> 因此，既然简洁是智慧的灵魂，
> 冗长是肤浅的藻饰，
> 我还是长话短说吧。
> 你们的儿子疯了；
> 我说他疯了；要是定义何谓真疯，
> 这本身不是发疯又是什么呢？
> 不过这就不用多说了。

他既知"简洁是智慧的灵魂"，却又咬文嚼字、不知所云，致使听者失去耐心，请他有话直说，少卖弄玄虚（102: "More matter, with less art."）。再如他正言厉色地告诫儿子对人对己都要忠诚、慎勿自欺欺人云云，但他本人却对亲生儿子都信不过，背地里派仆

---

① 《孟子·离娄下》："父子责善，贼恩之大者。"

人跟踪到巴黎剌探汇报他的行踪（II. i. 1—81），还忙不迭地把哈姆雷特写给女儿的情书拿来向国王邀功献媚，又自作聪明地设计让王后找哈姆雷特谈话，自己躲在幕后偷听，结果被哈姆雷特误作国王一剑刺死。俗话说："能言者未必能行。"真是可惜了他字字珠玑、头头是道的至理名言了！

莎士比亚写戏喜欢采用"情节束"，即在主线之外安排一条甚至多条副线，主线、副线彼此交错、相互映衬，从而起到深化主题的作用。例如《哈姆雷特》中同时安排了哈姆雷特、Laertes与挪威王子Fortinbras为父报仇的情节，三条线索一起拧成对复仇行为的伦理思考。再以"训诫"为例，第一幕第三场中不仅有父亲对儿子（Polonius-Laertes）的训诫，同时还有兄长对妹妹（Laertes-Ophelia）、父亲对女儿（Polonius-Ophelia）的训诫。父子、兄妹、父女这三种天伦关系共同构成一种级差性的家庭权力结构。法国学者福柯（Michel Foucault）认为"权力"产生于"话语"（discourse）机制，反过来我们也可以说"话语"投射并隐喻了"权力"。《哈姆雷特》第一幕第三场中父训子、兄训妹的场面正凸现了男性/父兄的威权—强势话语地位与女性/子女的服从—弱势话语地位。

我们先来看Laertes对Ophelia的训诫。尽管作者没有明说，但我们可以从文中判断Ophelia事先向哥哥吐露了她和哈姆雷特的感情进展，并为此征求过他的意见。Laertes对此坚决表示反对。他奉劝妹妹对王子的爱情表白不要当真，认为这不过是年轻人的一时冲动，就好像早熟的紫罗兰，鲜艳芬芳但不能持久（I. iii. 6—10）；他提醒妹妹，即便哈姆雷特的感情是真诚的，但他作为一国储君，在婚姻问题上没有自主权，也就是说他必须服从国家利益的需要，与门当户对的邻国王室联姻（22—31）①，因此不要相信王子的甜言蜜语，轻易委身于人而给自己带来羞辱（32—35）。末了他郑重告诫妹妹：不要放纵感情而被欲望所俘虏，"畏惧是最好的防护"，"贞洁的姑娘让月亮窥到自己的容颜也就够放荡了"（39—40 & 46）。

Laertes反对女子抛头露面，这和中国古人"妇人不会，会非正也"（《春秋谷梁传·庄公七年》）的说法如出一辙。这是一种再典型不过的男权话语。人类中心主义的突出表现之一就是男性中心主义：出于动物本能，男性渴求拥有对女性的绝对支配权，于是建构出一套男尊女卑的神话；为了捍卫这套秩序的合法性，"他"——包括"立人极"或"为世作则"圣哲和诗人（所谓"the legislator of mankind"或"unacknowledged legislators of the world"）——把"她"描述成了低劣、幼弱、缺乏理性的"他者"。在西方，"厌女"传统渊源有自也不绝如缕：古希腊人算是非常尊重女性了，但是像赫希俄德、苏格拉底、亚里士多德等冠冕人物尚不免认为女性比男性低劣②；文艺复兴时期的荷兰人文主义者伊拉斯谟（Erasmus）断言女人就是愚人③；十九世纪德国哲人叔本华坚持认为女性"构成次等性别，——在任何方面都逊于第一性的

---

① Cf. II. ii. 149: Polonius: "Lord Hamlet is a prince, out of thy star." 按婚姻讲究门当户对，中外皆然。如《左传·桓公六年》载："北戎伐齐，齐侯使乞师于郑。郑太子忽帅师救齐。……公之未昏于齐也，齐侯欲以文姜妻郑大子忽。大子忽辞，人问其故，大子曰：'人各有耦，齐大，非吾耦也。'"再如唐时大姓（所谓李、王、郑、卢、崔"七姓十一家"）之间"自为婚姻"，太宗下诏禁止，结果无济于事："然族望为时所尚，终不能禁，或载女窃送夫家，或女老不嫁，终不与异姓为婚。"（《资治通鉴·唐纪·高宗显庆四年》）

② 例如赫希俄德在《神谱》中说到天神宙斯"把女人变成凡人的祸害，成为性本恶者"（《工作与时日 神谱》，张竹明、蒋平译，商务印书馆，1991年，第44页）。柏拉图认为神创造了三种生物：男人，女人，禽兽，如果男人未能控制欲望感情，则将二次发生为妇人，如果仍然不能改正，则投生为禽兽（Timaeus, 42A—C），在《法律篇》中也说女性的天赋禀性比男性低劣（Laws, 781b）。亚里士多德也宣称男人本性相对优越而治人，女子本性相对低劣而治于人（Politics, 1254b）。

③ 伊拉斯谟：《愚人颂》，许崇信译，沈阳：辽宁教育出版社，2001年，第18—19页。

第二性"①，而尼采更是公然宣称女性"存在着生理上的弊端"②，"是那么迂阔、浅薄、俗气、琐屑骄矜、放肆不逊、隐蔽着轻浮"③……哈姆雷特也感慨地说"软弱，你的本性是女人"（I. ii. 146: "Frailty, thy name is woman!"），甚至当着恋人的面指斥女人水性杨花、矫揉造作（III. i. 153—160）。其实，"低下""软弱"这些女性特质（womanliness）在很大程度上——这里不排除某种两相情愿的"合谋"可能——不过是男性中心意识形态—话语建构的必然结果罢了。

这一点在Polonius对女儿的训话中表现得尤其突出。在父亲的追问下，Ophelia坦白说王子近来多次向她表达"爱慕"。听到这话，老头子一声断喝（I. iii. 106—107）：

> 爱慕？算了吧，你说话就像是一个
> 不知深浅的黄毛丫头。

和他的儿子一样，Polonius也断定哈姆雷特是在别有用心地玩弄感情。不同的是，父亲比兄长拥有更大的权威，因此训话的语气也就更加粗暴而不容置否。例如他盛气凌人地教训女儿说（110—112）：

> 咄，我来教导你！就当自己是小孩子罢，
> 你把这些虚情假意都信以为真了。

"就当自己是小孩子罢"，这不禁让我们想起汉儒对君夫人自称"小童"的解释："自称小童者，谦也。言己智能寡少，如童蒙也"（《白虎通·嫁娶·论王后夫人》）。既是孺子，又是女性，

---

① 叔本华：《论女人》，《叔本华论说文集》，范进等译，北京：商务印书馆，1999年，第485页。
② 尼采：《附录：看哪这人！》，《权力意志》，张念东、凌素心译，北京：商务印书馆，1991年，第48页。
③ 尼采：《超善恶》，张念东、凌素心译，北京：中央编译出版社，2000年，第147页。

女儿在父亲面前可以说是双重和加倍的弱势存在；除了俯首听命，她还能做什么呢？

不用说，这是一场单向度的、因此是不平等的"对话"。在这种不对等的对话关系中，"话语"本身蕴涵了某种权力结构，其中男性"说"而女性"听"。事实上"说"和"听"、"话说者"和"听话者"分别是"统治"和"服从"、"强势方"和"弱势方"的隐喻。法国语言学家海然热（Claude Hagège）指出："语言的实践反映一种并未公开宣布的霸权"，例如墨西哥阿兹台克人称皇帝为"tlatoani"，意为"发话的人"，这个词来自动词"tlatoa"，意为"说话"，它的同源词还有"tlatolli"（语言）和"tlatocayotl"（"政权"），这两个词的联合形式"tlatoacan"意为"最高国务会议"，也就是"说话的地方"①。汉语中也有很多这样的例子，如"不听话/听话""言听计从""听差""听任"（=无力管束或放弃控制）。现实生活中，领导讲话是"说"的人格化体现（他们发言的次序、长短和他们拥有权力的大小精确对应），而麦克风、高音喇叭之类则是"说"的工具化形式。

在上面的训话中，我们看到Laertes规劝妹妹"克己复礼"，Ophelia虽然不无意见，甚至忍不住反过来提醒哥哥不要像假道学那样，给别人指点上天堂的荆棘险路，自己却在花街柳巷留连徜徉（I. iii. 49—54），但她最终还是表示会把兄长的教导牢记心间（90—91）。紧接着我们看到Polonius对儿子训话，这时Laertes只能闷头聆听父亲的长篇大论而无置喙余地了（86）。最后是父女间的对话：女儿怯怯地陈述自己的想法，但父亲根本不听，悉数加以指责、否定，直到Ophelia表示一定会听话（141），这才止住话头。

可怜的Ophelia呵！她在生活中始终得是一个"听话的人"：父兄发话，她只有听从的份儿；就连哈姆雷特思想苦闷了，也要冲她——

---

① 海然热：《语言人：论语言学对人文科学的贡献》，张祖建译，北京：生活·读书·新知三联书店，1999年，第266—267页。

而且首先是冲她——指桑骂槐地发泄一通（III. i. 101—160）①。仅仅在一人独处的时候，也就是说没有男性在场的情况下，她才偷偷地难过了一番（161—172）。事实上，直到芳心破碎、神志失常后她才获得在公众场合（也就是男性空间）言说的权力（IV. v. 23—72）。福柯告诉我们，"疯人"在西方社会一向被视为"不正常的人"（福柯），也就是"非人"；可以说，直到成为"非人"这一刻，Ophelia才摆脱了"女人—弱者—听话的人"的身份，有了"说话"的权利。——然而她马上就死了，或者说永远沉默了！

《哈》剧中的另外几场对话也蕴含有类似的话语—权力结构。在第一幕第二场，老王的鬼魂开始向哈姆雷特发话时，他要求儿子谛听自己将要说的话（I. v. 6—7），而哈姆雷特的回答是："说吧，我自当聆听"（8）。在亚里士多德所谓"相认"（ἀναγνώρισις）②的这个场面中，对话一开始就从"追问—回答"模式转换成了"讲述—聆听"模式。"追问"体现了人对鬼（人的他者）的控制，而"聆听"则体现了儿子对父亲权威的认同。可以说，正是后一种话语关系为父子"相认"提供了适当的契机。第三幕第四场王后Gertrude和哈姆雷特的对话也是一个很好的例子。母亲本想训诫儿子一顿，不料儿子反唇相讥、咄咄逼人（III. ii. 383），自己反遭训斥；做母亲的又是羞愧又是惊恐，但却无力反抗，只得哀求儿子不要再说了（III. iv. 96 & 104—106）。这是一场男女／长幼两套话语权力之间的对抗；结果是尊长话语—权力不敌，男性话语—权力胜出，母亲的尊严在儿子的男性意志——或者说是儿子所

---

① 即如海涅所说："唉，弱者就是这样遭殃，每当一场巨大的冤屈落在他们头上，他们首先便向他们所有最好、最可爱的东西发泄他们的怨愤。而可怜的哈姆雷特首先毁坏了他的理智，那绝妙的珍宝，经过佯装的神经错乱投入了真正癫狂的可怕的深渊，并以尖刻的讽刺折磨他可怜的少女……"（海涅：《莎士比亚的少女和妇人》，绿原译，上海：上海文艺出版社，2007年，第118页）

② 亚里士多德：《诗学》，陈中梅译，商务印书馆，1996年，第89—90页。"相认"也译为"发现"，指悲剧主人公发现了改变自身命运的隐匿事实（往往是血缘关系、自己的真实身份，如Oedipus得知自己的王后Jocasta居然是自己的亲生母亲）；在这个意义上讲，"相认"等于情节的"突变"（περιπέτεια）。

代表的夫权——面前彻底崩溃①。

　　海德格尔有言：语言是存在之家②。家，甜蜜的家，温馨的家，舒适安逸的家……多么迷人的意象！但是不要忘记，只要有语言，就会有"说话的人"和"听话的人"，而这必然会构成某种权力结构。换句话说，只要话语存在，就有权力（广义的权力）的介入和滋生。从这个角度来看，语言也恰正是存在的牢笼。这时，我们对海德格尔的另外一句名言——人类始终"嵌"在语言的本质之中③，也许另有一番感受吧。

---

① 在中国传统社会中，却是长幼秩序——确切说是子女对父母的服从（孝道）——战胜了女性"夫死从子"的律令（妇道）。例如《红楼梦》第三十三回中贾母因贾政打宝玉而斥责贾政，面对母亲的斥责，贾政只有"躬身赔笑""跪下含泪说道""叩头哭道""苦苦叩求认罪"的份儿，并不敢还口（《红楼梦》，人民文学出版社，1982年，第458页）。当然，贾母是在丈夫去世（父权—夫权缺席）的情况下成了父权—夫权的代表，Gertrude则背叛了丈夫及其所代表的权力结构；现在哈姆雷特是代表父亲来谴责母亲，因此归根结底还是男权（确切说是夫权）在操纵着话语—权力游戏。

② 参见海德格尔：《语言的本质》，《在通向语言的途中》，孙周兴译，北京：商务印书馆，1997年，第134页。

③ 海德格尔：《走向语言之途》，《在通向语言的途中》，第228页。

6. 胡桃壳里的噩梦

　　Claudius凭直觉感到哈姆雷特突然神志失常——他宛转其辞地称为"转性"（transformation）——不是因为失恋，而是另有隐情，于是派遣王子的两名"发小"罗某（Rosencrantz）和吉某（Guildenstern）前去窥伺刺探（II. ii. 1—18）。老朋友见面煞是亲热，一时间"忘形到尔汝""惊呼热中肠"（240—242），但哈姆雷特很快就识破了他们的来意。在他逼问之下，罗吉二人只好承认自己是奉王命而来（283—302）。叔侄斗法，哈姆雷特赢了第一回合。

　　在他们把话说开之前，王子和这两位朋友有一段暗藏机锋的对白（II. ii. 256—268）：

　　　　哈：丹麦是一座囚牢。
　　　　罗：那么整个世界也都是了。
　　　　哈：是一座大囚牢，里面有许多囚室、监房和地牢，
　　　　　　丹麦是其中最糟的一座。
　　　　……
　　　　罗：嗨，那是您的雄心促成的。对您的心灵来说，丹麦是
　　　　　　太狭小了。

> 哈：上帝啊，我可以关在胡桃壳里而自认为是无限空间的君王——要不是因为我做噩梦的话！

哈姆雷特认为丹麦乃至整个世界都是一座囚牢，罗某乘机接过话头，说这是他心怀"大志"（ambition）所致。听到他这么说，哈姆雷特忍不住一声长叹："我可以关在胡桃壳里而自认为是无限空间的君王——要不是因为我做噩梦的话！"

这句话应当格外引起我们的注意：这是哈姆雷特装疯以后首次向旁人剖白心事（后来他孤身奋战，这种知己话就只向Horatio一人说了）。可惜，儿时好友已经变成"熟悉的陌生人"（这大约是Claudius始料未及的），罗吉二人竟未能听出其中的玄机。

细心的读者不难发现，王子在说上面这番话时，一连用了四个大有深意的隐喻："囚牢""胡桃壳""无限空间的君王"以及"噩梦"。在这四个隐喻中，哈姆雷特的精神品貌（moral physiognomy）得到了最初的、然而也是完整的揭示。下面，我们就来解析这些隐喻所可能蕴含的意义，并由此深入探索哈姆雷特的心灵世界。

（一）"囚牢"

说到"囚牢"，熟悉西方哲学的人多半会想到柏拉图的"洞穴"隐喻。在《理想国》（第七卷开篇）中，"苏格拉底"把现象世界或常识社会比喻为一个地下洞穴，洞中人——即蒙昧的常人大众——只能看到真实世界投射到洞中的阴影，也就是假象。按照"苏格拉底"的说法，这些人"从小就住在这洞穴里，头颈和腿脚都绑着，不能走动也不能转头，只能向前看着洞穴后壁"（514a—515b）。顺着他的话头，对话者"格劳孔"（Glaucon）指出这是"一些奇特的囚徒"；而这个"洞穴"，在"苏格拉底"看来，正是一个"囚室"（517b）。如果说受拘束、不自由是"囚牢"的本质,那么这个"洞穴"实际上是"囚牢",译解为"囚洞"也许更符合作者的原意。

如果我们所料不差,这就是哈姆雷特所谓"囚牢"的最初原型。

在后人的解读中,《理想国》里的"囚洞"隐喻往往被赋予单纯的认识论指向,就好像柏拉图所关心的是"解蔽"(《荀子·解蔽》)、"去宥"(《吕氏春秋·先识览》)或"正确的认识如何可能"这类问题似的;殊不知"束缚"和"局囿"首先是、而且归根结底是一种生存状态:"极高明"、认识善并不是故事的结尾,而恰只是故事的开始;"道中庸"、重返囚洞生活方才是人生在世的主题大义。即如"苏格拉底"所云,已经习惯囚徒生活的人乍然解除禁锢走出囚洞来到真实世界,会因为不适应天光、一时连阴影也都看不到而格外感到痛苦懊恼;更有甚者,当他发现阳光下的事物本相、回到地洞讲述他的见闻时,洞中的同伴势必会讥笑或惊诧于他的妄语邪说,群起而攻之,直至肉体消灭而后快。这样说来,先知先觉反倒成了一种罪过(hamartia)、人生受难剧的开场楔子,或者说命运的一道诅咒。由此可知,柏拉图同时是在伦理学和存在论的意义上使用这个"囚洞"隐喻的。

无知是痛苦的,但有知更加痛苦,因为这时我们面临着更大的无知。法国思想家帕斯卡尔(Pascal)曾经感叹:

> 我们尽管把我们的概念膨胀到超乎一切可能想象的空间之外,但比起事情的真相来也只不过成其为一些原子而已。……
> 让一个人返求自己并考虑一下比起一切的存在物来他自身是个什么吧;让他把自己看作是迷失在大自然的这个最偏僻的角落里;并且让他能从自己所居住的这座狭隘的牢笼里——我指的就是这个宇宙——学着估计地球、王国、城市以及他自身

的正确价值吧！一个人在无限中又是什么呢？①

他在说这番话时特别使用了"牢笼"（cachot）一词，这显然袭取了柏拉图的"囚洞"隐喻，并把"囚洞"的领域扩展到了整个宇宙。在帕斯卡尔看来，有限性是人性的本质，人类总是处于某种无知状态而永远无法走出囚笼：

> 看到人类的盲目和可悲，望着静默的宇宙，蒙昧的、抛闪给自身的人类在宇宙一角歧路彷徨，不知道是谁把他搁在这里、他来这儿做什么、死后他又会变成什么，而且不可能有任何知识，这时我就陷入了恐惧，就好像一个人在沉睡中被带到一个荒凉可怕的小岛，醒来却不知道自己在什么地方，也没有办法离开这儿一样。于是我惊诧人们何以对这样一种悲惨的状况不感到绝望。②

这里出现了一个新的隐喻："荒凉可怕的小岛"③。比照前后文意，"荒岛"显然是"牢笼"的另一表述和同位意象，但悲观的意味更加浓重：如果说柏拉图的"囚洞"尚有隧道通向外界，那么帕斯卡尔的"荒岛"则是一种前定的（"不知道是谁把他搁在这里"）、无法逃避的（"没有办法离开这儿"）生存绝境。换言之，人生就是一座"死牢"。

历史似乎有三重时间性：预演、发生和重现。大约六七十年前④，莎士比亚也通过哈姆雷特之口表达了几乎完全一样的想法。例

---

① 帕斯卡尔：《思想录》，何兆武译，北京：商务印书馆，1985年，第28—29页。参见Pascal: *Pensées*, Paris: Jean-Claude Lattès, 1988, p.31。

② 同上书，第328页。译文根据法文本（p.267）有所修改。

③ Cf. Hamlet II. ii. 308—309: Hamlet: "this goodly frame, the earth, seems to me a sterile promontory."

④ 《哈姆雷特》写作时间不晚于1600年，至迟在1600年底已经上演（参见裘克安：《莎士比亚年谱》，北京：商务印书馆，1988年，第150页）；《思想录》的大部分内容自1656年9月至12月完成，后经亲友整理，于1670年出版（参见陈兆福、刘玉珍编：《帕斯卡尔生平和著作年表》，《思想录》附录三，第511页）。

如帕斯卡尔认为宇宙是一个"狭隘的牢笼",哈姆雷特则说"世界是一个大囚牢,其中有许多囚室、监房和地牢"。再如帕斯卡尔反思"人类的盲目和可悲",悲叹"蒙昧的、抛弃给自身的人类在宇宙一角歧路彷徨,不知道是谁把他搁在这里、他来这儿做什么、死后他又会变成什么",哈姆雷特也沉吟"像我这样蠢动于天地之间的家伙能干什么?"(III. i. 137—138),"在死亡的睡眠中会有什么样的梦发生?"(III. i. 74.)不妨说,帕斯卡尔是哈姆雷特的哲学家版,而哈姆雷特则是帕斯卡尔的一个文学镜像。

不过,二者间还存在着一个微妙的、然而是根本性的分判,这就是帕斯卡尔认定人类是钉在原地百般挣扎也动弹不得的死囚,而哈姆雷特则认为我们至少有一处可以退守隐遁,这就是"胡桃壳"之内的广阔天地。

(二)"胡桃壳"和"无限空间的国王"

亚里士多德把人生分为"静观"与"行动"两种,认为"静观"是神之所为,也是人生的极乐(*Ethics*, 1177a; *Politics*, 1324a)。他所说的"极乐"指的是一种悠然自得、无待于外的生存状态,亦即"自由"。关于这一点,黑格尔在《哲学史讲演录》中有段话说得极是明白:

> 在思想的王国里自由地生活,在古希腊哲学家看来,是绝对目的本身。他们认识到,只有在思想里才有自由。①

显而易见,这是把意识从存在中抽离、回返自身并将意识与存在对立起来的一种做法。本来,抽离、回返和对立只是一个必要的、有待克服的中介或者说否定性环节,本身并不是

---

① 黑格尔:《哲学史讲演录》(第二卷),贺麟、王太庆译,北京:商务印书馆,1960年,第223页。

目的。儒家经典《大学》中说"知止而后有定，定而后能静，静而后能安，安而后能虑，虑而后能得"，"知止"（包括"定""静""安""虑"）即为"得"之手段。再以文学创作为例，"收视反听"只是"笼天地于形内，挫万物于笔端"的准备工作，一旦"情曈昽而弥鲜，物昭晰而互进"（陆机：《文赋》），它的任务即告完成，用黑格尔的话讲就是手段消解在目的中了①。至于老子讲"其出弥远，其知弥少"（《老子》四十七章），就有些过于偏激；而如果肯定这一否定环节而坚执不放，它就会固着为一个美妙空明的意念世界。例如文艺复兴时期荷兰人文主义者伊拉斯谟讥讽同时代的学者沉迷于琐碎无聊的学问，略有所得辄欢欣鼓舞，仿佛征服了非洲或者是占领了巴比伦，就算给他王位都不换②。与之相映成趣，王国维在《论哲学家与美术家之天职》一文中以赞赏的语气说道：

> 今夫人积年月之研究而一旦豁然，悟宇宙人生之真理，或以胸中惝恍不可捉摸之意境，一旦表诸文字、绘画、雕刻之上，此固彼天赋之能力之发展，而此时之快乐，绝非南面王之所能易者也。③

这和哈姆雷特所讲的"关在胡桃壳里而自认为是无限空间的君王"何其相似乃尔！正是在这一点上，我们说哈姆雷特虽然身为王子，却拥有哲人和诗人的灵魂。

诗人、艺术家、哲学家本性上都是理想主义者（idealists），他们留恋、礼赞这样一个世界是很自然的（虽然培根会认为这是他们的"洞穴妄念"④）。然而，正如叔本华所说，文学艺术只是暂时的

---

① 黑格尔：《逻辑学》（下卷），杨一之译，北京：商务印书馆，1976年，第441—442页。
② 伊拉斯谟：《愚人颂》，许崇信译，沈阳：辽宁教育出版社，2001年，第60—61页。
③ 王国维：《静庵文集》，沈阳：辽宁教育出版社，1997年，第121页。
④ 参见培根：《新工具》，许宝骙译，北京：商务印书馆，1984年，第29页。按"Idola"希腊文原意为"假象"，其义近乎佛家所说的"心魔""妄念"。

解脱、一时的安慰，并不能带来圆满常住的喜乐①，这个空灵妙曼的小世界是通过悬停或屏蔽现实而建立起的桃花源或乌托邦，需要靠极大的信力来护持，否则是很容易破碎而消散的。

说到这里，"胡桃壳"与"无限空间的国王"所指为何就不难理解了。按照精神分析学派的说法，"胡桃壳"表征了母体子宫的意象，而"胡桃壳"里面的桃仁活脱是大脑的形状；综合起来看，"胡桃壳"就是"子宫"和"大脑"的一个叠合意象。这样一来，"胡桃壳"里的"无限空间"就隐喻了一个封闭自足的精神世界，这个精神世界是一个以自身为目的的思想王国；而"我"，作为此间的唯一居民，便是拥有无上权威和绝对自由的"国王"了。

当"我"走进温暖而舒适的"胡桃壳"时，"风刀霜剑严相逼"的现实世界就关在了"胡桃壳"之外。这时节，尘世间的一切都变得那样遥远，那样模糊，那样渺小……

然而"噩梦"袭来了。

（三）"噩梦"

东晋时人孙楚《征西官属送于陟阳侯作》一诗中云：

> 莫大于殇子，彭聃犹为夭。吉凶如纠纆，忧喜相纷扰。
> 天地为我炉，万物一何小？达人垂大观，诚此苦不早。

这里说的"达人"显然是庄子。"莫大于殇子，彭聃犹为夭"一句几乎是《庄子·齐物论》中"天下莫大于秋毫之末，而大山为小；莫寿于殇子，而彭祖为夭。天地与我并生，而万物与我为一"的原话照搬。"天地为我炉，万物一何小"则兼取"天地与我并生，而万物与我为一"以及《庄子·大宗师》中的"子来"之语：

---

① 叔本华：《作为意志和表象的世界》，石冲白译，北京：商务印书馆，1982年，第370、439页。

> 夫大块载我以形，劳我以生，佚我以老，息我以死。故善吾生者，乃所以善吾死也。今大冶铸金，金踊跃曰："我且必为镆铘！"大冶必以为不祥之金。今一犯人之形而曰："人耳！人耳！"夫造化者必以为不祥之人。今一以天地为大炉，以造化为大冶，恶乎往而不可哉！

按此，诗中所说的"大观"即是庄子所鼓吹的等同死生、齐一万物的思想。等同死生、齐一万物，也就是泯灭真实、具体的生命感受（特别是痛苦感受），从而在主观上达到"逍遥""至乐"的境界，这无异于"关在胡桃壳里而自认为是无限空间的君王"；用弗洛伊德的话讲，这无非是生物惰性或"死亡本能"（Thanetos）的表现罢了①。然而，哲学家往往有意无意地把这种渴望回复初始状态（例如出生前在母体子宫内的生存状态，或者是人类"堕落"之前在伊甸园的幸福生活，"静止永恒的道理世界"则是一种更加隐蔽的变体形式）的本能冲动解释为一种崇高伟岸的情怀。德国哲学家费希特即为其中代表，他满怀激情地颂扬"理念"，声称：

> 理念是独立的、自己满足自己的和自己产生自己的。它要生活，它要生存，完全是为了生存而生存；它鄙视它生存中一切可能处于它自身之外的目的。……正如在整个人类中它决不追求世俗福利，而只追求绝对尊严——不是作为福利条件的那种尊严，而是完全自为的尊严——一样，在它表现于个人生活的地方，它自身完全满足于这种尊严而无须考虑成败。由于它不以成败为转移，由于它如同放弃感性欲望那样放弃功利，所以，对成功的毫无把握就绝不可能搅浑它的内在清晰性，而真正的失败也从来不可能引起它的痛苦。悲伤、痛苦或干扰怎么

---

① Sigmund Freud: *Beyond the Pleasure Principle*, trans. by C. J. M. Hubback, The International Psycho-Analytical Press, 1922, pp.29—48.

能进入这个自我封闭的生活圈子呢？①

费希特认为，人一旦超越成败和功利等等"自身之外的目的"，他就会进入纯粹的"理念"世界，自足、自为而"不喜亦不惧"。但问题在于，"不以成败为转移、放弃功利"恰恰是身负国仇家恨的哈姆雷特无法做到的。超越时空、不落因果的"理念"固然可以"鄙视它生存中一切可能处于它自身之外的目的"，然而坎陷在特殊存在中的个体生命又怎能遗世而独立、"躲进小楼成一统"、关在胡桃壳里称王？一如王子恋人的兄长Laertes所说，"他（哈姆雷特）的意志不属于他本人，他受制于自己的出身"（I. iii. 20—27）：作为王子，哈姆雷特必须对国家的命运负责；而作为人子，为父亲报仇更是责无旁贷的义务。尘世间的种种责任、义务和"不得已"②共同勾结成了此在的"囚笼"。在这种情形下，存在者委实"无所逃于天地之间"，——即便他遁入"胡桃壳"中，"囚笼"也会笼罩、萦绕、浃洽在这个"自我封闭的生活圈子"周围，时刻映入或投下噩梦的阴影。

通过上面的分析，我们可以想见哈姆雷特所谓"噩梦"的真实含义。首先，这个"噩梦"并不是罗吉二人所猜度的权力野心，而是指他父亲死后的诡异显灵、他于是领受的世俗义务以及他因此遭受的命运。对于鬼魂讲述的秘密，哈姆雷特不愿也不敢向朋友明言，最多只能向他们略微暗示一二；同时他心中也不无疑虑，因为这也许是魔鬼为引诱他陷入万劫不复之地而布下的圈套（II. ii. 602—607）③。尽管如此，他仍将鬼魂在荒野中的叮咛——这来自幽冥世

---

① 费希特：《现时代的根本特点》，沈真、梁志学译，沈阳：辽宁教育出版社，1998年，第51页。

② 参见《庄子·人间世》："仲尼曰：'天下有大戒二：其一，命也；其一，义也。子之爱亲，命也，不可解于心；臣之事君，义也，无适而非君也，无所逃于天地之间。……为人臣、子者，固有所不得已。'"

③ 黑格尔称之为对启示的"不信赖"，见《精神现象学》（下卷），贺麟、王玖兴译，北京：商务印书馆，1979年，第221页。

界的启示——认定为自己必须倾听的天道（I. v. 2—3 & 8—10）。于是，他左支右绌而心力交瘁（V. ii. 4—5 & 208—209）、"操心"不已却困魇在"在世"的噩梦之中。

不幸的哈姆雷特啊！

哈姆雷特也哀叹自己是一个"不幸的人"（I. v. 203 & V. ii. 236）。这种不幸在很大程度上来自于他的无知，以及面对无知所产生的无力感。哈姆雷特曾经反讽地将自己和神武的英雄海格力斯（Hercules）进行比较（I. ii. 152—153），似乎是自暴自弃，但他内心深处何尝不以大英雄自期！"让海格力斯做他会做的事吧"（V. i. 292）一句话就豁显了他的自我期许。然而，"时代脱节了"，"生来要重整乾坤"（I. v. 208—209）的英雄本人身陷梦魇，就像被捆绑、禁锢的力士，空有一身本领而无从施展。

可以说，哈姆雷特是被缚的海格力斯（Hamlet-Hercules Bound）。他孤悬于命运的尖峰危崖，身下虚凌存在的弱水深渊。他想要挣扎，却又不能太用力。最后，他疲惫了，认命了（V. ii. 216—221）：

> 死生有命，哪怕是一只麻雀。如果是现在，那就不是在将来；如果不是在将来，那就是现在；如果不是现在，那么将来仍会发生。做好准备是最重要的。既然谁也不知道自己会留下什么，那么及早离去又有什么呢？

费希特曾经说过，"理念"是一个时代的精神，没有理念的世界只是一具空洞的躯壳：

> 理念在它表现于生命的时候，能提供不可估量的力量和优势，是力量的唯一源泉；因此，一个缺乏理念的时代会成为一个软弱无力的时代；它还在从事的一切，表现它的生命象征的一切，都完全是苍白的、虚弱的和无精打采的。[①]

---

① 费希特：《现时代的根本特点》，第64页。

"一个软弱无力的时代"也就是一个失魂落魄的时代。这里说的"理念"是通过理性而升华、挺立的意志。正是由于缺乏这种理念—意志的支持,哈姆雷特产生了无力感和疲惫感。

(四)困顿与出走:哈姆雷特与浮士德的不同命运

经过仔细阅读的话,我们会发现《哈姆雷特》这部悲剧嵌套着"复仇"和"拯救"两大主题,而后者又与"追寻自我"或"自我认识"(精神的自身开展—完成)主题紧密结合在一起。作为复仇悲剧,《哈姆雷特》是一部完整的作品;但是"认识自我"这个悲剧行动却没有完成,或者可以说是以主人公的失败而告终的一部悲剧。在这个意义上讲,"拯救"主题的《哈姆雷特》是一部未完成的作品。

哈姆雷特去世后,他的挚友Horatio为他深情祝祷:"晚安,亲爱的王子,愿成群的天使用歌声伴你走向安宁"(V. ii. 378—379)。确实,哈姆雷特最终为父亲报了仇,并在临死前指定王位继承人,从而完成了自己的尘世义务,但是"自我完成"这项精神事业——这是他的"终身之忧"①——却远远没有完结。不知他死后可会升入他生前怀疑过的那个天堂?在那里,他得到喜乐安宁了吗?②

哈姆雷特带着深深的困惑与遗憾走了(V. ii. 351—353: "Had I but time—as this fell sergeant, Death, / Is strict in his arrest—O, I could tell you— / But let it be.")。但他的理想并没有跟着消逝,而是留在了世间,重新开始寻找自己的代理人。两个世纪之后,这个人出

---

① 参见《孟子·离娄下》:"君子所以异于人者,以其存心也……是故君子有终身之忧,无一朝之患也。"《论语·泰伯》记曾子言曰:"士不可以不弘毅,任重而道远。仁以为己任,不亦重乎?死而后已,不亦远乎?"对观二语,可知君子存心于"成仁",即成为我自己,这是他终生的事业。

② Cf. A. C. Bradley: *Shakespearean Tragedy*, The Macmillan Press Ltd., 1974, p.28 & p.29 n1.

现了：他就是歌德笔下的浮士德①。

在某种意义上讲，歌德的《浮士德》是作为"拯救"悲剧的《哈姆雷特》的重写、续作与完成。哈姆雷特渴望在"胡桃壳"中建立自己的自由王国，而浮士德却痛感"胡桃壳"里的世界是一座囚牢，认为只有走出这个胡桃壳—囚牢（nutshell-prison）才能接近、发现真正的"无限空间"。

剧情一开始，夜深人静困守书斋的浮士德感叹自己的世界是一个囚洞（Kerker）：

> 唉！我还要在这囚洞里苦捱？
> 该死的幽暗墙穴，
> 连可爱的天光透过有色玻璃
> 也暗无光彩！
> 更有这重重叠叠的书堆，
> 尘封虫蠹已败坏，
> 一直高齐到屋顶，
> 用烟熏的旧纸遮盖；
> 周围瓶罐满排，
> 充斥着器械，
> 还有祖传的家具堵塞内外——
> 这就是你的世界！这就叫一个世界！②

于是他下定决心走出书斋：

> 走！起来！到远方去！
> （Flieh! Auf! Hinaus in's weite Land!）③

---

① 歌德自1768年开始构思《浮士德》，最终于1832年完成该剧，先后持续六十四年；这里说"两百年"是取其约数而言。

② Goethe: *Faust*, Frankfurt am Main: Deutscher Klassiker Verlag, 1999, p.34. 译文参考了董问樵译本（复旦大学出版社，1983年，第23页）。

③ Goethe: *Faust*, Frankfurt am Main: Deutscher Klassiker Verlag, 1999, p.35.

他来到城外，目睹喧闹纷攘的世俗生活场景，由衷地感到"在这里我是人，在这里我能发现我自己"（"Hier bin ich Mensch, hier darf ich's sein."）①。

这是浮士德第一次走出小我世界。此后，他和魔王靡非斯特签订赌约，在后者的协助下阅历了从爱情到权力、从古典到浪漫的大千世界，不断开辟新的人生天地，又一再不满足于现状而出走。许多年之后，依旧是在一个夜晚，年届期颐、大限将至的浮士德发出了这样的人生感悟：

> 我已经熟识这攘攘人寰，
> 要离尘弃俗决无办法；
> 是痴人才眨眼望着上天，
> 幻想那云雾中有自己的同伴；
> 人要立定脚跟，向四周环顾！
> 这世界对于有为者并非默然无语。
> 他何必向那永恒之中驰骛？
> 凡是认识到的东西就不妨把握。
> 就这样把尘世光阴度过；
> 纵有妖魔出现，
> 也不改变道路。②

这是他对自己当年困守书斋时深夜所发感慨的正面回答，同时也是歌德对哈姆雷特的间接回应。此时此刻，"囚洞"和"天光世界"、"胡桃壳"和"无限空间"、"小我"和"大我"可以说完全融合在了一起。

浮士德溘然长逝后，他的精神开始最后一次出走——向天堂进发。魔王想要夺取他的灵魂，但是被众天使击退。胜利的天使托着

---

① Goethe: *Faust*, Frankfurt am Main: Deutscher Klassiker Verlag, 1999, p.52.
② Ibid., pp.441—442. 译文根据董问樵译本，第660页。

浮士德的"不朽部分",一边向天界飞升,一边曼声吟唱:

> 不断努力进取者,
> 吾人均能拯救之。①

歌德认为这几行诗蕴含了浮士德最终得救的秘密:"浮士德身上有一种活力,使他日益高尚化和纯洁化,到临死,他就获得了上界永恒之爱的拯救"②。永不知足、不断向上,这正是浮士德的"理念"或者说生命意志;用儒家的话讲,就是明明德而止于至善,即通过"日新""自强不息"的生命实践而达到"与天地合其德"(《易传·文言传》)、"上下与天地同流"(《孟子·尽心上》)的境界。通过一步一步走出小我、不断开拓存在的更高可能,他最终见证了理想的自我(用黑格尔的话讲,就是精神完成了自我认识)。在这个意义上讲,不是神恩拯救了浮士德,而是浮士德自己拯救了自己。在这时,哈姆雷特的人生理想——精神的自我认识与自我完成——终于得到了实现。

---

① Goethe: *Faust*, Frankfurt am Main: Deutscher Klassiker Verlag, 1999, p.459. 译文参考了董问樵译本(复旦大学出版社,1983年)。

② 爱克曼:《歌德谈话录》,朱光潜译,北京:人民文学出版社,1978年,第244页。基督教神学认为神恩是拯救的关键,而歌德将之实体化了。例如德国的埃克哈特大师(Johannes Eckhart)在他的《讲道录》中提到"恩典",认为它"乃是一种完完全全的运送","它的任务就在于将灵魂带回到上帝那里去"(《埃克哈特大师文集》,荣震华译,北京:商务印书馆,2003年,第262页)。在《浮士德》中,神恩作为天使出现,拯救因其"运送"而完成;但是从上面这段话来看,歌德格外强调了人类自身的努力,因此神恩似乎只是认可既成拯救事实的最后一道象征性手续罢了。

7. 人是何物

哈姆雷特告诉他的老朋友,为了向国王交差,就说他近来郁郁寡欢是因为厌世好了(II. ii. 304—308):在他看来,陆地是一块荒芜的海岬,而天穹不过是一团乌合的浊气(308—313)。说着,他把话题转向了人(314—319):

  人是多么了不起的作品!
  他有那样崇高的理性,无穷无尽的才能!
  举止宛若天使,悟性犹如神灵!
  啊,天地之英华,万物的灵长!
  可对我来说,这尘土的精华又是何物?

"这尘土的精华又是何物?"在此诘问声中,方才热烈欢快的"人类颂"戛然而止。哈姆雷特虽然没有明言——他只是讲"我不喜欢人"(319—320)——其实他心中已有答案:人无非是"造化的玩物"(I. iv. 57)、"十足的无赖"(III. i. 138—139)罢了。

"玩物""无赖",这与前面所说的"英华""灵长"云云形成何等强烈的反差!在这里,我们不仅看到"人之应然"与"人之实然"两种人性观的截然对立①，更感受到一种强烈的厌世情绪②。

作家笔下的人物往往是他的化身或代言人。在这个意义上，与其说哈姆雷特厌世，不如说莎士比亚有此感受而发为文字。之所以如此，除了作家的个体经验，更有时代精神的影响。我们知道，"天地之英华"和"万物之灵长"曾是文艺复兴时期欧洲人文主义者的普遍信念：从拉伯雷（François Rabelais）的"巨人"到马洛（Christopher Marlowe）的"帖木尔""浮士德"，人类意气风发，自我张大（self-assertion）到无以复加的程度；但是物极必反，由蒙田（Michel de Montaigne）发端，人类的自我意识渐趋幽暗而成为时代的精神，哈姆雷特的疑难即是这一"亢龙有悔"精神的症状表现。

宇宙间，人为何物？这是一个典型的"哈姆雷特问题"。这不仅是他那个时代的问题，也是一切时代的根本问题。古希腊神话说普罗米修斯用泥土按照神的形象造了人③，又说人性由神性和兽性混杂糅合而成，这一朴素的二元论思想对后世产生了深远的影响，并在不同历史时期以不同的话语或表述方式重复再现。如柏拉图笔下的"苏格拉底"认为人的灵魂秉具善恶两元，即"理"和"欲"两端，二者为主—奴关系，人既是自己的主人也是自己的奴隶，而以"理"治"欲"，人就可以成为自己的主人（*Republic*

---

① Theodore Spencer: *Shakespeare and the Nature of Man*, New York: Macmillan Company, 1951, p.94.

② 康德在论述"崇高"时附带谈及厌世问题，他认为有三种不同的厌世：第一种是"高贵的"厌世；第二种是"可鄙的"厌世；第三种可以说是一种无奈的选择，即"这些人虽然就好意来说是充分博爱的，但却由于长期的悲伤的经验而远离了人类的愉悦……虚伪，忘恩负义，不公正，以及在我们自认为重要和伟大的目的中的那种幼稚可笑，在追求这些目的时人们甚至相互干出了所有想象得出来的坏事：这些都是与人类只要愿意成为什么就能够成为什么的那种理念十分矛盾的，并且是与想要看到他们改善的强烈愿望极其对立的，以至于当我们不能爱人类时，为了不至于恨人类，放弃一切社交的乐趣显得只是一个小小的牺牲而已。"（康德：《判断力批判》，邓晓芒译，北京：人民出版社，2002年，第116—117页）哈姆雷特的情况比较复杂，似乎三种倾向都有，但更接近第三种。

③ Plato: *Protagoras*, 320c—322a. 参见奥维德：《变形记》，杨周翰译，北京：人民文学出版社，1984年，第3页。

430e—431b）。后代斯多亚哲人也认为人由动物本性和神圣理性混合而成①，即具有二元品性。文艺复兴时期的人文主义者更结合基督教神学深化了这一观点。如新柏拉图主义者马西留·费奇诺（Marsilio Ficino della Mirandola）把存在分为五个等级，其中"灵魂"处于第三等级，同时具有高级存在和低级存在的特性，既可以趋向"欲"，也可以趋向"理"，因此是二元的②。乔万尼·皮科（Giovanni Pico）亦认为人处于宇宙的中项，具有双重的和不定的人性，他通过自由选择而成为自己，既可以上升为神，也可以下降为兽③。莎士比亚在《哈姆雷特》中表述的人性观与之一脉而来（尽管他的知识来源非此一端④）。

哈姆雷特反问："这尘土的精华又是何物？"文艺复兴时期的人性观在此定格为对自身的怀疑和反讽。中世纪的基督教以上帝为中心而否定人性，如奥古斯丁在《忏悔录》开篇引《旧约·诗篇》和《新约·彼得前书》宣称：

"主，你是伟大的，你应受一切赞美；你有无上的能力、无限的智慧。"

一个人，受造物中渺小的一分子，愿意赞颂你；这人遍体带着死亡，遍体带着罪恶的证据，遍体证明"你拒绝骄傲的人"。⑤

这种自我否定意识在文艺复兴时期得到人文主义的反拨，但是

---

① 如爱比克泰德所说："人是由两种东西混合产生的，一种是肉体，与动物相通，一种是理性和智能，与众神相通。"（《爱比克泰德论说集》，王文华译，北京：商务印书馆，2009年，第29页。）

② Ernst Cassirer, Paul Oskar Kristeller & John Herman Randall, Jr. (ed.): *The Renaissance Philosophy of Man*, Chicago: The University of Chicago Press, 1948, pp.190—191.

③ Giovanni Pico: Oration on the Dignity of Man, in *The Renaissance Philosophy of Man*, p.224, 225, 230 & 235.

④ 有人指出这段话本出自15世纪西班牙学者雷蒙·塞邦（Raymond of Sabunde, ? —1436）《自然神学》（*Theologia Naturalis*）第95—99章的内容（E. M. W. Tillyard: *Shakespeare's History Plays*, New York: The MacMillan Company, 1946, p.7）。

⑤ 奥古斯丁：《忏悔录》，周士良译，北京：商务印书馆，1963年，第3页。

仍然通过历史—文化惯性而沉淀为某种"前有"（Vorhabe），并以"常言"的形式顽强"在场"。16世纪40年代，哥白尼在《天体运行论》中提出日心说，极大促进了16世纪以来的不可知论与怀疑论，也直接动摇了文艺复兴时期的人类中心主义①，于是产生了更大的、严重分裂的二元人性论。在某种意义上，它表象了时代的精神分裂症候：哈姆雷特对人类的嘲弄（包括他的自嘲）即是这一分裂的时代精神的文学映现。

四分之一个世纪前，蒙田曾在一篇著名的随笔中讥讽人类的狂妄自大：

> 所有创造物中最不幸、最虚弱也最自负的是人。（《雷蒙·塞邦赞》第2节）②

> 这个可怜而脆弱的创造物，连自己都不能掌握，受万物的侵犯朝不保夕，却把自己说成是他既没有能力认识、更没有能力统率起一小部分的宇宙的主宰，还有比这个更可笑的狂想吗？（《雷蒙·塞邦赞》第1节）③

已为哈姆雷特（莎士比亚）的反诘张本④。半个多世纪之后，法国哲学家帕斯卡尔也发出了同样的感慨：

> 人是怎样的虚幻啊！是怎样的奇特、怎样的怪异、怎样的混乱、怎样的一个矛盾主体、怎样的奇观啊！既是一切事物的审判官，又是地上的蠢才；既是真理的贮藏所，又是不确定与

---

① 参见卡西尔：《人论》，甘阳译，上海：上海世纪出版集团、上海译文出版社，2003年，第23—24页。
② 《蒙田随笔全集》马振骋译，上海：上海书店出版社，2009年，第2卷第110页。按：《雷蒙·塞邦赞》一文约创作于1576年。蒙田《随笔》英译本于1603年问世，译者是约翰·弗洛里奥（John Florio），莎士比亚或及见之。
③ 同上书，第107页。
④ 今天学界倾向于认为莎士比亚在1603年——这一年蒙田《随笔》英译本问世，译者约翰·弗洛里奥与莎士比亚同为骚桑顿伯爵（Earl of Southampton）门下，很可能彼此认识——之前已然读过这篇文章的译文手稿。

错误的渊薮；是宇宙的光荣而兼垃圾。①

这段话仿佛是哈姆雷特"反人类"言论的翻版②，或者说"翻版的翻版"。——甚至又一百多年后，人类依然为相同的问题所困扰。我们看到，歌德笔下的浮士德博士在书斋中研读"宇宙的符记"，深有会心而一时踌躇满志："我莫非是神？"（Bin ich ein Gott?）他念动符咒召来地灵，地灵也称他为"超人"（Übermenschen）。但是当他宣称自己与地灵相近时，竟被地灵嗤之以鼻。这个意外的打击顿令浮士德怅然若失：

> 我是神明的肖像，
> 自诩接近永恒真实之镜，
> 摆脱了尘世的凡胎，
> 在天光澄明中怡然自得；
> 自觉优于天使，自由的力量
> 已经穿流造化的经络，
> 具有创造力来享有神的生活。
> 谁知狂妄自大招致惩罚，
> 霹雳一声把我击垮！
> ……
> 我不像神！这让我感受至深！③

人不是神：人是欲望的动物，因此先天具有恶的因子。正是看准了这一点，魔鬼靡非斯特才敢于向上帝叫阵并自信胜券在握："从第一天到现在，世上的小神（按：指人类）就一直是老样"。

---

① 帕斯卡尔：《思想录》，何兆武译，北京：商务印书馆，1985年，第161、196页。

② 不同的是，这里不仅流露出道德的焦虑，也反映出一种认识的焦虑，用帕斯卡尔的话说就是"真正的人性、人的真正的美好和真正的德行以及真正的宗教，都是和认识分不开的东西"（帕斯卡尔：《思想录》，第201页）；因此当他说"人既不是天使，又不是禽兽；但不幸就在于想表现为天使的人却表现为禽兽"时，他想表达的或许是："人是无和全之间的一个中项"，"我们既不可能确切有知，也不可能绝对无知"（同上，第31、161页）。

③ Goethe: *Faust*, Frankfurt am Main, Deutscher Klassiker Verlag, 1999, pp.35, 37, 41 & 42.

但上帝恰恰是要假魔鬼—"恶"之力来推动人类向善——这刚好印证了悲剧第二部中远古怪物"斯芬克斯"给靡非斯特下的论断："无论对善人还是恶人，你都不可或缺"①。正如浮士德通过自身命运所证明的，人通过"恒常否定的精神"②不断认识自己、实现自己、超越自己，"不断向崇高的存在勇猛精进"③，最终可以克服"恶"（也就是自身的有限性）而"止于至善"。

诗人的观点得到了哲人的响应。康德认为人类历史具有长期的合理性与合目的性，即人类历史始于恶而止于至善，恶不仅是推进人类完善的必要手段，而且终将消融在未来的善中④。黑格尔同样注意到了这个被他称为"人格概念的高贵和低微"的问题。在他看来，"人就是意识到他的纯自为存在的那种自由的单一性"，即人自知其主体性（"人格的可能性"）；主体是人，但是人不等于主体，原因是"我作为这个人，在一切方面（在内部任性、冲动和情欲方面）都完全是被规定了的和有限的"；因此"人既是高贵的东西又是完全低微的东西，他包含着无限的东西和完全有限的东西的统一、一定界限和完全无界限的统一。人的高贵就在于保持这种矛盾，而这种矛盾是任何自然东西在自身中所没有的，也不是它能忍受的。"⑤不仅如此，黑格尔还提出"痛苦是生物的特权"⑥，这种痛苦就是"概念"与自身的分裂；在他看来，生命就是"概念"与其"客观化的特殊性"的自为分裂，因此：

> 某物在同一个观点之下，即是它自身，又是它自身的欠缺或否定物。抽象的自身同一，还不是生命力；但因为自在的肯

---

① Goethe: *Faust*, Frankfurt am Main: Deutscher Klassiker Verlag, 1999, pp. 26, 28 & 289.
② Ibid., p. 65. 这是魔鬼对浮士德的自我介绍，其实也正是"浮士德精神"乃至人性的一个写照。
③ Ibid., p. 205.
④ 参见康德：《历史理性批判文集》，何兆武译，北京：商务印书馆，1990年，第7、68页、第73—75页、第202页等处。
⑤ 黑格尔：《法哲学原理》，范扬、张企泰译，北京：商务印书馆，1961年，第46页。
⑥ 黑格尔：《逻辑学》（下卷），杨一之译，北京：商务印书馆，1976年，第467页。

定物本身就是否定性，所以它超出自身并引起自身的变化。某物之所以有生命，只是因为它自身包含矛盾，并且诚然是把矛盾在自身中把握和保持住的力量。但是，假如一个存在物不能够在其肯定的规定中袭取其否定的规定，并把这一规定保持在另一规定之中，假如它不能够在自己本身中具有矛盾，那么，它就不是一个生动的统一体，不是根据，而且会以矛盾而消灭。①

如果把矛盾对立的二元"肯定性"与"否定性"落实为"善"与"恶"，那么"人的高贵就在于保持这种矛盾"这句话意味着"唯有人是善的，只因为他也可能是恶的"②；进而言之，即人性中的"恶"（完善的缺乏与否定、"有限性"）成就了人性之高贵。在这里，两个世纪以来骚动不安的人类自我认识达到了平衡，分裂的时代精神得到了慰藉与弥合。

自我认识是一个永不停滞的动态过程，认识或精神的运动在取得瞬间平衡后不会停驻不前，而是会朝着新的甚至是相反的方向继续运动下去。按照皮亚杰（Jean Piaget）的说法，认识是一种连续不断的建构（自我中心化）—解构（去除自我中心）—再建构（重新自我中心化）过程，即"在循环往复的通路中发生作用的、并且具有趋于平衡的内在倾向的自我调节的作用"③；进一步说，"主体的活动，在认识层次上说（也许如同在道德价值或美学价值等等的层次上一样），要求有一个连续不断的除中心过程来把他从自发的心理方面的自我中心现象里解放出来，这样做并不就是为了要得到一个外在于他的完备的普遍性，而是为了有利于一个协调的和建立互反关系的连续不断的过程"④。这一观点似乎也可以用来描述西方

---

① 黑格尔：《逻辑学》（下卷），杨一之译，北京：商务印书馆，1976年，第67页。
② 《法哲学原理》，第144页。
③ 皮亚杰：《发生认识论原理》，王宪钿等译，北京：商务印书馆，1981年，第67页。
④ 皮亚杰：《结构主义》，倪连生、王琳译，北京：商务印书馆，1984年，第100页。

的人性论传统。如果说康德、黑格尔的人性观是中心化的、建构性的，那么19世纪以来叔本华、尼采、弗洛伊德、福柯对人的认识则是去中心的、解构性的。这两大运动趋势相互摩荡，自行建构并彼此拆解；而在前力已尽、后力未生的转折点上，在"前不见古人，后不见来者"的混沌中，认识主体（同时也是存在者）难免会歧路彷徨、无所适从，甚至"以矛盾而消灭"，成为人类历史祭坛上的牺牲。

哈姆雷特对人类的疑否（包括他的自我定位）即是前一平衡—中心已被打破、后一平衡—中心尚未建立时的认同危机的表征和产物。"从崇高到可笑只有一步之遥"，反之亦然：如果说哈姆雷特发现了人类的可笑与可鄙，那么歌德笔下的浮士德则重新为人类找回了自信与自尊。之后，是新的一轮幻灭与失落……人类，永远的"西西弗斯"和"奥德修斯"，就在这永无休止的摇曳、颠荡中，一再见证了自身的崇高与卑贱、伟大与渺小，以及二者的融合与分裂；而哈姆雷特，即是这样生存的人类的一个永恒镜像。

附论：
无知的黑洞

说明自己被害的真相后，老哈姆雷特的鬼魂像雾气一样消失了。这时Horatio等人追上来（他们的动作似乎也太慢了），急切地询问刚才发生的情况。看着他们，哈姆雷特欲言又止，最后含糊其词、意味深长地说了这样一句话："天地间你不知道的事情多着呢。"（I. v. 185—186: "There are more things in heaven and earth, Horatio, / Than are dreamt of in your philosophy."）

大约两百三十年前，意大利人文主义者彼特拉克曾在《论他自己的无知》（1370）一文中说："一个人（不论他是谁）所知道的，和他自己的无知——神的知识就不用说了——比起来根本不算什么。"①现在哈姆雷的感叹仿佛是这句话在历史长廊另一端的悠悠回响。不过彼特拉克旨在强调"真正的、最高的哲学是认识神"②，即神是人的最高知识对象，而哈姆雷特则暗示了人对命运的无知。

人对自己的命运是无知的，这一点被神志失常后的Ophelia一语道破："我们知道自己现在是怎样，但却不知道自己将来会如何"（Ⅳ. v. 44—45："we know what we are, but know / not what we may be"）。在最根本的意义上讲，无知正是一切悲剧的主题。

对于不可知的命运，我们能说什么？维特根斯坦告诉我们：对于不能说的事情，我们应当保持沉默③。他的意思是：逻辑是先天的，我们不可能思考非逻辑的东西，也不可能非逻辑地进行思考④。罗素认为维特根斯坦的观点是一种唯我论的表述⑤；确实，如果把这里的"逻辑"换成康德所说的"知性形式"，这一点就看得很清楚了，只不过康德强调的是"物自身"隔断了理念世界的入口，而维特根斯坦则提醒说认识走不出逻辑的牢笼，换言之"纯粹知性形式"本身构成了认识——同时也是存在——的大限。在这里，柏拉图的寓言就再一次被改写了：当我们自以为走出洞穴时，却发现自己置身于一个更大的洞穴；因此认识是绝对的黑洞，我们只是从一个洞穴走向另一个洞穴罢了！然而，"洞穴"只是一个隐喻，这里面蕴含着某种倾向性预设或价值判断，例如必然有一个光明世界、这个世界必然好于洞穴、因此我们必须走出洞穴等等。事实上我们

---

① Petrarca: *On His Own Ignorance,* in Ernst Cassirer, Paul Oskar Kristeller & John Herman Randall, Jr. (ed.): *The Renaissance Philosophy of Man*, Chicago: The University of Chicago Press, 1948, p.67. 彼特拉克的说法不过是中世纪神学家的老生常谈，如库萨的尼古拉早就说过：人类无法认识上帝即无限或绝对真理，绝对真理启示了我们无知中的晦暗——有学识的无知。（库萨的尼古拉：《论有学识的无知》1卷2章、26章，尹大贻、朱新民译，北京：商务印书馆，1988年，第6—8页、第58页）

② *The Renaissance Philosophy of Man*, p.80.

③ 维特根斯坦：《逻辑哲学论》绪论、命题6.53及7，郭英译，北京：商务印书馆，1962年，第20、97页。

④ 《逻辑哲学论》3.03、5.4732，商务印书馆，第28、69页。

⑤ 维特根斯坦：《逻辑哲学论》导论，第13页。

完全可以反过来理解这个隐喻，认为外面的世界是幽暗寒冷的永夜，我们只有回到室内才能享受到温暖和光明；或者，我们都走出洞穴而见识了天光（以及光天化日下的"自然"：一个远非美好、甚至是野蛮和危险的世界），但晚上又都回到洞穴，燃起了灯火，在憧憧人影的包围下，轮番讲述自己的所见所闻——就像哈姆雷特说的那样，身囿方寸而神御八极（II. ii. 266—267: "bounded in a nutshell and count / myself a / king of infinite space"）。

即便如此，问题依然存在：除了相信，我如何知道他人的叙述是真实的？对哈姆雷特来说，这个问题显得尤其迫切：我如何知道鬼魂所说的一切是真实的？这难道是魔鬼布下的陷阱或自身心灵走火入魔而产生的幻觉（Cf. II. ii. 602—607: "The spirit that I have seen / May be a devil; and the devil hath power / T'assume a pleasing shape; yea, and perhaps / Out of my weakness and my melancholy, / As he is very potent with such spirits, / Abuses me to damn me."）？即便鬼魂所说的一切都是真的，因此我可以而且必须复仇，然而这个"必须"或者说复仇的"自然正当"（natural right）又从何而得知？换言之，我何以知道我的复仇一定是善的（Cf. II. ii. 261—262: "there is nothing / either good / or bad, but thinking makes it so."）或一定会符合永恒正义呢？如果说，只有认识了自己才能认识命运、天道或永恒正义（尽性而后知命），而我认识了自己了吗？

在最后一幕，哈姆雷特告诉Laertes：疯狂害了他，疯狂是他的敌人（V. ii. 235—236: "Hamlet is of the faction that is wronged; / His madness is poor Hamlet's enemy."）。其实，他的真正敌人不是疯狂，也不是魔鬼，而是"无知"——对自身命运的无知、对命运本身的无知。面对不可知的命运，他无法解释而难以释怀，苦苦思索但心下茫然，于是一再延宕而陷入了认识的（同时也是存在的）"黑洞"……他最后能得解脱吗？这是一个"哈姆雷特的问题"；或者说，它构成了每一个人——至少是每一个自觉的人——的"哈姆雷特问题"。

8. 父仇焉报

第二幕第二场将终之时,哈姆雷特为自己一再延迟复仇行动而深感自责备(II. ii. 569—591):

> 而我,
> 一个软弱迟钝的家伙,就像在梦里一样,
> 对自己的大事全无想法:
> 一位国王被杀害、他的王国被篡夺,我也一声不吭!
> 我难道不是一个懦夫吗?谁骂我是小人,打破我的头,
> 拔掉我的胡子,然后吹在我的脸上?
> 谁拧着我的鼻子,公然撒谎让我乖乖地吞下?
> 我是该受这样的羞辱!
> 我是一个懦夫,没有胆量起来反抗,
> 否则我早拿这奴才的肠肚喂饱天上的兀鹰了。
> 卑鄙无耻的小人!
> 怙恶不悛、奸诈荒淫、灭绝人性的小人!
> 报仇啊!
> 我真是一头蠢驴!实在太棒了:
> 我亲爱的父亲被人杀害,天地鬼神都催促我为他报仇,

> 而我偏偏用诅咒发泄仇恨，
> 像娼妓一样，骂骂咧咧地躺倒，
> 贱人！
> 啊呸，呸！

在这里，哈姆雷特的"延宕"（procrastination）性格——据说这就是他的"hamartia"——显露无遗：就在他这样自怨自艾的时候，复仇再一次被延宕了。他这次的理由是：自己见到的鬼魂也许是魔鬼变幻的假象，而魔鬼常常利用人的软弱和忧郁（这在17世纪与"疯狂"是同义词①）把人引入万劫不复的深渊，因此鬼魂的一面之词不足为凭，复仇还需要有更加确凿的证据（II. ii. 607—608）。

黑格尔曾云：智慧女神的猫头鹰等到黄昏才展翅飞翔。他的意思是指思维（概念）总是晚于现实（历史）出现（"哲学总是来得太迟"）②。就像追着自己尾巴转圈的小狗一样，思维总是徒劳地追捕着现实；这个现实也可以是先前出现的思想（在黑格尔看来，思想最终必然外化为现实，因此现实必然曾经作为思想而存在），而后者又反思着更早的思想，这样存在就成了单纯的认识过程，思想者将陷入无休无止的思想反刍而永远无法走出自身。哈姆雷特的"延宕"即属于这种情况：他反复思索复仇的合法性问题，而复仇行为本身则被无限期地搁置了③。

哈姆雷特不仅是老哈姆雷特的独生子，同时也是丹麦王国的法定储君，因此他的复仇具有双重意义：既是为父亲复仇，也是为国

---

① Cf. Robert Burton: *The Anatomy of Melancholy*, London: J. M. Dent & Sons Ltd., 1932, p.120.
② 黑格尔：《法哲学原理》序言，范扬、张企泰译，北京：商务印书馆，1961年，第13—14页。
③ 后来他被解往英格兰，途中看到挪威王子Fortinbras兴兵征伐波兰，深有触动，再次谴责自己优柔寡断，痛下决心报仇（IV. iv. 33—68）。然而说归说，复仇行动又一次被延宕了。

家复仇①，而为父亲复仇同时就是为国家复仇，二者是等价的。他为自己的父亲"遭到无情的毁灭"而痛不欲生，这"毁灭"同时包括了他的"产业"和他的"宝贵生命"（II. ii. 572—574）。他把父亲的一枚印鉴藏在身边，在危急关头用它伪造国王的密信，将奉命护送（实为押解）他到英国受死的两名旧友送上了不归路，从而挫败了Claudius的阴谋，部分完成了自己的复仇任务；后来他经过一番波折回到丹麦，向挚友Horatio讲述起这段惊险的经历，并为自己的无情之举辩解说（V. ii. 68—73）：

> 你难道不认为这是我应当做的吗？——
> 他杀害了我的父王，奸淫了我的母亲，僭夺了我的王位，
> 而且设计谋害我的性命——
> 我这样做难道不是最有良心的做法吗？

从上面这段话可以看出，在哈姆雷特的心目中，复仇不仅是为父亲复仇，也是为国家复仇，二者都是理所当然、不容置否的正义行为。

不过我们要问：这种特殊的复仇需要理由吗？如果答案是肯定的，那么它需要何种理由？为什么需要理由？换句话说，是什么保证了这个理由的合法性？这个合法性从何而来？它本身是合乎理性的吗？

复仇本质上是一种以暴易暴的行为，因此不可能全然符合正义。黑格尔曾经在《法哲学原理》中指出：

> 犯罪的扬弃首先是复仇，由于复仇就是报复，所以从内容上说它是正义的，但是从形式上说复仇是主观意志的行为，主观意志在每一次侵害中都可体现它的无限性，所以它是否合乎

---

① 中世纪政治神学认为国王有两个身体：他（作为个人）的自然身体（body natural）和他（作为国王）的政治身体（body politic），后者即是国家（Ernst H. Kantorowicz: *The King's Two Bodies: A Study in Mediaeval Political Theology*, Princeton: Princeton University Press, 1997, pp.7—23）。

正义，一般说来，事属偶然，而且对他人来说，也不过是一种特殊意志。复仇由于它是特殊意志的肯定行为，所以是一种新的侵害。①

黑格尔认为复仇会导致冤冤相报的恶性循环，为了避免这种情况产生，有必要把复仇的权力交给作为普遍者（或者说"概念"）的第三方；后者"虽然是特殊的主观意志，可是它希求着普遍物本身"，即"要求从主观利益和主观形态下，以及从威力的偶然性下解放出来的正义"②。换言之，复仇只能是一种由国家（黑格尔称之为"地上之神"的暴力机构）代理执行的行为。"王制"（法律）神圣不可侵犯，因此复仇必须经过法律的中介代理、进入法律程序才能获得合法性。可是，如果法律机构不受理私人的复仇要求怎么办？清代学者赵翼论东汉"轻生报仇"之风曰：

> 夫父兄被害，自当诉于官，官不理而后私报可也。今不理于官，而辄自行仇杀，已属乱民。（《廿二史劄记卷五·东汉尚名节》）

这段话的重点是反对民众"自行仇杀"，但他同时也承认"官不理而后私报可也"。这就是说，在代理机构不作为（"官不理"）的情况下，个人可以自行复仇（"私报可也"），这种私人复仇行为是合法的。然而，即便是法律受理个人的复仇请求，复仇进入法律程序而合法化，它就是"自然正当"的了吗？法律并不足以保证复仇的"自然正当"（natural right），正如法律不能规定人性一样。归根结底，国法是人情的外化产物，因此复仇的最终依据只能在人性当中去寻求。

古人认为："父子有亲"，"父子之道，天性也。"就"子"

---

① 黑格尔：《法哲学原理》，范扬、张企泰译，北京：商务印书馆，1961年，第107页。

② 同上书，第108页。

而言，这种天性体现为"孝"。《中庸》称"夫孝者，善继人之志也"，又说"事死如事生，事亡如事存，孝之至也"，这样"孝"即意味着对父亲——无论是生前还是死后——意志的服从。这一点也许可以从生物学（例如基因—遗传理论）中找到"科学的"根据，但问题并不因此而解决：如果复仇出于本能的生理—心理冲动，那么它还能算作理性的行为吗？复仇离不开对以往经验的记忆、当下的隐忍、对未来结果的期待，其具体实施更需要审慎的筹划、冷静的判断、果敢的行动，因此复仇本身必然是一种理性行为；但是这种理性行为的根源未必是理性，而更多是一种非理性的生命冲动。

古人说"食色，性也"，即以"食色"为人生之"大欲"："食"是为了维持自身的生存，"色"的目的在于延续自身的生存（繁衍自身）。无论是维持自身还是繁衍自身，都可以说是"生生"本能的不同表现。"我要生！"这是生命的第一原则，也是最原始、最基本的生命意志。然而如果没有生命，生命意志也就无从谈起；那么人的生命从何而来？一名男子和一名女子性交，卵子受精，于是生命就出现了。可以说，人的生命开始于那颗幸运的受精卵；这颗受精卵意味着人类生命意志的实现，或者说是原始生命欲望的客体化①。换言之，生命并不是自由选择的结果，而是从一开始就打上了生命意志的暴力印记：汝生！这一生命意志——同时也是强力意志——是生命的真正"作者"，每一具体生命都承受并施加着这一意志。因此，"汝生！"和"我要生！"在很大程度上其实是同一个意志；每个存在者都是其制造者的生命意志的体现和延续，或者说它们干脆是一体的。

在各种人际关系中，父子关系格外被认为具有这种一体性。在这一点上，可以说是"东海西海，心理攸同"：东海哲人如黄

---

① 王充《论衡·物势篇》曰："夫妇合气，非当时欲得生子，情欲动而合，合而生子矣。"《后汉书·郑孔荀列传》记孔融语祢衡曰："父之于子，当有何亲？论其本意，实为情欲发耳。"此意古人已先言之矣。

宗羲认为"父子一气，子分父之身而为身"（《明夷待访录·原臣》）；西海哲人如叔本华则说父爱比母爱恒久，因为"父亲在孩子的身上发现了他内在的自我"①。当代女性主义批评也认为女性具有怀孕—生产的特殊经验，母与子血肉相连而具有存在意义上的换喻关系；相反，男性与其子女缺乏这种直接关联而体现为隐喻关系②。所谓"一气"，所谓"他内在的自我"，所谓"隐喻关系"，其实都是指精神生命的一体性。

然而自相矛盾的是，父子间的这种一体性往往表现为弗洛伊德所谓"俄狄浦斯情结"的对立冲突关系。例如在乔伊斯的小说《尤利西斯》中，渴望寻找精神父亲的青年学生斯蒂芬（Stephen）不无愤激地说："父性也许是法律的虚构。有哪个儿子的父亲是儿子爱他或他爱儿子的？""未出生的儿子破坏了美：出生后，他带来了痛苦，分去了爱，加剧了操劳。他是一个男人：他的成长是他父亲的衰亡，他的青春让他的父亲感到妒忌，他的朋友是他父亲的敌人。"③这番话其实是儿子心理的投射：他看到的父亲的敌意无非是他对父亲所怀敌意的映像罢了。

让我们回到《哈姆雷特》的文本中来。老哈姆雷特去世的时候，哈姆雷特正在普鲁士的威滕堡（Wittenberg）学习④。这一年他三十岁⑤。三十岁似乎已经不是求学的年龄了，而他这时候去威滕堡干什么呢？有论者指出："剧情开始时，哈姆雷特已届而立之年……他接受了各种文化教养，唯独没有关于行动生活（active life）的教养。强势的老哈姆雷特在位时，他那喜欢冥想的儿子从

---

① 叔本华：《论女人》，《叔本华论说文集》，范进等译，北京：商务印书馆，1999年，第489页。

② Dorothy Dinnerstein: *The Mermaid and the Minotaur*, quoted from Jonathan Culler: *On Deconstruction*, London: Routledge & Kegan Paul, 1982, p.60.

③ James Joyce: *Ulysses*, London: The Bodley Head Ltd., 1937, p.196.

④ A. C. Bradley: *Shakespearean Tragedy*, The Macmillan Press Ltd., 1974, p.344.

⑤ 后来墓地一场中，挖墓人说自己从哈姆雷特出世那天起干这一行，干了三十年（V. i. 136—137,139—140 & 153—154），我们由此可以推断出哈姆雷特的年龄。

来没有感到行动的召唤。他已经完全成年,然而在大学里游荡,学习哲学、爱好艺术并思考生与死的问题,但从未做过决断或做成某事。"① 在这段话中,"强势"(strong-willed)一词意味深长。我们不妨猜想,哈姆雷特之所以远走他乡,与其说是为了求学,不如说是一种自我放逐,目的是为了回避、忘记他那年老而大权在握的父亲的强势存在。在成年儿子的心目中,父亲被下意识地视为存在的缺席(在如不在,甚至是在不如不在):他拒绝拉康所谓的"二次同化",即对父亲这个代表法律/权威/秩序的他者和超我能指的认同②。然而父亲一死,情况立刻发生了变化:对立冲突的关系不复存在,父亲成为缺席的存在(不在如在);而通过记忆和想象,父和子在精神上更结为一体,"二次同化"于一瞬间实现完成(I. iv. 47—48: "I'll call thee Hamlet, / King, father, royal Dane.")。这时,父亲真正成了我的父亲:他的一切都是我的,包括他的生命意志。这样一来,复仇就是同一个生命意志的原始冲动及其自我完成,或者说某种基于非理性的生命本能、在非理性驱使下展开的理性实践。

哈姆雷特看到伶人借助"激情的梦想"(a dream of passion)而真实再现了古人的悲欢离合,不禁感慨系之(II. ii. 561—564):

> 赫卡柏是他什么人?他又是赫卡柏什么人,
> 居然为她伤心流泪?
> 如果他有和我一样动情的理由,
> 他又会怎样做呢?

人生宛若一场戏剧,其中情感戴着"理性"的假面粉墨登场,煞有介事、兴致勃勃地假戏真做而忘乎所以,然而隐藏在各色冠冕堂皇的"理性"假面下的无非是些"情感的梦想"罢了。哈姆雷特

---

① Edward Dowden: *Shakespeare, his Mind and Art*, quoted from A. C. Bradley: *Shakespearean Tragedy*, The Macmillan Press Ltd., 1974, p.84.

② 李幼蒸:《形上逻辑和本体虚无》,北京:商务印书馆,2000年,第199—200页。

在流放途中看到挪威王子Fortinbras率军攻打波兰，心下自忖（IV. iv. 48—58）：

> 巨大的榜样在激励着我：
> 瞧这支庞大的军队，
> 在一名娇弱的王子的带领下，
> 野心膨胀、意气昂扬而蔑视不可预见的结果，
> 仅仅为了一块弹丸之地，
> 就不顾性命，与命运、死亡和险境为敌。
> 真正的伟大不是任意寻衅，而是在荣誉受到侵犯时
> 为了芥豆之微的事情大动干戈。

哈姆雷特因此鞭策自己不要优柔寡断，立刻采取行动复仇（67—68）。然而，"巨大的榜样""真正的伟大"云云显然言不由衷，他接下来说这两万人为了"虚幻的、哄人的荣誉"而"和上床一样走向坟墓"（62—64）即暴露了他内心深处对待复仇的消极态度。复仇关系到当事人的"荣誉"，而"荣誉"不过是"神圣野心"（divine ambition）膨胀的产物；这样，复仇似乎只是一种经过"理性"美化的欲望。"哪里有傲慢和虚荣，哪里便有复仇的欲望。"[①]——也许，作为一名哲人，哈姆雷特洞透了"理性"的虚幻荒诞，于是意兴萧然、万念俱灰而选择了延宕？

如果说理性反思乃是"从无到无"的单纯否定[②]，那么，理性除了发觉自身的虚幻与造作之外，还能做些什么呢？但是生命，具体的、作为现象存在的真实生命，实在又离不开"情感的梦想"，否则就会陷入尼采所说的"颓废"状态[③]，用哈姆雷特本人的话说就

---

① 叔本华：《心理的考察》，秦典华译，《叔本华论说文集》，北京：商务印书馆，2010年，第296页。
② 参见黑格尔：《逻辑学》（下卷），杨一之译，北京：商务印书馆，第14—15页、第181页。
③ 尼采把"颓废"界定为"用理性对抗本能"，认为"坚决主张理性就是埋葬生命的危险的暴力"（尼采：《权力意志——重估一切价值》，张念东、凌素心译，北京：商务印书馆，1991年，第51页）。

是（III. i. 91—96）：

> 这样，思虑就把我们都变成了懦夫，
> 决断的血性
> 由于阴郁的思考而带上了病容，
> 伟大的事业因此偏离正轨
> 而失去了行动的本义。

9. 生与死

生命在其本能中既有肯定，也有否定。
生命了解肯定与否定是不可分的。
——尼采[①]

（一）

第三幕第一场自第64行以下，是《哈姆雷特》中最著名的一段独白：

生还是死？问题就在这里。
隐忍暴虐命运的摧残，或者
直面无量的苦难并消灭它们，
哪一种做法更加高贵？
死了，睡着了，什么都没有了；
于是说我们了结了烦恼
和生命必须遭受的千万种折磨。

[①] 尼采：《权力意志——重估一切价值》，张念东、凌素心译，北京：商务印书馆，1991年，第559页。

> 这是人们一心向往的结局。死了，睡着了。
> 睡——也许会做梦吧？哎，麻烦就在这里：
> 当我们摆脱了尘世的烦恼之后，
> 在长眠不醒中会做什么样的梦呢？
> 这肯定会让我们踟蹰止步。
> 正是这种顾虑使人生成为漫长的苦难。
> ……

独白的第一句，"To be, or not to be, that is the question"，总领下面长达三十二行的长篇独白，同时也是全剧的题眼和总纲，是本剧甚至是所有莎剧中最重要的一句台词。它的中文译文不下十种，例如朱生豪译为"生存还是毁灭，这是一个值得考虑的问题"，孙大雨译为"是生存还是消亡，问题的所在"，梁实秋译为"死后是存在，还是不存在——这是问题"，卞之琳译为"活下去还是不活：这是问题"，方平译为"活着好，还是死了好，这是个问题"等等。以上这几种翻译各尽其妙，但是严格说来都有不足之处。当然，这并不都是译者的责任，因为这句话事实上是不可译的。我们知道，汉语中缺乏冠词形式，更没有定冠词和不定冠词之分，因此在译"the question"时，上述译者或者忽略了定冠词"the"（梁译、卞译），或者译成了"a question"的意思（朱译、方译），或者增字添意（朱译），或者改变原文的语法结构而欠通顺（孙译），但是都未能准确译出定冠词"the"所具有的特定和专指意义。

然而，根本的问题还不在这里，而是出在对"to be"的处理上。在印欧语系语言中，诸如古希腊语、拉丁语、德语、法语，当然还有英语，"to be"同时具有"是""在""有"等多种意义。以英语为例，表示"是"者如：

This *is* a book.

表示"在"者如：

There *is* a book (on the desk etc.).

表示"有"（具有某种性质或效应）者如：

This book *is* interesting (dog-eared etc.).

事实上，"to be"是西方形而上学的出发点，古希腊哲学中的本体论范畴"τὸ ὄν"（being）就是从"εἶναι"（to be）发展来的[①]。笛卡尔有一句名言："我思故我在"（或可译"我思则我是"），这句话的拉丁文、法文、英文分别是：

1. Cogito ergo sum.
2. Je pense donc je suis.
3. I think therefore I am.

其中"sum"，"suis"，"am"均为表示本体（"是""在""有"）的动词。

那么"to be, or not to be"这句话中的"to be"是什么意思呢？在这句话中，"to be"单独出现，后面没有跟任何表语或状语，因此它表示本体的存在，意谓"生""实有""恒存"，即对存在及其意义的肯定。与之相反，"not to be"意谓"死""断灭""虚无"，即对存在及其意义的否定，同时还暗含有主动放弃现世肉体生命——也就是自杀——的意思。在本段独白第84—90行，哈姆雷特即明言了这一点：

谁愿意负荷生命的重担，
在沉重的压迫下呻吟流汗，
如果不是因为害怕死后

---

① 参见王太庆：《我们怎样认识西方人的"是"？》，《柏拉图对话集》，王太庆译，北京：商务印书馆，2004年，第714页。

>那个人们一去不返的未知国度？
>恐惧心理使意志惶惑动摇，
>于是我们宁愿在世间受苦，
>也不愿奔赴未知的忧患。

事实上他以前就动过自杀的念头（I. ii. 130—133）：

>但愿这过于坚顽的身躯
>融化、消释为露水一滴！
>或者那永恒的上帝
>不曾定下禁止自杀的法律！

现在得知父亲被害的真相后，他由冥想自杀转向了沉思存在：生是？死是？生死都是？都不是？由此可知，"To be, or not to be"首先是（尽管并不仅仅是）对生死这一根本问题的追问和沉思。

（二）

哈姆雷特的追问隐含了人类对于死亡的本能焦虑。这种焦虑不仅是一种认识的焦虑，更是一种存在的焦虑。出于这种焦虑，人类开始沉思生死问题；而正是在试图解答这个问题的过程中，出现了各种各样的生命哲学。

根据柏拉图的叙述，苏格拉底临死前告诉弟子：灵魂是存在的，生命不会断灭；从"生"中产生"死"，从"死"中产生"生"，生—死相互流转不已。"生"生"死"很好理解，为什么说"死"生"生"呢？苏格拉底用归谬法证明了这一点（*Phaedlo*, 72c—d）：

>如果产生的过程不是从对立的一方到另一方，然后再返回来，兜着圈子转，而是永远以一直线向前，没有返回或转折，

那么，你明白，到了最后一切事物都成了一样的，都达到同一状态，就根本停止产生了。

如果一切有生命的东西都会死，如果死者在死后始终处在那种状态中，岂不是到最后必然一切都是死的，没有一个是活的吗？因为如果活的不是从死的产生，而是从别的产生，而活的又必要死，怎能避免到头来一切事物都要同归于死呢？①

于是他认为人死后会变成灵魂，——灵魂是不死的，只不过"好人的灵魂存在得好些，坏人的灵魂存在得差些"，——然后因其业报重新转世，生成新的生命②。

照此，死对于"好人"来说并不可怕，相反倒是一件值得庆幸的事（Hamlet, III. i. 71—72: "'Tis a consummation / Devoutly to be wished"）。苏格拉底正是这样认为的。在柏拉图的《申辩篇》中，他对审判自己的人说（40d—41c）：

如果我们用另一种方式考察，那就会看到很有理由希望死是一件好事。因为死的状态有两种可能：死可能是绝对虚无，死者全无知觉；死也可能像人们说的那样，是灵魂从这个地方迁移到另一个地方。如果死是毫无知觉，像一场没有梦的熟睡，那就是近于绝妙的境界了。……另一方面，如果死就是从这里移居别处，如果传说无误，所有的死者都在那里，那还有什么比这更好的呢，法官们？……同这些古人交谈和往来，对他们进行考察，将是无法估量的幸福。③

苏格拉底深信自己死后会和古代的英贤们生活在一起，因为在他看来"一个好人无论在生时或死后都不会遇到不祥，神灵并不忽视他的幸福"（41d）④。毫无疑问，"神"和"灵魂"一道构

---

① 《柏拉图对话集》，王太庆译，北京：商务印书馆，2004年，第227—228页。
② 同上书，第228页、第276页以下。
③ 同上书，第53—54页。
④ 同上书，第55页。

成了他的生命哲学的基础：没有"灵魂"就不会有"生"；而没有"神"，"死"将是无所谓的事情，哲人在世之所为——按照"苏格拉底"的说法，"真正献身哲学的人所学的无非是赴死和死亡"（*Phaedo*，64a）①——就失去了意义。

一如苏格拉底，西塞罗相信人死后"或者感到很快乐，或者什么感觉也没有"②；同时，他表示自己愿意相信（而不是像苏格拉底那样坚信不疑）灵魂的不朽和转世③：

> 我认为人的灵魂是不朽的，即便我的这一观点是错误的，我也愿意这样错下去，因为这一错误给予我如此多的快乐，我不愿在我有生之年失去它。但是，像有些蹩脚的哲学家所认为的那样，如果我死后就没有知觉了，那么，我也用不着担心死后哲学家们会嘲笑我的错误了。此外，假如我们不是永生的，那么，一个人在适当的时候死去也是件值得欣慰的事。因为"自然"为一切事物设定了极限，人的生命也不例外。④

照这个说法，死非但不足惧，甚至还是一件令人向往的事情。由此可以看出，在西塞罗的生命哲学中，"死"的问题就是"生"的问题，灵魂不朽和转世的宗教信仰只是一种可爱并且有利的辅助假设罢了。

在这一点上，西塞罗和苏格拉底所说的"哲人"貌合神离，倒是更像17世纪时荷兰哲学家斯宾诺莎所描述的"自由的人"。后者在《伦理学》中提出："自由的人绝少想到死；他的智慧，不是死的默念，而是生的沉思。"⑤这和柏拉图说的"真正献身哲学的人所

---

① 《柏拉图对话集》，王太庆译，北京：商务印书馆，2004年，第216页。
② 西塞罗：《论老年 论友谊 论责任》，徐奕春译，北京：商务印书馆，1998年，第35页。
③ 西塞罗在别的著作中也表达了这种信仰，例如他在《国家篇》将近结束时（第6卷第28节）谈道："由于灵魂是唯一自动的力量，它就当然没有始点且是永生的。"（西塞罗：《国家篇 法律篇》，沈叔平、苏力译，北京：商务印书馆，1999年，第136页）
④ 西塞罗：《论老年 论友谊 论责任》，第40—41页。
⑤ 斯宾诺莎：《伦理学》，贺麟译，北京：商务印书馆，1983年，第222页。

学的无非是赴死和死亡"恰好形成鲜明的对照。斯宾诺莎是这样进行论证的：

> 自由人，亦即纯以理性的指导而生活的人，他不受畏死的恐惧情绪所支配，而直接地要求善，换言之，他要求根据寻求自己的利益的原则，去行动、生活，并保持自己的存在。所以他绝少想到死，而他的智慧乃是生的沉思。①

柏拉图认为不知"死"则不知"生"，而斯宾诺莎却认为知"生"不必知"死"。不妨说，柏拉图（以及中世纪基督教神学）正面肯定了"死"，而斯宾诺莎则正面肯定了"生"。

斯宾诺莎的《伦理学》写作于1662年至1675年，距离莎士比亚创作《哈姆雷特》大约六七十年光景。如果说"To be or not to be"这句话代表了时代转型中普遍存在的怀疑精神，那么斯宾诺莎则为时代立言，对这个"哈姆雷特问题"做出了肯定（"to be"）的答复。

（三）

哈姆雷特在沉思"生还是死"这个问题时，心中的顾虑主要有两点：其一，上帝禁止人类自杀；其二，人死之后并非"万事皆休"，也许会有"噩梦"出现。这两个问题可以归结为一个问题，即个体灵魂的归宿和朽与不朽问题。基督教认为人是上帝的造物，因此人必须向上帝负责，自己无权处置自己的生命；同时，人类具有与生俱来的"原罪"，每个人在上帝面前都是罪人，死后灵魂会受到上帝的审判：好人上天堂，罪大恶极者沉沦地狱而万劫不复，

---

① 斯宾诺莎：《伦理学》，贺麟译，北京：商务印书馆，1983年，第222页。

普通人则先在炼狱净罪（就像老哈姆雷特那样①），然后超度升天。

因此，对于基督徒来说，"to be or not to be"本不成为问题，或者可以轻而易举地回答："存，吾顺事；没，吾宁也。"（《正蒙·乾称篇上》）然而，这在哈姆雷特恰恰是不可能的选择：他"定在"于一个完全不同的现实世界。首先，他身负为家（父亲）国（王位）复仇的双重义务，虽有出世之想（II. ii. 266—267），但无法洒脱到"以死生为一条，以可不可为一贯"地"纵浪大化中，不喜亦不惧"（Cf. I. v. 208—209: "The time is out of joint. O cursèd spite / That ever I was born to set it right!" II. ii. 229—231: "You cannot, sir, take from me anything that I will more willingly part withal—except my life, except my life, except my life."）。其次，他从小接受的宗教观念也不允许他有这样的想法。哈姆雷特在威滕堡（Wittenberg）接受大学教育，而这里是马丁·路德新教改革的大本营，布鲁诺也曾于1586年到过此地，他们的革新思想不可能不对他的信仰产生冲击。另一方面，此时新教思想方兴未艾，但是尚未形成气候，还不足以取代旧有信仰；而天主教虽然受到质疑，却仍然是唯一的既定宗教信仰（the only established faith），舍此之外心灵没有任何现成的庇护所。这是一个亦新亦旧、方生方死的时代（Cf. I. v. 208: "The time is out of joint." IV. v. 103—104: "as the world were now but to begin, / Antiquity forgot"），即如柏拉图在一封信中向友人介绍雅典社会现状时所说：

> 我们的城邦已经不按照传统的原则和法制行事了，而要建立一种新的道德标准又极为困难。（《书简七》，325d）

而个人则如黑格尔在论古希腊的"居勒尼学派"时所说的那

---

① Cf. I. v. 14—17: "Doomed for a certain term to walk the night, / And for the day confined to fast in fires, / Till the foul crimes done in my days of nature / Are burnt and purged away."; 76—79: "Cut off even in the blossoms of my sin, / Unhous'led, disappointed, unaneled, / No reckoning made, but sent to my account / With all my imperfections on my head."

样：

> 在这里出现了希腊精神的逆转。当一个民族的宗教、法制、法律有效的时候，当一个民族的各个个人处在宗教和法度之中，与宗教和法度合而为一、共为一体的时候，是不发生个人自己应当做些什么的问题的。这可以说已经就在那里了，已经就在他本身之中了。相反地，当这种满足不再存在的时候，当个人不再处在他的民族的伦理之中，他的实质不再在他的国家的宗教、法律上面的时候，个人就开始关注自己了；他不再发现他所期望的东西，他不再满足于现状，不再满足于他自己的现状了。①

时代精神发生逆转、个人与自身现实（黑格尔所谓"民族的伦理""他的国家的宗教、法律"）相剥离而感到不满足和不安宁，这正是哈姆雷特的真实处境。在这个"此亦一是非，彼亦一是非"（Cf. II. ii. 261—262: "there is nothing / either good or bad but thinking makes it so"）的精神暗夜与信念荒原中，敏感如哈姆雷特者彷徨四顾，迷不知其所之，以至于失魂落魄、忽忽如狂，不亦宜哉！

哈姆雷特死后，他的挚友Horatio哀悼他说："一颗高贵的心碎裂了"（V. ii. 378）。其实，在他生前这颗心就已经碎了（Cf. III. i. 161: "O, what a noble mind is here o'erthrown!"）。

---

① 黑格尔：《哲学史讲演录》（第二卷），贺麟、王太庆译，北京：商务印书馆，1960年，第136—137页。

10. 哈姆雷特的命运

哈姆雷特认为人生是一场漫长的苦难历程：只要活在世上，我们就不得不忍受时运的暴虐和轻薄、强徒的胡作非为、高傲者的白眼、爱情被鄙弃的惨痛、法律的延误①、官府的侮慢、克己忍耐反被没有价值的人奚落（III. i. 78—82）……在这里，他简直就像是一名十六七世纪的"愤怒青年"，向我们诉说了人世间的种种苦楚和不幸。

有人也许会问：哈姆雷特身为一国储君，地位何等尊崇，生活何等安逸，怎么可能有普通民众的生活经验而产生这种愤世嫉俗的感慨？②显然是作者借题发挥，吐露自家胸中的不平之气罢了。此说不无道理，莎士比亚的确喜欢而且也善于通过剧中人之口表达自己对人生和社会的看法；但是如果说哈姆雷特因为是王子就不可能具有这种感受，或者因此断言这段独白游离于主题之外、人物性格显得不够真实，那就错了。

人们常常认为生活优裕的人不可能有痛苦，因此没有资格谈论痛苦，否则便是矫情。例如鲁迅就曾批评有些作家好以己度人，挖

---

① Cf. III. iii. 60—63: "In the corrupted currents of this world / Offence's gilded hand may shove by justice, / And oft 'tis seen the wicked prize itself/ Buys out the law".

② 例如布莱德利即认为这"绝不是他（哈姆雷特）本人的感受"。（A. C. Bradley: *Shakespearean Tragedy*, The Macmillan Press Ltd., 1974, p.126, n.1.）

苦说这好比乡下人认为皇帝是用金扁担挑水、农妇想象皇后天天吃柿饼一样；但是他本人也曾讽刺地谈到"一个家里有些钱，而自己能写几句'阿呀呀，我悲哀呀'的女士，做文章登报，尊之为'女诗人'"（《准风月谈·登龙术拾遗》）①，这也不过是想当然罢了。假如这名诗人是无病呻吟、"为赋新诗强说愁"，那么鲁迅的批评自然不错；可是如果她的痛苦是真实的呢？当然，她感到痛苦不可能是由于饥饿、寒冷或生活资料的匮乏，而多半是精神方面的原因，诸如失恋、自卑、抑郁等等，但这些感受对她本人来说一样真切实在，别人无权禁止她具有这种痛苦感受，更没有权利禁止她感到痛苦②。

痛苦是一种个人感受，如人饮水，冷暖自知。《红楼梦》第七十六回中史湘云和林黛玉有一段对话，就很说明问题：

> 湘云笑道："得陇望蜀，人之常情。可知那些老人家说的不错。说贫穷之家自为富贵之家事事趁心，告诉他说竟不能遂心，他们不肯信的；必得亲历其境，他方知觉了。就如咱们两个，虽父母不在，然却也忝在富贵之乡，只你我竟有许多不遂心的事。"黛玉笑道："不但你我不能趁心，就连老太太、太太以至宝玉探丫头等人，无论事大事小，有理无理，其不能各遂其心者，同一理也，何况你我旅居客寄之人哉！"③

黛玉所言甚是。不但红楼之内，红楼之外亦复如此。佛说人生有八苦：生、老、病、死、爱别离、怨憎会、求不得、五取蕴；这八宗苦，无论男女、老少、贫富、贵贱、种族、阶级，概莫能外。

---

① 《鲁迅全集》第5卷，北京：人民文学出版社，1981年，第275页。他所说的"女诗人"名叫虞岫云，是当时上海大亨虞洽卿的孙女。

② 中新网2005年10月21日转载台湾地区媒体新闻："台湾'最高检察署'检察官黄世铭的长女黄宜君，昨天清晨被发现在就读的东华大学宿舍阳台前上吊自杀。"据报道，黄宜君年初出版了她的第一本散文集《流离》，书中她以"细腻的观点写私生活、梦境、情妇、死亡、遗弃等主题，反思女性对情感、生活和伤痛的态度，用词大胆、坦白，风格独树一帜，被视为深具潜力的文坛新秀"。鲁迅如若在世，对此不知又有何评说。

③ 曹雪芹、高鹗：《红楼梦》，北京：人民文学出版社，1982年，第1087页。

面对痛苦，每一个人都是平等的。

另一方面，痛苦却又因人而异。昔人有言："圣人忘情，最下不及情；情之所钟，正在我辈"（《世说新语·伤逝》）。人之所以为人，在于有情，而痛苦的根源也正在于有情：有情，则感通；感通，则觉灵；觉灵，则欲求盛；欲求盛，则烦恼多有。质言之，感受力的高低决定了痛苦的大小，感觉越发达就越痛苦。即如叔本华所说，感觉是意志的现象，而"随着意志的现象趋于完美，痛苦也就日益显著"①，因此"真正的痛苦只是由于认识的明确性、意识的明晰性才可能的"②：

> 在植物身上还没有感性，因此也无痛感。最低等动物如滴虫和辐射体动物就能有一种程度很微弱的痛感了。甚至昆虫，感觉和感痛能力都还有限。直到脊椎动物有了完备的神经系统，这种能力才以较高的程度出现；而且智力愈发达，痛苦的程度愈高。因此，随着认识的愈益明确，意识愈益加强，痛苦也就增加了，这是一个正比例。到了人，这种痛苦也达到了最高的程度；并且是一个人的智力愈高，认识愈明确就愈痛苦。具有天才的人则最痛苦。③

简言之，认识和意识是与感受力同步发展的，因此拥有超常感受力的天才也就格外痛苦。

叔本华的观点引发了王国维的深衷共鸣。王国维也认为"天才者，天之所靳而人之不幸也"，原因是：

> 若夫天才，彼之所缺陷者与人同，而独能洞见其缺陷之处；彼与茕茕者俱生，而独疑其所以生。……然彼亦一人耳，志驰乎六合之外，而身局乎七尺之内；因果之法则与空间时间之形式束缚其知力于外，无限之动机与民族之道德压迫其意志

---

① 叔本华：《作为意志和表象的世界》，石冲白译，北京：商务印书馆，1982年，第424页。
② 同上书，第425页。
③ 同上书，第424—425页。

于内。而彼之知力意志，非犹夫人之知力意志也；彼知人之所不能知，而欲人之所不敢欲，然其被束缚压迫也与人同。夫天才之大小，与其知力意志之大小为比例；故痛苦之大小，亦与天才之大小为比例。①

这里他提到"因果之法则与空间时间之形式"，显然是受了康德的影响。本来康德告诉我们：人同时属于感觉世界和理智世界，同时受到自然规律和理性规律的支配；在第一种秩序中，人是自然的，而在第二种秩序中，人是自由的；这两种秩序能够而且必须统一。现在王国维从叔本华的立场出发，认为这两种秩序都是意志的现象，二者相互冲突、无法调和，个人"知力意志"越强，就越感到被阻遏、被限制，痛苦也就越大。

天才"所缺陷者与人同，而独能洞见其缺陷之处"：这一点正是我们理解哈姆雷特悲剧命运的关键所在。

哈姆雷特是怎样一个人呢？他可以说是时代的骄子，命运的宠儿：他的老朋友艳羡他高踞"命运冠冕的正中"（Cf. II. ii. 242）；他的恋人称赞他是"高瞻远瞩的朝臣，辩才无碍的学者，武艺超群的战士，众望所归的一国之英"（III. i. 162—163）；他生前深受国内人民爱戴②，去世后挪威王子福丁布拉斯（这是哈姆雷特的潜

---

① 王国维：《叔本华与尼采》，《静庵文集》，沈阳：辽宁教育出版社，1997年，第92—93页。

② Claudius向Laertes解释他为什么不能处决哈姆雷特，原因有二：首先，他深爱着Gertrude，一步也离不开她，而Gertrude没有哈姆雷特简直就活不下去（IV. vii. 13—18），因此他投鼠忌器；其次，老百姓都非常喜爱哈姆雷特，不但对他的缺点视而不见，甚至认为是优点（id, 18—23），杀他恐怕会犯众怒。之前他也曾满怀妒意地说："不明事理的大众都喜爱他，这些人用眼睛而不是根据明智的判断来喜欢一个人，他们不会考虑他的过错，而是会认为刑罚太重了"（IV. iii. 4—7）。如果不因人废言，他的话还是很有道理的。大众喜欢以貌取人，对政治人物也不例外。春秋时期郑国共叔段骄纵无礼，图谋不轨，但是百姓喜欢他，称他"洵美且仁""洵美且好""洵美且武"（《诗经·郑风·叔于田》）。再如三国时孙策顺利平定江东，据说是因为他"为人美姿颜，好笑语，性阔达听受，善于用人，是以士民见者，莫不尽心，乐为致死"（陈寿：《三国志·吴书一·孙破虏讨逆传》）。可见对政治人物来说，"洵美且好""美姿颜"是其个人魅力的重要来源——他们由此具有某种"明星效应"而成为大众崇拜的偶像——甚至可以说是一种"克里斯玛"（charisma）。在这个意义上讲，政治是一种表演：它不仅具有观赏性，而且需要被观赏；或者说，"seeming"等于"being"。

在对手和镜像人物）叹惋他本会成为一名杰出的王者（Cf. V. ii. 421—422）。然而，高踞"命运冠冕的正中"、成为万民瞻仰的一国之君并不是哈姆雷特的真正理想。他声称自己可以"关在胡桃壳里而自认为是无限空间的君王"（II. ii. 266—267），并且由衷地赞美 Horatio（III. ii. 66—75）说：

> 你浑若无事地忍受一切苦楚，
> 对命运的苛待和优遇都一视同仁；
> 这样的人是有福的，
> 他的情感和理智调理得十分停当，
> 命运无法随意排遣他。
> 给我这样一个不为情所役的人，
> 我会把他放到心间、置于心灵的中心①，
> 就像我对你一样。

Horatio 是哈姆雷特的知心好友（Cf. III. ii. 64—66 & 73—75），或者说就是他的"另一自我"（I. ii. 162: "Horatio—or I do forget myself!"），在他身上，哈姆雷特与其说发现、不如说投射和寄托了自己的理想人格（确切说是斯多葛哲人式的人格②）。他对 Horatio 的赞美——"情感和理智调理得十分停当，命运无法随意来排遣他"③——正表达了他自己内心深处的真实理想，这就是超越特殊而

---

① 《管子·内业篇》云"心以藏心，心之中又有心焉"，《心术下》又称"心之中又有心"。《大乘起信论》揭"一心二门"之说，以为"依一心法有二种门"，"一者心真如门，二者心生灭门"；然"是心从本已来，自性清静而有无明"，"心真如者，即是一切法界大总相法门体"。哈姆雷特所谓"my heart's core"，"my heart of heart"者，其心中之心、真如之心欤？

② 黑格尔指出：斯多葛哲学"摈弃一切"，"对于一切东西、一切直接的欲望、感情等等一概漠不关心"；"斯多葛派哲学的伟大处即在于当意志在自身内坚强集中时，没有东西能够打得进去，它能把一切别的东西挡在外面"（黑格尔：《哲学史讲演录》（第三卷），贺麟、王太庆译，北京：商务印书馆，1959年，第35、37页）。

③ 斯多葛哲人认为最高尚的人（即斯多葛哲人）"不被任何激情所压倒"而"满心欢喜地接受一切对他发生和作为他的份额分配给他的事物"（奥勒留：《沉思录》，何怀宏译，北京：生活·读书·新知三联书店，2002年，第21页）；哈姆雷特所谓"浑若无事地忍受一切苦楚""不为情所役"，与之同揆。

有限的生命，"纵浪大化中，不喜亦不惧"，成为一个自由的人。

不幸的是，哈姆雷特受制于自己的出身，意志不属于个人（I. iii. 18—19）。这样他就具有双重的身份和命运：一方是他的出身和世俗义务（id., 21—25: "on his choice depends / The safety and health of this whole state, / And therefore must his choice be circumscribed / Unto the voice and yielding of that body / Whereof he is the head."），另一方则是他的天性与精神追求（II. ii. 266—267: "I could be bounded in a nutshell and count / myself a king of infinite space"）。二者虽然有被动接受与主动选择之分，但它们都是先定的必然命令和欲罢不能的生命程序。黑格尔曾经断言"在真正悲剧性的事件中，必须有两个合法的、伦理的力量相互冲突"①；现在哈姆雷特一个人身上同时出现了两种相互冲突的合法伦理力量（布莱德利所谓"内在冲突"或"灵魂交战"②），他自身即结成了一个悲剧性的反讽。

可以说，哈姆雷特的命运自身分裂了。这就是为什么他一方面以大英雄海格力斯自期（V. i. 292），觉得自己应当有所作为；一方面又由衷地向往"胡桃壳"里的世界，悲叹自己必须担负起治世的任务（I. v. 208—209），结果坎陷于两种命运之间，无法取决也难以自拔③，成了一个"不幸的人"。

"不幸的人"，这正是哈姆雷特对自己的清醒认识（I. v. 203 & V. ii. 236）。帕斯卡尔曾经说：

> 人的伟大之所以伟大，就在于他认识自己可悲。一棵树并

---

① 黑格尔：《哲学史讲演录》（第二卷），第44页。
② A. C. Bradley: *Shakespearean Tragedy*, pp. 11—12。
③ 在这个意义上，Claudius忏悔时的哀鸣，"like a man to double business bound, / I stand in pause where I shall first begin, / And both neglect"（III. iii. 44—46），恰是哈姆雷特生存处境的真实写照。参见歌德的评论："他（按：即哈姆雷特）在重载下毁灭了，这重载，他既不能负担，也不能抛弃；那种责任对他来说，是神圣的，而又是太沉重的。……他那样辗转、徘徊、提心吊胆、瞻前顾后，不断被人提醒，自己也不断回忆，最后差点从思想中失去了目标，而任何时候都没有重新感到快活过。"（歌德：《威廉·麦斯特》，董问樵译，上海：上海译文出版社，1999年，第240—241页）

不认识自己可悲。

　　因此，认识自己可悲乃是可悲的；然而认识我们之所以为可悲，却是伟大的。①

这番话也完全适用于哈姆雷特。哈姆雷特是一个"独能洞见其缺陷之处"的自觉者。通观全剧，我们发现几乎所有人都生活在一种不自觉的、缺乏反思的天真状态之中，如Polonius刺刺不休地宣讲"简洁是智慧的灵魂"，Ophelia沉醉于虚幻的爱情，Gertrude安然享受不伦婚姻带给她的幸福生活，Claudius自欺欺人地扮演着英明君主的角色，只有哈姆雷特一个人始终清醒地觉察到自身（小我）的可悲，并进而同情地感受到他人（非我）的不幸与痛苦，即"常常将自身的痛苦转化成对于人类普遍状况的思考"②。——因此他会感叹"时运的暴虐和轻薄、强徒的胡作非为、高傲者的白眼、爱情被鄙弃的惨痛、法律的延误、官府的侮慢、克己忍耐反被没有价值的人奚落"，乃至对全体人类（大我）产生了悲悯（Cf. I. iv. 55: "We fools of nature"; II. ii. 318—319: "And yet to me what is this quintessence of dust?" & III. i. 137—139: "What should such fellows as I do / crawling between earth and heaven? We are arrant / knaves all"）。可以说，哈姆雷特是一个痛苦的觉者，他的痛苦与不幸在很大程度上正是由他的自觉造成的。

这是一种超越的、普遍的同情，或者说是一种更大的自觉（大觉）。人类历史上许多杰出人物都有过这样的生命感受和心理体验。如儒家讲"仁者己欲立而立人，己欲达而达人"（《论语·雍也》），"大人者与天地合其德"（《易传·文言传》）、君子"上下与天地同流"（《孟子·尽心上》）、"民，吾同胞；物，吾与也"（张载：《正蒙·乾称篇上》）；佛家讲"无缘之慈、

---

① 帕斯卡尔：《思想录》，何兆武译，北京：商务印书馆，1985年，第175页。
② 威廉·哈兹里特：《莎士比亚戏剧中的人物》，顾钧译，上海：华东师范大学出版社，2009年，第84页。

同体之悲"，以普度众生为己任；耶稣也说"爱你的敌人"（*Luke* 6：27），情愿牺牲自身为全人类赎罪。哈姆雷特悲天悯人，也有同样的情怀。然而，他身为一国储君，遭逢杀父欺母、篡位夺国的无妄之灾（Cf. V. ii. 69—72: "killed my King and whored my mother, / popped in between the election and my hopes, / Thrown out his angle for my proper life, / And with such cozenage"）而落入极端紧张、不容转圜、"虽欲不为是不可得"（柳宗元：《宥蝮蛇文》）的生存境域，于是只能放弃自己的人生理想、重新回到现实世界去完成因偶然而成为必须的尘世义务。

这样，哈姆雷特的命运便绾成了一个无法解释的死结。为了更好地说明这一点，我们不妨拿他和苏格拉底与释迦牟尼这两位哲人做一比较。

先来看苏格拉底。据柏拉图《克力同篇》（*Criton*）记载，苏格拉底被雅典法庭判处死刑后，他的朋友劝他逃跑，但他拒绝了。朋友们对此感到不可理解，认为这样做不仅会毁掉他本人，而且也会毁掉他的儿子，因此是一个"最偷懒的办法"，对他这样一个正直的人来说是可耻的。对于上述责难，苏格拉底的回答是：他在心灵深处听到了"最神圣的法律"的呼唤，后者告诉他不要把子女、生命一类的事情看得比道义更加重要，因此他宁肯赴死（45d & 54c）①。在苏格拉底看来，践行自己的哲学是生命中的头等大事，为此他可以放弃一切，包括赡养家庭的责任，而无所愧怍。就这样，他成功地化解了自己临处的道德困境，从而在命运面前开释了自己。

我们再来看释迦牟尼。释迦牟尼本是迦毗罗卫国的太子，十六岁成婚，十九岁（一说二十九岁）出家修行，三十岁（一说三十五岁）时证道成佛。就个人而言，他实现了与生俱来的、不容已的理

---

① 参见《柏拉图对话集》，王太庆译，北京：商务印书馆，2004年，第59—60页、第70—71页。

想,成就了自身;但是从家庭、民族和国家的角度来看,他逃避了同样是与生俱来的和不容已的责任和义务,因此是不道德的。例如宋代理学家二程兄弟就曾责难说:

> 1. 佛者一黠胡尔,佗本是个自私独善,枯槁山林,自适而已。若只如是,亦不过世上少这一个人。却又要周遍,谓既得本,则不患不周遍。要之,绝无此理。(《二程遗书·二先生语二上》)

> 2. 佛逃父出家,便绝人伦,只为自家独处于山林,人乡里岂容有此物?……释氏自己不为君臣父子夫妇之道,而谓他人不能如是。容人为之而己不为,别做一等人;若以此率人,是绝类也。(《二程遗书·伊川先生语一》)

程氏兄弟从儒家伦理立场出发,坚持修身、齐家、治国、平天下的进路,认为释迦牟尼的做法只是"自适"而无法"周遍""率人",因为这不仅在理论上自相矛盾("自己不为君臣父子夫妇之道,而谓他人不能如是","容人为之而己不为"),而且会导致"绝人伦""绝类"的灾难性后果。二程的说法不无偏激甚至隔阂,但他们的确击中了问题的要害。对于"外道"的指责非难,佛教有一套自圆其说的解释。《佛说未曾有因缘经》即是一例。本经开头部分记叙释迦牟尼派遣大弟子目犍连(即国人熟知的那位"目连")"往彼迦毗罗城,问讯我父阅头檀王,并我姨母波阇波提,及三叔父斛饭王等",同时交给他一项重要任务:说服他出家之前的妻子耶输陀罗送他们的儿子罗睺罗前来跟他修道[①]。目犍连如命前往,经过一番波折终于见到耶输陀罗并向她传达了佛意。耶输陀罗的回答是:

> 释迦如来为太子时娶我为妻,奉事太子如事天神,曾无一失。共为夫妇未满三年,舍五欲乐,腾越宫城,逃至王田。

---

① 《大正新修大藏经》(第十七卷),东京:大正一切经刊行会,昭和三年,第575页。原文四字一顿,标点为笔者试加。下引同。

> 王身往迎，违戾不从，乃遣车匿白马令还，自要道成，誓愿当归。披鹿皮衣，譬如狂人，隐居山泽，勤苦六年。得佛还国，都不见亲，忘忽恩旧，剧于路人，远离父母，寄居他邦。使我母子守孤抱穷，无有生赖，唯死是从，——人命至重，不能自刑，怀毒抱恨，强存性命，虽居人类，不如畜生。祸中之祸，岂有是哉！今复遣使，欲求我子为其眷属，何酷如之！太子成道，自言慈悲，慈悲之道应安乐众生，今反离别人之母子。苦中之甚，莫若恩爱离别之苦；以是推之，何慈之有！①

目犍连无法，只好请来王后劝导耶输陀罗。耶输陀罗仍不肯从命，并且悲愤地反诘说：

> 我在家时，八国诸王竞来见求，父母不许。所以者何？释迦太子才艺过人，是故父母以我配之。太子尔时知不住世出家学道？何故殷勤苦求我耶？夫人娶妇正为恩好，聚集欢乐，万世相承，子孙相续，绍继宗嗣，世之正礼。太子既去，复求罗睺，欲令出家，永绝国嗣，有何义哉！②

这番话说得何其沉痛，又何其严正，可谓掷地有声！一般人定然无言以对，但这难不住佛陀。他一开始就告诉目犍连说：

> 因复慰喻罗睺罗母耶输陀罗，令割恩爱放罗睺罗，令作沙弥，修习圣道。所以者何？母子恩爱，欢乐须臾，死堕地狱，母之与子，各不相知，窈窈冥冥，永相离别，受苦万端，后悔无及。罗睺得道，当还度母，永绝生老病死根本，得至涅槃，如我今也。

这番话其实预先回答了耶输陀罗的第一个责难：佛并不是要

---

① 《大正新修大藏经》（第十七卷），东京：大正一切经刊行会，昭和三年，第575—576页。
② 同上书，第576页。下引同。

"离别人之母子",而是要度化他们,使之"永绝生老病死根本,得至涅槃"。耶输陀罗不是问佛"何慈之有"么?这就是佛的"慈悲之道"。现在这番话没有说服耶输陀罗,于是佛又当机"遣化人空中告言"说:

> 耶输陀罗!汝颇忆念往古世时誓愿事不?释迦如来当尔之时为菩萨道,以五百银钱从汝买得五茎莲华上定光佛。时汝求我世世所生共为夫妻。我不欲受,即语汝言:"我为菩萨,累劫行愿,一切布施,不逆人意。汝能尔者,听为我妻。"汝立誓言:"世世所生,国城妻子及与我身随君施与,誓无悔心。"而今何故爱惜罗睺,不令出家学圣道耶?

这就回答了耶输陀罗的第二个责难:原来,"往古世时"耶输陀罗追求佛陀,为此她立下誓言"世世所生,国城妻子及与我身随君施与";现在佛只是按照这个誓约行使自己的正当权利罢了。多么高明的解释!既然是因缘注定的前世宿业,耶输陀罗也就释然了:

> 耶输陀罗闻是语已,霍然还识宿业因缘,往事明了如昨所见,爱子之情自然消歇,遣唤目连,忏悔辞谢,捉罗睺手,付嘱目连,与子离别。

就这样,佛圆满地解释(开脱)了命运,或者说使自身命运成了可解释的(可开脱的)。

能够解释命运的人或命运能够得到解释的人是有福的。然而,哈姆雷特的命运恰恰是无法解释的。我们不妨设想一下,如果苏格拉底和释迦牟尼的父亲也遭人陷害死于非命,他们是否还能常驻喜乐安宁的精神世界,一如既往地继续自己的哲学事业呢?恐怕很难。退一步讲,即便他们还能用"心灵的呼声""前世因缘"之类的说辞一了百了地解释命运、开脱在世的责任,这些解释也很难对哈姆雷特发生作用了。时代不一样了。苏格拉底和释迦牟尼均相信生命可以轮回再来,但哈姆雷特从小接受的信念却是:生命只有一次，我们并没有重新来过的机会。基督教所说的"afterlife"并非指"来世"或"来生"，而是指人死后灵魂接受审判、根据生前功过上天堂或下地狱之前的存在；现在他甚至对这一点也产生了怀疑（Ⅲ. i. 72—76: "To die: to sleep— / To sleep, perchance to dream—. Ay, there's the rub, / For in that sleep of death what dreams may come / When we have shuffled off this mortal coil / Must give us pause"）。按照黑格尔的说法，世界历史是"精神"的展开过程，这种向前进展的精神是"一切人内在的灵魂"，但它是"不自觉的内在性"，由"伟大的人"即所谓"世界历史个人"或"世界精神的代理人"引向自觉①；现在哈姆雷特把时代精神引向了自觉②，或者说时代精神通过它的代理人哈姆雷特表达了自身，而这个自觉的意识就是："To be, or not to be, that is the question"。这显然是一种怀疑的精神。——怀疑不等于怀疑主义，即如黑格尔在介绍古代怀疑论哲学时所说：

> 古代的怀疑论并不怀疑，它对于非真理是确知的；它并不只是徘徊不定，心里存着一些思想，认为有可能有些东西或许还是真的，它十分确定地证明一切非真。换句话说，怀疑对于它乃是确定的，并没有期望得到真理的打算，它并不是悬而不决的，而是斩钉截铁的，完全确定的；不过这个决定对于它并不是一个真理，而是它自身的确定性。这个决定乃是精神自身的安宁和稳定，不带一点悲愁。③

---

① 黑格尔：《历史哲学》，王造时译，上海：上海书店出版社，1999年，第19页、第30—34页。

② 在剧本中，这不仅表现为他本人的自觉，也表现为他唤醒了其他人的自觉：例如他训斥Ophelia，使之结束天真状态而产生了痛苦的自觉（Ⅲ. i. 171—172: "O, woe is me / To have seen what I have seen, see what I see!" Ⅳ. v. 44—45: "we know what we are, but know not / what we may be."）；Claudius看到哈姆雷特授意演出的戏后，良心受到折磨而被迫正视自己的罪恶灵魂（Ⅲ. iii. 39: "O, my offence is rank, it smells to heaven" etc.）；再如Gertrude遭到哈姆雷特的训斥，由是看到了自己灵魂中"无法消除的污点"（Ⅲ. iv. 97—99: "Thou turn'st mine eyes into my very soul, / And there I see such black and grainèd spots / As will not leave their tinct."）等等，不一而足。

③ 黑格尔：《哲学史讲演录》（第三卷），第111页。

怀疑主义本身构成一种信仰，而怀疑则不然，它——

> 只是不确定，乃是一种与确认相对立的思想，——一种举棋不定，一种悬而不决。怀疑包含着心灵和精神的一种分裂，它使人惶惶不安；这是人心中徘徊于二者之间的状态，它给人带来不幸。①

简言之，"怀疑是安宁的反面，安宁则是怀疑论的结果"②。对心灵来说，信仰既是束缚，也是必要的凭护。哈姆雷特因自觉而怀疑一切，这固然打破了信仰的结，但同时也就失去了存在的解，于是他的命运成了一道不可解的、甚至根本无解的难题。

就这样，哈姆雷特裸然一身和命运怪兽遭遇了。他哀叹自己的不幸，但是已经无路可逃。他被迫仓促应战，但是深知对手无比强大，自己注定会失败。他竭力抗争，但是力气逐渐衰竭。而就在扭打和僵持的同时，他绝望地、清醒地等待着（甚至是企盼着）那个必然的结局——或者说最终解决，也就是死亡——的到来："If it be now, 'tis not to / come; If it be not to come, it will be now; if it be not now, yet it will come; The readiness is all"（V. ii. 217—220）。在此之前，他只能默然忍受（Cf. V. ii. 365: "in this harsh world draw thy breath in pain" & 377: "The rest is silence."）。

遭遇和忍受：这就是哈姆雷特的命运。在某种意义上，这正也是一切人的命运③。

---

① 黑格尔：《哲学史讲演录》（第三卷），第110页。
② 同上书，第119页。
③ 斯多葛哲人教导世人："你是天生被创造出来忍受这一切的，你要依赖你自己的意见使它们变得可以忍受，通过思考这样做或者是你的利益，或者是你的义务。"（奥勒留：《沉思录》，第124页）可惜，哈姆雷特无法做到这一点。他因此成了一个"荒谬的人"：如加缪所说，"他知道自己的自由是有限制的，知道自己的反抗没有未来，知道自己的意识是要消亡的，他带着这样的意识在生命的时间长河中进行冒险活动"或者说"反抗"，而反抗"就是人不断面对自我而在场。它不是向往，而是无希望地存在着。"（加缪：《西西弗神话》，杜小真译，北京：商务印书馆，2018年，第65、52页）

附录一

关汉卿和莎士比亚：中英戏剧传统比较考察之一

谁是中国的莎士比亚？老实说，这是一个典型的伪问题。姑且不论此问所蕴含的文化地方主义色彩与殖民心态，——今天我们需要的是平等的对话而不是单向度的攀附，——莎士比亚只有一个，尊某某为中国的莎士比亚，恰恰证明他不是。也许这样提问更恰当些：在中国文学史上，有哪一位作家，与莎士比亚的生活与创作时代相仿，个人的经历与个性接近，创作题材与风格类似，并在本国或世界文坛中具有等同的影响和声誉？这样提问相对严谨一些，但是仍有漏洞，如作家的声誉与其创作成就往往并不相符，而且忒啰嗦了些。为方便讨论起见，下文暂时沿用"某某是中国的莎士比亚"这一约定俗成的提法，遵循上述原则对下述中英剧作家做一番比较考察，想来读者自能意会。

（一）汤显祖是中国的莎士比亚吗？

20世纪中叶，赵景深先生在《汤显祖与莎士比亚》一文（以下简称《汤》文）中指出：汤显祖是中国的莎士比亚，因为二者"生卒年相同，同为东西二大戏曲家，题材都是取之他人，很少自己的想象创造，并且都是不受羁勒的天才，写悲哀最为动人"①。

这是中西作家比较研究中较早的一篇论文，其发轫之功，自不可没；而"汤显祖是中国的莎士比亚"这一说法日后深入人心，几乎成为定论，直到今天尚在影响着人们的研究思路，如徐朔方、周锡山等人的同名论文就有近十篇之多。不过，今天我们再细玩该文，不难发现这个提法并不是无懈可击，如文中列举的几条理由并非汤、莎二氏的本质类同点，其具体论证亦漏洞颇夥，令读者甫一阅毕而疑窦丛生。顺此思路写作的论文，虽多方补充经营、局部论证亦能言之成理，其立论大端终不免有些先天不足。看来重新评价、认识这个今天仍很通行的"话语"，还是很有必要的。

我们现在便不妨将之逐条推敲一番。

赵氏认为，汤显祖（1550—1617）与莎士比亚（1564—1616）"生卒年相同，这是相同的第一点"，并引《中国近代戏曲史》的话说："东西曲坛伟人，同出其时，亦一奇也"②。按以同年而为同行，固甚难得，然以世界之大，同年甚至同日月生卒者不知凡几；何况汤显祖与莎士比亚生卒年份并不全然相同。若准此例，则王士禛（1634—1711）与德莱顿（John Dryden, 1631—1700）亦为同时，再如龚自珍（1792—1841）与雪莱（Percy B. Shelly, 1792—1822）同生而丁尼生（Alfred Tennyson, 1809—1892）与惠特曼（Walter Whitman, 1819—1892）共逝，这几位同行也都大可一比了；但他们又有何本质上的类同点呢？维·日尔蒙斯基说过："我们可以而且应该把在相同社会历史发展阶段生成的类似文学现象进行比较"③，

---

① 原载《文艺春秋》1946年2卷第2期，引自北京大学比较文学研究所编：《中国比较文学研究资料（一九一九—一九四九）》，北京：北京大学出版社，1989年，第283页。
② 同上，第278页。
③ 维·日尔蒙斯基：《比较文艺学》，列宁格勒科学出版社，1979年，第7页，转引自陈惇等主编：《比较文学》，北京：高等教育出版社，1997年，第211页。

但在时间上平行的社会并不总处在相同的历史阶段。这一点对于文学来说尤其是如此。

其次,《汤》文认为"汤显祖与莎士比亚都在戏曲界占有最高的地位。这是相同的第二点。"①西方戏剧并非戏曲,这且不论;莎翁确是雄视百代的大剧作家,——本·琼森(Ben Jonson)的诗赞"自豪吧,我的不列颠,你拿得出一个人,欧洲所有的剧坛都向他致敬"即代表了后世莎评的主流意见,——但汤显祖在中国剧作家的排行榜上,恐尚非头号种子。《汤》文云:"汤显祖是明万历年间的大戏曲家,虽不能说像莎士比亚那样有世界的声誉,但是在中国的传奇方面,不能不说是首屈一指"②。此言非虚,但明传奇之前,尚有作为"中国最自然之文学"③的元杂剧,再往前溯更有金院本、诸宫调,传奇又怎能代表整个中国戏曲呢?因此,传奇大家亦难称戏曲作家第一人了。

复次,《汤》文指出:"在题材方面,他们俩都是取材于前人者多,而自己创作的少。"④以下有精当的论述,如莎剧中《亨利五世》《麦克白》等取诸史实或传说,《罗密欧与茱丽叶》《威尼斯商人》等汲化于欧洲各国故事,特别是意大利的"小说"(Novella);汤剧则包括"四梦"在内,无不胎托于唐人传奇及元杂剧。斯论极是。莎翁的"拿来主义"举动之大,竟使"大学才子"之一的罗伯特·格林(Robert Greene)于辗转病榻之时兀自规劝马洛(Christopher Marlowe,1564—1593)等同行勿再作剧,因为"有一只用我们的羽毛装点自己的暴发户乌鸦"("For there is an upstart Crow,beautified with our feathers")。不过,莎氏的前辈如基德(Thomas Kyd),同时代人如马洛、琼森等又何尝不是如此?不过视野较狭、气魄稍逊罢了。古罗马作家贺拉斯(Horace)曾鼓

---

① 《中国比较文学研究资料(一九一九—一九四九)》,第279页。
② 同上书,第278页。
③ 王国维:《宋元戏曲史》,上海:华东师范大学出版社,1995年,第121页。
④ 《中国比较文学研究资料(一九一九—一九四九)》,第282页。

励剧作家采用古典题材，认为"从公共的产业里，你是可以得到私人的权益的"①。在中国，文章向为"天下之公器"，"填词"虽是"文人之末技"，然亦"乃于史传诗文同源而异派者也"②，戏剧与稗官正史关系之密切，恰似同胞兄弟，剧家作剧，欲不资鉴前人亦不可得矣。试以杂剧大家关汉卿为例，在他所作六十余种剧中，取诸野史、小说的就有《薄太后走马救周勃》《关大王独赴单刀会》等近三十种；它如《感天动地窦娥冤》《温太真玉镜台》等"旦本"戏，也都渊源有自，并非纯然向壁而造者。即以取材而论，汤显祖取用的多是唐传奇等文人作品，与关、莎二氏迥然有别。显然，这第三点理由亦难以成立。

《汤》文列出的第四条理由，是"莎士比亚的戏剧是不遵守'三一律'的。……汤显祖也是不肯遵守规律的，他所谱的曲常与曲律不合"，他们"都是不受羁勒的天才，这是相同的第四点"。③此论似是而非。"醉酒的野蛮人"（伏尔泰语）莎士比亚所蔑视的，是古板教条的欧陆戏剧传统，为此他甚至被认为"断送了英国的戏剧"④：他在"斗鸡场"中展开了河山万里，在"木头的框子里"（见《亨利五世》开场白）埋伏下了百万貔貅，摧肝裂胆之际突来科诨调谑，喋血鸣镝之处忽见筋斗杂耍……所有这一切，都维护、发扬了英国戏剧"是大众娱乐的综合艺术品种"⑤这一本土传统。而汤显祖作为文人剧作家，他所致力反抗的却是本国戏曲"本色"派之"家数"。如他在《与宜伶罗章二书》中再三致意："《牡丹亭》要依我原本，吕家改的，切不可从。虽增减一二字以

---

① 贺拉斯：《诗学·诗艺》，北京：人民文学出版社，1982年，第144页。
② 李渔：《闲情偶寄·结构第一》，引自郭绍虞主编：《中国历代文论选》（一卷本），上海：上海古籍出版社，1979年，第294—295页。
③ 引自《中国比较文学研究资料（一九一九—一九四九）》，第280—282页。
④ 伏尔泰：《论悲剧》，引自马奇主编：《西方美学史资料选编》（上卷），上海：上海人民出版社，1987年，第580页。
⑤ 王佐良：《白体诗里的想象世界——论莎士比亚的戏剧语言》，《外语教学与研究》1984年第1期，第2页。

便俗唱，却与我原本做的意趣，大不同了。"为了维护剧本的"意趣神色"（汤显祖：《答吕姜山》），他不惜"拗尽天下人嗓子"（汤显祖：《答孙侯居》），甚至为此和沈璟大打笔墨官司。他的创作取向与莎翁可以说恰好相反：莎士比亚致力在舞台上展现剧作的壶中世界，汤显祖却把目光投向案头，得意于在剧本中施展他的袖里乾坤。

《汤》文举出的最后一条论据是："汤显祖与莎士比亚的戏剧悲哀的地方，都极能动人"；尽管"莎士比亚所作虽非全是悲剧，汤显祖也许竟不曾写过悲剧"，但后者之"《牡丹》《紫钗》二记实有写成悲剧的可能"，因此二人的戏剧天才都在悲剧中得到最大发挥[①]。此说又差。姑不言汤显祖到底创作过悲剧与否（因为"可能"并不等于事实），也不论莎剧中的崇高悲剧感与汤剧中缠绵悱恻的"动人""悲哀"是否为一谈，我们单是来分析一下二人剧作中的人物形象与主题，就足以说明问题了。莎剧中展现的，或是溺爱失察、刚愎自用的耄聩君王，或是因谗生妒、转爱成恨的摩尔大将，或朝廷新贵由于野心膨胀而做法自戕，或青春王子愤激家国惨变而留连感伤……可以说，其中的人物性格、主题思想都达到了"极大丰富"的程度。这一点前人之述已备，毋庸赘述。相形之下，《汤》文作者首肯的《牡丹》《紫钗》二剧，充其量不过是鲁迅论《红楼梦》时所说的言情"小悲剧"，至于《南柯》《邯郸》二记更是直接抒发"人生如梦"的主题，人物、主题相对单一，整体上看与莎剧迥然异趣。

此外汤、莎二氏的差异亦不在少数，如剧本数量多寡悬殊；莎翁不仅是大剧家，也是开领一代诗风（Shakespearean sonnet）的大诗人，而汤氏诗作虽多，却非以此道见长……这些且不论，《汤》文列举出的五点理由，均非确凿无疑，在此基础上得出结论说"汤显祖是中国的莎士比亚"，不免有些轻率了。

---

① 引自《中国比较文学研究资料（一九一九—一九四九）》，第282—283页。

陈寅恪先生曾在《与刘叔雅教授论国文试题书》中指出："盖此种比较研究方法，必须具有历史演变及系统异同之观念。否则古今中外，人龙天鬼，无一不可取以相与比较。荷马可比屈原，孔子可比歌德，穿凿附会，怪诞百出，莫可追诎，更无所谓研究之可言矣。"① 赵景深先生固非穿凿为文，但自郐而下，皮攀肤附、"私掖偷携强撮成"的比较文学研究不在少数。这类文章在茶余饭后作为佐谈之资尚可，但若用于严肃的文学研究，"仅仅对两个不同的对象同时看上一眼就作比较，仅仅靠记忆和印象的拼凑，靠主观的臆想把一些很可能游移不定的东西扯在一起找类同点，这样的比较绝不可能产生论证的明确性"②。

但这绝不是说作家比较研究全无可能或毫无意义。恰恰相反，作家作为创作主体，是文学作品研究中相当重要的一环。别林斯基说得好："每一部艺术作品一定要在对时代、对历史的现代性的关系中，在艺术家对社会的关系中，得到考察；对他的生活、性格以及其它等等的考察也常常可以用来解释他的作品"③。作家比较的前提，并不是要不要比较、能否比较，而是因何比较、如何比较。

先说第一点。法国比较文学学者（如卡雷）认为比较作家须研究"作家生平之间的事实联系（rapports de fait）"，对于同气连枝的西方各国文学来说，这个看法自然是不错的，但中西（欧美）文学在20世纪初以前几无接触，相互辗转之影响固然极少，"事实联系"更是"遇之匪深，即之愈稀"，若照以上实证思路，中西作家的比较研究只能是一条短小逼仄的死胡同，在此基础上的作品比较乃至诗学比较亦势将成为沙地上筑起的象牙塔……事实上，东西方特别是中西比较文学研究已形成国际性大趋势，比较文学事业若没

---

① 陈寅恪：《陈寅恪集·金明馆丛稿二编》，陈美延编，北京：生活·读书·新知三联书店，2001年，第252页。
② 巴尔登斯柏格（Fernand Baldensperger）语，引自张隆溪选编：《比较文学译文集》前言，北京：北京大学出版社，1982年，第4页。
③ 别林斯基：《关于批评的讲话》，引自伍蠡甫、胡经之主编：《西方文艺理论名著选编》（中），北京：北京大学出版社，1985年，第297页。

有中国参予，不过是一只跛鸭。正如美国比较文学学者纪延所说，"只有当世界把中国和欧美这两种伟大的文学结合起来理解和思考的时候，我们才能充分地面对文学的重大理论性问题。"[①]也许，绝少"事实联系"的两大文学传统之间不期而遇的契合，反而更能深刻、有力地揭示"一切文学创作和经验是统一的"这个命题的真理性。当然，这样的比较工作需要更为敏锐的头脑、更为艰巨的劳动，但也更富有挑战性、更具有研究价值。

那么应如何开展比较呢？首先一点，比较者必须具有"历史演变与系统异同之观念"。这里，我们不妨对"系统"概念稍作引申，即把作家及其作品放置到特定历史条件与社会背景这一文学外的大系统中去考察。在我看来，这应当是比较工作的第二条原则：在这两个座标上座标值相近甚或相反的作家、作品，方才具有比较的可能与价值。

其实这两条原则并不新鲜，前人之述已备。孟子云"知人论世"，西方历史实证主义学者亦强调从作者的生平、作品产生的时代背景下研究、评价作品。法国学者泰纳（Taine）更认为文学创作的发生、发展取决于（作家的）种族、环境和时代："如果你想看到地里将有一次劳而有效的收获，就得在历史这块地里深耕细作。"[②]对此，丹麦文学评论家勃兰兑斯（Brandes）有一段精辟的发挥：

> ……尽管一本书是一件完美、完整的艺术品，它却只是从无边无际的一张网上剪下来的一小块。从美学上考虑，它的内容，它创作的主导思想，本身就足以说明问题，无需把作者和创作环境当作一个组成部分来加以考察；而从历史的角度考虑，这本书却透露了作者的思想特点，就像"果"反映了

---

① 引自乐黛云：《比较文学与中国现代文学》，北京：北京大学出版社，1987年，第40页。
② 泰纳：《英国文学史·导论》，引自朱雯等编选：《文学中的自然主义》，上海：上海文艺出版社，1992年，第35页。

"因"一样，这种特点在他所有的作品中都会表现出来，自然也会体现在这一本书里，不对它有所了解，就不可能理解这一本书。而要了解作者的思想特点，又必须对影响他发展的知识界和他周围的气氛有所了解。①

当然，他们都是从实证角度谈比较研究的，对于异源、异质的中西文学来说不一定完全适用，但若将类型学研究、平行研究方法结合起来，辅助参伍，则不失为稳妥有效的研究方法。

综上所述，对作家进行比较研究，在首先考察作品的文学性之外，须同时考察其生活时代、创作环境、创作个性等因素。基于以上认识，我愿提出"关汉卿与莎士比亚是互为镜像的中英两大戏剧传统代表作家"这一命题，具体论证如下。

（二）关汉卿和莎士比亚

说到关、莎二氏的比较，我们立刻面对一项不利的事实：他们的生活时代相隔甚远，竟达三个世纪之多。

事实上，时间与历史的发展并不是同步的。各国的政治、经济、文化进程并不均衡，因此大可不必胶柱鼓瑟，刻求作家生卒年月的一致。马克思曾指出，存在着历史的相似现象，是可以造成文学和艺术的类似发展的，即类似的历史条件可能产生出类似的艺术作品②。关汉卿虽然年长莎士比亚三百岁，但他们生活、创作其中的社会却处于类似的历史发展阶段，呈现出相似的转型时代精神。

我们先来看莎翁的时代。莎士比亚身历伊丽莎白一世（1558—1603）、詹姆士一世（1603—1625）两朝。这是一个民族扩张、商

---

① 勃兰兑斯：《十九世纪文学主流》（第一分册），张道真译，北京：人民文学出版社，1980年，第2页。
② 柏拉威尔：《马克思和世界文学》，梅绍武等译，北京：生活·读书·新知三联书店，1980年，第546页。

业繁荣和宗教大论战的时代。《至尊法案》（1534）推翻了罗马教廷的宗教权威地位，代之而起的是英王即"英国国土教会的最高统治者"这一新的权威。其后多年的宗教纷争，亦在坚持至尊王权的前提下得以折冲和解。内政稳定下来的英国开始把目光投向外界，在1588年击溃西班牙"无敌舰队"后，更逐渐成为欧洲政治、经济和世界贸易的龙头。这个时期的英国，可以说正处在神权与君权国家、封建农业社会与近代工商业社会、民族与世界性国家的交接点上。

社会的发展与变化，带来了英国文学的黄金时代，而戏剧则是这个时代的骄子。从1580年起，六十年内，英国产生了数十位卓有成就的剧作家，见于记载的剧本有一千部左右。莎翁与其同行们的创作，从不同的时空角度折射出这一时代的光怪陆离的色彩。遗憾的是，这一时期剧本文学化、戏剧歌舞化的趋势（琼森的创作即是典型的例子），尤其是从欧洲大陆吹来的诸如"三一律"等复古风尚，渐渐掩翳了这一光芒，致使后来戏剧日趋诡丽而生气渐少，莎剧中回荡的那种"盛世元音"难以为继，渐至化为一两声呜咽惨叫。不用到英国资产阶级革命胜利、清教徒当政后封闭伦敦剧院，实际上就已经曲终人散了。①

我们再看关汉卿。关汉卿的生活和创作时代，正值胡马南渡、在包括中国在内的广大亚欧地区建立起蒙古族贵族专制统治的元朝。中国无意中——也许是不情愿地——被抛进世界历史发展轨迹。然而，表面上的大一统并不意味着民族矛盾的缓解。元统治者于施行四民等级制之外，从开国至仁宗延祐朝近四十年间废止科举，汉人知识分子地位低下，有道是"八娼九儒十丐"（谢枋得：《叠山集》），华夏文明可说是处在一个"脱节的时代"：中国也正面临着原始游牧文明与封建农耕文明，汉人与胡人生活习俗，佛

---

① See Gamini Salgado: *English Drama: A Critical Introduction*, London: Edward Arnold Ltd., 1980, pp.85—86 & p.131.

道思想与儒教思想、民族国家与世界性国家的相峙、对撞①。

元杂剧作为一种来自民间的文艺样式，于此文化断层中勃发，可谓正得其时。首先，由于蒙古族贵族专政，废行科举，致使"中州人每沉抑下僚，志不获展"（胡侍：《真珠船》），大批失意落魄文人成为杂剧作家，形成中国文学史上罕见的专业文人创作队伍。其次，由于蒙元统治者虔信佛教（喇嘛教），失势的儒学在政治、文化、意识形态领域中风光不再，元杂剧得以保持、发扬其大众文化本色，成为具有原生性质的"最自然之文学"与戏剧形式。后世戏剧如传奇、昆曲，偏重于格律、意趣等文学性，每有繁缛典丽之弊；而乱弹、皮黄，则侧重娱乐歌舞，又往往失之于俚俗不文；只有元杂剧，处在中国戏曲发展历程中一个"文质彬彬"的阶段，形成了中国古典戏剧的一座高峰。当时有姓名可考的剧作家有八十余人，见于记载的作品达五百余种。这一盛况是空前绝后的，足可与伊丽莎白一世时期至1642年的英国戏剧相揖让而毫无逊色。

综观关、莎二氏的生活与创作时代，不难发现，二者虽一呈上升态势，一现下降轨迹，但二者相交于一点：其座标值，一为"断"，即该时期与之前的时代形成某种断层；其二为"变"，即本时期是本民族文化连续性发展中的一个突变点，因而呈现出若干相应的临界状态特征（如英国戏剧中的"巴洛克风格"即是其表征②）。这两个特点在很大程度上决定了当时中英文坛的气候，也是以关剧为代表的元杂剧与以莎剧为代表的英国文艺复兴时期戏剧得以激扬灿烂的源泉。

不过，关汉卿与莎士比亚能成为震古烁今的戏剧大家，除了受到时代与社会的影响，亦得力于他们独特的生活与创作经历。

有趣的是，对于二者的生活和创作经历，我们均知之甚少。先

---

① 参阅韩儒林：《元朝史》，北京：人民出版社，1986年，第4、6、9页，第11—14页及第四章第五节，第五章第四、五节，第九章第一、四节，第十章各处。

② 参见杨周翰：《镜子和七巧板》（中国社会科学出版社，1990年）中《巴洛克的涵义，表现和应用》一文。

说莎士比亚。由于资料不足，有的研究者甚至怀疑有无莎士比亚这个人或莎剧的作者是否就是此公①。好在近四百年来英国社会一直安定，婴儿出生受洗、成人婚丧记录及各色法律文件、账目、登记册等保存完整，通过这些材料，我们勉力亦能勾勒出莎翁的生平大概。可惜这些材料零碎漶漫，缺少莎氏从故乡到伦敦这一关键时期的记载，不少剧本的创作时间难以确定，至于作者的创作意图、理论思想更是无从查考。不过，莎翁比他的中国同行已是幸运多多。对于关汉卿，我们知道他大致生活在金末元初时期，但具体年代却是一个谜，而有限的记载也时相抵牾，致有人认为有大小两位关汉卿。至于关氏的籍贯，研究者们更是聚讼不已：或曰大都人（钟嗣成：《录鬼簿》），或曰解州人（邵远平：《元史类编》），或曰祁之伍仁村人（罗以桂：《祁州志》）……今人大多认为关氏原籍祁州，后离乡赴京作剧成名，或近于真实。不过中国人素喜攀扯名人点缀本地风光，这场官司恐怕还会继续打下去。而关氏在大都的活动虽然记载稍详，但除了关氏本人及其与友朋的诗作往还、回忆之外，资料亦付阙如。

关莎二氏均来自民间，本非庙堂人物，当时自不会有人为他们撰写什么年谱、行传；这对研究者来说是一大遗憾。然而正因如此，他们的思想、心灵——这具体表现为个性与作品风格——浸渍弥漫着朴素的大众性与真气淋漓的原生风貌。

关汉卿与莎士比亚，当然不是"玩"戏剧、一不留神玩成了戏剧大家，但他们也不是发愤著书、志在美刺、自觉担任时代书记员的正统派作家。不错，他们是文人（men of letters），但他们首先是世俗中人（men of the world）。如关汉卿曾在"金末以解元贡于乡，后为太医院尹"，后来据说因"金亡不仕"（蒋一葵：《尧山堂外记》），这才成了专业剧作家。关氏为人"滑稽佻达"（王国

---

① See Michell, John F.: *Who Wrote Shakespeare?* London: Thames & Hudson Ltd., 1996, pp.37—38. 其中列出的莎剧作者有30余人之多。

维:《元戏曲家小传》),《录鬼簿》的作者称他"心机灵变,世法通疏";关氏本人也曾豪迈地自述"我是个普天下郎君领袖,盖世界浪子班头","我是个蒸不烂、煮不熟、捶不扁、炒不爆、响当当一粒铜豌豆"("南吕一枝花·不伏老")①;这是自嘲,同时也是一幅逼真的自画像。

关汉卿亦是相当不错的诗人,现有散套若干传世,并曾有一曲"南吕一枝花"相赠名旦朱帘秀。莎士比亚是英国诗人中可数之白眉,亦曾为一"黑夫人"(Dark Lady)大作十四行诗;从这二十七首诗来看,称作者一声"浪子"并不算是过分。当然,关莎二氏生活经历中的相似处远远不止于此。莎翁虽非"少也贱"(其父曾出任市财务官),但少小便辍学随父学习手艺,干活补贴家用。后一度任乡间学校教员,不过他为人师表的意识淡薄,据说曾不止一次伙同不三不四的朋友,到附近大户(Sir Thomas Lucy of Charlecot)的林苑中偷鹿,为躲避有司追究而遁往伦敦闯滩,从为剧院看马开始,打杂工、赶零碎角儿,渐至正式登台,担纲"宫内大臣剧团"(Lord Chamberlain's Men)的主演、股东和剧作家,直到成为环球剧院(the Globe Theatre)的"经理"(housekeepers)之一,每年坐拥二百五十镑,厕身贵游,买屋刻稿,俨然名士矣②。

个人生活经历的丰富多姿,对关莎二氏创作心理、创作风格无疑影响至深。关汉卿的早期活动我们不甚了了,但从其为人、文风来看,他和莎翁一样,都是来自乡村,久历世情,登台演戏、下台写剧而扬名京城内外。莎氏际遇似优于关氏,但他们作为演员兼剧作家,稿酬菲薄不说,其职业在当时也是属于不入流的行当③。因此他们虽是严格意义上的文人,却非株守书斋、青春作赋的"名

---

① 王学奇等:《关汉卿全集校注》,石家庄:河北教育出版社,1988年,第772页。
② 参见裘克安:《莎士比亚年谱》,北京:商务印书馆,1988年,第122、125、127、135、137、145、147、170页。
③ See C. T. Onions (ed.): *Shakespeare's England*, Vol II, Oxford: Clarendon Press, 1917, p.240 & 242.

家",而他们的作品自然也不会是散发头巾气的案头清供。德国哲学家狄尔泰以为"富有想象力的诗所具有的最一般特征,在于它来源于丰富多彩的生活感受、来源于人生的经验,而不是文人们从书本到书本的抄袭"①,这一点正是关莎二氏超出同侪后辈的奥妙所在。

时代与个人生活经历的影响是重要的,而他们成为戏剧花园中"一根最高的枝条"(泰纳:《艺术哲学》),还得力于他们的创作小气候。

还是先来看关汉卿。在元杂剧作家中,关氏年辈最高,作品最多,成就也最大。这一点早有公论,如贾仲明补撰《录鬼簿》,以"凌波仙"一曲凭吊关氏,赞之为"驱梨园领袖,总编修师首,捻杂剧班头"。以今人眼光来看,尊关汉卿为"杂剧之父"应不为过。不过,伟大的艺术家并不是一枝独秀的光杆儿牡丹,在他周围还聚集了一大批优秀的剧作家,如时有"莫逆之交"之目的杨显之(杨氏常为关氏剧本进行"后期制作"而得外号"杨补丁"),与关氏"相亲如故者"的梁进之,与关氏风格酷似的"小汉卿"高文秀、"蛮子汉卿"沈和甫等。此外,关氏作为"玉京书会"的灵魂人物,不仅与伶人(如朱帘秀)等往还密切,他本人亦"至躬践排场,面傅粉墨"(臧晋叔:《元曲选·序二》)。关汉卿能成为"杂剧创作的中心作家""本色派的第一流人物",②这些经历应该说起到了重要的作用。

如果用中国古典戏曲术语来描述莎士比亚,那么他无疑是一名"本色派"作家了。和关汉卿一样,莎氏本人也是一名演员兼编剧。他的演技如何,我们不甚了了③,但他的剧本(确切讲是脚本)

---

① 狄尔泰:《诗的伟大理想》,引自《西方文艺理论名著选编》(下),第558页。
② 青木正儿:《中国近世戏曲史》,王古鲁译,上海:上海文艺联合出版社,1954年,第54页。
③ 据说他曾经在《哈姆雷特》中饰老王的鬼魂,在《如愿以偿》中出演亚当一角(*Shakespeare's England*, Vol II, pp.248),并在琼森的两部作品中扮演过角色(阿尼克斯特:《莎士比亚传》,第153、180页)。

无疑是人类文明所达到的制高点之一,对此历代诸家的惊叹赞美贬备,委实无庸赘言;我们只需知道,莎翁能成为不世出的天才,他的前辈、同仁以及后起之秀,诸如李利(John Lyly)、格林(Robert Greene)、皮尔(George Peele)、洛奇(Thomas Lodge)、纳什(Thomas Nashe)、马洛、基德这些所谓的"大学才子"以及弗莱彻(John Fletcher)、博蒙(Francis Beaumont)这些年轻的同行居功甚伟。如他们创制了素体诗、复仇悲剧、伟人悲剧、浪漫主义喜剧、历史剧、宫廷喜剧、传奇剧(tragic comedies),而莎翁则博采诸家成果,更加纯熟老到地驾驭这些形式,从而真正全面奠定了英国戏剧的传统。莎剧无论从剧本数量上还是从戏剧样式上都超迈前贤①,而后者主要活跃于16世纪八九十年代,并"在英国戏剧走向成熟的发展途中抛弃了戏剧"②:格林于1592年病故,1593年马洛被杀,1594年基德去世,而李利则于1594年后告别了剧作生涯③……依此而论,莎士比亚一如关汉卿,亦是开风气而集大成的剧作家。

关汉卿和莎士比亚的名字分别代表了中英戏剧的最高成就。事实上,关莎二氏创作成就之高,几令后学难乎为继。詹姆士一世时期的英国剧坛风行华丽而空洞的假面歌舞剧(the Masque),例如当时的文坛盟主琼森就创作了四十部音乐歌舞剧④,而彼时之悲剧创作,亦钟情于恐怖、暴力、乱伦、通奸一类耸人听闻的题材,整个剧坛呈现出所谓"巴洛克"的怪诞风格。与之相似,杂剧在元朝后期逐渐衰微:内容上战斗性和现实性的锋芒减弱了,宣扬封建和出世思想的劝善剧、神仙道化剧甚嚣尘上;在艺术上亦偏向曲词的工

---

① 洛奇、纳什、基德各有剧作一种传世;皮尔、格林各五种;马洛七种;李利最多,然亦不过八种。"大学才子"们剧作共有二十八种传世,而莎氏一人就有三十七种。另外"大学才子"除李利外都只运用一种戏剧形式写作,而莎剧则几乎包括了当时所有的戏剧类型。
② 张泗洋等:《莎士比亚引论》(下),北京:中国戏剧出版社,1989年,第105页。
③ 阿尼克斯特:《莎士比亚传》,安国梁译,郑州:海燕出版社,2001年,第68—69页。
④ 即便是琼森本人,也曾批评"妆绘和木匠活成了假面剧的灵魂"("Painting and carpentry are the soul of masque", *Shakespeare's England*, Vol II. p.332.)。

丽华美和情节的曲折离奇，杂剧全盛期那种朴素、生动的风格剥落殆尽，陷于颓唐趣味的流弊渐起①，余风直熏染至明代前期的剧坛。

"时运交移，质文代变"（《文心雕龙·时序》），这大约也是艺术兴衰的一个规律吧；而在关莎二氏的剧作中流溢出来的那种元气淋漓的原生性，恰是后代作家可望而不可及的天才标志。马克思反对剧作家把人物写成"时代精神的传声筒"，曾提出"莎士比亚化"这一概念；我国学者则将莎士比亚的风格总结为"题材的多样化，剧型的多样化""众多形象鲜明的人物"及"五颜六色千变万化的万花筒式语言"。②笔者认为，这几条规则亦完全适用于关汉卿的剧作。为方便讨论起见，本文将使用"原气淋漓的本色派风格"来统一描述关莎二氏的创作风格。下面，我们不妨就以此为切入点，对他们剧作中的语言、题材和人物形象等方面略作一番比较。

关汉卿被誉为"本色派的第一流人物"（青木正儿）。"本色派"与"文词家"或"名家"相对而言，两者的区别首先在于语言。明人王骥德所谓"曲之始，止本色一家"，"自《香囊记》以儒门手脚为之，遂滥觞还有文词家一体。夫曲……一涉词藻，便蔽本来"（《曲律·论家数》）即是。关汉卿"作为当行的剧作家，创造出适合于场上演出的'场上之曲'，与专门写'案头之曲'的'名家'大异其趣。"③正因为这个原因，正统文人对关氏的评价历来都偏低，如《太和正音谱》的作者朱权就认为："观其词语，乃可上可下之才。"确实，关剧中的语言固然丰实生动，但同时也稍显纷乱粗犷。关剧作为演出脚本，"文字在剧本上的书写随意性较大。且有些方言土语，市井用语，甚至有音无字，便出现重音不用形的现象"，"又由于服从于唱腔音律的需要，造成词序颠倒，词

---

① 宁宗一、陆林、田桂民编著：《元杂剧研究概述》，天津：天津教育出版社，1987年，第128页。
② 陆谷孙编：《莎士比亚专辑》，上海：复旦大学出版社，1984年，第3—5页。
③ 李汉秋、袁有芬编：《关汉卿研究资料》，上海：上海古籍出版社，1988年，第4页。

语重叠或语法失常等现象"①。应该说这些现象确实都存在,然而它们决非"俚腐"的"本色之弊"(王骥德:《曲律》),而是恰恰证明了关汉卿具有原生性的本色风格。关剧语言可以说达到了"语求肖似"(李渔:《闲情偶寄》)的境界,即"根据生活本身所提供的语言来反映现实,充分为剧情和人物性格服务"②,而不是大掉书袋,让剧中人一律之乎者也,片面地追求戏剧语言的典丽。

"一切强有力的东西;都被称为粗鄙的"③,司汤达曾这样形容当时的法国戏剧欣赏标准。对此褊见陋识,古今中外不知多少天才作家为之扼腕永叹!莎士比亚总算比关汉卿幸运些,甫逝世便有琼森献诗,被赞为"时代的灵魂""我们剧坛的喝采对象";但琼森也不无惋惜的提到这位"诗人中的诗人"文化不高,"只懂得一点儿拉丁文,希腊文更少","但愿他改过一千行"。莎翁殁后很长一段时间内,世人对他的剧作评价并不很高,多为其"野蛮"、不雅驯感到遗憾,而其中头一款罪状往往就是莎剧的语言。如德莱顿认为莎翁"以辞害意""硬把日常使用的字句粗暴地使用",④伏尔泰亦认为"文笔太铺张",断言"这位作家的功绩断送了英国的戏剧"⑤。事实当然不是这样。我们知道,莎士比亚是首屈一指的英语语言大师;在他使用的一万七千余(一说据电脑统计为29 066,最大数字达43 566)词汇中,既有高古时髦的古罗马语、法语、意大利语,也有百姓习用的方言土语,甚至实在不登大雅的粗话。即以《哈姆雷特》一剧为例,其中我们不仅可以读到典雅的素体诗,玄奥的思索和评论,也可看到平实的口语化散文和粗野俚俗的市井人语。确实,莎翁对于文字游戏(如双关仿辞)有着非同寻常的爱好,时或堆叠缛丽的辞藻而遭后人嗤点,不过我们须知,莎剧同关

---

① 《关汉卿全集校注》,第2页。
② 游国恩等:《中国文学史》(三),北京:人民文学出版社,1964年,第198页。
③ 《拉辛与莎士比亚》,引自伍蠡甫主编:《西方文论选》(下卷),上海:上海译文出版社,1979年,第153页。
④ 《莎士比亚引论》(下),第373、379、387页。
⑤ 伏尔泰:《论悲剧》,引自《西方美学史资料选编》(上),第580、584页。

剧一样首先是舞台演出脚本，写作时并未计划出版，粗枝大叶、遗漏重复、臃肿花哨的毛病在所难免。其实，莎氏本人对文词派作家的夸张其辞也很不以为意，他曾借哈姆雷特之口加以抨击（III. ii. 17—24），并且在第三幕第二场"戏中戏"中予以丑化模仿。莎剧语言与所谓"绮丽体"（Euphuism）是大异其趣的（莎氏在《爱的徒劳》一剧中使用了这种文体，同时又对它进行嘲讽；在《亨利四世》上篇第二幕第四场中更是痛快地讥讽了这种风格）。前面所说的莎剧语言的不足之处，我认为在某种程度上倒是展示了作者汪洋恣肆、"不择地而出"的语言天才。

关剧与莎剧语言中这种酣畅淋漓的原生性，在各自的戏剧传统中不仅罕逢其匹，甚至后继乏人。莎翁封笔后，琼森接掌英国剧坛之牛耳，但他把自己的作品当成文学经典看待，为剧本文学化献力甚伟，并在1616年出版了《作品集》（Works），这部文集"成为英国剧本文学化进程中的一座里程碑"①。而元杂剧，则自关汉卿之后（特别是在元后期）日趋典丽，作者往往着意于格律词藻的雕镂，词曲的文学性孤立地看有出蓝之势，但作为戏剧语言则生气剥尽、"不能复化"（《文心雕龙·通变》），而且往往喧宾夺主，诗"味"浓郁而剧"情"消隐。这一趋势自《香囊记》后加速发展，终于在传奇剧大师汤显祖那里由附庸成为大国，完成了文学的又一轮文质循环。

这种文和质的区分也体现在关莎二氏作品的体裁与题材上。莎士比亚一生作剧凡三十八部，计历史剧十部，喜剧十四部，悲剧十部，传奇四部；各种戏剧样式在他手中无一不被运用得出神入化。中国古典戏剧的分类自成一派，关汉卿的剧作既有"公案"（如《窦娥冤》《鲁斋郎》）、"风情"（如《救风尘》《望江亭》），也有历史剧（如《单刀会》《哭存孝》），几乎涵盖了当时几乎所有的戏剧样式。他们的剧作题材，更是洋洋乎万取一收，

---

① Stanley Wells: *Literature and Drama,* London: Routledge & Kegan Paul Ltd., 1970, p.46.

蔚为大观。在中英两国戏剧史上，剧作样式如此完备、取材如此广阔者，除去关莎二氏，不作第三人想。

题材的广泛，在优秀剧作家手中，必然导向人物形象的丰富多彩。关汉卿和莎士比亚都是描绘当时社会众生相的大手笔。关剧里的人物，有官吏（如包待制、钱大尹），有武将（如关羽、李存孝），有文士（如裴度），有贵妇（如邓夫人、刘夫人），有权贵贼臣（如鲁斋郎、桃杌），有地痞无赖（如杨衙内、张驴儿），有风尘女子（如赵盼儿、杜蕊娘），三教九流应有尽有，五行八作活灵活现。莎剧更为我们提供了文学殿宇中最壮阔的一条人物画廊。据统计，莎剧中出现的人物有名者达七百余，有台词的角色竟达1 378人之多！以种族分，有欧、非、犹太、摩尔、阿拉伯；以国别论，有英、法、德、意、丹麦、希腊、罗马、埃及；以时代言，有远古、中古、近现代；从职业上看，上至帝王将相，中有农工商兵，乃至倡优叫花，林林总总，无所不包。非但如此，关莎二氏笔下人物，性格真实多样，有厚度、有深度。"莎士比亚所表现的一切人物，都揭示高度人格化的、拥有个性结构的生命"[①]，狄尔泰曾如是评价莎剧中的人物；歌德亦赞叹说："没有比莎士比亚的人物更自然的了！"[②]而关汉卿，作为"中国最自然之文学"——元杂剧的首座，比诸莎氏"神一般的"（伏尔泰语）人物塑造功力亦不遑多让。前文所说的"莎士比亚化"，其实正是"本色"或"原生性"的一种表述方式，亦可称为"关汉卿化"，因为关汉卿的创作也体现出同样的特点。

与其它描写单一身份类型主人公的剧作家（如马洛与汤显祖）不同，关汉卿与莎士比亚塑造的是复合的、多元的、立体的人。为说明这一点，我们不妨从两人笔下的浩瀚人物形象中截取"妇女形象"这一切片，看她们是如何体现了作者的原生性风格的。

先说莎剧。从上古史诗到中世纪的浪漫传奇，欧洲文学中的

---

① 狄尔泰：《诗的伟大理想》，引自《西方文艺理论名著选编》（上），第556页。
② 歌德：《莎士比亚纪念日的讲话》，引自《西方文艺理论名著选编》（上），第426页。

妇女形象多属陪衬（如珀涅罗珀），或类"起兴"之由头（如海伦），即使被尊奉为女神，其地位实与宝物、圣杯相去不远，不过是男性主人公政治、爱情游戏中的人格化猎物或彩头罢了。这一局面到了文艺复兴时期有所改观，而到了莎翁手中就更是一番新天了。莎剧中的妇女确实占据了舞台的"半边天"，如《温莎的风流娘儿们》中的培琪大娘、《亨利五世》中的快嘴桂嫂、《麦克白》中的麦克白夫人、《李尔王》中的里甘、《威尼斯商人》中的鲍西娅、《特罗伊洛斯与克瑞西达》中的克瑞西达……她们年龄不一，性情各异，来自社会各阶层；更重要的是，这些人物无论贤愚善恶，无一不是活生生的"有着内在的活力和对自身强烈的意识"（狄尔泰语）的"这一个"，而非声容举止经过男性想象力统一包装的阴性符号或青春、美丽的简单拟人化。

再看关剧。中国文学除了《诗经》、乐府外几乎是清一色的男性世界，妇女形象几成绝响，偶或出现一些春闺少女、高楼怨妇，而且多半是被蹭蹬失意的男性作家拉来自况，借以渲泄其不遇、不售的怨艾牢骚。这种现象到了唐传奇、宋金话本等俗文学中略有反拨，然亦往往囿于小家碧玉私会情郎、风尘女子慧眼识英雄一类，即便有侠女、神女一类角色出现，重点亦往往在其"侠"、其"神"而非其"人"特别是女人的身份。关汉卿扭转了这一局势。在他的十三种"旦本"杂剧中，关氏创造出不同年龄、身份、性格的女性形象，如大义替死的童养媳窦娥、智斗登徒的再醮寡妇谭记儿、老辣热忱的风尘女子赵盼儿……她们不再是在情天恨海中春啼秋怨的单调扁平人物模型（stereotype），而是被还予了本来面目的真实女人。

关剧与莎剧中的妇女形象不仅数量众多、性格丰富多样，而且往往是作者的代言人（surrogate）或心目中的理想人物[①]。薇奥拉、鲍西娅、德斯狄莫娜、米兰达、窦娥、谭记儿、燕燕、赵盼儿……

[①] 严格说来，关汉卿的时代并不具备产生"新人"的社会历史条件，但不可否认，这些可爱、可敬的女性形象构成了剧本世界中的"亮点"，我们不妨将此视为作者在社会转型期的人格价值取向。

这个名单还可以再开下去。这一现象绝非巧合，个中情由也不难索解：在等级森严的古代社会，无论是西方神权国家，还是东方的君权国家，妇女都处在等级金字塔的底层，如西方常以男女欢爱象征人对神的皈依，而中国素以夫妇之道譬喻君臣伦常。当这社会处于转型的边缘，当人们因其身份、地位动荡变化而对自身存在意义和价值进行反思时，他们很容易对同样不幸的妇女产生认同、理解、同情乃至礼赞。较早觉醒的人，如中下层文人，往往因之提笔作文，通过塑造妇女形象来排攮胸中块垒，抒发一己的愤懑不平。——《十日谈》《红楼梦》就是很好的佐证。关莎二氏均生活在一个大变革的时代，他们的中下层生活经历与佻达放浪的个性等各方面条件辐凑聚变，使他们得以创造出新一代的女性形象。

可惜的是，他们塑造的这些"新女性"形象却被后辈所忽视甚至歪曲：她们好不容易逃出海角危塔、重锁香闺来到人间世界的前台，旋又被一支笔逼回宫室、沙龙和闺房的背景中。例如琼森重拾中世纪"性情剧"（Humorous Plays）的人物塑造手法，而海伍德（Thomas Heywood）则惯于把戏核置于夫—妻—情夫的三角关系上[1]，致使妇女形象单调雷同，失却莎剧人物的那种原生性和真实性。无独有偶，在"后关汉卿"时代，才子佳人剧风行于世，如白朴的《墙头马上》、郑光祖的《倩女离魂》、乔吉的《两世姻缘》等等，无复关剧中的多元立体品貌。这是戏剧的退步还是它的必然发展趋势？是时代风习使然还是作家个人趣味的结果？不管怎么说，关汉卿与莎士比亚笔下的女性形象，恰如一道闪电划破长空，虽只戛然一现，却震烁百代、弥足珍贵。

关莎二氏剧作中的女性形象先谈到这里。此外二氏笔下人物相似之处甚多，如追求个性解放、赞美治世雄才等等，指不胜屈。东坡咏庐山诗句云："横看成岭侧成峰"，这正是原生性作家作品的

---

[1] Ifor Evans: *A Short History of English Drama*, London: MacGibbon & Kee, 1965, pp.67—68 & pp.78—79.

绝好写照。然而,他们不论如何"远近高低各不同",有一点在本质上是相同的,即具有充盈、结实、元气淋漓的原生性风格。关莎二氏剧中的人物形象是这样,语言、题材、体裁亦复如此。中英剧坛诸家中创作相契如斯者,似无第三人。贤如汤显祖,他的"临川四梦"创作别是一工,可以说是"用写诗的手法写戏"①,其内容也可归为"两情相悦反礼教、士子顿悟成丹道"两端,与关莎二家相较,尽管自成家数,却无多少可比性。

因此我们可以有把握地说:在中英戏剧传统中,关汉卿与莎士比亚是最具可比性的代表性作家。当然,这并不意味着二者全然等同;事实上他们之间尚存在着许多差异,有些差异甚至还是根本性的——仅以剧本形式而论,就有对表演性与文学性、诗体与散文体的不同侧重等等(这将是下文要讨论的问题)。然而,差异的存在正是比较研究的一个重要前提:比较对象若浑然不类,固无法比较,但如两粒豌豆般相似,也就无需比较了。钱锺书先生云:"比较不仅求其同,也在存其异,是所谓'对比文学'。正是在明辨异同的过程中,我们可以认识中西文学传统各自的特点。"②研究者能味斯语,则思过半矣。

关汉卿与莎士比亚是中西比较文学研究的一组理想对象,二人创作的契合与歧异揭示了戏剧这一艺术形式与文学样式的本质规律与分化可能。本文提出:"关汉卿与莎士比亚是中英戏剧传统中互成镜像的两位代表";这一论点若能成立,那么中英乃至中西戏剧的比较研究将获得一块坚实的基石。我对此深怀信心。

---

① 游国恩等:《中国文学史》(四),第79页。
② 张隆溪:《钱锺书谈比较文学与"文学比较"》,引自朱维之主编:《中外比较文学》,天津:南开大学出版社,1992年,第144页。

附录二

文学和表演：关于中英戏剧传统的一个比较考察

中西戏剧比较是一个有趣的课题。有的人认为二者是互不影响、各成体系的系统，除了进行主题学的研究外，其它问题都缺乏可比性，或者不比自明。事实上，二者之间绝非"缺乏可比性"，其具体差异只有通过比较方能凸现出来。元杂剧与英国文艺复兴时期的戏剧、关汉卿与莎士比亚的戏剧创作，就是极好的研究对象。如果我们承认"比较"是获得真知的一个有力手段，那么关剧与莎剧为我们认识中西戏剧各自的特点及二者间的异同，提供了可信的例证。

（上）楔子

下面我们就不妨从一个小题目入手，即对关剧与莎剧中的开端部分做一番考察。为方便讨论起见，这一开端部分在本文中统称为楔子。

元杂剧的体制一般为四折一楔子。杂剧中的楔子，上承唐宋时期的"致语"（又名"乐语""念语"，是由"参军"或优长在表演前所致的骈文颂词）和宋话本的"入话"（也叫得胜头回，原是说书引子），下启明清传奇的"家门""开场""传概"①，而独盛于元。在《元曲选》所收的一百种杂剧中，有楔子的共六十九种，占三分之二强。在关汉卿现存的十八种剧作中，有楔子者共十二种（包括"双楔子"和"头折"）。有时元杂剧没有"楔子"或"楔子"居于剧中，但开始时总要由登场人物"自报家门"的。在明代中期以后，随着北杂剧的衰落，楔子渐渐销声匿迹了，但广义上的楔子，即戏剧结构中的开端部分，仍以"引子"，"定场诗"，"自报家门"等其它形式保存下来，并在后代一脉相承的表演形式（包括明清传奇，清中后期之"乱弹"如京剧）中作为一种程式而大量地运用。楔子与中国传统戏剧关系十分密切，可以说是它的一个基本形式特征。

　　但这并不意味着只有中国传统戏剧才有楔子或类似的戏剧表现手法；它只不过是完整地保存至今并且尚在广泛运用罢了。楔子的运用在西方戏剧中亦有悠久的历史。古希腊公元前六世纪的酒神颂歌中即出现了歌队领队（Chorus），由其与歌队通过唱、白来结构敷演情节。后领队逐渐发展成一个演员，可与剧中人交谈，起着类似剧情介绍与评介的作用。在文艺复兴时期的英国，歌队的任务由一个演员来担任，由他来朗诵开场白与收场白，进行幕间评论并预告即将发生的事件。莎士比亚的前辈如基德（Thomas Kyd）在《西班牙悲剧》（*The Spanish Tragedy*）中，其同时代剧作家如马洛（Christopher Marlowe）在《浮士德博士的悲剧》（*Doctor Faustus*）中，稍后的琼森（Ben Jonson）在喜剧《狐狸》

---

① 亦名"副末开场"，"开宗""标目""提宗""开演""叙传""首引""家门大意""家门始末""开场家门""敷演家门""传奇纲领""本传开宗""梨园鼓吹"等等。其中亦由非剧中人"副末"一人登场，用一首或两首诗简介剧情，同样只有"报幕"性质，不能算是正戏。

（*Volphone*）都运用了这一手法。莎士比亚本人有时也运用楔子（Chorus，Prologue，Induction），但与关剧相比数量有限，且大部分集中在第一创作时期（1590—1600）的历史剧与悲剧作品中[①]，在中后期剧作中就很难见到了。

关剧与莎剧分别是中、英戏剧黄金时期的巅峰之作，它们之间的异同代表并体现了中英乃至中西戏剧理论与实践的共同规律与深刻分歧。亚里士多德在论及悲剧的"整一性"（Wholeness）时云，一出完整的悲剧，必须由开端、发展、结尾三部分组成（*Poetics*，1450b）[②]。我国元代杂剧作家乔吉对杂剧的结构，亦曾提出著名的"凤头、猪肚、豹尾"的要求，即所谓"起要美丽，中要浩荡，结要响亮"（陶宗仪：《南村辍耕录卷八·作今乐府法》）。中西戏剧一致强调开端在戏剧结构中的重要性；但开端应是怎样的，或何为好的、合适的开端，莎士比亚与关汉卿在各自的创作实践中给予了不同的答案。这些相异之处，在其剧作里楔子的运用（如数量、组成、表演人员、手法与正戏的关系等）中均有具体的凸现。

下面我们不妨具体分析一下《感天动地窦娥冤》与《亨利五世》两剧中的楔子并就二者的异同做一番比较。

请先来看《窦》剧中的楔子。楔子起始，由"卜儿"（类似京剧中的老旦演员）饰剧中人蔡婆"带戏上场"，首先念了四句定场诗："花有重开日，人无再少年；不须长富贵，安乐是神仙"，向观众泛泛介绍自己所饰角色的老年妇人身份。然后是自报家门："老身蔡婆是也……家中颇有些钱财"，进一步向观众介绍了自己的籍贯、家庭及婚姻状况。接下来蔡婆追述穷书生窦天章因无力偿银、欲卖女窦娥为蔡婆童养媳一事。这时冲末、正旦扮剧中主角窦

[①] 这几部作品是：《罗密欧与茱丽叶》（剧首致Prologue）；《特洛伊洛斯与克瑞西达》（Prologue）；《亨利四世》第2部（Induction）、亨利五世（剧首的Prologue、其余各幕首和剧末的Chorus）及第三创作期（1609—1613）中的《亨利八世》（Prologue）。这部作品实际上是第一时期历史剧的收束。

[②] Aristotle: *Poetics*, translated by Gerald F. Else, The University of Michigan Press, 1970, p.30.

天章、窦娥父女上场。窦天章亦念了四句定场诗后自报家门,向观众介绍自己的姓名、籍贯、职业、卖女原由等。下面是窦天章与蔡婆相见,商议卖女借银事;剧情即从此展开。之后三人同下,楔子结束;第一折正式开戏则已是十三年后的事情了。

  下面我们再来看《亨利五世》中的Prologue。在篇幅不大的整个开场白中,只上了一名并非剧中人物的致辞者。开场白由素体诗(blank verse)形式写成,首先按照史诗体例的俗套赞美缪斯并吁请灵感,继而为舞台条件的简陋而向观众道歉:"在座的诸君,请原谅吧!像咱们这样低微的小人物,居然在这几块破板搭成的戏台上,也搬演什么轰轰烈烈的事迹。难道说,这么一个'斗鸡场'容得下法兰西的万里江山?还是我们这个木头的圆框子里塞得进那么多将士?"接着又吁请观众"来激发你们庞大的想象力吧,就算在这团团一圈的墙壁包围了两个强大的王国……我们提到马儿,眼前就仿佛真有万马奔腾……把我们的帝王打扮得象个样儿,这也全靠你们的想象帮忙了;凭着那想象力,把他们搬东移西,在时间里飞跃,叫多少年代的事迹都挤塞在一个时辰里。"①至此,致辞者在剧中的任务完成,在他下场后,演出正式开始。

  观察以上两段楔子,我们发现二者间颇有一些共同之处,如它们都在剧首出现,简略地介绍剧情以使观众熟悉剧中环境(如历史背景、地点)与人物;但更多的、更引人注目的是二者间的不同。

  我们先来看看它们在戏剧结构中的地位的作用。俄国形式主义学派的中坚人物鲍里斯·托马舍夫斯基在谈到"戏剧情节分布的构成"时认为:"开端……在剧初必须造成适于详细讲述的局势。戏剧的处理办法是引入一个开场人。由他在演出前向观众交代开头的情景。随着求实细节印证原则的兴趣,开场人的角色被溶到了剧中,其职能由开场人物之一来担任。"②这个说法也大致适用于

---

① 《莎士比亚全集》(五),北京:人民文学出版社,1978年,第241页。
② 《俄国形式主义文论选》,方珊等译,北京:生活·读书·新知三联书店,1989年,第155页。

元杂剧中的楔子，尤其是其中"自报家门"的开场方式。但有一点需要特别指出，即杂剧如《感天动地窦娥冤》中开场人与剧中人溶为一体，并不是为了"求实"以换取逼真的戏剧效果，正像莎剧如《亨利五世》力求逼真（莎翁甚至为未能做到这一点而再三申歉）而特设一名非剧中人致辞者。后者在开场白与正戏间起到一种"切换"（switch）作用，即将舞台切割成两层泾渭分明的表演时空（与观众同时同地的舞台和虚拟的剧中时空），而元剧楔子中演员甫一登台已是剧中人物，在"向观众交代开头的情景"时用的是第一人称。在西方戏剧中大多用第三人称，特例如基德之《西班牙悲剧》楔子中的"魂子"上场云："I was a courtier in the Spanish court, my name was Don Andrea ..."这里的Don Andrea虽是剧中人物，但饰其"魂子"的演员却随后坐下，与观众一起观剧了，所以这番致辞其实起了剧情提示的作用，它向我们介绍了剧中参与剧情发展的各个人物，但是与剧情发展毫无关系。莎剧亦复如是，不过将魂子的任务交予了致辞者。更重要的是，关剧楔子具有"造成适于讲述的局势"的完全功能，而莎剧开端的任务一分为二，大部分信息要由文字叙述（如人物表、舞台说明）来传达。关汉卿之后的剧作家们有时采用"副末开场"的开端形式，然不废"楔子"及"自报家门"等手法（典型如洪昇《长生殿》的开端），而西欧剧作家们，自莎士比亚以下，愈来愈倚仗剧本文字说明，干脆抛弃了"楔子"（代表作家如萧伯纳，有时竟以长达几页的篇幅精细地描述故事背景）。

中西戏剧楔子的差异流变，实在引人注意。为什么关剧与莎剧中的楔子存在着这样的差异？换言之，为什么中西戏剧中的开端采取了不同的形式？为解答上述疑问，我们不妨在中西戏剧这两个庞然大物身上竖剖一刀，看看它们经络血脉的走向。

"歌舞之兴，其始于古之巫乎？"[①]王国维认为，中国戏曲亦

---

① 王国维：《宋元戏曲史》，第11、4、15页。

可上溯到初民的宗教仪式。"后世戏剧,当自巫优二者出";二者,一"乐神"一"乐人",共同构成了中国传统戏剧中的骨架与雏型。不过,中国的戏剧主要还是为了娱众。无论"乐神"还是"乐人",娱乐性始终是中国戏剧的第一要义;因此在中国戏剧中,歌舞表演成分占了大半江山。

中国戏剧的另一特点,就是"美"。清末京剧大师谭鑫培在谈表演心得时云:"戏中作工以哭笑为最难,以其难以逼真也;然使果如真者,亦复何趣旨哉?"[①]这里的"趣旨"指的正是艺术之美。为了达到"美"而不是"真"的目标,则需借助夸张写意、程式等虚拟性手段,这样就形成了中国戏曲艺术"坦白承认演戏","表现形式的程序化"与"戏是生活的虚拟"等一整套独特的理论体系与"既不泥真,亦不认假""既要观戏,又要赏艺"的戏剧审美观。

我们不难发现,中国戏剧的这些特点,无论其娱乐性或歌舞、虚拟,都是针对其舞台演出而言的;舞台演出而不是剧本创作占据着中国传统戏剧的中枢地位。中国戏剧剧本的创作确曾数度操纵在"文人"手中,但并未形成气候;象汤显祖那样斤斤于"意趣神色"(《答吕姜山》)等剧本文学性的作家实属凤毛麟角,大多数创作人员都是像关汉卿那样游离于士林之外的落魄知识分子。正统的所谓"文人"偶一兴至也会游戏笔墨,但他们更多的时候只是戏剧的欣赏者或批评者,并未真正加入创作队伍。而且更重要的是,不论哪类作者的作品,几乎全部是为演出而创作的,所谓"词藻工,句意妙,如不谐里耳,为案头之书,已落第二义"(王骥德:《曲律·论戏剧》),"无声戏"式的案头剧(closet drama)在"五四"前的中国少而又少。

可以说,中国戏剧的表演性纯度很高,文学剧本在很长一段

[①] 陈彦衡:《说谭》,戴淑娟等编:《谭鑫培艺术评论集》,北京:中国戏剧出版社,1990年,第147页。

时间内不过是附丽于表演,与身段动作、音乐伴奏等平行的一种舞台演出文字记录罢了。作为叙事文学与抒情文学相结合之文学样式的戏剧,在中国始终未得到充分发展。所谓"填词之设,专为登场",戏剧表现的任务,差不多全部要落实在演员的表演之中。这就是为什么杂剧楔子中人物要化好妆,穿好行头"带戏上场",同时却又以剧外人(如作者)的口吻向观众介绍"开头的情景",并通过繁重的表演(如《窦》剧楔子中上场人物念"白"、作"科"甚至唱"曲"),将"适于详细讲述的局势"展现出来。

反观莎剧的楔子,则其为一可有可无的附件,除去对剧情的简介或暗示,它与正文无多大关系,即使删去也毫不影响演出效果。可以说它只是作为一种历史遗留下来的僵化仪式依靠惯性而被运用着。致辞者如人格化的"谣言"等剧外人物除去朗诵一段素体诗外并无其它表演任务,他起的作用类似报幕员(这种表演方式倒是比杂剧楔子更为接近中国唐宋时期的"致语""参场");而且在莎剧中运用"楔子"者不过聊聊五出,随着逼真摹仿原则如"三一律"在英国剧坛的兴起①,致辞者也渐渐溶入剧中而消失了。十八世纪以后,此类"楔子"就几乎完全绝迹了。莎剧的楔子正好体现了这一转型期的特点。

我们知道,西方戏剧是摹仿的产物,它自诞生后不久便发育成一种成熟的文学样式,剧本创作与舞台演出剥离而并行,享有与戏剧演出同等重要的地位。如古希腊有专门的赛诗会,听众通过作者的朗读来评定剧本的优劣;古罗马喜剧作品中,亦有一部分是专门向公众朗读而不是为了上演而创作的。至于中世纪的戏剧,也不一定都要在舞台上演出,在多数情况下只是为朗诵而作,因此究其质是一种"叙述体"(genus narratinum)。这一特点深刻影响了西方后世的戏剧创作(如莎氏同代人本·琼森的创作及浪漫主义时期大

---

① Ben Jonson在 *Volphone* 的 Prologue 中声称:"The laws of time, person, he observeth, from no needful rules he swerveth",即从侧面证实了这一点。

量涌现的案头剧），从而构成西方戏剧的一种传统。

西方作家喜欢把作品拟作一座小小的傀儡戏台，或把戏剧视为用人物的语言和动作建构起来的立体文学世界。这样，与中国戏剧强调"美"与虚拟不同，西方戏剧走的是一条皈依逼真再现（verisimilitude）、力求如实描摹世态人情的道路。亚里士多德认为"一切艺术都是摹仿"，"戏剧是对行动中的人的摹仿"[①]；古罗马诗人西赛罗论喜剧时所说：喜剧是"生活的摹本，风俗的镜子，真理的反映"；莎翁本人也曾借哈姆雷特之口说："自有戏剧以来，它的目的始终是反映自然，显示善恶的本来面目，给它的时代看一看自己演变发展的模型。"（《哈姆雷特》第三幕第二场）。新古典主义时期"三一律"横行欧洲剧坛不必说了，甚至在挣脱"三一律"的束缚后，易卜生揭橥的现实主义戏剧及二十世纪初企图"建立正在进行的生活"的自然主义戏剧中，对逼真摹仿的要求（如"第四堵墙"理论）更是发挥到了极致。

诚然，莎士比亚的戏剧是对当时欧洲大陆戏剧传统的一个反动。限于物质技术条件，伊丽莎白时期的剧场采用类似中国传统"三面光"式的裙式（skirt）舞台，不可能像现代镜框式舞台（picture stage）那样把观众与演员隔离开来，故演员可以直接同观众交流，而且在"喝醉酒的野蛮人"（伏尔泰语）莎士比亚的剧作中，我们发现的是"一种混杂的艺术品种"，其中几乎包括了当时流行的所有大众娱乐形式，但莎剧几乎在对"三一律"表示蔑视的同时很快就文学化了：莎剧毕竟只是西方戏剧大树的一枝而已。

文学化是莎士比亚时代英国剧坛的一个必然趋势。出于经济方面的考虑，莎翁的同辈剧作家如海伍德（Thomas Heywood，1570—1641）尚认为"为了在印刷品中追求不朽的名声，那么可没有什么钱好赚的了"，马斯顿（John Marston，1575—1634）等人也认为"一个剧本不过是失去灵魂的尸体"；在他们看来，戏剧艺术是种

[①] Aristotle: *Poetics*, p.15 & 20.

综合艺术，而"文学性"只是其中一个因素，戏剧剧本并不同于专供阅读的文学作品"①。但这种观点在出身上层、受过高等教育的观众与剧作家的双重推动下逐渐发生了变化。本·琼森就把他的剧作当成古代经典作品一样看待，为剧本文学化不遗余力，并且在1616年出版了他的剧作（*Works*）——这成为剧本文学化的一个划时代的标志。

莎翁的创作时代，就正处于这样一种转型期。莎剧中的几个楔子写得算不上高明，甚至很草率，很快就退化成了打印在剧本上的文字叙述：1603年的四开本与1623年的对开本几乎毫无例外地在首页列出了人物表及故事发生之场所及时代的简介。本来楔子的作用是为了"减轻开端的负担"，由演员通过叙述或表演来"造成适于详细讲述的局势"，但在莎氏时代，这部分任务显然已经开始由文字叙述来承担了。

"宣物莫大于言"（张彦远：《历代名画记》），倒是凭着文字之功，直到今天我们还能欣赏到莎剧的精妙。但这不等于说，我们在莎剧剧本中发现了的就是一部完整的莎剧。虽然塞缪尔·约翰逊声称"时间的洪流经常冲刷其它诗人们的容易瓦解的建筑物，但莎士比亚像花岗岩一样不受时间洪流的任何损伤"（《莎士比亚戏剧集序言》）②，这不过是文人从文学的角度来说罢了。事实上，时间照样冲刷走了莎剧的舞台表演成分，只留下其"文学性"部分安然不动，而且随着时间流逝而越发地凸现出来，甚至被误认为这便是莎剧的全璧了。欣赏莎剧的最佳场所其实是在剧院；若地下有知，莎翁对上述诸家买椟还珠式的言论，真不知做何感慨。

---

① Stanley Wells: *Literature and Drama*, London: Routledge & Kegan Paul Ltd., 1970, pp.40—41 & pp.45—46.

② 塞缪尔·约翰逊：《莎士比亚戏剧集序言》，引自《莎士比亚评论汇编》（上），北京：中国社会科学出版社，1979年，第46页。又，许多著名评论家都蹈此覆辙，如坎贝尔（Thomas Campbell）曾云：《麦克白》有的部分我爱读，而非在舞台上看演出；兰姆（Charles Lamb）认定莎士比亚的悲剧只宜阅读不宜上演，而歌德断言莎士比亚属于诗，"在舞台史中他只是偶然的出现"。

不过请注意，虽然莎剧在当时以表演为指归，其文学剧本的功能与地位仍极其重要，几乎就等于演出本。据说有的演员拿到莎氏剧本几乎一字不改拿来演出，这在中国戏剧演员是匪夷所思的。因为在我国戏曲传统中，文字决不代表着戏剧表演的全部或主要力量；与之相反，西方戏剧的力量在很大程度上体现在文字（剧本）中。有时对文字的迷信甚至导致对戏剧的误读。例如马洛的名剧《马耳它的犹太人》（*The Jew of the Malta*）曾在很长一段时期内被认为是作者"最糟糕的作品"，如爱略特（T. S. Eliot）就认为它是"一场闹剧"，1964年在伦敦重排上演该剧时，许多评论家都认为这是一场"冒险"①。结果出乎大多数人的预料，演出获得了巨大成功，从此马洛的戏剧天才方真正为世人重新发现。

不幸，很多中国戏曲大师都罹受了马洛的命运，关汉卿就是其中之一。关汉卿和他的同行们，如所谓的"关、王、马、郑、白"杂剧五大家，开创了中国戏剧史上第一个文人编剧的时代。他们对中国戏剧传统的影响是深远的。但正如前文所述那样，氍毹毯上的演出才是中国戏剧的中心。明清传奇、昆曲剧（曲）本大多朗朗可读，具有颇高的文学性，但并未获得像西方戏剧中文学剧本那样的正统地位，文学化也始终未能成为中国戏剧发展的大趋势，虽然文学化进程在中国戏剧史上也曾提上日程，如明末的汤（显祖）沈（璟）之争便是当时戏剧文学与戏剧表演两大派之间的论战。火并的结果，是具有中国特色的折中："倘能守词隐先生之矩矱，而运以清远道人之才情，岂非合之两美乎？"（吕天成：《曲品》）话虽如此，然而从此后数百年间的戏剧实践来看，中国戏剧无疑是沿着舞台表演的大方向前进的。词章典丽的昆曲渐趋没落，充斥了俚言"水词"的"乱弹"（京剧是最典型的代表）却受到包括文人学者在内的广大观众的喜爱，即是明证。

对舞台表演的重视，甚至达到"填词之设，专为登场"的程

---

① Stanley Wells: *Literature and Drama*, pp.86—87.

度，与对文学剧本和剧本文学性的重视，甚至以文学技法庖代戏剧手法，这些都构成了中西戏剧的一个重要分界点。

现在不妨回过头来概括上述分歧对关剧与莎剧中楔子的影响。如前所述，本文所讨论的楔子即广义上的楔子，是指戏剧的开端。作为戏剧结构的有机组成，"开端"的任务无非是介绍剧中人物的姓名，剧中人之间的关系，时间地点—社会背景，补叙往事，初步展现人物性格并设置伏线，预示或开展冲突；简言之"在演出前向观众交代开头的情景"以"造成适于详细讲述的局势"。关剧与莎剧的楔子在这一点上的功能是相同的。

但是，中西戏剧对于舞台表演与文学剧本的不同侧重使得关剧和莎剧的楔子表现出不同的形态。关剧的开端，不管有无楔子，开始总要由登场人物同时也是剧中人"自报家门"。这种手法，虽然有人认为"太近老实，不足法也"（李渔：《闲情偶寄》），但它对于戏剧的表演却是一种十分适宜的手法。由于中国戏曲观众具有"既不泥真，亦不认假"的欣赏习惯，登场人物可以同时肩负起表演剧中人与介绍剧中人的任务而不会担心受到指摘；又因为中国戏曲以歌舞为主，观众看戏时更关注其中的技术成分，他们需要迅速地了解大概剧情，以便集中精力欣赏表演。莱辛讨论"诗与画在构思与表达上的区别"时指出，如果诗人运用熟悉的故事和人物为题材，在表达上"就是抢先了一步，诗人能愈快地使听众了解，这就能愈快地引起听众的兴趣"[①]。这一点对于剧作家又何尝不是呢？为了使观众尽早尽快地了解剧情以便充分欣赏表演，在开端部分让演员通过表演，同时简介剧情与剧中人，这应当说是一种极为精简和有效的手法。

西方剧作家（如布瓦洛、狄德罗、果戈理）也认识到了这一点，但却把开端的任务交给了文字。西方戏剧始终是对现实的摹仿，这就要求演员尽可能地真实再现生活。这种传统中培育出的剧

---

① 莱辛：《拉奥孔》，朱光潜译，北京：人民文学出版社，1979年，第66—67页。

作家与观众，怎能容忍"由剧中人代理剧情介绍人"这种不真实的手法呢？在这种情况下，甚至在剧中引入一个开场人来向观众"交代开头的情景"也是有损真实的。于是，西方强大的戏剧文学传统把戏剧开端的任务交给了剧本，通过其中的文字叙述来介绍人物姓名、生活关系、故事发生的时间与地点等等。这样，开端的任务实际上被剧本中非表演性的文字部分承担起来，而表演性的楔子也就不得不退避三舍乃至销声匿迹了。

莎剧的楔子正处在这样一种尴尬的处境之中。一方面是重视舞台表演的英国本土戏剧传统，另一方面却是与西方文学传统共振而生的对剧本文学性的重视，这就使得莎剧中的楔子一分为二，其功能分别体现在开场白及人物介绍、舞台提示之中。从表演的角度讲，莎剧的楔子与关剧相比无疑显得有些笨拙累赘，但若从剧本的文学性角度讲，"自报家门"式的楔子确实有些简单直露甚至原始，所以莎剧更能赢得读者的掌声也就不足为奇了。

以文字和以表演来建构戏剧的开端，哪一种方式更为高明或较为可取？寻求这个问题的答案其实并无多大意义。我们知道，包括戏剧在内的任何一种艺术形式都与本国的文化传统息息相关，凡是满足了某一时代观众审美需求的艺术形式便是好的艺术形式。其次，进化论的观点并不完全适用于艺术，如唐诗宋词分别表达满足了当时及后代的艺术趣味，但我们绝不能因为宋词后出便认为宋词的艺术成就高于唐诗。简言之，凡是适应特定时空条件的艺术形式便是好的艺术形式。真正的问题也许是：如何使艺术形式适合民族与时代的要求呢？

其实历史已经给了我们这方面的启示，即东西戏剧间的相互影响与借鉴分别壮大丰富了各自的戏剧理论与实践。如布莱希特受到京剧表演的启发，结合古代西方戏剧的传统（如歌队）表现手法，在《伽利略传》《高加索灰阑记》等创作中成功地运用了楔子、定场诗、自报家门等程式，创立了"叙事剧"（Episches Theater）这一戏剧类型。中国则在五四时期从西方移植来戏剧文学这一文类，舞台上出现了话剧这种西方戏剧形式，对中国传统戏剧的表演产生了很大的冲击。如《原野》的序幕：

> 大地是阴沉的，生命藏在里面。泥土散着香，木根在土里暗暗滋长。
>
> 巨树在黄昏里伸出乱发似的枝桠，秋蝉在上面有声无力地振动着翅膀。……

像这样优美富含诗意的开端在中国传统戏剧中是极为罕见的，这里的楔子可以说完全文字化了。再如20世纪末上演的京剧《曹操与杨修》中，"报子"一角揉合了古希腊戏剧歌队及元杂剧"冲末开场"的开端方式，也对传统的开端方式进行了革新尝试。

小小的楔子，反映了中西戏剧对于文字与表演的不同侧重，体现出中西戏剧传统深层结构的异同。正确认识它在中西戏剧中的运用特点与演变，对于完整理解中西戏剧、借鉴吸收西方戏剧来发展本国戏剧传统，都是不无启发的。

（下）诗·乐·剧

现在我们来讨论中西戏剧作为一种文学样式，其文本存在形式即文体的一个差异。

如果说，戏剧是西方文学的骄子，戏曲在中国倒像是个血缘可疑，来路不明，躲躲闪闪欲寄身"文学"篱下而不得的流浪儿。我们读西方文学史，差不多从一开始便接触到了戏剧。根据亚里士多德的看法，摹仿这种"人的天性在人类文学童年生产出抒情诗、史诗和戏剧诗这三种最初的、也是最基本的文学样式。"[①]古希腊、罗马戏剧的黄金时代过后，在中世纪西方戏剧曾一度岑寂，但并未

---

① Aristotle: *Poetics*, p.20.

销灭:它潜藏在教会仪式中(如唱诗、弥撒)并在文艺复兴时期苏生、壮大;后虽几经跌宕,这条血脉却始终传流不息,直到今天。因此说,作为叙事文学与抒情文学结晶的戏剧,铸就了西方文学巨鼎的一足。

亚里士多德的论断在中国却遇到了麻烦。首先,如前文所述,中国传统戏剧文本对形体、语言表达的依赖性极大,在很大程度上未能摆脱舞台表演的附庸地位而成为纯粹的文学形式。其次,戏剧晚至金元才出现(尽管几乎同时也高度成熟),而更晚至民初王国维氏方将之揖入文学庙堂。他认为元杂剧是"中国最自然之文学",并强调"元剧最佳之处,不在其思想结构而在其文章"[①]。但问题也就随之而来:"元剧最佳之处"当指剧中之曲,而"曲"向被目为"诗降而词,词降而曲"(黄星周:《制曲枝语》)这一系统的衍化物,那么代表中国古代戏剧文学的杂剧,到底是"诗"的胜利还是"剧"的凯旋?如其兼美二者,那么哪一方起的作用更大?二者的关系又是怎样的?

一、诗体与散文体

中国戏曲有一最醒目的文体特点,即没有产生像西方戏剧那样的散文文体。还让我们来看关剧与莎剧这组试验品。莎剧文体可分为散文(主要是对白)、素体诗、押韵对句与格律诗;后三者均为诗体,其中以素体诗为主,广泛用于独白、对白、开场白与下场白。关剧则采用多宫调、多曲体的联套方式,一剧中每折均由一"套数"或"套曲"组成;对白多为散文体,但也有用诗体的(如《窦娥冤》中窦娥斥责欲再嫁的婆婆时便唱了《后庭花》等四支曲子)。关剧中的曲子,不仅可以抒情,还可以叙述,具有多种表达功能。

关剧与莎剧均属诗剧(poetic drama),但"诗"在二者及二者所代表的戏剧传统中,份量两样,走势亦大不相同。虽然诗体在

[①] 王国维:《宋元戏曲史》,第121页。

西方从古希腊到今天一向被认为是戏剧的合适语言媒介，不仅在新古典主义剧作家手中曾再度辉煌，20世纪亦出现许多优秀的诗剧作家（如Maxwell Anderson、T. S. Eliot、Christopher Fry等人），但散文表达事实上已成为西方戏剧语言的主流形式。早在伊丽莎白一世时期的英国，李利（John Lily）就创造出号称"绮丽体"（Euphuism）的散文喜剧，到18世纪，李洛（George Lillo）又首创"散文体家庭剧"，而随着真实主义（Realism）兴起，王政复辟时期的喜剧对话均采用散文体，此后散文便逐渐成为西方戏剧的主要表达方式，至19世纪下半叶易卜生出，散文体语言在西方戏剧创作中更取得了完全胜利。

戏剧语言散文化，是西方戏剧流变的一个特征，而莎剧则体现出这一语言媒介转型期间的某些特点。如《哈姆雷特》一剧中散文道白已占有不小的比例。典型如墓地（五幕一场）一折，道白多为散文甚至口语；而在戏中戏（三幕二场）中，作者甚至对雕镂堆砌的诗剧体皮里阳秋地予以丑化摹仿。总的来说，莎氏作品中已出现"诗"从"剧"中剥落的迹象，诗与散文的界限开始变得模糊了（如素体诗有不工整的变体出现）。

杂剧的重心无疑是在曲子。即以元剧首座关汉卿的杰作《窦娥冤》为例①，该剧说白特繁，是关剧中最为散文化的一部作品。据笔者统计，曲文占全剧五分之一强（21%）。其余诸作中曲文所占比例当在百分之五十上下（极端的例子是《关张双赴西蜀梦》与《诈妮子调风月》残本；前者所存惟曲，共四十一首，后者除去少量对白，共有曲五十六首；两剧大意从这四五十支曲子中也还能揣度出来）。即便是最为散文化的《窦》剧，也有四十一只曲子，这些曲文是全剧精华，并占去了大部分的演出时间②。

---

① 根据《关汉卿全集校注》，下引同。
② 对于杂剧的演出，我们从由之一脉相承而来的京昆戏曲中约略能获得一些了解。如程砚秋主演的《窦娥冤·法场》一折，全部表演时间约二十分钟，而演唱由"滚绣球"衍化来的一段反二黄慢板就用了十二分二十秒（据程氏1954年静场录音）。

杂剧是以金代北方民间俗谣俚曲为基础，吸收宋代大曲和诸宫调及宋杂剧，金院本舞台表演而形成的艺术形式，与诗歌可说渊源有自。与西方不同，中国戏剧不但没有随着时代趋向散文化，反而加强了本身的诗体特征。关汉卿之后的杂剧、传奇，越来越向"诗"靠拢，出现了一大批所谓的"文词家"及文人剧。其代表如汤显祖，虽以"琼筵醉客"关汉卿的精神传人自居，但观其剧作，更多地像在读抒情诗而非阅读剧本，具有革新思想的汤氏恰恰在形式上采取了向诗歌输诚的反表演或非表演道路。事实上，不论是临川派还是吴江派，本色派还是文人派，几经文质代变的中国戏曲几乎均为诗体创作。

黑格尔在其《美学》一书中曾把诗分为两种，其一为上古时期一般艺术性散文还未发展成熟之前就已存在的原始诗歌，其二是散文化的生活情况和语言都已完全发展成熟时发展出来的诗歌（《美学》第三卷下第3章）。事实上，几乎所有的文类都是源出第一类诗歌的母体，经过散文化后而成形。西方文学便体现了这一规律，戏剧则是典型的例子。

耐人寻味的是，中国文学的散文化进程很早就启动了。就《诗》《书》《礼》《易》这几部现存最早的中国古籍来看，其中只有《诗经》一书纯是诗歌作品，其余各书不是诗、散混合，就是已很成熟的散文。事实上，诗（黑格尔所说的第二类诗）与散文的区别在魏晋南北朝时期还成为热门的话题。南朝宋人颜延年认为，文章无韵者为"笔"，有韵者"文"，刘勰在《文心雕龙·总术》中虽直斥其非，却也承认"今之常言，有文有笔"。真正明确界定了"文—笔"的是梁元帝萧绎："不便为诗""善为奏章"谓之笔，"吟诵风谣，流连哀思者，谓之文"（《金楼子》）。后世多承用此说，所谓"有所记述之为文，吟咏性情之为诗"（元好问：《遗山先生文集·杨叔能小亨集引》）或"诗以道性情"（杨慎：《升庵全集·诗史》）等等即是。

令人费解的是，即然在中国文学中诗、散对垒森严，为何戏剧的主体却是兼任叙事，抒情功能的诗（曲）呢？换一个角度来问，为什么"诗"在戏曲中的势力如此之大，以致于中国传统戏剧始终未能产生西方式的散文体戏剧呢？进一步追问，这一现象反映了我国戏曲、文学乃至文化的一个什么特点？

在问题的旋涡中，我们又向下卷深了一层。

二、诗与乐的离合

"乐"也许是将我们渡出问题之海的船筏。

顾炎武曾经指出："古人必先有诗，然后以乐和之"（《日知录·乐章》）。我们可以在《尚书·尧典》中为之找到凭据："诗言志，歌永言，声依永，律和声。八音克谐，无相夺伦，神人以和。"如果说这里讲的"乐"还难以断定是否即为上古戏剧，那么《吕氏春秋·仲夏季·古乐》篇中"昔葛天氏之乐，三人操牛尾，投足以歌八阕"的记载，无疑展现了一幅再生动不过的原始戏剧表演画面。

所谓"古曰诗颂，皆披之金竹"（钟嵘：《诗品》），"乐为诗心"（《文心雕龙·乐府》），中国诗歌与音乐互为表里。虽然到了文学自觉魏晋，文学自身的音节韵律开始受到重视（如《世说新语·文学》载："孙兴公作天台赋成，以示范荣期，云：卿试掷地，要作金石声。'范曰：'恐子之金石声，非宫商中声。'"），但诗人们仍往往从纯音乐的角度衡定文学本身的音乐性。稍后如沈约即标榜"音律调韵"之"秘"，认为"夫五色相宜，八音协畅，由乎玄黄律吕，各适物宜，欲使宫羽相变，低昂互节……妙达此旨，始可言文"（《宋书·谢灵运传》），而后人索性认为"诗在六经中，别是一教，盖六艺中之乐也"（李东阳：《麓堂诗话》），干脆将诗与乐等量齐观。较诗后出的曲子词、长短句、诸宫调乃至杂剧、传奇、花雅诸部，全封承袭了这一天然密切关系。有时诗对乐甚至还具有能动的反作用力，如明戏剧家王骥德便认为"盖曲之调,犹诗之调",曲之美听,在乎声调,"其法须先熟唐诗……机括即熟,音律自谐(《曲律·论声调》)。中国传统戏剧中诗与乐之关系密切如此。

不过,诗、乐与表演的结合,也是古代西方戏剧的特征。亚里士多德的《诗学》开宗明义,认为戏剧(包括悲剧与喜剧)"凭藉节奏、话语和音调进行摹仿"①。此话不假。古希腊酒神节宗教仪式上载歌载舞、连唱带念的合唱(chorus)蕴育了悲剧的雏型(choir song→tragedy)②,而喜剧亦是从歌曲(komos: the song of the gay revelers)发展而来,二者均有乐器伴奏。古罗马戏剧祖述希腊,然其本土之原始戏剧"萨图拉"(satura)亦胎托于诗歌"Fescennine Verses"③。中世纪的教会仇视世俗娱乐,戏剧一度岑寂,但恰恰正是教会内部极类戏剧的仪式(如弥撒)和音乐造就了日后戏剧的苏生勃发④。17世纪初意大利歌剧(Opera)的兴起,也不过是力图再现古希腊戏剧中音乐特色的结果。《悲剧的诞生》的作者说悲剧中的灵魂——音乐——消逝而悲剧衰亡,这句话正好从反面说明西方古代戏剧与"乐"的关系是何等密切。

尽管中西戏剧与"乐"都有如此之深的渊源,但到了后世,在各自的代表作家关汉卿与莎士比亚的剧作中,"乐"的成分此消彼长,分量大不一样。就拿关剧中曲文比例最低的《窦娥冤》来说吧,全剧有四套共四十一支曲,它们担负着推动情节、展开动作的功能,从文学角度看也是全剧的精华(如"滚绣球")。而莎剧中极富音乐性的《第十二夜》也不过由小丑Feste穿插了六支歌曲(O Mistress Mine; Hold Thy Peace; Three Merry Men; Fare-well, Dear Heart; Hey Robin; When I was a little Tiny Boy)以及几段器乐演奏而

---

① Aristotle: *Poetics*, pp.15—16.
② H. J. Rose: *A Handbook of Greek Literature*, London: Methuen & Co., 1956, p.103.
③ Margaret Bieber: *The History Of the Greek And Roman Theatre*, Princeton: Princeton University Press, 1939, p.65 & 301.
④ Ifor Evans: *A Short History of English Drama*, p.21.

已，不仅数量远逊《窦》剧，而且与全剧进程无甚关系，只是作为严格意义上的歌曲存在着，其地位颇似咖啡屋里的背景音乐。其它莎剧（如《爱的徒劳》五幕一场，《麦克白》剧中三女巫的巫咒曲，《哈姆雷特》剧中奥菲莉亚投水前的哀歌）就更是如此了。

一言以蔽，关剧中诗、乐、剧是融融泄泄的三位一体，莎剧中三者却是"杂而不越"，各自为政。二者的差异不可谓不大矣。这一差异中最引人注目之处则是诗与乐的离合。在中国戏曲中，"乐"总领歌诗，贯穿古今：演员尤其是主角要在音乐伴奏下，将诗（曲）文演唱出来。而西方戏剧早有古希腊时起就已出现了诗与乐的疏离，并且愈演愈烈（后世歌剧出现便是其后果）。不错，古希腊演员于掌握道白工夫以外，还需按节歌唱，有时为了表现狂喜、迷乱的剧情，也要进行舞蹈表演，但诗歌乐舞尤其是诗与乐似乎并未形成浑然的一体。希腊戏剧在以合唱（chorus）为主体的早期阶段，已出现在合唱间隙歌队领队（exarchos）与剧中人的对白。后世悲剧由此生发而歌队式微（其直接表现就是舞台上乐队的位置渐被侵消），领队不再由职业诗人担任，从此合唱音乐一蹶不振。①古罗马时期的剧作家塞内加创作了大量纯供阅读的案头剧，这也许是一极端现象，却被文艺复兴时期及以后的剧作家所继承发扬。莎剧中的诗不消说是"事谢丝管"的了，琼森倒是创作了不少假面歌舞剧，但这并不是严格意义上的戏剧②，而不少浪漫主义剧作家们更因"自信几行素体诗就可以构成一台戏"而折戟沉沙③。此后欧洲剧作家与观众对写实的兴趣与日俱增，非但乐亡，诗亦亡矣。直到本世纪方有若干诗剧作家出来，力图恢复戏剧中"乐"的精神，但那与古希腊戏剧中"乐"的精神已然是貌合神离了。

---

① Margaret Bieber: *The History Of the Greek And Roman Theatre,* pp.18—20. Gilbert Murray: *A History of Ancient Greek Literature*, London: D. Appleton and Company, 1897, pp.208—209.

② 将假面剧推向大成的琼森本人也不无讥讽地说过："彩妆与砌末成了假面剧的灵魂"。按假面剧源自查理二世时期之宫廷化妆舞会，并在詹姆士二世统治时期盛极一时，多为王家婚诞或外交庆典仪式。

③ Ifor Evans: *A Short History of English Drama*, p.144.

三、音乐与作为戏剧灵魂的"乐"

现在我们追到了问题的核心：乐。中西戏剧生发流变异同的全部秘密，也许就蕴含在这粒种子之中。

中西戏剧从一开始对于"乐"的理解就有些两样，而随着时间推移，这一罅隙更日渐断裂成为鸿沟。前面谈到中国戏曲中"乐"总歌诗，这话其实低估了"乐"的作用。《礼记·乐记》云："诗言其志也，歌咏其声也，舞动其容也；三者本于心，然后乐器从之"。"乐"不单单是人声或器乐发出的音乐，它更是一种戏剧的精神。《尚书·尧典》云"八音克谐，无相夺伦，神人以和"，《礼记》云"乐者，天地之和也"，此处所谓"和"是指戏剧或前戏剧（仪式）中的"乐"。从上古巫舞（王国维说）、庙堂之颂（刘师培说），到汉时之"东海黄公""西方老胡"，北齐至唐的"代面""钵头""踏谣娘"，及宋金元之院本、杂剧，明清至近代的传奇、花雅诸部，直到现代的京昆与地方戏曲，乃至20世纪末兴起的MTV均秉此精神而来。

"乐"不单组织、而且超越了文字、舞蹈和音乐；"乐"是戏剧中文字、舞蹈与音乐的缘起与旨归。中国"最自然之文学"——元杂剧的成功，正来自"乐"这只看不见的手的始终在场。可以说，在中国传统戏剧中，我们看到了诗与乐、诗与剧、剧与乐的密合无间。

西方戏剧却是另外一番风光。古希腊戏剧源乎宗教庆典仪式中的歌舞；希腊语中的"诗"（aoide）原义即是"歌"，而二者均属"乐"（mousike）的范畴。悲剧缪斯Melpomene与"歌舞"（molpe）一词同源，这表明悲剧不仅要"说"，更要"唱"，许多古希腊悲剧（如Oresteia）即以molpe终场[①]。可见，早期戏剧极富"乐"的精神。

---

① W. B. Stanford: *Greek Tragedy and the Emotions*, London: Routledge & Kegan Paul, 1983, p.49.

歌队（chorus）则为这一"乐"的精神在戏剧中的人格化体现，如其领队往往同时兼任诗人、演员、歌手、演奏家以及领舞。但是在雅典民主政体兴起后，歌队渐趋非职业化而渐渐不歌，代之而起的是渐趋繁重的说白，舞蹈也日趋草率；歌队开始在剧中担任真正的、活生生的角色，而原始歌队也就消失得更快了①。可以说，歌队作为古希腊戏剧灵魂，随着力求写实之悲剧的发展，不可避免地走向了没落，而后世悲剧的衰变亦由此远埋下了伏笔。

事实上，即使在古希腊戏剧最具"乐"的精神的全盛期，文字与音乐也并未妙合无垠。亚里士多德认为悲剧成分有六：情节、性格、思想、言辞、唱段与场景，他不单将诗从乐中析离，并且显然认为"言辞"表达意思的"潜力"远比唱段这一"装饰成分"重要（《诗学》第6章）。确实，虽然如古典作家所承认的，演说家与演员的言辞，在共鸣韵律方面与歌同质，但在雅典戏剧黄金时期，"言辞"的地位至高无上。当时器乐要伴和人声，公元前五世纪末，一个名叫克勒索克斯（Krexos）的音乐家引进了"衬腔（复调）音乐"与"辅韵伴奏"（heterophonic and pararhythmic accompaniments），文字本身的音乐性与器乐就此两分②。另一方面，虽然戏剧中的音乐成分经过埃斯库罗斯与索福克勒斯时代的衰落而在欧里庇德斯手中有所回升，但歌队中的"乐"却一去不返了。如自索福克勒斯之后，埃斯库罗斯式集诗人、演员、演奏者及歌队领队于一身的多功能角色逐渐分化解散③，"乐"的原始精神从此也就消失了④。

如果说，中国原始戏剧的精神是"乐"，是"神人以和"及"天地之和"的"和"，是诗、乐、舞的浑然一体，那么古希腊戏剧却体现出诗与剧、诗与乐、乐与剧的离析走势，即"和"的破坏

---

① Gilbert Murray: *A History of Ancient Greek Literature*, p.213.
② W. B. Stanford: *Greek Tragedy and the Emotions*, p.63.
③ Margaret Bieber: *The History Of The Greek And Roman Theatre*, pp.158—159.
④ Gilbert Murray: *A History of Ancient Greek Literature*, p.209.

与消失。前面讲过,元杂剧全面继承了上古原始戏剧中"和"的精神;与之相反,文艺复兴时期及之后欧洲戏剧,却继承甚至加速了古希腊戏剧中诗—乐—剧的离心倾向。

莎剧即是比较典型的例子。与同辈后学片面强调音乐舞美(如琼森的假面剧)或剧本文学性(如浪漫主义剧作家)不同,莎士比亚努力在他的戏剧综合诗文、音乐、舞蹈表演来娱乐当时的观众,如《第十二夜》中的歌曲及类乎molpe的终场、《爱的徒劳》第五幕第一场、《罗密欧与茱丽叶》一场五幕中的假面舞会等即是。不过,莎剧并未成为中国戏剧那样的表演形式:独树一帜的英国本土戏剧终究仍是欧洲戏剧传统的一个分枝,其对于逼真摹仿的重视掩没了对"和""乐"的追求。莎翁本人曾借剧中人物之口,要求演员准确、自然地反映社会生活(《哈姆雷特》三幕二场),这就足以说明问题了。

西方近现代诗剧作家继承古希腊、罗马及文艺复兴时期的戏剧精神,力求在作品中突出"音乐"特色,但也没有真正达到中国戏曲或古希腊早期戏剧中"和"的精神。以萧伯纳为例,他本人精通乐理,早年写过音乐评论,但其剧作仅具"歌剧式的结构"而已,大众通过阅览其剧本来品味文字的音乐之美,这与古希腊诗剧作品多为悦"耳"而非娱"目"颇有不同。其他作家如爱略特、布莱希特等人也都未能真正解决戏剧中"乐"也就是"和"的难题。他们注入的是歌曲、配乐、伴舞或音乐的结构、节奏诸成分的杂合,但不是"乐",更非"和"。他们的创作,与汤显祖虚心接受帅机、王骥德等对《紫箫记》文辞太过的批评,洪升与音律专家毛玉斯及徐麟合作以求"审音协律,无一字不慎"及孔尚任在创作《桃花扇》时"每一曲成,必按节而歌,稍有拗字,即为改制"的做法,形成了鲜明的对比。

四、美与真:不同接受者的反动

现在,我们对以关、莎二氏为代表的中西戏剧传统之异同试做一全景回顾。二者分歧大抵有以下三点：

首先，中西戏剧"本事"（story）载体不同。中国戏曲文学先天发育不足，是依赖性很强的副/准文类。戏曲的剧本类似唱白的底本，只提供大致框架，其中"空白点"极多，往往依赖演员的再创作方能成活。甚至有这样一种有趣的现象，即戏剧文学创作的兴盛竟会导致舞台表演的萎缩，继而又会导致剧本创造的式微。而在西方，戏剧是与史诗、抒情诗鼎足而三的文类。如亚里士多德认为"悲剧即使不借助动作也能产生它的效果，因为人们只要凭借阅读，便可清楚地看出它的性质"①，再如黑格尔认为诗是艺术之王，而戏剧则是诗中之王（《美学·序论》）。无论从理论上还是从实践上看，西方戏剧都接近于一种叙述体文类。

其次是中西戏剧文学对诗体与散文体的不同侧重。中西戏剧起初均为合乎韵律的诗体创作，但西方戏剧语言因重视逼真摹仿而日趋散文化，中国戏曲却与诗歌长相厮守，一再从民间文艺形式汲取元气而冲破诗词格律的羁束，从而拓展了诗国的的疆域、丰富了诗的表达能力（抒情与叙事）。这构成了中西戏剧语言/叙述方式的不同。

再次，中西戏剧对"乐"的理解与实践大相径庭。"乐"是戏剧的母体，这一点中西皆然。但在中国戏曲中，"乐"一以贯之地作为灵魂而发挥作用，无论它作为文学创作还是舞台艺术。而"乐"在西方戏剧中呈离散态势，"乐"或"和"在戏剧中的缺席使之分化为歌剧、舞剧、叙述体话剧（诗体或散文体）及哑剧、音乐假面剧等等各得一体、各自为政的亚剧种。

上文分析表明，中西文化对"和"的不同认识，导致了中西戏剧的殊流异相。奇怪的是，为什么中西戏剧同作为上古歌舞音乐合一之仪式的衍化产物，竟会对"和"采取大相径庭的认识与实践呢？换言之，中西上古戏剧雏型中的核心因素"和"有何不同，为

---

① Aristotle: *Poetics*, p.74.

什么会产生这一不同?

先看第一个问题。中国美学的特点,体现为"高度强调美与善的统一","强调情理的统一"等伦理因素的"和","以和为美的思想最为典型地体现了中国'古典美'的理想"①;"美"是"和"的核心,是"和"的旨归与外现。反观之下,西方文艺美学诸概念——无论是"理念""摹仿""渲泄""太一"或"崇高",无论是镜式外观或灯式内摄,无论是人与神的合一、摹仿作品与摹仿对象的逼真、表现作品与心灵的契合——往往将"真"作为艺术的环中之义。"美"与"真"构成包括戏剧在内诸多中西艺术品种的内在面貌,更决定了它们的发展路线与趋势。

为什么会产生这样的不同?这个答案恐怕得到戏剧的接受者即观众身上去寻找。读者接受批评认为文学作品并非纯然自足的客体,其发生、存在与发展的效果均取决于作者与读者的共谋。戏剧可以说是典型的例子。"剧本只有在舞台上才有生命"(果戈里),没有观众就没有戏剧,而中西戏剧的观众或预期观众是大不一样的。

上古戏剧起源于部落内全民性的宗教仪式,而所有的宗教仪式都服务于交际的目的。这一"交际"不仅包括"天人相和""人神克谐"这种由上及下,宗教性的交流,也包括"乐者为同"(《礼记·乐记》)、通过艺术相互传达感情的横向性、世俗性交流。

中西戏剧的核心"和"对此两方面各有侧重。古希腊戏剧源出赛神,演出并非纯为娱乐,而是作为宗教仪式的一部分来教化大众,如演出地点必须选在诸神圣地,甚至在公元前三世纪出现的演员公会也是一个宗教组织②。"诗人为演出所作的剧本这一工作是'教化'(didaskein)"③,这样戏剧实际上成了一种国家政治生

---

① 李泽厚、刘纲纪:《中国美学史》(第一卷),北京:中国社会科学出版社,1984年,第24—25页、第101页。

② Margaret Bieber: *The History Of The Greek And Roman Theatre*, p.307.

③ W. B. Stanford: *Greek Tragedy and the Emotions*, p.64.

活制度。如政府向富户征收"公益税"（tax of public service）来组织全民性的免费演出，同时观看戏剧演出也是公民的义务。在古罗马，戏剧渐渐成为固定的庆典演出，政府举办赛诗会鼓励创作，或大兴土木兴建"全国最辉煌的建筑"——剧院[1]。中世纪仇视世俗娱乐的教会扼杀了戏剧，恰从反面证实了上层社会对戏剧的控制。在"戏剧仿佛是社会中心"[2]的文艺复兴时期英国，戏剧家们（如莎士比亚、本·琼森）不仅隶属王室贵族（类似中国古代士大夫的家班），他们的创作亦非纯然"虚静无执"（negative capability），而是以大众尤其是上层观众为剧家之心（《温莎的风流娘儿们》的创作缘起就是例证）。欧洲自从文艺复兴到19世纪之前，文化领导权总体上掌握在政府手中。英国政府从1737年至1843年实施的"禁演令"（Licensing Act）及全欧性的检查制度（censorship）即说明了国家对戏剧的控制。至于19世纪以来浪漫主义戏剧、自然主义戏剧的兴起，也是由上而下的"交际"，不过这一权力在民主化历史进程中从教会、贵族转移到资产阶级知识分子手中罢了，主流社会对戏剧的主导性质则始终如一。

中国戏曲则来自民间，并具有最典型的民间性。在宗教意识淡薄、世俗力量强大的古代中国，戏剧或宗教仪式很快变形并消融到各种政治、伦理礼仪中去了。苏轼曰："八蜡，三代之戏礼也。"（《东坡志林卷二·祭祀》）王阳明说："《韶》之九成便是舜的一本戏子，《武》之九变便是武王的一本戏子。"（《传习录·下》）即发见此意。孔子悲叹礼坏乐崩，并不是像尼采那样悲悼"乐之精神亡，剧亦偕亡"，而是喟叹一种政治制度的崩溃。在他开创并在后世成为国家意识形态的儒学思想中，"敬鬼神而远之"的入世、现实主义态度进一步扫荡了宗教仪式在社会生活中的功能。戏剧既失去庙堂教化的战略地位，便只能成为一种在野的、世

---

[1] W. B. Stanford: *Greek Tragedy and the Emotions*, p.11.
[2] Ifor Evans: *A Short History of English Drama*, p.106.

俗性的、偏重娱乐的艺术形式,而身处江湖之远的作者与观众便取得了对戏曲的主导权。这样,在中国戏曲发生与发展的过程中,我们看到的是一种由下而上的作用力而不是相反。

不同的文化语境造就了不同的作者与观众,而不同的作者与观众又对各自的文化传统进行着修正与塑形。诗与乐在中英戏剧传统中的不同境遇,可以说验证了这一简单然而经常被人忽略的事实。

参考文献

西文部分

TEXTS

1. *The Oxford and Cambridge Edition of Shakespeare's Hamlet, Prince of Denmark* with introduction and notes for students and preparation for the examinations by Stanley Wood and Rev. F. Marshall, London: George Gill & Sons, 1904.
2. *The Arden Edition of the Works of William Shakespeare: Hamlet*, edited by Harold Jenkins, London / New York: Methuen, 1982.
3. *Hamlet,* edited by Ann Thompson & Neil Taylor, London: Arden Shakespeare, 2006.
4. *The RSC Shakespeare: The Complete Works*, edited by Jonathan Bate and Eric Rasmussen, *New York*: Palgrave Macmillan, 2008.

REFERENCES

1. Arendt, Hannah: *Lectures on Kant's Political Philosophy*, Chicago: The University of Chicago Press, 1992.
2. Bradley, A. C.: *Shakespearean Tragedy*, London: The Macmillan Press Ltd., 1974.
3. Bloom, Harold: *Shakespeare: The Invention of the Human*, New York: Riverhead Books, 1988.
4. Burton, Robert: *The Anatomy of Melancholy*, London: J. M. Dent & Sons Ltd., 1932.
5. Caesar, Michael (ed.): *Dante: The Critical Heritage*, London: Routledge, 1995.
6. Cassirer, Kristeller & Randall, Jr. (ed.): *The Renaissance Philosophy of Man*, Chicago:

The University of Chicago Press, 1948.
7. Castiglione, Baldesar: *The Book of the Courtier,* trans. by George Bull, Penguin Books, 1976.
8. Culler, Jonathan: *On Deconstruction*, London: Routledge & Kegan Paul, 1985.
9. Freud, Sigmund: *Beyond the Pleasure Principle*, trans. by Hubback, C. J. M., The International Psycho-Analytical Press, 1922.
10. Frye, Northrop: *Anatomy of Criticism*, Princeton: Princeton University Press, 1957.
11. Frye, Northrop: *The Double Vision*, Toronto: University of Toronto Press, 1991.
12. Goethe: *Faust*, Frankfurt am Main, Deutscher Klassiker Verlag, 1999.
13. Ingarden, Roman: *The Literary Work of Art: An Investigation on the Borderlines of Ontology, Logic, and Theory of Literature*, Evanston: Northwestern University Press, 1973.
14. Joyce, James: *Ulysses*, London: The Bodley Head Ltd., 1937
15. Kantorowicz, Ernst H.: *The King's Two Bodies: A Study in Mediaeval Political Theology*, Princeton: Princeton University Press, 1997
16. Lucian: *The Works of Lucian of Samosata*, translated by Fowler, H. W. and F. G., Oxford: The Clarendon Press, 1905.
17. Plutarch: *Plutarch's Lives*, trans. by Arthur Hugh Clough, Philadelphia: The Pennsylvania State University, 2003.
18. Sacks, Sheldon (ed.): *On Metaphor*, London: The University of Chicago Press, 1980.
19. Spencer, Theodore: *Shakespeare and the Nature of Man*, New York: Macmillan Company, 1951.
20. Strauss, Leo: *Persecution and the Art of Writing*，Chicago: The University of Chicago Press, 1988.
21. Tillyard, E. M. W.: *Shakespeare's History Plays*, New York: The MacMillan Company, 1946.
22. Weber, Samuel: *Benjamin's -abilities,* Cambridge, M. and London: Harvard University Press, 2008.

中文部分

1. 《丛书集成新编》，台北：新文丰出版公司，1985 年。
2. 《大正新修大藏经》，东京：大正一切经刊行会，昭和三年。

3. 《鲁迅全集》，北京：人民文学出版社，1981 年。
4. 曹雪芹、高鹗：《红楼梦》，北京：人民文学出版社，1982 年。
5. 方以智：《东西均注释》，庞朴注释，北京：中华书局，2001 年。
6. 顾炎武：《日知录集释》，长沙：岳麓社，1994 年。
7. 李幼蒸：《形上逻辑和本体虚无》，北京：商务印书馆，2000 年。
8. 钱锺书：《管锥编》，北京：中华书局，1979 年。
9. 钱锺书：《谈艺录》，北京：生活·读书·新知三联书店，2008 年。
10. 王国维：《静庵文集》，沈阳：辽宁教育出版社，1997 年。
11. 闻一多：《神话与诗》，上海：古籍出版社，1956 年。
12. 叶嘉莹：《中国词学的现代观》，长沙：岳麓书社，1990 年。
13. 朱熹：《四书章句集注》，北京：中华书局，1983 年。
14. 朱自清：《诗言志辨》，上海：古籍出版社，1956 年。

译文部分

1. 埃克哈特：《埃克哈特大师文集》，荣震华译，北京：商务印书馆，2003 年。
2. 爱比克泰德：《爱比克泰德论说集》，王文华译，北京：商务印书馆，2009 年。
3. 爱克曼：《歌德谈话录》，北京：朱光潜译，北京：人民文学出版社，1978 年。
4. 奥古斯丁：《忏悔录》，周士良译，北京：商务印书馆，1963 年。
5. 奥勒留：《沉思录》，何怀宏译，北京：生活·读书·新知三联书店，2002 年。
6. 奥维德：《变形记》，杨周翰译，北京：人民文学出版社，1984 年。
7. 布鲁姆：《莎士比亚笔下的爱与友谊》，马涛红译，北京：华夏出版社，2012 年。
8. 柏拉图：《柏拉图对话集》，王太庆译，北京：商务印书馆，2004 年。
9. 但丁：《神曲·地狱篇》，田德望译，北京：人民文学出版社，1990 年。
10. 费希特：《现时代的根本特点》，沈真、梁志学译，沈阳：辽宁教育出版社，1998 年。
11. 弗洛伊德：《弗洛伊德后期著作选》，林尘等译，上海：上海译文出版社，1986 年。
12. 伽达默尔：《真理与方法》，洪汉鼎译，上海：上海译文出版社，1992 年。
13. 歌德：《浮士德》，董问樵译，上海：复旦大学出版社，1983 年。
14. 歌德：《歌德文集：威廉·麦斯特》，董问樵译，上海：上海译文出版社，1999 年。
15. 哈兹里特：《莎士比亚戏剧中的人物》，顾钧译，上海：华东师范大学出版社，2009 年。
16. 海德格尔：《在通向语言的途中》，孙周兴译，北京：商务印书馆，1997 年。

17. 海涅:《莎士比亚的少女和妇人》,绿原译,上海:上海文艺出版社,2007年。
18. 海然热:《语言人》,张祖建译,北京:生活·读书·新知三联书店,1999年。
19. 荷马:《伊利亚特》,陈中梅译,广州:花城出版社,1994年。
20. 赫西俄德:《工作与时日 神谱》,张竹明、蒋平译,北京:商务印书馆,1991年。
21. 黑格尔:《逻辑学》,杨一之译,北京:商务印书馆,1976年。
22. 黑格尔:《法哲学原理》,范扬、张企泰译,北京:商务印书馆,1961年。
23. 黑格尔:《精神现象学》,贺麟、王玖兴译,北京:商务印书馆,1979年。
24. 黑格尔:《历史哲学》,王造时译,上海:上海书店出版社,1999年。
25. 黑格尔:《美学》,朱光潜译,商务印书馆,1979年。
26. 黑格尔:《小逻辑》,贺麟译,北京:商务印书馆,1980年。
27. 黑格尔:《哲学科学全书纲要》,薛华译,上海:上海人民出版社,2002年。
28. 黑格尔:《哲学史讲演录》,贺麟、王太庆译,北京:商务印书馆,1959年。
29. 怀特海:《科学与近代世界》,何钦译,北京:商务印书馆,1959年。
30. 卡西尔:《人论》,甘阳译,上海:上海译文出版社,2004年。
31. 库萨的尼古拉:《论有学识的无知》,尹大贻、朱新民译,北京:商务印书馆,1988年。
32. 康德:《道德形而上学原理》,苗力田译,上海:上海人民出版社,2005年。
33. 康德:《历史理性批判文集》,何兆武译,北京:商务印书馆,1990年。
34. 康德:《判断力批判》,邓晓芒译,北京:人民出版社,2002年。
35. 康德:《任何一种能够作为科学出现的未来形而上学导论》,庞景仁译,北京:商务印书馆,1978年。
36. 莱辛:《拉奥孔》,朱光潜译,北京:人民文学出版社,1979年。
37. 刘小枫主编:《人类困境中的审美精神》,上海:东方出版中心,1994年。
38. 蒙田:《蒙田随笔全集》,马振骋译,上海:上海书店出版社,2009年。
39. 米诺瓦:《自杀的历史》,李佶等译,北京:经济日报出版社,2003年。
40. 尼采:《悲剧的诞生》,孙周兴译,北京:商务印书馆,2012年。
41. 尼采:《超善恶:未来哲学序曲》,张念东、凌素心译,北京:中央编译出版社,2000年。
42. 尼采:《权力意志》,张念东、凌素心译,北京:商务印书馆,1991年。
43. 帕斯卡尔:《思想录》,何兆武译,北京:商务印书馆,1985年。
44. 培根:《新工具》,许宝骙译,北京:商务印书馆,1984年。
45. 皮亚杰:《发生认识论原理》,王宪钿等译,北京:商务印书馆,1981年。
46. 裘克安:《莎士比亚年谱》,北京:商务印书馆,1988年。

47. 叔本华：《叔本华论说文集》，范进等译，北京：商务印书馆，1999 年。
48. 叔本华：《作为意志和表象的世界》，石冲白译，北京：商务印书馆，1982 年。
49. 斯宾诺莎：《伦理学》，贺麟译，北京：商务印书馆，1983 年。
50. 维特根斯坦：《逻辑哲学论》，郭英译，北京：商务印书馆，1962 年。
51. 西塞罗：《国家篇 法律篇》，沈叔平、苏力译，北京：商务印书馆，1999 年。
52. 西塞罗：《论老年 论友谊 论责任》，徐奕春译，北京：商务印书馆，1998 年。
53. 亚里士多德：《诗学》，陈中梅译注，北京：商务印书馆，1996 年。
54. 伊拉斯谟：《愚人颂》，许崇信译，沈阳：辽宁教育出版社，2001 年。

后记一

在复旦外文系读书时，我师从陆谷孙教授精读了莎士比亚的两部戏剧作品：《第十二夜》和《哈姆雷特》，留下了深刻的印象。此后每年都会重读《哈姆雷特》，逐渐积累了一些想法。2002年夏我到外地旅行，途中突然迸出一个念头：写一本关于《哈姆雷特》的书吧！第二年秋我动笔写作，两年后终于完成。这便是本书的缘起了。

在写作过程中，我经常会问自己这样两个问题：我为什么要写这本书？我为什么要这样写？现在写作已完成，不妨对上述问题略做分说，算是"卒章明义"——读者视之为作者的自我辩护，也未尝不可。

《哈姆雷特的问题》是我的第二本书。它在很大程度上是一个示范性的写作，其示范对象正是作者本人。德里达曾经说存在着两种类型的写作：一种是书的绝对模式，即"以自我转动的卷轴形式结集的整体知识"；另一种是片断性的书写，即"不在自身上以书或者绝对知识的形式结集的书写"，或曰作为"文本开始"的"某种印迹组织"①。德里达并不认为前者是唯一可行的写作方

---

① 德里达：《书写与差异》，张宁译，北京：生活·读书·新知三联书店，2001年，"访谈代序"第8页；"省略/循回"，本书第526页。

式，相反他表现出"对可自我关闭的整体"的怀疑。他的怀疑不是没有道理的。在中国学术界，这种"绝对模式"有时以"规范化的学术写作"的面目出现，代表了学术写作的正确道路，几乎成为一种意识形态。对于青年学生来说，接受学术规范的训练肯定是必要的（我本人就是一名受益者）；在某种意义上，写作学位论文的过程也正是一个接受学术规范训练的过程。但是有一点：硕士、博士论文的写作规范并不等于学术规范的全部。现在研究生论文无一例外要求创新，然而前人论述已备，为了寻求突破，写作者不得不从某个细枝末节入手（所谓"小切口"）向下深挖（所谓"大截面"）；其结果，可能是知识的专精化，也可能是知识的狭隘化。在极端情况下，专精之学会成为另一种意义上的"后现代碎片"，明察秋毫却不见舆薪，甚至歧路亡羊（用解构主义的术语讲就是"différance"），用力愈勤而离真知愈远。更重要的是，学术规范并不等于学术本身。学术规范只是一个工具，为写作目的服务的工具，本身并不是目的；如果以工具为目的，为规范而规范，那么目的和工具就会一并异化而两败俱伤，学术规范成为学术的戏仿（parody），而学术成为学术规范的反讽（irony）。

学术论文并不是学术写作的唯一方式。学术写作可以是，而且应当是多种多样的。无论是"片断性"的写作（如钱锺书的《管锥编》），还是"绝对模式"的写作（如黑格尔的《逻辑学》），只要持之有故、言之成理而有所发明，均可视为学术著作。正是在这个意义上，《哈姆雷特的问题》是一个自我示范的作品：我希望通过写作本书，为自己寻证一种新的言说方式。这种言说方式就是阐释。

《哈姆雷特的问题》是一个阐释，确切说是一个比较文学的阐释。比较文学不等于文学比较：它的研究对象未必是文学，而它的研究方法也不仅仅限于比较。按照我的理解，比较文学与其说是一种研究方法，不如说是一门认识论，即在交流前提、互动关系、对话逻辑中，通过会同与对治的方法，更好地认识自我与他者及其共同临对的某些问题。其次,在我看来比较文学可以分为三个发展阶段(同时也是三种研究模式):第一个阶段,是对异质文化及其语言载体的译介与阐释;第二个阶段,是这些译介和阐释所构成的文学—文化关系及相关研究;最后,是对文学—文化关系研究进行反思而上升为理论(比较诗学),同时作为阐释实践进入新一轮的文化互动。可以说,阐释是比较文学的灵魂,它不仅是文学—文化关系研究的对象,而且创造着新的文学—文化关系。《哈姆雷特的问题》正是处于第一阶段的阐释,阐释的对象就是哈姆雷特——作为人类/人性(humanity)一个镜像——的问题。

那么,什么是"哈姆雷特的问题"呢?首先,哈姆雷特的问题是人的问题。《哈姆雷特》是一部形而上的问题剧:如果说萧伯纳、易卜生、奥尼尔的戏剧应时对症地反映了特定时空中的社会问题,那么《哈姆雷特》则揭示了一切人生存中的永恒困境与根本困惑(我想这也是莎剧在中国始终没有大红的原因)。因此,哈姆雷特的问题也就是我的问题。在阐释活动中,阐释者于阐释作品的同时也阐释了自己。这种阐释也就是存在论意义上的自我解释——解说、解答、解决、解放、解脱、开解、调解、化解、拆解、了解、释放、消释、开释……直至和解与释然;通过这种解释,我成了我。

经典是有待解释的另一个我(他我)。《哈姆雷特》无疑是一部经典,哈罗德·布鲁姆甚至说莎士比亚(他指的是莎剧,其中自然包括《哈姆雷特》)是西方经典的中心。然则何谓"经典"?(与之相关的问题是:我们为何要读经典?)在我看来,经典之为经典,首先在于它的保守性。在国人眼中,"保守"差不多是抱残守缺、故步自封、不思进取、裹足不前、顽固不化的同义词,甚至被视为"进步""革命""现代"的反面。这不过是时代大叙述召唤出的一种"市场偶像"[①]罢了。其实,"保守"意味着保有、

[①] 培根认为:文字强制和统辖着理解力,把人们引向无数空洞的争论与无谓的幻想,是为"市场偶像"(参见培根:《新工具》,许宝骙译,北京:商务印书馆,1984年,第21、31页)。

保藏、保存、保护、保养、保育、守护、守望、守卫，实在是一种基本的生存方式。以个人为例，我一出生就有一个已经过无数代适应、选择、进化和遗传的身体，这个身体是我"营生"的原始资本，首先要保守住它，岂能因其不够健壮或美好就丢弃不要呢？一个民族、国家或文化同样也有它的身体和原始资本，也就是"本体"。这个本体有如一枚种子，贮存以往、承载当下并化育将来（用黑格尔的话说就是"回忆把经验保存下来了，并且回忆是内在本质，事实上它也是实体的更高形式"①）。而经典，就是护守这枚种子的储存器；通过阅读经典，我解释了生命的本体，从而保有、滋养了我自己。

《哈姆雷特》正是这样一部经典。因此，解释《哈姆雷特》意味着解释我自己。我在解释，也在被解释；我解释，因此我是；我就是我的解释。这个解释与生命同步，面向多种可能敞开，不断生发而无有穷已。而《哈姆雷特的问题》，不过是方今之我——自我解释的一个印迹（trace）罢了。

既然是印迹，就免不了随写随扫、"以不同形相禅"和不断延异的命运；但其所以如此，不正是出于对"环中"或"圆心"的企慕么②？在这个意义上，解释乃是黑格尔所说的那种"自己爱自己的游戏"③：解释因由此爱，也指向此爱；解释是此爱所为，并与此爱共在。走笔至此，即以一首小诗结束本文，读者会心不远，一笑可也：

> 银汉灭明无量寻，氤氲三弄凤凰琴。
> 乘龙曷待昆仑岛？燃犀还聆流水音。

2006年2月下旬于北京大学中关园

---

① 黑格尔：《精神现象学》（下卷），贺麟、王玖兴译，北京：商务印书馆，1979年，第274页。

② Jacques Derrida: *Writing and Difference* (translated by Alan Bass), London: Routledge & Kegan Paul, 1978, pp.295—299.

③ 黑格尔：《精神现象学》（上卷）序言，第11页。

后记二

在这篇后记中,我想特别感谢一个人——复旦大学的陆谷孙先生。

十二年前,我还是一名本科生,正准备考研。一个秋雨绵绵的下午,我到复旦大学了解情况,一进校门就在西侧的"名师风采"宣传栏中看到了陆谷孙教授的图片。图片上的陆先生正在讲课,头发花白,目光清朗,愉快而自信地打着手势,一派名师风范。我心头一震:这不正是我要找的老师吗?我一定要做他的学生!

事与愿违,我来到复旦后,陆先生并没有带我这一届的硕士生。当时他担任外文系主任,同时主持《英汉大词典》的编写工作,还坚持给本科生上基础课,实在太忙了。记得派定导师和研究方向后,我径直走到陆老师面前,心有不甘地说:"我想找您做导师!"听到这话,陆老师轻轻叹了一口气,注视着我,语气诚恳地回答说:"张沛啊,我今年不带学生了。你不要太看重师生名分,你上我的课,一样可以跟我学的呀。"唉,我还能说什么呢?

就这样,我的如意算盘落了空,未能拜在自己景仰的老师门下学习。不过有失就有得,我听从陆老师的建议,跟随夏仲翼先生学习西方文论,大开眼界,并进而对比较文学产生了兴趣,为日后进入北大深造打下了基础。——这是后话不提,且说我当时对未能进入陆门耿耿于怀，决心"偷师学艺"：学他的真功夫，而且还要比他的正式弟子学得更好！现在回想起来，这真是少年意气；但是对青年来说，意气也许能转化为志气，不见得总是坏事吧。

于是，只要陆先生开课，无论是本科生的课还是研究生的课，我都去听。两年下来，我先后选修了陆老师的英美散文、莎士比亚戏剧精读等课程。陆老师的讲课艺术是超一流的！他嗓音浑厚，有如黄钟大吕，而且语音纯正、用词典雅（别忘了他可是辞典编纂专家！），再加上博洽的学识、洒脱（北京土话叫"飒"，也就是谡谡有林下风气的意思）的风度，简直达到了无美不具的境界。因此，他的课堂总是人气旺盛，常常是本系的、外系的甚至外校的学生、青年教师乃至慕名而来的社会人员汇聚一堂；而陆老师，作为"the observed of all observers"，一定是神采飞扬、妙语连珠，并不时有"随心所欲不逾矩"的发挥；而听讲者，也无不欢欣鼓舞，跟着他一道神游灵魂的故国而流连忘返……

不用说，我在陆老师的课上学到很多东西，小到一字一词的读音，大到立身处世的道理，至今不能忘怀。他极少缺课，偶尔因开会不得不停课，事后也一定补上。"我是一个教书匠"，这是他的一句口头禅。记得有一天上课，正讲到酣处，突然有几名新闻记者进来，冲着讲台咔嚓、咔嚓地照个不停。陆老师开始没好说什么，过了片刻，看见这些人还在忙活，便停下来有些不快地对他们说："老兄，这里正在上课，你们先出去好吗？"还有一次，也是正在上课的时候，一位朋友来看他，站在教室门口向他打招呼。陆老师点头示意而已，继续给学生上课。我想，在陆老师心中，上课一定是最重要的事，所以他才会这样吧。

然而，日常生活中的陆老师极富人情味，据我看是少有的深情人。他自言平生最得意的事情是"我是我父亲的儿子"。在他住处的显眼位置上，一直摆放着父亲的遗像，每到除夕他都会取下揩拭一番，鞠躬行礼，然后奉上一杯清茶，独自默坐追思。陆老师也十分重视师生友情。杨岂深先生去世后，他神情黯然，大异平时，后来竟因此发病。对于青年学子，陆老师更是关爱有加。当时他做系主任，每日早八点必来"坐镇"办公室；办公室的大门始终敞开，学生可以随时来向他咨询问题。我曾多次来这里请教疑难，陆老师从未表示过厌烦，总是亲切地、甚至饶有兴味地和我讨论问题，有时还会向我提问，启发我进一步思考。我平生发表的第一篇学术论文，还有我的硕士论文选题，包括本书附录的两篇文章，都是在这样的谈话中逐渐成形的。

后来我将离开复旦时，作为临别纪念，特意请一位老朋友同来旁听陆老师本学期为四年级本科生上的最后一堂英美散文课。课间休息时，陆老师踱过来询问我考北大的情况，关切之中隐隐流露出挽留的意思。下课后这位老朋友跟我说："看得出陆先生很重视你。"我回答说："你不知道，他对每一个学生都是这样的。"确实，和陆老师在一起，你能从他的眼神和语气中感到他在真心关注你，会觉得自己很受重视，是大有希望的可造之才。这说来简单，然而非情深者不能为也。为人师者，如果没有这种深情，则不过是一台讲课机器罢了。

《哈姆雷特的问题》这本小书可以说是我和陆老师师生情谊的见证。去年我给学生开"欧美文学经典导读"，讲《哈姆雷特》，第一堂课我就告诉学生：本人当年在复旦大学陆谷孙先生开设的"莎剧精读"课上学习了这部作品，受益良深。我这么说不是为了炫耀，而实在是发自内心的感念。我用本书作讲义，一边上课，一边修改。定稿后，我把一些重要章节寄给陆师审阅，他放下手头正在进行的《英汉大词典》修订工作，认真审读一过，并提出了中肯的修改意见。我请先生赐序，他也欣然命笔，很快就写好寄来，并风趣地说："We're quits now"（我们两清了）。怎么会"两清"呢？说学生又欠了老师一笔债还差不多。陆师在序中称本人"审问慎思""素心笃志"云云，我愧不敢当，惟愿以此自勉，作为对老师的回报。

不觉离开复旦八年了！临别时，陆师曾赠诗一首：

> 深巷柳依依
> 新雏贴地飞
> 明年寻故旧
> 能否识荆扉？
>
> 书赠张沛惜别
>
> 陆谷孙敬识
> 1998年4月于
> 复旦大学

直到去年十一月，复旦百年校庆后不久，我才有机会重访母校。不用说，复旦变化很大。在我印象中，复旦是温厚从容、蕴藉风流的，正如北大雄浑阔大、沉潜激扬一样；现在看来，这似乎是一种"机械的、静止的、形而上学的观点"（借用政治教科书语，一笑）。复旦本非"荆扉"，而我——现在是"老鸟"了——有些不识故旧倒是真的。幸好，变化中有不变者在；无此不变者，变化将不知伊于胡底。会议结束后，我专程拜会陆、夏二位先生，就感受到了这个不变者，或者说保守的精神。事实上，这也是一国文化命脉的保守者——大学的精神。所谓"道不虚行"，精神需要人来践履，否则无以呈现；而陆老师，可以说正是这样一个典范。在这个意义上，他对我的帮助和影响就绝不仅仅限于学业方面了。

听到上面这番话，陆老师一定会说：我只是一名教书匠，你把我理想化了。确实，我在陆老师身上投射了自己青年时的理想；但人是需要理想的，不是么？何况，是陆老师本身焕发出理想的光华，我不过有幸见证了理想的真实性罢了。对于这样一位"教书匠"，怎能不叫我充满感激和敬意呢！

2006年3月上旬于北大中关园

新版后记一

硕人之藚,永矢弗谖

大约在2006年7月间,我有一次和陆谷孙老师通话,向他汇报最近研读莎剧的心得,最后问道:"陆老师,您能否用一句话概括您对莎剧的整体感受?"陆老师的回答脱口而出:"终归寂灭。"这个答案完全出乎我的意料,我当时如受重击,刹那间感到虚无洪荒之力的巨大冲压,很久之后——甚至现在——都不能释然。

十年之后,2016年7月26日,多年未见的硕士同学高永伟教授突然来电,告说陆老师脑梗病危。第二天上午,我赶到上海新华医院19号楼5层的重症监护病房,看到了已然昏迷不醒的先生。病房很安静,只有监测生命表征的仪器在旁不断闪烁。我默立床前,内心涌动抽搐,什么也说不出来,"终归寂灭"这四个字在脑海中反复轰鸣。8月1日下午,我来到龙华最后送别陆老师,望着大厅中静静躺卧的先生,感觉自己的一块生命也粉碎寂灭而归于了虚无。

时至今日,我仍然无法正面这一现实:陆老师走了,"I shall never look upon his like again"。现在,只有对老师的回忆——这回忆构成了我的一部分真实生命经验——与我同在,并继续给我力量。在这个意义上,陆老师并未远去;对我而言,对一切爱他和被他所爱的人而言,他依然还在。

这里需要说明一点:我虽受业于陆先生,却不是他的及门弟子。当初我报考复旦外文系研究生，本意是想追随陆先生学习莎士比亚，但他此时全力以赴主持《英汉大词典》的编写工作，莎研方向下不再招生，我的愿望未能实现。不过，他后来为研究生开设了莎剧精读课程，我全程选修跟听两个学期，受益匪浅。越年我报考北大，亦请陆师写推荐信，先生慨然应允，并题诗赠别。后来我任教北大，继续以"a serious amateur"的身份关注和介绍莎剧，期间与陆师多有交流，自认为是先生莎研一脉的教外别传弟子，并得到了先生的认可，我也为此深感自豪。我在北地经常称说先生的品行学问，此间师友每有误会，我必郑重解释，以免攀附之嫌，同时心中也有一种想法，认为师生之谊，首在知心：苟能知心，则胡越可为肝胆；不能知心，则同室无非路人。确切说，师生之间应该是一种"友爱"加"对手"的关系：所谓"友爱"，是指师生之间齐心合德而"当以同怀视之"；所谓"对手"，是指师生之间实为"过去之我"与"未来之我"异代同时、惺惺相惜的凝望对话和当仁不让、惟道是从（Amicus Plato, sed magis amica veritas）的竞争赶超。昔日禅宗大德声言"见与师齐，减师半德；见过于师，方堪传授"，即深得其义。

  话虽如此，先生之学广大深闳，"庾信文章老更成"而"暮年诗赋动江关"，令后学者瞻望弗及而心悦诚服。陆老师平生服膺钱锺书先生，自言"我辈的学问若能及钱杨的百分之一，足矣！"我于陆师亦有同感。作为先生门墙之外的不肖弟子（陆师尝以尼采名言勉励后学："尼采讲过宗师与弟子的关系，称'子将背其师，盖渠亦必自成大宗师也。'张年而立，可不勉欤！"其实恐怕也是失望多于欣慰吧），我对老师的道德文章拳拳服膺，一见心折，继而心仪，终于"心死"：无论为人为学，我都永远不可能达到先生那样高远和纯粹的境界了！

  后来我在北方生活工作，未能侍奉先生左右而随时聆听教诲，平时只能通过电话邮件问候请益。尽管如此，先生待我亲切如故，我仍能与先生有旦暮会心的交流。(……)

事实上,先生不仅以其言、更以其行——所谓行胜于言——亲证了"真人"和"仁者"的生命境界:他是孺慕的人子和慈爱的父亲,是感恩念旧的学生和仗义长情的同事,是光风霁月的师长和恢弘博雅的学者,是不辞辛苦穿行语林辞海而乐在其中的wordsmith(陆师自我定位为"称铢度寸的微观型学人"),是不畏浮云秉笔直书的自由思想者,也是"常为大国忧"而"有恨无人省"的批判现实主义爱国者(董桥先生戏称陆师为"愤老",颇为传神)。(……)2011年8月,我到上海看望先生,将话题转向他正在主持编写的《中华汉英大词典》,还顺便考较了我几种汉语表达(例如"就势")的英文译法。我正心中暗喜廉颇未老,赞叹陆老师确实"编出了自我实现的乐趣",先生又话锋一转,谈到布拉格、昆德拉、生活在别处、故乡的陌生人、本土流亡,而后陷入了沉默。我读懂了先生的寂寞、孤愤和绝望,但是强颜欢笑,故作不解而问:您说"本土流亡"这个词该怎么译?是"domestic exile"吗?如果用"in-exile",或者干脆用"inile",您看怎么样?如果是集体流亡,可以仿照"wed-in / cook-in"之类而用"exile-in"吗?如是等等,直到先生神色稍霁,我才告辞出来。在回来的路上,我心中隐隐作痛,似有一种不祥的预感,但未敢以告人,只是暗自沉吟,同时也自欺欺人地想:陆老师如果身边有家人陪伴照顾,他的心情和健康状况一定会比现在好许多——而这无疑是国家之幸和学界之福!

这是我当时的想法。现在看来,陆先生几乎是自觉而悲壮地选择了向死而生的有限未来此在。古希腊哲人认为"Ήθος ἀνθρώπῳ δαίμων"(命自性出/性者命也),而能够掌控自己的命运(δαίμων),中国古人所谓"惟克天德,自作元命",这是怎样的一种天性修为(ἦθος)呵!正是通过这样一种决绝的选择,陆先生在沉默中爆发燃烧,不仅"编出了自我实现的乐趣",更实现了生命的内在超越。

一个如此高贵和杰出的灵魂是不会随着肉体的消亡而"终归寂灭"的!我宁愿相信——而且此时此刻,我也确实感到——陆老师只是去了另一个世界,一个类似于"盗梦空间"的平行世界(χώρα ἔκστασεως):

Denmark's a prison.
Then is the world one. (*Hamlet*, II. ii)

There is a world elsewhere (*Coriolanus*, III. iii)
Where souls do couch on flowers. (*Antony and Cleopatra*, IV. xiv)

O brave new world, that has such people in't! (*The Tempest*, V. i)

在这个世界里,被缚的普罗米修斯终于获得了解放,而漂泊海上的奥德修斯重新回到了故乡。作为这个世界的幸福居民,陆老师一定还在关注着我们;而我们,作为必死者与后死者,同时作为见证者和铭记者,也将从他的关注中继续获得精神的护持与灵魂的滋养:

If thou didst ever hold me in thy heart,
Absent thee from felicity awhile,
And in this harsh world draw thy breath in pain
To tell my story. (*Hamlet*, V. ii)

The weight of this sad time we must obey;

Speak what we feel, not what we ought to say. (*King Lear*, V. iii)

So our virtues lie in the interpretation of the time. (*Coriolanus*, IV. vii)

谨以此文,纪念我的老师陆谷孙先生逝世一周年。

2017年7月初写于北大中关园寓所

新版后记二

《哈姆雷特的问题》初版于2006年，迄今已逾一纪。当时书生意气，一心想着自出机杼另辟蹊径，尝试用中国传统诗话和札记、随笔的形式反向阐发西方经典，但是"力与愿矛盾"，出版后恒觉若有所失。诚如哈罗德·布鲁姆所说：走到莎士比亚之外来更好地理解莎士比亚是危险的（"going outside Shakespeare to apprehend Shakespeare better is a dangerous procedure"）[1]——可惜我未能及时领悟这一点！虽然读者宽容，而我始终不能释怀，总想有机会改正。适逢中文系出台学术奖励政策，于是我申请了年度科研资助，修订出版这本十多年前的"少作"，以为往昔之"坟"与今日之"药"（德里达所谓"φάρμακον"）。

"克力同，我们欠药王爷（Ἀσκληπιός）一只公鸡，别忘了还上呵。"

"我会的。你看你还有什么要说的吗？"[2]

那就再说几句。此次修订，除了改正一些细节，主要有两项

---

[1] Harold Bloom: *Shakespeare*: *The Invention of the Human*, New York: Riverhead Books, 1988, p.719.

[2] *Phaedo*, 188a.

变动。首先，原书正文15章，新版删去了第3章、第7～9章、第12章等半数以上内容，重新编为10章，旧版就此作废。古人云"书贵瘦硬"，又称"学贵博而能约"，本人不才，愿事斯语。其次，新版增加了《哈姆雷特》全剧英文注释，大体采撷成说，间下己意而与中文论述互为表里，以备初学专业者使用。事实上这也是我在北大讲授"莎士比亚戏剧专题"课程、特别是悲剧专题《哈姆雷特》时使用的底本和部分讲义。笔者当年跟随陆谷孙先生研习莎士比亚戏剧，陆师文本精熟，批郤导窾、发微抉隐如入无人之境，听众手追心摹、目不暇给而感动欢喜。事后想来，这大概就是昔人所说的"ἔκστασις"境界了吧！我由此认定文本——特别是原文文本（当然这不仅限于文学文本）——是文学教学和研究的物质基础，而"理论"特为其上层建筑或"继而成之"。本书的英文注释部分在一定程度上代表了我对《哈姆雷特》"文学文本"的基本理解和掌握。我以此向老师的在天之灵汇报和致敬，同时向我的学生与未来同道示范和传承一种方法和信念。

  北京大学比较文学与比较文化研究所孟来燕硕士为剧本分行并编辑整理了英文注释部分，博士生陆浩斌同学通读校对了书稿清样，陈瑶同学覆核了征引文献和全文。青年们的工作十分出色，甚至超出了我的预期——it is a wise teacher that knows his students. 我在此向他们表示感谢，同时也希望他们从中有所收获，并在此基础上超越前人：这是后来者的权利和义务，也是学生对老师的报答。

  最后，感谢本书责编郝妮娜女士为此书付出的辛劳。这是我第五次与北大出版社结缘："What's past is prologue"，"greatly instructed I shall hence depart"。

  文之将终，抄录旧年习作小诗三首，抒发此时心意——"文青"故态，博雅君子一笑置之可也：

一

江湖笑傲缅渔樵，野寨扪谈堪寂寥？
多情随喜耽三界，可惜菩提事业萧！

二

灯传教外是吾禅，高蹈何烦佩芷兰。
能识南华挥麈尾，悠游濠上是何缘？

三

春光旖旎为谁来？已负董家园外梅。
朗润湖山今又是，会邀陶令赴天台。

2018年7月17日写于北京大学中关园住处
2020年1月10日改定于昌平瑞旗家园寓所